MW01230643

In memory of my m

To my father, who taught me poetry.

In remembrance of my aunt — my second mom.

Dedicated to all my fur- and feather-babies, along with the countless homeless fur-babies.

Thank you to all of those who pick up this book and give my words a chance.

For my husband, who is my soulmate.

Inner Light

No need to ask for directions,
The way is hidden inside your soul.
Just follow your inner light,
And that will guide you home.

Christine Ryan, Spirit Guide

First printed in the United States of America, 2017.
ISBN: 978-0-5783-4324-2 (paperback)

www.EtherealRomance.com

This is a work of fiction. Names, characters, places and incidents either are the product of the author's imagination or are used fictitiously. Any resemblance to actual persons, living or dead, events or locales is entirely coincidental.

The Ruler's Soul

Christine Ryan

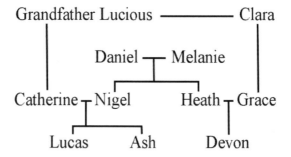

Chapter 1
Lucifer Watches

He could manifest himself as a human form if he chose, but now was not the time; he did not wish to impose himself on Rosemary's Earthly experience unless deemed necessary. It would be best if circumstances solved themselves.

He would wait. Lucifer would watch.

The missing piece of his reason for being felt like it slipped back inside of him, and made him whole.

In his past, long before his position as ruler of Hell, Lucifer had experienced several human lives. All of those lives had been shared, in some capacity, with his only love. He had purposely lost track of her soul after assuming his new position, but her father's passing and her grief had led him back to her. Her name was Rosemary. She lived in Wolfe County, Massachusetts.

He watched.

She now sat on the wooden swing underneath her willow tree.

Lucifer thought back to the moment this beautiful soul had reemerged into his orbit, when Rosemary had sat beside her father's bed at the hospital. Tears had moistened her cheeks as her father, Frank, slept. Lucifer had felt her sadness.

When he had first arrived at her ailing father's bedside, he immediately recognized Rosemary. It would be impossible not to know her soul, even in her unfamiliar human body.

1

After a few days of drifting in and out of consciousness, Frank's body quietly induced a coma. The coma allowed his soul time to transition from human life to human death.

Before the coma had disallowed his consciousness, Frank and his daughter had reminisced about Rosemary's childhood years. They spoke of her first friends, pets and hobbies. It had been pleasurable for Lucifer to learn of her present life's journey. Then, a glistening flow of wetness had steadily streamed her cheeks, as her father had taken his last breath. The awaiting escort had then guided the departing soul.

It was not usual protocol to keep watch over the deceased's descendant. Lucifer had completed his job, guiding Rosemary's father to Hell, but then Lucifer had returned.

His energy, locked in position, had hovered about her.

Each soul, enlightened with all-knowing awareness, possessed the ability to observe without human eyes. It seemed as though a thousand eyes saw in a thousand directions, with Lucifer's own acute perception. But his focus was on Rosemary.

Darkness was now beginning to encompass Earth. She looked frozen in place, on her wooden swing beneath the willow tree. Her feet mechanically moved under the swing and kept it in slow, rhythmical motion. Her blood-red eyes, worn from grief, stared into nothingness.

It pained him to see her like this, and he couldn't leave, even though he was invisible to her. There was no one here to watch over her now. He would have to protect her.

He knew what she longed for: she wanted answers to her suffering.

There was suffering on Earth and in Hell. Each soul, no matter whether occupying Earth or Hell, must look within to find healing and peace. Lucifer felt as though his core twisted in torture as he watched Rosemary struggle. He was connected to her soul.

"Is someone there?" she called out.

She could sense his presence. He knew she felt connected to him.

If Rosemary could see Lucifer's orb, it would appear as a glowing ball of energy; a bright, translucent nucleus, covered by a thin yet resilient membrane. It would look as though the membrane were lit from within, as a soft, green aura encircled the membrane.

Rosemary finally rose and went inside her house.

Now, at three o'clock in the morning, she lay awake in bed.

She had fussed over tucking the covers in all around her, changed positions several times, moved her pillow...

Lucifer could not leave until she fell asleep, finally at peace.

Two green, glimmering eyes beamed straight at him, studying the obscured figure. The cat could see him. The golden feline, perched on the foot of the bed, stared.

Just yesterday morning – a humid, hot Saturday – Rosemary had kissed her father's forehead for the final time.

The mourners who joined her had been a small group. Her friend, Sharon, and a couple of her father's long-time co-workers had attended the short ceremony and burial. Sharon had taken Rosemary's hand and held it, as they watched the coffin being lowered into the ground.

Mark, Rosemary's boyfriend, had also been in attendance. He had obligatorily stood by her side, but remained unemotional. He had not offered a gentle word nor a comforting touch, though he had agreeably conversed with Frank's co-workers. Frank had been the last of Rosemary's living relatives familiar to him.

A few hours had passed now. The alarm clock on Rosemary's nightstand was the only indicator of time to Lucifer. Between the different planes of Earth and Hell, only eternity existed. Her eyelids scrunched fitfully, as Rosemary turned on her side.

"Mama!" she called out from her sleep.

If he were human, Lucifer would place the palm of his hand on her forehead. He'd smooth back strands of her hair, move his lips to her hairline and kiss her. He would gaze into the depths of her hair as his lips caressed the soft, brown tresses. The color reminded him of walking through a thick forest of oak trees; he saw tall tree trunks, scattered hues of chestnut, bronze and tan. He saw touches of golden leaves, which glimmered in the sun, in her highlights. Even warm reds of the sunset tinted throughout. She was the most beautiful, gentle soul he had ever known. Rosemary graced Earth as its most stunning woman.

Exhaustion seemed to have now swept her away, to a peaceful unconsciousness.

When he was assured her closed, warm, hazel eyes were calm, Lucifer descended into the core of the universes. His soul returned to Hell.

"Why are you still in bed?" Mark asked, as he pulled on Rosemary's turned shoulder.

She opened her eyes and repositioned herself onto her other side, looking at him.

Lucifer's vibrations were linked to the grief of a human's soul, which was ready to transform and be escorted to Hell. Never before had Lucifer sensed a healthy person's sad emotions, nor been able to hear a healthy person's thoughts. He had been connected to Rosemary's sorrowful emotional state ever since he watched her tending to her ailing father. Lucifer's energy was so sensitive to hers that he actually felt the soreness which crept up the back of her neck, to her head. A heavy pressure accumulated behind her eyelids and tears pooled in the corners of her eyes.

"I'm sorry you lost your father, Rosemary," Mark said, "but he would want you to live your life. There is no sense dwelling in self-pity." He sat down beside her and rubbed her knee, through the covers. "It's best to just get right back to life after a setback." He took her hands and assisted her to a seated position.

"You think this is a setback I'm going through, Mark?"

"We have to see your dad's lawyer. We need to get his estate figured out."

"Mark, I can't get out of bed today." She rubbed her eyes with the flatness of her fingertips, and wiped her face and nose. "I'm grieving, Mark. I need to take care of myself now."

He gave her knee a little squeeze. "I know the other day was hard for you, I know you lost your dad, but these things always get better when we get right back up and in the swing of life. We need to think about getting this house ready to show soon."

"I love this house. I'm not selling this house," she said.

He ignored her statement, holding his jawline between his thumb

5

and forefinger. "I've got to go show a house right now," he said, looking down at his watch. "Have yourself ready by four p.m."

There followed a loud thud, as Mark pulled the bedroom door shut behind him.

Rosemary slid back down in the bed, under the covers.

Now that he had located her soul, Lucifer could not fully return to his duties as the ruler of Hell, until he was assured that she was safe in this human lifeform. Her essence could not be entrusted to Mark. The man did not emanate a healthy spiritual energy toward her.

As Rosemary rested on her back, Samantha the cat took her place on her human's chest. Although the feline eyed Lucifer, Samantha sensed her human's grief and stayed with her.

Looking up at the ceiling fan, watching it turn, Rosemary focused on the color her father's casket had been, as it was being lowered into the earth. The arguments she and Frank had regarding her relationship with Mark were now forefront of her mind. Lucifer's core cringed as he stayed connected to the darkness of her thoughts. She now concentrated on the very last argument, which had led to the two-month-long separation of father and daughter, preceding Frank's death; only three weeks before Frank's passing had they reunited. The sound of silence, after abruptly disconnecting a phone call with her father, had begun the estrangement.

Rosemary's eyelids now tightly closed, as tears seeped from underneath. Her whole body felt rigid, as she remembered the last words before the disconnection:

"My whole life, Dad, I wished I'd had a different father!"

Rosemary inhaled a deep breath and held it in her lungs, as those words now seemed to clunk around in her head.

For most of her life, she had felt belittled by her father's disapproval. The insult she bestowed upon him had been in response to his threat to never be in the same room as Mark. Frank had vehemently voiced his distaste for her choice of a partner. Only recently had she realized that the heated discussion was only a father's desperate outpouring of concern for his daughter's well-being. And defending her relationship with Mark had not been worth the strained relationship with her father.

A loud chime rang from the cell phone on the nightstand.

Samantha moved to her human's lap, as Rosemary took a seated position and reached for her phone. The cat then jumped onto the tree beside the bed, and scratched the sisal rope.

"Hi, Share," Rosemary answered. There followed a pause as she listened to the caller.

"I'm okay, but I need to talk to you," she said into the phone; "I finally made a decision about Mark. Can we meet at noon?"

Chapter 2

Lucifer's Apparition

"Rose, for whatever reason, he can't show you affection," Sharon said.

Rosemary's best friend was sat across from her, at the little coffee shop in town. They occupied an outdoor table beneath the awning, sharing a bagel with their drinks.

Lucifer watched, his energy fused with Rosemary's. He would feel buoyant when her life force released the burden of negativity.

It was a humid afternoon and Sharon wore a lightweight blouse. The frilly-cap sleeves fluttered around the top of her thin arms with any movement.

"I know. I don't think he would be that type of person with anyone. But I need a man who *can* show affection. I would enjoy that in a relationship," Rosemary answered.

Sharon had called her friend "Rose" ever since meeting her, ten years ago. She had known Frank, Mark and Josephine, Rosemary's mother. Rosemary usually addressed her best friend as "Share". She had known Sharon's mother, brother and grandmother since the beginning of their friendship. Share was 5'8" and, in Rosemary's opinion, paper-thin – not skinny on purpose, just naturally smaller-framed. Sharon's shoulder-length, dark-brown hair hung down the back of her neck.

"You need a man who can show you affection," Sharon began again. "Mark didn't even give you a hug at your father's funeral. He didn't even hold your hand, Rosemary! You know how I feel about your relationship with him; I've always been honest with you. But you have to make your decisions in your own time."

Sharon then looked directly into Rosemary's eyes and firmly stated: "I think now is the time; you should leave him. You aren't happy." She took a sip from her cup of coffee. "I hate to be harsh, but I think you need honesty. You sounded serious this time."

"Share, I have been…" Rosemary lowered her head toward the table and cradled her face inside her palms. "Maybe I have avoided grieving for my mother; having a boyfriend kept my mind occupied on other things…" Her own voice sounded fuzzy, captured inside her self-made cocoon. She lifted her head and looked sheepishly at her friend. Rosemary had expected to see pity in Sharon's eyes, but they were focused.

"Well, couldn't you have picked a better boyfriend?" Sharon asked, teasingly.

"Yes."

They both chuckled.

"Most men at my age are married. The pickings are slim," Rosemary added.

"It's better to face your grief and be alone, than to be with someone like him. I love you, Rose; I want the best for you. Now is the time. You are being pushed by raw emotions right now – please follow your gut," Sharon said.

"Mark can be very rude," she then plainly stated, her face showing no signs of delicacy. "I noticed his rudeness right away: the time we went on a double date and met at my house, Mark took the remote control from the table and changed the channel on the television, without even asking if Marten minded. In my house! My fiancé was watching his football game!"

A touch of reddish freckling then quickly appeared on Sharon's cheeks. She enfolded her nose between the palms of her hands. "Rose, I'm sorry. I don't mean to hurt your feelings. Your dad just passed…"

"It's okay. I'm okay. You're right," Rosemary said. "I do appreciate the truth. I wish I had appreciated my father's opinion."

"Rose, my fiancé talks to my mom with sincerity and hugs her. He shows me, my family and my friends affection. You say you want those things."

Lucifer had stayed connected with Rosemary's energy throughout the conversation. Her mind was out of alignment with her soul, which, like each and every other soul, wanted to thrive through a peaceful mindset. Her relationship with Mark was upsetting that alignment. Any negative emotion would attract negativity.

Lucifer would stay close to her. He would feel it in his core when she remembered the reason for her soul transforming into human form: to experience life in a way which expanded oneself and the world in a positive manner.

"Mark rarely sits next to you," Sharon persisted; "he either stands alone or sits on a chair by himself."

Rosemary closed her eyes as she focused inward. "I know, you're right," she said, and looked at her friend. "I did try to communicate my need for closeness, but now… I don't see a future with him. I can't wait a second longer; I have to break up with him. Like you, my father tried to advise me, but I only heard his disappointment in me. Share, you are right."

Rosemary inhaled a deep breath. She held the breath for a long moment, then slowly released it.

"I think that Mark has given me a distorted sense of stability. His unemotional stance on life gave me a feeling of safety, because I usually reacted overemotionally to stressful situations. He calmed me with his blasé attitude." She inhaled another deep breath, and felt her t-shirt stick to her chest with the rise. Sweat beaded on her skin.

"It seems I was still being a rebellious little teenager, in my thirties," Rosemary continued. "No – a brat! But it hurt my feelings that my dad thought I wasn't taking care of my own life. I wanted him to be proud of me, for once in his life. I just wanted him to focus on the good."

She gestured to Sharon, reaching a hand out to her. "We co-own an animal shelter; that is a labor of love – why couldn't he have just concentrated on that? Our work at our animal shelter is so rewarding."

"Sometimes parents can be critical, but they just want the best for us. I think your father just wanted you to be happy, in all areas of your life, and he knew you were not happy with Mark. Anyone with eyes can see you two are not meant to be."

"The passing of my father has given me a weird sense of strength," Rosemary said. "I miss him horribly. I don't know how I'll get through the day. But his passing has reminded me that life is too short to not be at peace. I want to make my life better, in his honor… and my mother's."

Sharon smiled. "That makes me happy."

Lucifer felt his aura thicken with dark colors, as he tuned into

Rosemary's change of mood.

Rosemary moved her fingers through the sides of her hair. She lightly gripped a section of strands and pulled her brows together. "Sharon, I've decided to break up with Mark, because he scared me last week. I would have broken up with him sooner, but with my dad in the hospital…"

"What happened?" The whites of Sharon's eyes showed, as her lashes rose.

"The day before my father was put in the hospital, an incident happened at Mark's house. A co-worker closed a deal with Mark's previous clients – Mark learned that information from a phone conversation – and he slammed the phone on the table, then shoved past me; he didn't realize his shoulder bashed into me as he passed. Then he punched the wall of his living room."

Sharon's brows pulled upward, as her eyes widened further. "You leave that son of a bitch now, Rosemary! Your mom would say that, too."

"I know."

"I know you still feel guilt… about what happened when you two first met… but…"

Rosemary nodded her head in agreement.

"But, Rose, you need to take care of yourself now," Sharon said.

Lucifer knew that there was a painful experience, so deeply embedded in Rosemary's consciousness, that he could not discern it.

"Rose, I have never trusted him," Sharon said. "I've heard him raise his voice and use a sarcastic tone toward you before but, Rosemary, this pushing is something very serious. It could escalate –

though, it is abuse in itself! And punching a wall is sadistic! Has he been physical before?"

"He's never been as violent as to punch a wall, but he has inadvertently pushed past me before."

"How can I help?" Sharon asked.

"Just by being here, listening to me, you are helping." The bridge between Rosemary's eyebrows tightened, as she scrunched her face.

"I'm telling him it is over today."

Sharon reached for Rosemary's hands across the table and held them. "I love you, Rose. You can do this. Would you feel safer if I were there with you?"

"Thank you, but I'll be okay. I'll have my phone with me, it will be daylight, and my neighbor Mrs. Travis will be home."

"Call me as soon as it's over."

Lucifer felt his whole essence relax. A calm energy smoothly flowed through him. Rosemary was going to end her connection to Mark.

If she were in a loving relationship with an honorable man, Lucifer would not feel the need to watch over her. Had he found her soul by chance? Or had his core known that she was in need of spiritual direction? Maybe it had been a magical reconnection, designed by the heavens? No, it was her father's death that had brought Lucifer to his love's side. Or, possibly, he had sensed that she was unaligned with her soul. There was no romantic intervention orchestrated by the universes.

Lucifer would continue to refrain from inserting himself into her life, unless he deemed it necessary for her safety.

*

A loud bang woke Rosemary from her sleep. The front door slammed, as Mark entered the house and shut it behind him.

Lucifer would remain close to Rosemary. He would be there if she needed him.

She tightened her eyes shut, as she inhaled a deep breath.

Mark bumped into the doorway as he walked into the bedroom. He almost fell over as he fumbled, trying to unzip his pants. Teetering on one foot at a time, as he took each leg out of his pants, he almost fell over again. Samantha jumped off the bed and exited the room.

"Mark! You woke me! It is so late. You need to go home!"

The room soon reeked of digested alcohol, which now wafted from his body with a loud belch. He pulled open the covers on the bed and climbed inside. Mark pressed up against Rosemary's back and reached around her, to clasp a breast.

"No!" she said. "You've been drinking. I can smell it. Please leave this room."

He kissed the back of her neck and cupped her breast tighter.

"Mark, I don't feel good." She pushed his hand away.

He reached under her gown.

"Mark! No!" Rosemary pulled his wrist away and turned to face him. "I thought you were going to be here at four. It's almost two a.m.!" Rosemary had planned on a confrontation with him earlier in the day. It was now too late, and he was too drunk to start the discussion.

Still, even though she wished him to go home, she did not want to be the reason he caused a car accident.

14

"I took... client out," Mark said, slurring his words. "I know... lawyer is important. We'll... go tomorrow."

Rosemary turned back around. After a few moments of silence, his heavy breathing turned into snoring, muffled by his pillow.

Nausea stewed in her stomach, lying so close to him. She quietly got out of bed with her pillow and went to the couch.

Her backside met the cushion with a heavy sigh of relief. She was free from his presence for the moment. Later today she would feel liberated.

Rosemary pulled the throw blanket down from the top of the sofa and lay there. Bending from her waist, she tucked the thin material around her legs; her toes felt safely cocooned with the edge folded underneath them. In the limited space, her arms were tucked close to her body, as if she were a mummy.

Physically, she felt safe.

But the pit of her stomach seemed to burn and churn, as if a simmering pot of stew. This man was disgusting, she now realized. She'd had so many dinners with him, so many social gatherings; this repulsive man had been allowed into her bed on so many occasions...

Not a second longer. Not another day would go by with him in her life. When morning arrived...

She gazed at the tank that housed her father's betta fish; it was set on a black metal and wood stand, with a bottom cabinet. The aquarium light was turned off, but a muted floor lamp cast an orange glow over the room. The brilliant blue fins and body of the solo fish were mesmerizing, and induced visual relaxation, as it stilled underneath live greenery, above gravel and caves.

Samantha took her place on her human's chest.

"Hi, pumpkin," Rosemary whispered.

The cat settled her body weight of about twelve pounds, as if it were an extra protective covering. Deep purrs ensued.

Lucifer watched.

He wanted a better life for Rosemary. She deserved to be with an individual who aspired to reach a higher spiritual level as a couple. He now observed her sleep. It was obviously not a peaceful rest, as her eyelids squeezed together and her jaws clenched...

Rosemary opened her eyes and immediately wondered if Mark was still there. Lucifer was able to feel her anxiety. She stretched her neck as she looked toward the kitchen wall clock. It was late in the morning.

Being still, Rosemary listened. There was no noise. She breathed out through her nose with relief; he had left without waking her. She figured Mark was at work; even after a binge the night before, he was usually able to make it to work on time the next day.

The sunlight cast a bright light through the east window, and Rosemary continued to lie on the couch with Samantha. Sharon had persuaded Rosemary to take a leave of absence from work, for a grieving period. The animal shelter would survive without Rosemary for a few days.

Mark had never once kissed her goodbye in the morning, as she slept. She had never awakened to the touch of his lips on her forehead, as he left for work. If Lucifer were her boyfriend, he would kiss her before he left for work and when he got home. He would kiss her at least once an hour, for every waking moment he had the pleasure of her company. He would wrap his arms around her whenever it looked as though she needed comfort. Whenever tears touched her eyes, a smile crossed her face or her brows scrunched together, he would give her a tight hug and kiss her forehead. Lucifer knew that she wondered what it would be like to have a man who wanted to kiss her goodbye, and would call just to hear her voice on his lunch break.

Rosemary lifted Samantha from her chest and set the cat on the top of the couch. Sitting upright, her head felt as though it weighed twenty pounds. Closing her eyes caused lightheadedness.

She wondered how Mark would take the news when she ended the relationship. Hopefully, his anger would only drive him to leave with swiftness. Maybe his car tires would squeal as they turned out of her driveway.

She got up to feed the cat and fish, then got herself a bowl of cereal. Walking through her quiet home, she realized that she enjoyed the stillness. Spending time alone would be okay. Mark brought a negative energy to her personal space. Not that he lived with her full-time, but his presence lately had been excessive, and had helped her become conscious of his negative influence on her mood. His late-night arrivals at her home, after mingling with clients, had increased in frequency. Mark's alcoholism had become more apparent and intolerable.

Lucifer watched as Rosemary moved about the rooms. She settled back on the couch, where she sat quietly. A picture of her mother framed her mind's vision. The heaviness in the air surrounding Lucifer seemed to lighten, as Rosemary's thoughts changed direction.

She now looked out through the sliding glass door in the kitchen. A view of the small wood decking; then green grass and a nearby willow tree, soothed her emotions. She watched a small chipmunk chase a large squirrel down the trunk of the tree; the chipmunk lived underneath the decking. A birdbath and feeder in front of the willow allowed observation of the cardinals, blue jays and sparrows; the piercing call of a blue jay sounded through the house, as the bird flew over the lively chipmunk and squirrel.

This house had belonged to Josephine, Rosemary's mother. Though it had been built in the 1970s, the home was made in a mock-1930s design, and there had been additions, such as the wooden decking outside the kitchen. Josephine had left the home to her only child.

Rosemary was the first daughter to the first daughter to the first daughter to the first daughter of the first daughter. Josephine had thought it special to be the first female born to each generation, going back to Rosemary's great-great-great-grandmother, Helen MacMillan. Helen had been a tough Southern woman, who once blasted a warning shot from her rifle at a pack of wolves, outside her hillside cabin. She surely wouldn't have wanted her great-great-great-granddaughter to submit to Mark.

Rosemary picked up the five-by-five, framed picture of her mother on the coffee table. Looking into her mother's eyes in the photograph, Rosemary wondered if there was disappointment from beyond. Was her mother looking down on her from the heavens, with tears in her eyes, that her only daughter had made a mess of her life? Josephine had told stories of women's strength. Rosemary had not felt strong for some time. Today would be the beginning of change.

Mark did not appreciate this cozy, three-bedroomed house, and wanted Rosemary to sell it. Frank's estate money, and the profit from the intended sale of Mark's modest home, would afford them a prestigious cohabitated residence.

Rosemary had never verbally agreed to reside with Mark, and her lack of clarity in rejecting that idea puzzled her. His tendency toward anger may have caused apprehension of disagreeing with him. For a 38-year-old woman, Rosemary supposed she should have had better judgment.

Lately, it had been difficult for her to look in the mirror. Familiarity with her reflection had been missing. The detachment in her eyes scared her.

Josephine would be disappointed to witness her daughter's unhappiness. She had believed that an eager soul found its way into a human body in order to enjoy the experience.

Rosemary wiped the corners of her eyes, as a moist itchiness began to migrate. How had she made such a mockery of her life?

The voice of her truth would now have to be recognized. She would make a promise to herself to become bold. Rosemary's name meant strength, to her mother, and she was determined to realize the significance of it.

"You are *not* breaking up with me! What would you do without me? Who would take care of you? You can't even pay your electric bill without me reminding you," Mark yelled.

Lucifer felt the stress of Rosemary's heart pounding against her chest. His energy, so responsive to hers, felt as though it were inside her body. A rush of adrenaline raced through her veins and caused a pulsating headache. Her pupils dilated.

"Mark, I wish you well but, with my father's death, I am seeing things more clearly now – more simply. We just aren't good together," Rosemary said.

"Oh, really?"

"I am thankful for our time together. I have learned so much from being with you... about what I need in a relationship. We are just too different."

It was early evening, and beginning to dim outside the window. She looked toward the front door. "I need my key, please."

"Your key?" he asked.

"To this house."

Mark looked at her, his eyes worn... maybe, watery? "You know, I do care for you, Rosemary," he said.

It was slightly hurtful to look into his blue eyes, and she glanced aside. "I know..." she softly began, "hopefully you have learned—"

A stained-glass vase seemed to appear in mid-air, as it swiftly glided through the dining room and crashed against the soft, yellow-painted wall of the living room. Jagged pieces of glass fell to the floor, beside the vintage upright piano.

Rosemary concentrated. She willed tears to refrain from forming, as she watched her mother's heirloom piece crumble to the floor in a chaotic pile.

"It's just a thing," her mother would say. "It's not things that are important; it's the love that binds all things which is important."

Now was a time to look at this moment with clear understanding. Mark didn't healthily love her. He had just broken the one thing that he knew had immeasurable sentimental value to Rosemary.

She heard a shout leave her throat as an unsettling glare moved across Mark's face. His outreached arms then pushed the rocking chair beside the couch toward her. The wooden chair shoved her backward.

Her head bounced off the oak floor as she tripped, trying to move away. She felt a thump, then a dull ache.

Lucifer moved near the front door and forced himself into a meditative state. His focused energy began to take a new shape…

A red aura circled his orb, as it transformed into a vision of him with dark hair and eyes. He projected an apparition that resembled a human form, dressed in period clothing, from his past human life as Lucas: dark-brown, wool pants and a cotton shirt. Lifting an arm to his face, Lucifer felt the substance of his jaw, then he walked toward Mark with useable legs. The adrenaline and heightened emotions of both Mark and Rosemary had left his materialization unnoticed.

"Leave her be!" Lucifer hollered.

Mark turned around and sharply breathed in. In his widened eyes the whites noticeably showed, as a six-foot-tall, dark-haired man stood there in front of him. The apparition appeared solid, and would feel so to the touch.

Lucifer saw through the new form's eyes. His essence spoke through the form's mouth. He could feel through fingertips, though only for a brief time. There were no lungs, nor heart, nor blood in his veins.

"I didn't hurt her!" Mark said. "She… fell. We were arguing."

21

The apparition stood right in front of him, leaving no space between them. "Let me tell you who I am," Lucifer said: "I am the man who will crush the life out of you if you ever touch her again."

"I won't. I didn't. I didn't hit her. I…"

Lucifer moved his face to almost touching Mark's. His dark eyes turned red and held Mark's, as a red tunnel extended from Lucifer, transmitting a flow of energy through the man's essence. "Don't ever come back here again," Lucifer said. The power of the words reached Mark on a soul level, and became embedded in his human brain. "Give me the key to the house."

Mark shakily took the requested item off his keyring and set it in the palm of Lucifer's hand. Then he left.

Lucifer turned to Rosemary. He knew his eyes had returned to the dark color he usually projected. The red hue felt as though it rapidly pulled back inside his core, through his provisional eyes. The color of movement had been depleted from his energy.

Rosemary's eyes were open wide, pupils enlarged. She was lying on the floor. She sucked in a gulp of air as the strange man walked toward her.

"It's okay," Lucifer said calmly, "I'm here to help you."

She flattened her palms to the floor and attempted to push herself to a seated position, against the wall.

"Let me help you," he said. Lucifer crouched beside her and lifted her by her underarms.

She looked at him as she sat against the wall, her darkened pupils still expanded. He lifted his palms in submission, still crouched beside her.

"I won't hurt you. I'm your neighbor. I was walking by and heard screaming coming from this house."

"My neighbor?"

"Yes. I'm Lucas," Lucifer said. "I'm your new neighbor. I just moved into the house next door."

"The house next door has been vacant for years. You bought that house?"

"Yes."

"Oh, I didn't know it had been sold."

"How does your head feel?" he asked.

She tentatively pressed her palm to the side of her head, and moved her fingers underneath her hairline. When she pulled her fingers away and looked at them, they were stained red, with droplets of blood. She sucked in another gulp of air.

"You'll be okay," he said; "it's not bad. Stay right there; don't move. I'll go get something to stop the bleeding."

Lucifer got up and checked the bathroom cabinets. He found a first-aid kit and took a washcloth. He had already become accustomed to the layout of the house. The open floorplan allowed an easy flow from the living room to the dining area to the kitchen. A long hallway provided access to the back bathroom and bedroom. The wooden stairs ascending from the living room led to two bedrooms and another full bath, on the second floor. A red paisley carpet covered the middle of the yellow-oak stairway, and seemed to gracefully make its own way upstairs.

He returned to her. "Is it okay if I help you?"

She slightly nodded her head in compliance.

23

He knelt in front of her and gently lifted a section of her smooth hair. Holding her hair in place, he compressed her wound with the moistened washcloth. "This is just cool water and soap."

"Thank you for your help," she quietly said.

"No thanks needed," he smiled at her. "This won't look pretty, but it'll do the trick." He dabbed an antibiotic ointment onto a sterile pad, and secured it against her head. Slowly, he then circled her head with a roll of gauze.

Lucifer helped her stand and walked with her to the couch. He got a cup of water from the kitchen. When he returned to her, tears were beginning to fill her eyes.

"Here, sweetheart, take this," he said. He placed a mild pain reliever in her hand and gave her the cup of water. "It's just the medicine from your cabinet."

She turned it over in the palm of her hand and read the label on it. "Thank you."

She looked through the sliding glass door, at the willow tree. It seemed to calm her, and she inhaled a deep breath. Being dusk, a muted light showed through. Placing the pill on her tongue, she put the rim of the cup to her lips and swallowed the medicine.

He stood in front of her. Not meaning to stare, he realized his eyes held hers in their gaze.

"You can sit down," she told him.

"Thank you." He sat on the couch beside her.

The cat jumped up on the couch's arm, next to Lucifer.

"Hi, friend," he greeted.

Rosemary set the cup on the coffee table. "This is Samantha," she said. Then she asked: "When did you buy the house next door?"

"A few weeks ago," he said.

He took her hand and cupped the back of it. He then placed a gold key in her palm. She folded her fingers over it.

"Don't worry, he won't be back. I made sure of that," Lucifer said. The color of Rosemary's hazel eyes seemed to deepen, as she looked at him. "Do you want to talk about it?" he asked.

"About Mark?"

"You are special, and you should always be treated with care," Lucifer said. "A man should never raise his voice or hand to a woman."

"I was breaking up with him. That's why this happened." She looked downward. "I'm so sorry you had to get involved in this."

"Rosemary, please don't feel that way."

"Did I tell you my name?" she asked. Her eyelids squinted and her eyes moved sideways, as she attempted to review their conversation so far.

"I guess another neighbor told me your name," he said.

Then, Lucifer stood. "I'll be back in a few moments." He went into the kitchen and carried the garbage pail to the living room.

"Oh, Lucas, you don't have to do that," Rosemary called out from the couch.

"No problem," he called back.

As he studied the large pieces of broken glass, he wondered if they could be glued back together; the base of the vase was still intact. The temporary sensation of touch from his fingers rolled over the thick objects. A pink aura circled the pieces and they held an intense energy.

25

His fingers slowly turned them in his palm and he felt great love. He was sure that energy was meaningful to Rosemary. He decided to store the pieces in a plastic bag, and went to the kitchen to find one, as he hauled the garbage pail back.

"This might sound silly, but I'd actually like to keep the broken pieces," she said. She watched him start back toward the remains with a bag.

"My thoughts exactly," he said.

"Would you please set the bag in the cupboard in the dining room?" she asked.

"Yes, I will." Lucifer fitted the smaller pieces into the foundation of the vase, then secured everything in the bag. A traditional walnut piano stood upright, above him, a matching bench nestled underneath it. Joyful, lively energy radiated from the vintage pieces of furniture. He set the bag in the dining-room cupboard. Lucifer then returned to the couch and sat beside Rosemary.

He focused on her eyes. "Please tell me you will never have anything to do with that man again," he said.

"I won't," she said, softly. "He broke my mom's vase. He knew how special it was to me. It had been handed down to my mom from my grandmother."

"No man who loves a woman would hurt her that way."

"I know."

He picked up the cell phone that was set on the coffee table in front of them. "Here," he handed it to her, "I'm not leaving 'til you call someone to come stay the night with you."

"No, no, I'm okay," she said.

"You have been through a frightening ordeal, and you could have a concussion. I'd feel better if you called a friend to stay with you tonight."

"Honest, I'm already feeling better."

"You are coherent." He turned on the floor lamp, then studied the pupils of her eyes; they shrunk in the light and now looked normal. "Follow my finger," he said, and her eyes moved properly. "Do you feel nauseous? Or dizzy?"

"No."

"Is your vision okay?"

"Yes."

"Stand and make sure you can walk without feeling lightheaded," he said, helping her up.

She steadily walked to the front door and back.

"Good," he said. "But I'm still not leaving 'til someone gets here to stay with you." He firmly held her gaze, as they returned to their seats.

"I'm fine," Rosemary said, with a sarcastic chuckle. Still, her brows pulled together tightly, as she dialed a number into her cell phone. It was obvious that she felt pressured and embarrassed, as she spoke into the receiver. "Hi, Share…" Rosemary began, her mouth tight.

Upon ending her conversation, Rosemary turned to look at Lucifer. "She's coming – my best friend, Sharon."

"Good. I'll stay here 'til she arrives," he said.

"I'm sure you have things to do. I'll be okay alone for a few minutes."

"I'm not leaving you alone. I'll leave when your friend gets here."

"I know you think I'm stupid, but…" Moisture touched the edge of

Rosemary's eyes and made them glisten.

"Why on Earth would you say that?"

"Because I was involved with someone like Mark."

"No, I do not think you're stupid." His eyes narrowed and his brows squeezed together. "I think Mark's stupid. He had a beautiful woman and did not treat her with love."

As he held a direct gaze, she lowered her eyes. He touched his fingertips to her chin and lightly lifted it, then released it when her eyes met his. "When one's mind becomes out of alignment with her soul, she can make decisions that are harmful to her. Maybe you just need to sit and relearn what your soul wants. You need to take care of yourself, that's all."

Rosemary blinked hard, and again broke the direct gaze into Lucifer's eyes. Was his advice too harsh? Too intricate?

He gestured toward the kitchen; "You have a green thumb."

Succulent plants lined her windowsill, and a table alongside it. The midday sun had cast brightness onto the tops of the greenery, earlier that day. They flourished under Rosemary's care. He recognized the connection she felt to all living things; she naturally shared a kinship with her plants, her willow tree and cat. A handful of pretty feathers were set in a small china bowl on the sill: dove feathers, a blue jay feather...

"Jade is my favorite," Rosemary said. "I call the jade plant 'Moon'. She is glorious. My plants keep me company – along with Samantha."

The golden cat had jumped onto the back of the couch, and she now perched herself above their heads. Her green eyes quickly darted toward the glass door, to watch a couple of squirrels running across the deck, in the dim outdoor light. One corner of Rosemary's mouth turned upward in a half-smile. The moisture in her eyes evaporated.

"You will probably find this odd…" she started, "but my mom, Josephine, was an earthy person, and named me after the herb, rosemary. She said rosemary was a strong, evergreen shrub; it holds its strength in the winter months. Rosemary stays green and fragrant, even in the winter, as long as the temperature remains moderate. Beds of rosemary always lined Mama's back-door walkway, like petunias line most folks' entrances." A small breath exhaled from her nose. "The rosemary is still there today. I do like the smell as I go out the back door."

Lucifer blocked out everything except the vision of Rosemary's face, as he looked at it. He felt himself engaged by her story. Even with gauze wrapped around her head, she looked beautiful.

"And Mama's favorite color was green – especially in winter," Rosemary said. "Green was the color of life to her; abundance." She chuckled. "Sure enough, the rosemary, green and erect, almost always pokes through the white snow."

"I love that story: the meaning of your name," he said. "I don't think it's odd at all."

"The willow tree is named Audrey: Audacious Audrey. My mom gave the humungous tree a bold name because of its size. Plus, she named it after her cat, Audrey.

"I like the sound of your name. Lucas. Lucas…?" she said, tilting her head to one side, clearly wanting to know his last name.

His provisional eyes glanced upon the closest object in their line of sight: the light-brown coffee table.

"Lucas Brownwood."

"That's charming. Such an awesome name." Her lips curved up in a small, sweet smile. "I'm Rosemary Winters."

The home was decorated with many period pieces – probably family heirlooms and other 1930s-style furniture. The white-oak wood of the coffee table and desk added warmth to the fresh, white wall paint. A pale yellow accent wall distinguished the living room, along with a large, natural, woven rug. He looked down at the cream-colored plush cushion of the sofa; it had obviously been a newer purchase. An end table provided the spot for a vintage-looking mahogany record player. The coffee table was opposite them, an oval rug underneath. The organic colors resembled scenes of a forest.

"Tell me more about your mother, Rosemary Winters."

She glanced toward the piano. "My mom loved music. She was a member of her high school choir; she had a baritone singing voice. She would play the piano and sing. And, she would swing beneath the willow and sing…"

Rosemary quietly snorted as she looked at him. "I did not inherit her musical gifts. But I crave hearing her play and sing for me once again, if only for five minutes. My mom passed about two years ago – and my dad just five days ago." Moisture seemed to polish her eyes in varying shades of brown. Trust and innocence were transmitted through those windows to her soul; her loss, pain and love were honest. Rosemary spoke matter-of-factly, as though in shock.

"Rosemary, I'm so sorry. I'm here for you if you ever need anything," Lucifer said. "Tell me about your father."

"He loved Asia. He traveled there for business. He'd bring me back gifts. To my dad, Buddha represented the notion that we each need to carry our innate gifts and laughter with us, wherever we go. He called me Rosy, his little rosebud. He thought pink was the color of love. He always got me rose-colored flowers."

Rosemary looked toward the fish tank, next to the television, and she softly groaned. "I told my dad not to buy betta fish from a pet store, which stored them in a tiny container; that is inhumane. Betta fish live free, in marshes, ponds or streams. Some are stolen from the wild, like hermit crabs."

She closed her eyes for a moment, then she said, reopening her eyes: "Don't get me started on hermit crabs! They are stolen from their home, where they could live for forty years, with the proper diet and environment. Hermit crabs need very, very deep, damp sand to burrow under, in order to molt." Angry wrinkles now formed on her forehead. "Those torture chambers some poor crabs are kept in aren't big enough for a single ant. I wish people would do research before buying a pet. Poor fireflies are put in jars. What human would want to be boxed up or put in a jar? It's really disgusting how some humans treat critters, their Earthly companions."

Her face then softened, with a childlike pout. "I'm sorry... I went off on a tangent. It's just... animal welfare is very dear to my heart."

"I agree a thousand percent," Lucifer firmly stated.

"I told him not to buy from that pet store," she continued, "but my dad told me that he felt so sorry for the guy in that tiny bowl, suffering. My dad had such a gentle heart, he couldn't help himself; he bought the last betta there. He named it Rambo, and got Rambo a seventy-five-gallon tank." She chuckled, looking at Lucifer. "Oh, my gosh, it was a

31

big ordeal getting this tank here, but it had to be done. I collected the water in buckets, and got movers that knew how to handle a fish tank.

"My dad passed from cancer," Rosemary said, then inhaled deeply. "He found out one day and passed five days later. I'm glad it was quick for him. My mom's illness worsened over the last few years of her life. Her blood disease exhausted her."

Rosemary softly snorted again. "Silly…" she said.

"What's silly?"

"That I feel so comfortable telling you everything I just told you. I must have bombarded you with all that information. I don't even know you."

"I asked," he said. "And… you do know me: I'm your neighbor, in the house right beside you."

"Thank you, Lucas." She inhaled deeply, then bit down on her lower lip. "That was a very nice thing you did for me today: saving my life."

"Your life is precious, my dear."

She looked at him with an odd gaze, as though hearing that statement from a man for the first time.

Sharon soon arrived at her friend's home and, after a short introduction, Lucifer left the two alone.

He headed toward his pretend house, where he would be squatting while human. He had decided that he would truly become a human being for a brief period. He had to ensure that Rosemary didn't encounter any more trouble with Mark, and so would need a place to stay, close to Rosemary. The abandoned house next door to her would suffice. Just in case the women glanced out of the window, he projected his image to walk across her open lawn.

He had introduced himself as Lucas because his current title, Lucifer, would have horrified her. Lucas had been his first human name. The name Lucas was a derivative of Lucious, meaning "light". His first human name had been given to him by his first blood-grandfather, Lucious.

Becoming human would be a process. After one more meeting with Rosemary, in the morning, he would begin the laborious transformation.

Chapter 3

Rosemary Remembers

"Rose, are you really okay?" Sharon asked, for the second time. Sitting next to Rosemary on the couch, she lightly touched a hand to her friend's gauze-encircled head.

"Yes," Rosemary faintly said. Her voice seemed to crack from dryness, and she swallowed hard to moisten her throat. "I am okay," she returned, with firm pronunciation. She mindfully pulled the edges of her mouth upward. "I will be better than okay now."

Only a best friend would recognize Sharon's lounge clothes; the long-sleeved cotton shirt and form-fitting sweatpants, flared at the hem, would be presentable to any passerby. Rosemary looked down at her own clothes. She thought her spaghetti-strap top still looked neat. Her casual, loose-fitting jeans added balance to the snug shirt.

She lifted her hand to her chest. Inhaling a deep breath, her forearm rose and fell. Rosemary felt almost whole inside. Her heart felt as though it were already on its way to recovery. Her soul felt at peace. She was beginning to find her strength. Life would be changed; she would be completely alone. Being alone would not be as frightening as not listening to her soul.

"Did you call the police? Should we take you to the hospital?" Sharon asked.

"I'm okay. I don't need to go to the hospital," she smiled, to assure her friend. "I don't even have a headache." Rosemary's eyes strained a narrowed gaze from the lie. "You don't need to worry anymore, Share, I am taking care of myself now."

It seemed that the back of her eyes hurt, as she rolled them up toward the ceiling corner, in thought. "I will consider filing a police report, but I think Lucas scared the shit out of Mark; he won't be back. He practically ran out of here."

"Tell me what happened. You said you broke up with him. That bastard hurt you?"

"I did break up with him – respectfully; he came over, after work today. He did not take it well. He pushed the rocking chair into me and I fell."

Sharon shook her head and puckered her red-stained lips in a tight ball.

"I just have a little cut," Rosemary assured her.

"You definitely should file a police report. I will take you tomorrow."

"I'll think about that. But Lucas took care of him. I honestly don't think Mark will be back."

"Who was this guy, Lucas? He's living next door now? He bought that scary old house? He helped you?"

"Yes, Lucas is my new neighbor. He said he was walking by and heard screaming."

"Thank God he did."

"Yes. Mark deliberately shoved the chair into me. I fell... then I remember this stranger. It was Lucas." Her eyes ached a little more, and they narrowed again as she tried remembering every detail of the event. "Lucas scared the shit out of him, somehow."

"Good. Maybe that's what Mark needed: to see a man protecting you!"

Sharon rose from her seat. "We need some coffee." She turned her head to look at Rosemary. "Then, I want the whole story!"

"No, you need to go to bed. I'll be okay. You can have my bed; I'll watch television on the couch. I can always sleep upstairs, in my old bedroom."

"I'm here to keep you company – Lucas made sure of that," Sharon said, with mock ridicule. "He does seem to be a nice person, but very protective! Your new neighbor is also very cute – did you notice?"

The bluntness caused a small smile to form on Rosemary's mouth. "I did notice."

She lifted her hand back to her chest. "Share, it finally became clear in my head today: Mark has never cared about my best interests. He wanted me to sell my mom's house, and he knows I love it here. He was anxious to hear how much my dad's estate was worth." Her arm waved toward the yellow back wall. "He broke my grandmother's vase! He knows I treasure it. He does things he knows will hurt me. That's not love."

Sharon's red lips formed a large smile. She moved her hand to Rosemary's knee and patted it. "Put your feet up. I'm going to go make that coffee." She headed to the kitchen. "I'm so proud of you, Rose, finally taking care of yourself." Her words were practically obstructed by the clanking of mugs.

"Do you think I'm stupid?" Rosemary called.

Sharon momentarily stepped out of the kitchen and studied her friend. "Why would you say such a thing?"

"Because I stayed with him for so long. Almost one year."

Sharon returned to the coffee pot and raised her voice. "No, I think you are finally taking care of yourself, and getting rid of things that are bad for you."

The familiar smell and sound of brewing coffee was a comfort to them both, Rosemary was sure.

"I'm going to make a whole pot of coffee, then we'll watch a movie," Sharon called from her spot.

"No, you need to go to bed, Share. You will be at the shelter by yourself tomorrow."

"I'll be fine. My mom is going to help out at the shelter until you come back; she will help walk dogs and clean. Now, be a good girl, put your feet up and turn on the television."

Loud clanking continued from the kitchen, as Sharon wiped counters and washed a few dishes. Rosemary lifted her legs and rested the heels of her feet on the coffee table. She inattentively gazed out of the glass door, toward the darkened willow, and was surprised by the thoughts that surfaced: they became focused on Lucas. She had felt unusually safe in his presence, despite having only just met him. It had been uncharacteristic of her to allow a stranger into her home, her thoughts and her space, but the fight with Mark had been traumatic. They had been extraordinary circumstances.

Lucas was very attractive, but conveyed a brotherly impression. Maybe the connection she had felt with him was on a friend level, not sexual, and therefore she felt no anxiety. He had protected her as if a brother. She had felt an overwhelming sense of trust in him.

Maybe Lucas did have boundary issues, though. It had felt a bit intrusive when he handed her *her own* cell phone and compelled her to call Sharon, but she regarded his invasiveness only as concern for her well-being.

Lucas said that Rosemary's mind was out of alignment with her soul. *"When one's mind becomes out of alignment with her soul, she can make decisions that are harmful to her. Maybe you need to just sit and relearn what your soul wants,"* he had said. It had been an odd thing for a man to say to a woman he had just met for the first time. Yet, he seemed absolute in his assessment of her. How had he known exactly the right description of the current disorder in her life? Was he sensitive to human psychology? Spirituality?

Rosemary now gazed at the framed picture of her mother on the coffee table. She tried her hardest to look into the eyes of that loving face. Picking up the frame, moisture built in her own eyes, as she thought how wonderful it would be to share even five minutes with her mother. As Rosemary lifted the picture to her chest and cradled it, she allowed emotion to fill her. Usually, it was easier to reminisce in the safety of her bedroom, under covers. Soft lips touched her fingertip as she kissed her flesh; she then pulled the picture away, to rest that finger on her mother's image.

Rosemary replaced the frame in its place, then walked to the bathroom. She looked in the mirror, at her bandaged head. A brownish-red color stained the gauze, in a small patch. A slight bruising was forming near her left eye, close to the cut. Her reflection looked foreign. Her former face seemed to have been stripped from her skin.

A wrong turn had been taken in her life, and left her unsure of her strength. What foolishness had fogged her perception enough to remain with Mark for almost a year? Truly, perhaps being involved with a man kept her mind busy, and off the grief of losing her mother.

Rosemary had met Mark at the hospital in the adjacent town. She had been donating blood, and he was, too – she figured he was a decent person if he would do such a thing. She donated in honor of her mother, and thought that he must have a similar reason. Later, she learned that he had donated in honor of his grandfather, who had passed from leukemia. That one empathetic gesture had been ingrained in her memory and, it seemed, her heart. Rosemary and Mark casually dated for a couple of months. She liked his confidence, his assertiveness; he talked to anyone, and felt comfortable in any establishment. They exclusively dated after that. Before she realized it, almost a year had passed.

There had been signs of Mark's anger issues. He would ignore Rosemary's conversation at the beginning of their relationship, and minor irritations, such as her asking him to listen, would cause his raised voice. He had also expressed irritation toward a waitress, when told his meal choice wasn't available. And, once, he had disallowed another vehicle a safe merge onto the freeway, because it had attempted to pass him.

Rosemary had become rebellious of her father's disdain for her boyfriend. Had Frank thought his daughter not intelligent enough to discern an unhealthy relationship? Maybe if his disapproval had been spoken only once, there would have been a quiet space for her to make the correct decision on her own…

Her lungs now held a gulp of air, as she remembered the night Mark had punched the wall. At the time Mark smashed his fist against his gray-painted drywall, the ghastly shivers that seemed to cling to her bones signaled the time for her departure. She had witnessed his visceral anger. Then the hardness of his shoulder roughly banging into her had upset her footing, nearly knocking her off balance.

She now released the held breath through open lips. From this moment forward, she would make wiser decisions for her life. The change would happen now. She had ignored her own needs. It seemed, now, that the only direction would be an arrow pointed inward. The injury that marked her face was in plain view, and would serve as a reminder. She would remember, in time, what it felt like to have positive expectancy in her life. The scar would only be temporary, and it felt as though her soul would heal along with her body.

The event of the recent passing of her father seemed to cling inside of her gut, as though it were a black cloud waiting to release its rain. It hovered there, but did not blacken her whole core. She knew that the rain would come after the thawing of her numbness. Right now, her small triumph made her joyful. Her father was happy that his daughter had finally become conscious of her ill-lived life, she was sure.

She would remember what it was like to be her former self, before her mother's passing. Her soul would remember. For the first time in a long time, an easy smile naturally separated her lips and widened her mouth. It had depth. It felt nice. A tingle of exhilaration seemed to travel through her bones and awaken her senses. She used to feel girly, sexy, funny, lighthearted, trusting and loved – she knew she'd feel that way again.

It felt as if a weight had been lifted from her soul. She felt weightless, ridding herself of negativity. Her mind visualized this present moment of her life as a single feather, floating freely in the breeze.

Still, she missed her mother. Tears quietly rolled down her cheeks, and she looked at the reflection of her gauze-encircled, reddened, bruised, wet face.

Walking back to the living room, Sharon met her. Rosemary felt warm, strong arms wrap around her back. The cocoon felt safe.

Rosemary heard a soft knocking on her front door, as she stirred a cup of coffee in her long, white robe. She set the cup on the living room table. It was eleven a.m., on Wednesday. Sharon had left for work a couple of hours prior, having had only a two-hour nap. Rosemary tentatively walked toward the door.

A short, quick breath was lost in her chest, as her heart thumped hard. The key from Mark had been returned to her...

She reached the entrance and held her breath, as she looked out through the peephole. It was Lucas.

"It's Lucas, Rosemary," he huskily called out.

She exhaled her stored breath and opened the door.

"Lucas, hi," she said, stepping aside in her slippers. "Come on in, but you'll have to excuse how I look."

"You always look beautiful, my dear." He studied her bandaged head. "I thought I'd come by and see how you're feeling today, neighbor. Maybe you will let me take off the gauze and see how your wound is doing?"

"Oh, you don't have to—"

"I insist," he said.

He walked inside, bent over, took off his dressy, moccasin-style shoes and walked into the living room. Rosemary had large feet for a woman, and was pleased to distinguish, through his socks, the ample width and length of Lucas's.

Lucas was clad in dark-brown, wool pants, creased down the middle, and a pressed white cotton shirt. It looked to be the same outfit as yesterday; Rosemary couldn't be positive. But he was always neatly dressed.

Whatever reason had brought him into her life, she was thankful. Somewhere deep inside of her, she knew that she was meant to have met him. She sharply breathed in at the weirdness of her thoughts.

Samantha was perched on the top of the couch, and Lucas gave her a pet on the head. "Hi there, friend," he softly greeted. Then he asked, turning to Rosemary: "How are you feeling, sweetheart?"

When she moved her head in any direction, a dull ache followed. "I do have a little headache now. But that's to be expected."

"I'll be right back," he said. He walked to her bathroom, then returned with a bottle of medicine. Lucas opened the top of the container and handed her a pill.

My goodness, he is a take-charge type of person. Maybe a little too assertive…? Rosemary was in too much discomfort to complain, and took the pill with her coffee. After she swallowed down the medicine, Lucas stepped directly in front of her and began examining the bandage.

She hadn't been able to attach the right words to her feelings last night, but now they came to her. The intensity of Lucas's attention could feel as though he was bombarding her personal space. His focus swarmed every inch of her, as if a flock of incessant birds. She sensed his sentiment was sincere, and there was no fear, only a feeling of being overwhelmed; he did not respect boundaries. Being in her robe, feeling vulnerable, she was not comfortable with him being so intimate with her.

He moved closer and his black eyes studied her face, her head. He was close enough to smell her, see her flaws... she hoped she didn't reek of body odor. Was the skin surrounding her eyes dull and wrinkled? Slowly, he unrolled the bandage. His breath cooled her forehead, as he intently bared her injury. When he breathed out, it smelled fresh, like a winter breeze. He moved even closer. His face looked as though it would be smooth to the touch. The olive-colored skin was clean-shaven, with no blemishes. There was no distinct smell of aftershave. Rosemary's eyes ached as she moved them sideways, to see his closeness.

"Your wound has stopped bleeding," he said. He gently held her hair in place. "It has formed a nice scab. You can leave the bandage off, but be careful to remember not to bother this area."

His long fingers entangled her hair, and his fingertips placed five points of a cool, light pressure on her scalp. She noticed his fingernails were clean and neat, as his hands reached for her.

"Thank you for checking it," she said.

"Of course." His black eyes, which had inspected her wound, now focused on her eyes. His gaze seemed to pierce beyond them and through, to the back of her skull. His smooth, black hair looked soft, as it feathered behind his head in a close cut; the looser waves on top would look boyish if they were tousled. The olive skin of his cheekbones seemed to set the stage for those dark eyes of his. His mouth looked strong…

"Would you like a cup of coffee?" she asked. "I just made a pot. Being home all day, I might just drink the whole thing if you don't have some."

"Sure, I'd love a cup." He followed her to the kitchen.

"Good morning, Moon," she said, as she tenderly pinched a thick leaf of the jade plant between her thumb and forefinger.

She turned to Lucas. "Actually," she said, "I was going to stop by your house today."

She caught the beginning of a thin smile tip the corners of his mouth, as she moved to the cupboard and pulled a mug from it. A rich, nutty aroma filled her nostrils as she poured the steaming, dark liquid into the cup.

Rosemary handed Lucas the coffee. "I wanted to properly thank you for your kindness," she said. "I don't know what would have happened if you hadn't magically shown up, like an angel."

His smile sharply dissipated. "I'm no angel," he said. A small smile then reappeared on his face. "You are the angel, my dear. I'm glad I happened to be walking by your house at the right time," he said.

She watched Lucas hold the mug just under his nostrils and inhale deeply. "Would you like milk or sugar?" she asked.

"No. Black is good." He closed his eyes as he continued the long whiff. The attentiveness was intriguing.

"Anyway, I was going to stop by your house today, to ask you if you'd like to come over here for dinner this Sunday evening? I thought I'd show my appreciation for what you did for me, by making you a home-cooked meal," she said.

"That sounds like Heaven; I'd love that. Thank you, Rosemary." The edges of his mouth turned up in a smile… No… a grimace?

Whenever he moved his lips, something seemed to stir inside her. The movements of his mouth appeared very intentional. Anytime he moved any part of his body, it looked to be deliberate.

"I do have to tie up some loose ends at work, in California," he said; "I will be gone for a week. Can we have dinner next Sunday?"

"Of course," Rosemary said. She walked toward the couch. "Let's sit down." The open-concept home allowed an easy flow from room to room.

Lucas seemed to enjoy looking at all the antiques and wall hangings. Josephine had been an amateur artist, and Rosemary had framed most of her mother's sketches, drawings and paintings. She had signed all of her work in calligraphy. Her favorite subject was nature; a simple pencil sketch of a rosemary shrub hung in the kitchen, and an acrylic painting of the willow tree decorated the yellow wall in the living room. Several crayon, charcoal and pen drawings of nature and animals graced the bedroom, bathroom and hall walls.

Lucas followed Rosemary, then sat down beside her. "Your home is old-fashioned, with modern touches. It has a joyful aura about it," he said.

"Thank you," she snickered. "The home does need a *modern* pole barn. There has never been a garage on the property."

"Yes, a lifelong endeavor," he breathed.

45

"What do you like to eat?" Rosemary asked.

"Anything home-cooked will be delicious."

"What do you like to drink with dinner?"

"I'm not picky: water, coffee, soft drinks..."

A comfortable silence graced the air for a few moments, as they sat there.

"What...?" he began, looking toward the glass door.

"What?"

His line of vision continued past Rosemary. "You have a visitor."

Rosemary followed his gaze and saw a small, gray head bobbing up and down, in front of the sliding glass door. The bright sunlight of late morning framed the view of the creature. The top of its narrow, gray head tapered to a peak at the nose, with whiskers. Small, round, black eyes looked intently inside the house, as the head continued to bob.

"That's Nancy," she said.

"You name the squirrels?"

Rosemary turned from watching Nancy to look at Lucas; the squirrel's black eyes locked on his. Lucas's expression seemed one of fascination.

"Yes. She wants breakfast; I didn't feed them yet this morning." She felt a smile soften her face. "Doesn't everybody feed the squirrels?"

"Some people feed the squirrels, but not everybody has squirrels with names knocking on their door."

The largeness of his widened eyes brought a chuckle from Rosemary, accompanied by an audible snort. "Nancy has a yellowish coloring around her eyes and nose," she said. "She'll tap on the glass door with her little paw."

"That little paw has long claws, you know."

"Better to grip nuts! I toss out walnuts, which I get in bulk at the grocery store. The walnuts are in the shell. I like them, too! I have a nutcracker for me. I get a variety of shelled nuts and peanuts. I also give the squirrels apples, grapes and strawberries. Some birds like the nuts and fruit, too."

Rosemary got up and tossed Nancy a handful of nuts, kept in a bag in the kitchen cabinet, then returned to her seat beside Lucas. They watched the squirrel eat its treat, and Rosemary felt the muscles of her face loosen with an easy smile, as Nancy gnawed on a walnut. "It's good for them," she told Lucas. "It's a habit that is vital to keep their teeth healthy."

"You know so much about animals," he said, in a convincingly sincere, low voice.

"Nancy likes to sit in the sun and crack open her nuts by the steps of the deck. I'll give the birds some seeds in a little bit."

Nancy's tail flipped up behind her head. The squirrel had a stripe of brownish fur down the middle of its back and fluffy tail, from which silver tips of hair stood erect on both sides.

The black squirrel that usually accompanied Nancy now cautiously approached the steps. The white fur on the tip of the tail caused the animal to resemble a skunk.

Rosemary continued looking out the glass door but not really focusing on anything. "I can't wait to get back to work tomorrow," she said.

"Are you sure you're ready? Do you need more grieving time?"

"I'm ready. Work is my family."

"What is your occupation?"

Samantha jumped onto the plant table, next to the kitchen windowsill. The various succulents that were set on the table slightly jiggled with the impact of the pounce. Samantha didn't bother the plants; she just rested in the perfect sunspot, beside the jade and aloe vera. The jade plant towered above the cat. It was about three feet tall and spread the width of about three feet. Thick, green leaves sprouted in every direction.

"Sharon and I co-own an animal shelter near town. Sharon has veterinarian technician certification, and she used to work at a veterinarians' office. I have a business management degree." She chuckled. "We both love animals, so thought a shelter made sense, with our backgrounds. When my mom passed, she left me a little money and Share was able to get a small loan. We have fun," she said, smiling.

Lucas's eyebrows pulled together, forcing a deep line between them. "Do you have volunteers at your shelter?" he asked.

"Yes, sometimes. Anyone who shows up is welcome to help out. We always welcome volunteers."

"How long have you owned the shelter?"

"About two years now."

"I will happen to have some extra time on my hands, when I get back from California in a week. Would it be okay if I volunteered at your shelter? Next Thursday morning?"

"Of course! We can always use the help." Rosemary felt the ends of her mouth pull slightly outward, as she tilted her chin up to Lucas.

48

"That's nice of you."

She rose from her seat. "I'm going to fill my cup," she said.

He followed her into the kitchen, and Rosemary poured the coffee. It looked as though it were a chocolate ribbon, flowing from pot to cup. She then added sugar and milk. "My mom always said: 'Give me a little coffee with my sugar and milk, please.'"

Lucas's elbow pressed against the counter, as he held the mug in his hand. Rosemary scrunched her brows together as she looked at him.

"Are you going to renovate your house? That will take up a lot of your time," she said, starting to walk toward the dining table. Lucas followed. They sat across from one another at the table.

"I will work slowly on the house renovation. It's a hobby. It will be a lifelong endeavor," he answered, a thin smile etching his face. "I'd like to volunteer some of my time to a good cause, though... like your animal rescue."

"I never asked you. Sorry. Last night, of course, was hectic, to say the least. What is your occupation?" she asked. He seemed to be an intellectual, not a layman.

Lucas quickly broke eye contact. His face tilted downward. He had been looking directly at her and now seemed to draw back. His thumb and forefinger traced the edge of his mouth. He reconnected eye contact. "I'm an engineer," he said, in a deep, gruff voice.

"My dad was an engineer! A mechanical engineer. What kind of engineer are—"

"I plan, manage, try to improve things," he quickly supplied.

"Did work bring you here? To Wolfe County?"

"No, I'm currently on a leave of absence." He shifted in his seat and looked uncomfortable. "I thought I needed a break. Thought I'd buy a fixer-upper and restore it. Sort of a hobby of mine."

"Where do you live?" She shifted in her seat. "I mean, where did you live before here? California?"

"I like to travel, so I don't stay connected to one place, but my last residence was in California."

Samantha jumped on the dining table and sat directly in front of Lucas. She serenely fixed her gaze on him, her back now facing Rosemary.

"'Mantha! Get down from there!" Rosemary yelled at the cat.

"Oh, she's okay," Lucas said. "We are becoming friends." He ran his fingers along the length of her back and she remained fixed.

"Well, I can see you're good with cats; Samantha rarely visits with my company. But she's not allowed on the table." Rosemary picked up the cat and placed her on the couch. Then she returned to Lucas.

"I love all animals," he said. "But I don't believe they are *just* animals; they are fellow souls."

"Yes," Rosemary thought out loud, "I've always considered animals to be our equals. They each deserve the love and respect any human does. Like any vulnerable soul, they need our protection."

"Ha!" Lucas bellowed. A hearty chuckle sounded from his nose, his lips forming a high-curved smile.

Rosemary felt her eyes widen with the loudness of his continued laughter.

Why?

"There's a little boutique in town called 'Samantha's Closet'," he said; "does your cat own that store?"

"Ha!" Rosemary now matched the volume of his laugh, her lips parted. It felt good. The smile on her face felt naturally initiated, from deep within her soul. The laugh came forth from inside her chest, and the sound and vibration felt foreign; too much time had passed, in the last couple of years, without organic laughter. "Why, yes, my Samantha does own that boutique. She is a very fancy girl and sells only the finest lingerie."

"Ha! I did peek in the window. It does look fancy."

Lucas pushed his chair back and stood. "I'd better get going now," he said. He lifted the coffee mug to his nose and inhaled once more, then walked to the kitchen. Rosemary followed and watched him set his mug in the sink. He then walked toward the front door.

"Well... Rose Petal..." Lucas's eyebrows lifted, as if they had asked a question. "Do you mind if I call you Rose Petal?"

Rosemary looked at him. His eyes were dark and unwavering. He was serious. *Why would he want to call me Rose Petal?* She didn't know how to respond.

He didn't wait for her answer. Bending over, he put on his shoes. Then, he looked up at Rosemary. "I will see you at the shelter next Thursday morning," he said.

"You... you take the dirt road here, a mile up," she began, with a creaking in her voice. "It's... it'll be on the right. It's just about a mile west of town. It's called Wolfe Rescue. We start at nine a.m."

"I'll see you there in a week, Rose Petal," he said on his way out.

He turned back. "Please take care of yourself until then," he gravely added.

"I will," seemed to emerge from her lips, in a whisper.

51

Rosemary locked the door when he exited. Then she walked to the kitchen sink and set her cup in it, next to his. As she looked down, she noticed that his was still full; he hadn't taken a sip. Thinking back, she remembered him bringing the cup to his nose and smelling it, but she did not remember him taking a drink.

She felt her forehead lift, as she pondered the reason. He didn't like the smell of it, so he didn't drink it...?

Chapter 4

Rosemary's Work

It had been a week and two days since her breakup with Mark. The past week of work had alleviated her grief. Even though she was still mourning the recent loss of her father, Rosemary woke the following Thursday morning feeling energized, with new perspectives about life. It felt as though a fresh vitality had been breathed into her.

She had hardly been able to recognize the woman she had become with Mark, and it had been difficult to look in the mirror. Negative emotions of anxiety and depression had once plagued her; now she could see a glimpse of her former self being restored. Life before Mark and before her mother's passing was a positive experience. She had chosen to stay in a relationship that was detrimental to her well-being, most likely to bypass grieving.

Talking about her mother with Lucas had seemed to ease some of the pain that came with reliving those heartfelt memories, which were able to bubble up softly, like a gentle water fountain. Some of the aching was released sweetly, in a manageable way, with someone who took an interest and didn't rush the slow pace. Things Rosemary hadn't thought of in two years now seemed to resurface, and she relived her mother's memory with joy.

For now, she wanted to take pleasure in this good mood. But what was special about this day?

She smiled. She knew exactly what might be different about today.

Her thoughts turned to Lucas.

He would be at the shelter this morning. His demeanor had projected honor, and she trusted his words as truth.

She looked through her closet. Standing in front of her bedroom mirror, she tried on her favorite work t-shirt; it had the shelter's logo printed on it. Sharon had designed a cat and dog emblem on the front, with *"Wolfe Rescue"* printed across the back. Then Rosemary pulled the shirt off, over her head, and replaced it on its hanger. She pushed aside a string of other shirts, looking for the raglan top with brown, capped sleeves and a white bodice, which clung to the curves of her body. There it was. She pulled it off the hanger and laid it on the bed.

Looking in the mirror, only a tiny, light-colored bruise remained near her hairline. It could be covered with a little make-up. Rosemary thought herself attractive for a brunette. Since her mid-twenties, she had covered gray roots with color matching the true hue of her natural strands. In younger years, she assumed that most men fantasized about blondes, so her mother had dyed her hair a medium-blonde color.

Josephine was five-foot-five-and-a-half inches and thin, at 125lbs. Her features were delicate, with her oval face, slender fingers and size-eight feet. Rosemary appreciated her own figure, though it was more of the athletic type. She was half an inch shorter than her mother and, at her current weight, about fourteen pounds heavier than her mom. She had recently lost about fifteen pounds, due to anxiety concerning her estranged relationship with her father and his subsequent illness. She had needed to lose the extra weight, having gained it during her discontented relationship with Mark. Her stomach had become round with the weight gain; it wasn't flat, like Sharon's. There were still a

54

few more pounds that needed to be shed, to reach her goal of 135. Once in a while, she'd get discouraged at her image in close-fitting garments, but, for the most part, was proud of the recent achievement.

Rosemary had inherited broad shoulders from her father. For a female, she also considered her hands and feet a large size. Lucas's hands appeared larger than hers, though she'd have to hold hers up to his to check. His feet had looked larger than hers in his socks.

Opening her lingerie drawer, she thumbed through an assortment of bras and underwear. Her favorite push-up bra would help her look extra curvy today, but it would get soiled; a day's work at the shelter always produced sweat. The sports bra would be more practical. A small smile tugged at one side of her face, as she looked at the fancy undergarments. The thought of a man seeing them on her let her know that there was the notion of future romance in her life.

Rosemary fastened the sports bra across her chest and fitted the raglan top over her head. She then gathered her hair into a band. Putting her hair up into a bun, she could be ready for a casual day in a few minutes. Lip gloss, blush and mascara could be applied in short order.

Now a better understanding of healthy living would become her focus. She felt her smile pull the edges of her lips up wider, as she continued sorting her thoughts. With Mark rid of from her present, hope for a healthy, loving partnership with a man was beginning to bud in her mind. Most men, she hoped, would find her easygoing.

Sharon's fiancé was proof to Rosemary that nice men truly existed. At home, Marten quite often waited on Sharon, bringing her refreshments. He held her hand while they walked. One time,

Rosemary remembered, he had paid close attention to Sharon's footing on the ice-coated sidewalk, as he held her close to his side. Sharon periodically received texts from Marten, throughout the workweek, expressing his love. Rosemary wanted to be in a relationship with a partner who thought of her in her absence.

The passing of Rosemary's father helped her to relearn how short one's time truly is on Earth. Mark's lack of concern for her had aided the realization that she wanted a partner in life who did care for her. Even casual dating would be different from her past, because of these new perspectives. She would no longer waste her time with someone who did not make her laugh, treat her like a lady and make her feel special.

She had considered what it would be like to kiss Lucas. She liked him, but each time they interacted he emitted a brotherly vibe toward her. He was a little pushy, but she sensed that came from a protective spirit. Lucas spoke with certainty. His words held seriousness, and Rosemary felt he would follow through with his promises. His voice carried a sincere tone, and the rhythm in which he spoke was almost hypnotic; a smooth cadence. She felt safe with him. Not that false sense of safety by acting unemotional, like with Mark. Rosemary felt secure with Lucas because she knew she *could* be emotional; she could actually feel things without being ridiculed. And she knew that if she collapsed, from being overwhelmed in times of grief, Lucas would be there for her. He would offer comfort. He would literally carry her, if need be…

*

Rosemary turned her white pickup truck into the shelter's parking lot, on Thursday at nine a.m.

Sharon's cousin owned a custom-business-sign company, and had supplied the eighteen-foot pole sign, which greeted customers from the small front lawn; it read *"Wolfe Rescue"* in red letters, with the same cute cat and dog logo that Sharon had designed. Rosemary looked up at it now and smiled.

It had been a pleasant ride here. Rosemary had enjoyed driving slowly, with an open window, down the dirt backroad, her 'fifties music playing. The late summer breeze now glided inside the cab and moved sweetly through her hair, as she pulled into her usual spot, farthest from the entrance.

An unfamiliar vehicle was parked near the entrance; she figured it would be Lucas's. It was a shiny, black sports convertible. *Hmm, edgy and vintage*. Lucas sat on the bench overlooking the parking lot.

Rosemary figured that she had blushed, because her face felt warm, and she smiled unreservedly, for no good reason. She glanced sideways at him through her window.

He stood as she opened her door and walked toward him.

Her eyes seemed to relish the view of the handsomely dressed man. Lucas wore a simple, short-sleeve, white blouse. His pants had a herringbone design, with a seam down the middle of each leg. He didn't look dressed for work. Well, maybe for work at a desk.

"You're here. A week from last Thursday," Rosemary called to him.

"I said I would be."

Lucas's warm hand curled around her upper arm, as he met her. He

57

was a few inches taller than her. He smelled of spice: rich clove. He held a large, brown coffee mug in his right hand, half full of dark liquid; a strong aroma of coffee beans wafted directly from the mug. The sides of Lucas's mouth were turned up in a big smile.

"Good morning, Rose Petal. I like a girl in a truck."

"Good morning, Lucas. My truck is very special," she started, with a sly grin: "it has pink underbody lighting, which makes the truck girly. And an L.E.D. strip under each of my bumpers. It was used… I bought it like that."

Still smiling, he lifted the mug toward his curved lips. He held the rim to his nose and inhaled deeply. He then tilted it to his mouth and closed his eyes, as the liquid passed from the mug through his lips. Rosemary could hear him swallowing, with audible gulps, watching his throat move. When he lowered the mug, Rosemary saw that most of the dark liquid was gone. Why did it strike her as intriguing to watch him swallow his coffee?

His dark eyes sparkled toward her. "How are you feeling, Rose Petal?" he asked, his voice a husky yet silky tone. His vocal waves seemed to swirl into the air, like the steam rising from his cup of coffee. The vibrations of his voice seemed to penetrate her body and curl around her internally, as if they were velvet ribbons.

"Good, thank you."

He stepped close in front of her, and studied the wound on her head. Her nose held the whiff of musky cologne, or aftershave; she didn't remember that scent from him before. "Your cut is healing nicely." His warm thumb and forefinger pressed her temple and forehead, as he steadied her for a closer look. "Even your bruise is lightening."

58

It was as though she were now feeling his warm touch for the first time. Her heart fluttered. Why? She forced a smile and noticed the tightness of her face. Inhaling a deep breath, she realized that she needed to lighten the seriousness of her mood. She backed up a little from him, but he still touched her.

He had made her nervous, for the first time. Maybe because she had admitted to herself that she was definitely attracted to him. Yet. the tenseness of her body alerted her that now was not the time to consider a relationship other than friendship.

His heated fingertips curved around her chin, as he tilted her face backward. She felt as if she were his puppet, and she relished the feel of his warm skin touching hers. She had no previous memory of his warmth.

His eyes seemed to pierce into her brain. "Looks real good," he said, sipping again.

Hmm... That's why it had been intriguing to watch him drink his coffee: as he held her, she realized that she had never actually seen him do so before. At her house, he had left his full cup of coffee in the sink. Hadn't he liked her brand?

Her eyes moved up toward his, as he continued to hold her. She tipped her head away and moved back again, to break his hold.

"You were serious about volunteering," she said.

"Yes. My words are my character."

"Well, follow me," she said, walking to the side entrance of the red-brick building. She turned to momentarily look at him. "How was your business trip to California? Was it a business trip? Or personal?"

"Everything went well... as planned. It was a business trip. I had to tie up a few loose ends at the job I was leaving. I helped train the new guy to take my place."

"Sounds important." A loose smile clumsily pulled at her mouth, as she fumbled with her keys.

"Nothing is more important than your work here," he replied.

She unlocked the door and they walked into the large backroom. Deep yelps and high-pitched barks were unleashed when the lights were switched on, awakening the dogs.

A large table was set at the front of the room, near the entrance. Pegs held an assortment of leashes, above the table. Large walk-in pens lined both sides of the room, a few feet from the table; they resembled small bedrooms and included mattresses, toys, and food and water bowls. A few of the pens had newspaper lining some of the floor, for bathroom accidents. Little Chihuahuas, a big St. Bernard and other canines, variously-sized in between, occupied the enclosures. All of their faces moved toward the latched doors.

Rosemary watched Lucas's eyes scan the length of the space, as he began to slowly move down the cement walkway, the long rows of pens on either side of him. Right now, the shelter housed twelve dogs. He stopped and looked at each animal. The pups on both sides of him watched his movements. Some whined softly and a couple panted, with their tongues hanging and drool dripping.

"You must have a calming effect on animals," Rosemary said. "Usually they go crazy, barking and jumping when anyone new walks in here."

"Every being feels vibrations," he said. "Animals are particularly good at reading the character of a person, because animals rely more on

60

their senses; they pick up on vibrations. If a person is not calm, that will make an animal nervous."

"I believe that," Rosemary said, as she now followed behind Lucas.

"I also believe that animals have a wider range of intellect than previously thought," he continued, his voice heavy with seriousness. "Animals can smell, see and sense malevolence. They also know kindness when they encounter it. They can sense a wide range of emotions and physical ailments, in any species."

"I agree," she said.

He stopped walking and she stood beside him, in front of a pen.

"This is Lucy," Rosemary said. The white Chihuahua looked up at them, her little head tilted to one side, as though trying to understand the conversation. "She has diabetes," she continued. "We give her daily insulin shots."

A smile formed easily on her face, as she felt both sides of her mouth turn upward. "Lucy is getting healthy. Since we've had her on a nutritious diet, her diabetes is improving. The doctor said she will be able to come off the shots soon. She will be placed in a loving home as soon as she gets the doc's okay."

Lucas returned her smile. "What a heartwarming ending for Lucy's difficult past." Rosemary nonchalantly studied the darkness of his eyes, as they turned to her. They didn't scare her; their depth of color felt peaceful. "Thank goodness she's in your care now."

Rosemary began to slowly continue down the middle aisle, behind Lucas. "When a new animal arrives, we have them quarantined and checked out by the veterinarian." She waved her arm toward the private room; "There's a good-sized space just the other side of this room, behind that wall. We have also kept pregnant animals in there, for privacy."

She nodded her head toward the mixed shepherd they now stood before. "This is Jerry Lee. He had mange. With the doctor, we helped him get through it."

"You're a blessing to these animals."

"They are a blessing to *us*," she said. "They are a treasure that most shelters aren't able to keep, because of the sheer volume of homeless animals. We are privately owned, so we can control our volume and help the sick ones; larger shelters don't have the time or room to keep animals if they are sick, because they take in so many. If we have a chance to help a stray animal, we do. We do our best to treat each one that finds its way here. I can't tell you how many flea baths we've given, or how many animals we've treated for worms, or injuries.

"A big orange cat, Tom, was brought in by a volunteer. Tom had been hit by a car and had a broken leg, and other injuries. We took him to Dr. Greene and the doc fixed him up. Tom ended up with a forever home."

She breathed in slightly and held it, with puckered lips. On the exhale, the edges of her mouth rose. "I feel joy when a little soul finds its way here and we save *that* one."

Lucas was intently gazing at her, listening to every word she spoke. His black eyes searched deep into hers. "You are such an amazing person. There is no one like you. You are special; unique; one of a kind, Rose Petal."

She pulled her bottom lip into her mouth and lightly bit down on it, then began walking again. "Thank you, but there are many wonderful people who do rescue work."

As they made their way to the very last pen, in the back of the room, the dog inside hung his head and shook when they approached.

"This is Chuck," Rosemary said, softly. "We just got this guy a couple of weeks ago. He limps a little. We had Dr. Greene do an exam, and the doc thought there might be bruising. Maybe from abuse. The owner claimed that Chuck bit someone, and considered euthanizing him, but brought him here instead. I don't know if I believe that story; maybe the man invented it, as an excuse to dump the dog here."

Rosemary's mind now replayed the vision of Chuck's owner jerking the leash and speaking angrily toward the dog. Spit had spewed from the man's mouth with his angry words. Her face scrunched in disgust as she described the scene to Lucas.

"Chuck was brought here with matting and fleas," she continued. "We had to muzzle the poor guy to brush and treat him. He didn't snap at us, but he jerked away. We used one for safety, but I don't think he would have bitten."

Her eyes moved from the trembling dog to Lucas. "Like you, I believe an animal can sense vibrations," she said. "Chuck was probably never shown affection. We will give him the time he needs." She returned her gaze to the dog, who stood about thigh-high, his long, reddish-brown nose dipped to the floor.

"He won't leave his enclosure to go outside yet," she continued. "We have a gated yard outside that door." She pointed to the metal exit beside Lucas, at the very end of the building.

"We can go inside his pen and clean it," Rosemary said, "and we can give him water and food; he just cowers in that back corner, behind his bed."

A mattress with a bedsheet was set in the middle of the pen. A couple of layers of clean newspaper were set on the floor, beside the mattress. The dog now hovered between the wall and bed.

"We can go inside the pen and do whatever we need to do," she repeated; "we just can't approach Chuck. He'll stay in that corner and shake. He's never lunged toward anyone, nor even lifted a lip. I think he just needs a little time to get used to being here. But we are trying to find him a foster parent, with a quiet home. I was considering fostering him…" she lowered her eyes, "but, my father…"

Lucas gave an understanding nod.

"Obviously Chuck can't be adopted now, but we will take care of him; he will be okay," she said, gently. "We're going to hire a trainer, to work with him and rehabilitate him. He is handsome, isn't he? He is a mix: part German Shepherd."

Lucas crouched down in front of the barrier. "Chuck is very handsome." He thoughtfully studied the frightened animal. "Do you mind if I try to work with him?"

"That's nice of you, but we are hiring a professional."

The dog lifted its eyes to Lucas, but still shook.

"I'm really good with animals," Lucas said. "Maybe I could start out slow, just sit outside of the pen and spend time with him? Maybe after we do the chores?"

"Sure," she said, "I guess experiencing human contact from someone as calm as you could be beneficial."

Lucas stood. Then he chuckled, as he turned toward the enclosure beside Chuck's: Lula May, a large St. Bernard, stood watch there, with her teddy bear hanging from her jowls.

"My love," Rosemary told him, and he smiled.

"Sharon will be here in a few minutes," she said. "She takes care of cleaning the dog pens and letting each one outside in the yard. I help take them for walks when I'm done with my chores: cleaning the cat cages and the sanctuary. Both Sharon and I sweep and mop the entire place every day, after our chores are done. Sharon is the technology person; she does most of the internet stuff, the webpage... I help out with the office stuff, making calls and inputting some stuff on our database. Sharon is also good with the financial stuff: bills... We both give the animals their medicine and keep track of the administration on a log. We have a computer program to organize the medical records."

Then she softly clapped her hands together. "Let's get started!"

"I'm ready to learn," he said, following her down the walkway.

"We will clean the cat room, then I will show you the rest of the shelter."

She felt her ponytail bob behind her, as she turned back to him. "I'll tend to a cat cage and you can watch me. Then you can do one yourself."

"Okay, sounds good, Rose Petal."

Why does he insist on that choice of name?

She felt his eyes on her backside, as he followed her through a short hallway that opened into another large room: the area which contained the cat cages, for new or sick felines. This time, mewing harmonized as the lights were turned on; pointed ears and whiskers protruded as little heads lifted; sets of green and gold eyes watched. Some cats rubbed their bodies against the cage doors, begging for attention. The encased cages lined two walls, halved by the corner. The three-by-three-foot enclosures were three rows tall and five rows wide.

Rosemary turned to Lucas; "All of these cats are new, so we have to keep them here until we know the status of their health and temperament. Then we can move them to the sanctuary, where there is space for them to play and live a relatively normal life, until adoption; I'll show you the cat sanctuary later. It's nice to move them into that room, when they have been given a clean bill of health and a temperament test. We'll have to clean that room, too. It has fifteen cats now, but that number constantly fluctuates."

Just inside the cat area, where they now stood, a small storeroom contained supplies for the animals and shelter. Opposite the supply room, a deep sink provided a space to wash small animals and soiled materials. Rosemary opened the door to the stockroom and Lucas followed her inside. It was a long, narrow space. She turned on the light, which revealed shelves packed with most items any cat or dog would need: varieties of canned and dry food, different-sized bowls, toys, litter boxes, bags of litter, grooming supplies, and accessories that were accepted as donations or bought for specific needs. The right-hand side was dedicated to cats and the left to dogs. A large container of ready treats was on either side. In the back, various different-sized crates were stacked against the wall.

A packed cart was sat in the front of the room. Rosemary gathered a few more supplies and set them on the cart.

"You're welcome to come in here anytime, to get something you need. Would you please grab about twenty litter scoopers for now?" she asked Lucas.

"Of course."

She collected a few litter boxes, a mini broom, a dustpan, a few small bowls, a watering can and an empty pail. Two large containers of dry cat food, which were continuously filled, were arranged on the cart, along with a large container of fresh litter. A couple of kitten toys and clean, folded towels had been stacked on the food cartons. Cleaning supplies were tucked in between everything, and a few more newspapers were added to the already stacked supply. Then, loaded with the supplies, Rosemary gingerly pulled the cart from the storeroom, to the middle of the cat area. She filled the watering can with water from the deep sink.

"We have a laundry room down the hall, off the cat area," she told Lucas, pointing toward it.

The small tires of the industrial-sized garbage can loudly rolled across the floor, as Lucas pulled the requested item to the work area. Then Rosemary opened the first cage, as Lucas watched. She had to stand on a footstool to reach the top level of enclosures.

"Hi, pumpkin," she cooed, as the cat inside rubbed its head against Rosemary's hand. Its name, Molly, was printed on a five-by-eight index card attached to the cage door, enclosed in a clear plastic binder. All of the cages and pens had the animals' names, approximate ages and health concerns listed.

"I like that all of these animals are given an identity," Lucas said.

Rosemary turned to him and felt the corners of her mouth lift. "Yes, we give them all a name, if they don't already have one as soon as they get here. They are all unique and special."

She lifted the binder. "We call these the presentation pages. Sharon and I gather as much information as we can from our vet and surrenderer."

Still turned to him, she felt the skin on her face heat as he stood attentively, watching her. She cleared her throat. "Never leave a cage door open unattended," she said, noticing her voice change to a deeper tone. "It's easy to forget not to latch it when you're cleaning, then have to leave to get something. Cats have gotten out, and it's a long day capturing them."

"Okay, I'll remember to keep the doors closed," he said.

"We are in the process of researching a more humane housing for the new kitties. There is double-compartment cage housing; modular condos with glass doors, a separate litter area and a resting shelf. There are even cat runs, which are obviously roomier."

Rosemary pulled the litter box from the cage and stepped down with it. She took a scooper from the cart and held the pan over the garbage can, as she discarded the soiled spots. Then she set the used scooper into the deep sink, to be washed.

"We use a fresh scooper for each cat's litter box," she said, "just in case a new cat has parasites; we wouldn't want anyone else catching them! We treat them all when they first get here, but we want to be safe and do a recheck," she added.

She replenished the pan with fresh litter, from the container on the cart.

"Also," she said, setting the litter box on the floor, "we never fill the pans too high; the litter would go all over." She stepped back on the footstool, but turned to look at him. "If a pan is too soiled to spot clean, we just replace it with a brand-new one."

"Okay," Lucas said.

"Oh, we wash and replace all litter boxes on Mondays."

"Okay."

She realized she was bestowing information as though he were going to run the shelter himself tomorrow.

Soiled newspaper that lined the bottom of the cage was now pulled and discarded. The towel, used for a soft bed, was shaken over the garbage can, to free loose food and litter. Food and water bowls were set on the floor, next to the cleaned litter box. Rosemary then stepped back up the stool and used the mini-broom to sweep debris from the cage base. She had to maneuver the broom around the playful cat inside.

"If an animal is too aggressive, we can transfer them to an empty cage while cleaning theirs."

"Okay," Lucas said.

Rosemary smiled at him, as she discarded the stray pieces of food and dirt from the dustpan into the garbage. "Any questions yet?" she asked.

"You are explaining everything perfectly."

She gathered a couple of sheets of newspaper from the cart. "We use this to line the bottom of the cages; it makes the cage a little warmer, rather than just cold steel." Once again stepping on the stool, Rosemary arranged the newspaper inside the enclosure. She then closed the door and started back down the stool.

"No, stay up there," Lucas said. "Let me help: I'll get what you need and hand it to you."

"Thank you. Can you hand me the litter box?"

"Of course, Rose Petal." He handed her the requested item. "What else do you need, sweetheart?"

"Would you please drain the water bowl in the empty pail, then refill it with water from the can?"

"Of course." He handed her the water bowl. "Refill the food bowl?" he asked.

She turned to him. His eyes were focused on her. "Would you please fill it halfway, with food from the container labeled *'Adult'*? The other container is labeled *'Kitten'*."

Lucas moved to the cart and eyed the containers. "Oh, I see," he said. He filled the food dish, then handed it up to Rosemary.

"Thank you," she said.

The cage was clean and refreshed, and Rosemary requested a couple more items. The cat now stood on the folded, comfy towel, eating breakfast. Rosemary set a plush ball with a rattle inside on the blanket. Then she petted Molly for a few moments, before closing and locking the cage door. She stepped down off the stool.

"We always place the food and water bowls on the opposite side of the litter box. We wash and replace all food and water bowls on Tuesdays."

She pulled her lower lip between her teeth, as his eyes now focused on her mouth. Or, was that her imagination?

"We make sure each animal has a toy, bed, food and water," Rosemary said, then bit down on her bottom lip again. "Oh, if a cage is really soiled, we can use cleaners, of course; we can take the cat out and really clean it good. We can mix a little bleach with water."

She moved her eyes to his. "Any questions? I think I covered most everything." She drummed her fingertips along her puckered lips, and he watched.

"Towels are in the laundry room – I'll show you where that is. Bowls, paper towels, extra food and litter are in the stockroom."

Four five-foot-tall, freestanding cat cages were stationed behind them, against the storage room wall. Four kittens were perched on one of the independent enclosures' second-tier platforms. Rosemary walked to them. "These cages are cleaned the same way, of course. They provide a little extra room for a litter of kittens, or a couple of cats from the same household."

She stuck her finger inside the cage, with the kittens, and one of them playfully swatted at her. The cat's little black paw wrapped around the finger and held it.

"We had to bottle feed these guys when we first got them, because their mama was sick," she said. "The mama recovered and, once the kittens were weaned, the mama got adopted, along with one of her babies!"

She looked toward the next tall cage, filled with two older, orange cats. "These guys, Sammy and Peeko, were surrendered to us after their owner passed," she said. "Poor things. Still, they are sweet and will find a good home. They have to go together, though."

She looked back at Lucas. "We get a lot of our cats and dogs through owner surrender, or family surrender, if an owner passes. We get most owner surrenders if family is moving, animal is sick and owners can't pay for it, animal gets too big or animal is disobedient." Rosemary breathed out, heavily. "Or, should I say, if the *owner* is disobedient."

71

She walked to the freestanding cage on the far right, and undid the latch to the door. The large tabby jumped up onto the perch closest to Rosemary, and stuck her head out of the opening. "Hi, Tulip," Rosemary greeted.

The tabby's face looked flat, with a squashed nose. Rosemary gently lifted its chin, as she stroked the sides of Tulip's jawline. "This kitty was surrendered to us because she has kidney disease; the young family couldn't afford the treatment. Tulip needs special food and frequent veterinarian visits," she said, petting the cat. "She will be moved to the sanctuary as soon as she's feeling better."

She turned to Lucas. "We give Tulip subcutaneous fluids to help hydrate her and help her body flush out toxins. Would you like to help me, Lucas, to give her fluids now? We can continue the cleaning right after."

"Of course."

"Thank you. It's a two-person job. Since she came right up to me, I figure it's a good time to do it."

Tulip stepped toward Rosemary's waiting arms, and was gently pulled from the cage. Rosemary carried the cat to the clean, empty table, flush against the back wall of the cat room. Lucas followed her. Rosemary took a clean towel from the bottom cabinet of the table, and placed it on top of the cold metal. Then she set Tulip on the tabletop, which smelled of antiseptic.

"Can you please hold her here for a minute, while I get the fluids?" she asked.

"Of course," he said.

As she walked toward the supply room, she listened to Lucas softly talking to Tulip. "You're a beautiful girl," he was saying. "You're so pretty, my friend."

Rosemary backed out of the supply room, pulling a two-hook, metal I.V. stand, its wheels rolling across the tiled floor. From the six-foot pole hung a translucent bag of clear liquid. The long tubing connected to the bag wrapped around the short arm of the hanger. Using her free hand, Rosemary stopped next to the deep sink and filled a shallow bowl with warm water. She then pulled the equipment beside the metal table and set the bowl behind the cat. A section of the long tubing was placed inside the warm water. Pulling a couple of treats from her pants' front pocket, Rosemary placed them in front of Tulip and coaxed the cat down onto her belly, on the towel.

"She tolerates this treatment pretty good," she told Lucas. "Please, just gently hold her in this position."

The cat's head bobbed as it munched on the treats.

Rosemary pinched up a small section of loose skin on the back of the cat's upper neck. She then slid a thin, silver needle, with the small opening pointing upward, into the crevice of the tented fold.

"Please roll up the dial on that," she asked Lucas, as she pointed to the white, plastic roller-clamp. "The roller regulates the flow," she said.

The needle, now under the cat's skin, was attached to the length of plastic tubing that extended from the bag. The liquid moved smoothly from the bag, through the tube, and was fast forming a mound under Tulip's fur. When done administering fluids, the clamp would be rolled down to discontinue the flow. The bag was hung a few feet above the cat, to provide quick administration. Rosemary pointed behind the cat;

"The fluids pass through that bowl of warm water, which makes the temperature more comfortable for Tulip.

"This is subcutaneous fluids," she continued. "It goes under the skin and the body slowly absorbs it. A bulge usually forms under the skin, until it is all absorbed, which can take a few hours. Intravenous fluids have to be given by a veterinarian, because they actually put a needle into the vein to give fluids. For acute situations, that is best, but for long-term home care, this is good for kidney cats, because they need a little help to manage and prevent dehydration. They usually produce more urine than usual, and may not drink enough to compensate for the fluid loss, which can make the kidney disease worse."

A see-through plastic chamber allowed a view of the liquid, dripping from the bag to the tubing. Rosemary eyed the top line of the fluid, lowering inside the bag. The ascending numbers on the bag, 1-10, each represented 100 milliliters.

"We give Tulip one hundred milliliters of fluid every other day now," she told Lucas. "So, we started giving her fluids today, when the top line of fluids was at four. See how the top line is moving downward, toward five?"

"Yes."

"Tulip was brought to us weighing twenty-six pounds," Rosemary began, still eyeing the progress of the descending line. "We have been feeding her one quarter-cup of grain twice a day, soaked in warm water for moisture, and a small portion of wet can food daily. She has lost one-and-a-half pounds since her arrival here two months ago." She looked at Lucas. "That's a lot to lose, for a cat! You don't want a cat to lose too much weight too fast; it's not good for them.

"Her previous owners favored free-choice feeding; grain was always left out. But some cats don't properly regulate their portions that way. Thankfully, with her new food and eating schedule, Tulip's kidney values have already improved."

"How do you think she feels, with her kidney disease?"

"I think she feels way better with her weight loss. Cats can live normal, healthy lives with kidney disease, with proper care; we just give the kidneys a little extra help. The food supports kidney function."

Rosemary looked back up at the bag. "We are done. The line has lowered to five."

"Do you want me to roll down that dial now, to stop it?" he asked.

"Yes, please."

Once the dial was rolled down, to clamp the tubing, Rosemary pulled out the needle. To help minimize leakage, she pinched the skin on the cat, where the fluids had entered. Rosemary preferred to discard used needles into the plastic, screw-top bottle after each treatment. She opened the cabinet below the table and pulled out the bottle, along with a packaged needle.

"We keep all of the sub-q fluid equipment in the cabinet, right here below the table," Rosemary told Lucas. She put the used needle in the bottle, then directly opened the packaging of the new needle. The hub of the new needle was placed inside the tubing, with the hard plastic cover over it, for easy future use.

"Good girl, pumpkin," she cooed. "You are all done today."

Tulip daintily walked the length of the metal table, with the end of her tail tipped upward in a rounded arch. The crease of her front paws became pronounced, when the toe bones extended with each step. The sweat from Tulip's footpads had left a trail of little paw marks on the silver tabletop. Lucas lowered his forehead to match the height of the cat's, and was greeted with a soft bump as she butted the top of her head against him. Rosemary then picked up the cat and carried her back to the cage. The front of Tulip's body reached for the top-tier platform when placed inside, along with a well-deserved treat.

Lucas pulled the I.V. stand back inside the storage room. "That was very informative," he stated, as he rejoined Rosemary.

She smiled. "Sharon helps me with Tulip if there are no volunteers." She then asked: "Ready to clean? Try a cage on your own?"

"I will try a cage on my own," he said. "You'll be right here if I need you."

His deep, velvety voice curled through her again. A rush of warmth heated the skin on her throat and face. He was so good-looking – more good-looking than she had remembered from their last meeting; his dark hair and eyes embellished his high cheekbones and slender lips. The reaction of being attracted to him made her feel uneasy.

She would have to revisit these thoughts when she was safely alone in her home.

"Yes, I'm right here if you have any questions," she told him, looking into the piercing blackness of his eyes.

He opened the door to a top cage, a few rows down from her. He didn't need a stool. "Hi, Misty," Lucas said, holding his nose to the cat's inside. The cat sniffed him and then rubbed against him; he chuckled and sneezed at the same time. He slowly slid his fingers down the length of Misty's back. "You are the prettiest girl here," he whispered. "Let's get your space nice and clean."

Rosemary was impressed with Lucas's meticulous attention to detail. He worked more quickly and proficiently than other beginner volunteers; it looked as though he had been employed here for years. Rosemary was also impressed with his patience and care for the animals; he talked to each one he visited. Each female was told that she was the prettiest girl, and each male was the most handsome boy. Each one's head was gently patted.

He began to now open the last cage in the last row, she noticed. That cage was separated from the other filled cages. There were a couple of unoccupied enclosures in between.

"Hi, friend," Lucas gently greeted.

"Be careful," Rosemary warned; "slow movements with him. That is Angel. He is semi-feral. We got him from animal control. They were going to euthanize him, because they deemed him afraid of humans. He came to us in a catch-and-release cage, from Bravetown Animal Control. We took him directly to the vet, to be on standby for a neuter operation. When cats are neutered or spayed, they become less aggressive and restless, without all those hormones. They fight less and don't mate, and are therefore less likely to spread disease. Plus, they won't get testicular, uterine and ovarian cancer. Anyway, the veterinarian sedated him through the cage. When Angel was asleep, they tested him for feline leukemia virus and feline immunodeficiency virus. When the tests came back negative, they neutered him."

Rosemary walked to where Lucas was stood. "I have caught and released a few feral cats on my property, with a catch-and-release cage, to get them neutered," she said. "It's called T.N.R., which stands for 'trap, neuter, release'. I did release them back on my property after getting neutered, because they were truly feral.

"There is a debate around T.N.R. Some think it doesn't go far enough to help the individual cat, because it's released right back to the dangers of the outdoors. Not only is the cat at risk of danger, but the cat is not native to North America, and kills animals that our native animals need to eat. It is unnecessary and harmful for anyone to allow their cat access to the outdoors; they kill our birds, mice and other critters, and upset the food chain and ecosystem. That is true but, the way I see it is, if a cat is truly feral, terrified of humans and can't be kept inside a home, at least with T.N.R. there is less harm done to our ecosystem, because at least they aren't reproducing. But I wish T.N.R. could afford to do a more precise job at distinguishing truly feral cats from stray cats. Stray cats simply don't have a home, but are friendly with humans. They need to be kept inside."

"Some people feel it's not right to keep their cats indoors," Lucas said. "They feel that would rob the cat of its instincts."

"Well, like I said, cats aren't native to North America; they kill our native animals if left outside. A cat can satisfy its instincts with play. If a person doesn't supply their cat with the right toys and interactive play, then they shouldn't have a cat. Any animal adopted should be treated as a family member, and supplied with the correct enrichment, nutrition and habitat. People need to do research. Young cats and dogs need extra playtime and exercise, otherwise they will have play aggression, and act out from all that pent-up energy.

"And, by the way, people don't allow their dogs to roam, so why cats? Outdoor cats live much shorter lives than indoor cats, because of the risks of being hit by a car; being stolen; fighting with other cats; dogs, coyotes and hawks; extreme weather; being shot by a mean human; disease; infections; injuries; animal traps; poison; eating a poisoned mouse; and many other horrific scenarios."

Lucas had not interrupted the long speech she had given countless times, to any open-minded person who would listen. He now lifted a corner of his mouth, while studying her. "Yes, cats were first domesticated in Egypt, in around two thousand B.C. They were domesticated wildcats. Felis sylvestris lybica, the African wildcats, were tamed." His seductive smile now lifted both ends of his thin lips.

She felt her lips twitch slightly as she smiled. "You know history. Thank you for listening. I know I can get preachy, but I feel so passionate about animal welfare."

"I appreciate your intellect regarding animal welfare. I learn so much from you," he deeply replied.

Rosemary moved her fingers through her bangs, and shifted her glance back to the red cat. "Anyway, no one can touch Angel right now. If you try, he will swipe a claw at you."

"Awe, I'm not afraid of handsome Angel," Lucas said huskily, in a low voice. "We will eventually become friends."

"Take it slow," she warned again. "We named him Angel to inspire peace and love."

ʹ "Hi there, friend," he continued, talking to the cat. "No worries, just cleaning up for you." Rosemary stood and watched. The red cat pressed its side against the back of the cage, as Lucas opened the door. Red fur stiffened on Angel's back, and the small, black pupils in his green eyes shrunk, with a wide stare, as Angel's ears flattened backward. His head turned in the direction of Lucas's every movement, but the cat didn't hiss or paw at the intruder this time; Rosemary had been swiped by his paw on a couple of occasions, with a sting.

"We can give Angel the time the animal control couldn't. We're hoping he becomes accustomed to humans, with consistent interaction," she said, then smiled. "He seems to already be coming around. Look at you: you still have your hand!"

"Of course I have my hand; Angel wouldn't harm me." Lucas spoke slowly and softly, as he pulled the litter box from the wall cage.

Rosemary resumed cleaning cages.

"Is Angel separated by a couple of rows because he doesn't like other cats?" Lucas called out to her.

"Being right next to another cat might be stressful for him. But, also, Angel had a little discharge from his eyes and nose, so Dr. Greene prescribed an antibiotic. We originally kept Angel in the private room. We haven't noticed any more discharge or sneezing so, after two weeks of being on the medicine, we brought him out."

"How did you give Angel his medicine? I know you are a miracle worker, but..."

"Ha! We slipped the tablet in his wet food and he ate it." She inhaled, deeply. "He'll eventually come around. We just need patience."

After attending to the rest of the cat cages, Rosemary went to the front lobby. There was a raised reception area, that looked out into the lobby and greeted customers. It was bordered by a circular-paneled wall and contained two desks, opposite one another. Rosemary went to her desk, as Lucas wheeled out the cart and garbage can. Lucas's volunteer application form sat on top of her stacked paperwork.

"I filled out most of your volunteer form," she told him, turning toward him. "When you get a chance, I just need your phone number on here."

"Sure," he returned. "I lost my phone amidst my travels, but will give you my new phone number as soon as I get one."

As she now turned the doorknob to the sanctuary, Lucas looked at the introduction poster taped to the wide, long window looking into the room. Pictures of each cat inside the room were pasted to the poster, with each of their names and approximate ages. The sizeable window provided customers a look inside. As Rosemary and Lucas entered, differently-sized felines of various colors looked up at them. It was an approximately 600-square-foot space, that currently accommodated fifteen residents.

"Sorry to wake you," Rosemary said to one cat, which yawned wide and stretched. The humans' legs were soon circled with furry bodies.

Rosemary turned on the overhead lights from the wall switch, but four long windows that lined the east side of the room provided plenty of daytime brightness; the sun now practically flooded the windowsill seats with warmth. Dark blinds were tightly rolled to the top of the frame.

A pungent odor wafted from one of the several litter boxes. "Who did a fresh stinker?" Rosemary joked.

She then turned to Lucas and explained the procedures for cleaning the sanctuary: "In here, we clean litter differently. Because they all share the same litter boxes, we only need one scooper; we don't need a separate scooper for each box."

Toting a small, plastic bag, she cleaned the soiled litter from one large box while Lucas did another. They each cleaned eight. Sets of green and gold eyes watched, as the toys and beds were picked up from the floor and placed on the wide windowsill seating that bordered the east side. Litter boxes were stacked against the corner wall. The tiled floor was then swept and mopped. The cats knew the routine and kept on top of the seating, or cat trees that got moved around with the cleaning. The food and water dishes were replenished.

Lucas had taken the broom, mop and garbage pail from the room, while Rosemary now sat on a section of window seating, next to one of her favorite cats, which lay in a bed. Fiber-filled, cozy beds and toys were scattered the length of the seating, which was itself cushioned with removable padding. The late-morning sunrays shone through brightly, behind Rosemary, as cats chased one another across the floor, jumped onto cat trees and scratched posts, while munching on the remaining food, placed in several bowls around the room.

Lucas reentered the room, walked over to Rosemary and stood in place, tall and broad-shouldered. He smiled down at the cat she sat next to. "What is this one's name?" he asked.

"This is Goose." The corners of her mouth pulled upward, as she remembered naming him. "He has always been a goofy guy... silly. I had to give him a fun name, 'cause he has a sense of humor. Once in a while, he'll just jump up and run around the room."

Rosemary had a small smile on her face, talking about the first days of Goose's residency here. She now felt the edges of her smile fade, as she caught herself worried about his future. "I want him to have a loving home. He's a little older now, so he's slowed down a bit," she continued, "but sometimes he'll chase after his tail, like a dog." Her fingers gently curved along the bottom edges of Goose's ears.

The cat was white with gray circles, seemingly painted in various spots on his body. Gray markings covered both of his eyes, as though a mask. The white fur pointed up to his forehead.

"This open room is the best environment for a hopeful adoptive family to visit with the cats; people can sit in here and relax. They can interact with the kitties in here, and see which one they share a connection with. Some cats will cuddle up on your lap; some will let you brush them; some will run around the room while you play with them…" Rosemary said, looking up at Lucas.

She then looked around the room, making sure everything was in place. A few barrels were positioned around the room. One tall barrel, set on the floor, contained long wands with colorful fabric, feathers and teasers on the ends. A short container on the window ledge was filled with an assortment of brushes, combs and grooming supplies. Another bin was full of small playthings, such as faux mice, balls and plush toys. Four five-foot-tall cat trees provided a spot to scratch posts, climb ramps, jump onto perches or sleep in cubby holes. Baskets lined with towels were scattered around the room, for a comfy bed. Long nylon tunnels were connected and ran the length of the floor. Large scratchboards provided a good place for a nap or exercise. There were also a few electronic motion toys and tall scratching posts. Various-sized shelves traveled up one wall, as though a ladder; one white cat now rested on a high shelf. Rosemary looked at the white cat and smiled.

"Cats are vertical creatures; they prefer height to horizontal space. They like to look down and observe."

Lucas took a seat beside Rosemary, and the white cat, Alva, climbed onto his lap. He bent forward and kissed the top of her head, then rubbed her belly as she flopped to her side.

"My Samantha wasn't comfortable in here," Rosemary said. A bright sunray distorted her view of Lucas and she shielded her eyes, with one hand curved over her forehead, as she turned toward him. "I ended up taking Samantha home, because I didn't want her to spend the rest of her life in a cage. She doesn't get along with other cats, so she had no desire to stay in here. And she's a bit standoffish around most humans."

"What a lucky girl Samantha is," Lucas said.

"Older cats, cats with disabilities or illnesses and shy cats are the ones that have a hard time getting adopted," Rosemary softly said. "We've been lucky here, finding almost everyone a home, because we can afford to spend the time caring for sick animals and making them better – then, when they are adopted, the new owners just need to maintain the animal's health. We are always here, if anyone needs future help, advice or needs to return an animal."

Rosemary looked over at Goose, still beside her in his cozy bed. "Goose is our senior resident," she said. "He's older: about twelve or thirteen years old, and he's one of the first cats we got. He was pawing at the window of a local restaurant, and they called us. We always check for microchips on strays, and we will put up a *'Found Cat'* sign in our lobby. Anyway, Goose has been a resident here for about two years. He seems happy. His favorite spot is on this bed. He loves it when the sun warms through the window, right here."

It was time to get up and finish the morning chores, before opening the doors. Rosemary gave Goose a few more pets while, on the floor, a couple of young cats took turns licking one another's heads with their rough tongues.

"This week, I need to brush and trim everyone's nails in here," she said. "I trim the cats' nails and Sharon trims the dogs' nails, once a month."

"I'll help you," Lucas said.

"Thank you." She turned and looked at him. He had a sober expression, his eyes steady, the line of his mouth straight.

Rosemary gave Goose a quick kiss on the top of his head, then stood. "Time to finish cleaning the rest of the place," she said.

After having attended to the cages, cat sanctuary and dog room, the three of them – Rosemary, Lucas, and Sharon – began to sweep and mop the entire building.

Sweat dripped from underneath Rosemary's hairline, as she squeezed her mop dry in the bucket; a mild disinfectant odor wafted from the collected dirty water. When she had rolled out the bucket and mop at the start, the water had been clear. Now, it had turned almost black.

Lucas passed her. He was carrying a bulky, overloaded garbage bag outside, to the dumpster. When he opened the door and walked back inside, he was smiling. His stride was relaxed. His dark hair, usually combed in place, was tousled to perfection. The left front corner of his white shirt remained tucked inside his pants, while the rest of the shirt hung loose. His normally rigid cheekbones loosened in an easy grin.

"Where do I dump this water?" he asked Rosemary. He stepped next to her and began to pull the mop and bucket. "You're done, right?"

"Yes, thank you. We usually just pour it down the deep sink drain," she said. "The gunk will be caught in the filter."

"Okay."

He pulled the equipment to the sink and lifted the heavy bucket. It was filled with water and very heavy, but he picked it up as if it were a piece of paper.

Rosemary had followed and now stood next to him. She watched the murky water pour down the drain. She watched the muscles under his skin contract. He wasn't extremely muscular, but his arms seemed strong, as they held the bucket upright. Nearly done, he glanced over at her with a thin smile.

"Thank you for helping out today," she told him, clearing the frog in her throat. "It is nice to have a strong man around here, for a change. You can push that mop and bucket around much faster than us girls."

"No, thank *you*," he returned, as the last of the murky water splashed the walls of the sink: "thank you for allowing me to experience this today. It was an education. I never knew anything about what it took to run an animal shelter." It looked as though he then winked – did he wink? "Maybe I'm physically stronger, but you girls are inspiring, doing this day in and day out." Lucas set the equipment beside the sink.

Rosemary took a look around the room they stood in. It was clean and the cats were satisfied, with full bellies. Some were licking their paws, others were curled up on their beds, with their tails folded around them.

"Would you like to help me walk some dogs?" she asked.

"Of course!"

The front door of the shelter was now open to the public, so Sharon minded the front desk area, while Rosemary and Lucas began to walk the dogs.

New volunteers were not allowed to leave the premises with dogs, but Lucas was entrusted with the responsibility. He had practically saved Rosemary's life, after all, and he was her neighbor.

The dogs' walking gear hung on pegs, over the table near the side door. Rosemary helped Lucas pick out the appropriate-sized collar for Shelby, who would be his first walk.

"When the collar's on, you should be able to slide a finger between the dog and collar; that's how you'll know it's not too tight," she told him.

As Rosemary selected the leash, she noticed a little spider crawling along the table, underneath the hung leads. She directed the black spider into an available bowl with a piece of paper, then took it outside.

"That was a kind-hearted act," Lucas said when she returned.

"If not for acts of kindness, human integrity is threatened," she said.

He smiled, but his black eyes didn't move from her. His smile playfully broadened as he continued to look into her eyes.

"Shelby is waiting," she said, her mouth pulled up on one side in a half-grin.

She watched him prepare his first dog to be walked on a lead. Shelby sat patiently, her tail swishing on the floor, as the collar and leash were secured on her; Lucas whispered sweetly to the little, mixed-breed terrier. Shelby then practically hopped along to the exit. Bright sunlight filtered into the building, as the door opened to the outside.

Rosemary passed Lucas a few times, as they both exchanged one dog for another throughout the day.

She felt her mouth turn up in a smile, as she now picked out a large-sized collar. The smile held as she walked to her favorite dog's pen. This would be her last walk of the day.

"Hi, sweet Lula May," Rosemary softly greeted. "Our turn."

The organic smile had seemed to emerge from deep in her soul, as the edges of her mouth pulled upward a little more. She giggled at the image of Lula holding her brown teddy bear under her floppy jowls. She bent over and kissed the top of the St. Bernard's wide head, her lips pressing upon tufts of the brown-and-white coat. She gave the dog a light hug, as her arms gathered around high, furry shoulders.

"Sit," Rosemary said to the dog. The teddy was dropped, as the pup's big, furry butt lowered to the floor, then Lula May allowed the collar to be placed around her neck, and herself led out from the pen. Turning corners with the large breed felt a bit like steering a horse, Rosemary figured. No other animal here compared to this one's size.

"Sit," Rosemary reiterated, as they approached the side door. Again, the big, furry butt lowered to the floor. Rosemary opened the door to brightness and warmth, then she led the way outside. The trees, the big, blue sky, the breeze and the distant view of a small, quaint town never ceased to bring feelings of gratitude.

The mile-long dirt road led the way to a paved road, edged with a sidewalk. The walk was peaceful; Lula May never pulled the lead and her strides were in rhythm with Rosemary's. Rosemary inhaled the fresh air deeply. She felt the muscles of her calves pull gently with the slight slope of the ascending sidewalk, as they neared town. They seemed to walk into the sun; it felt warm on Rosemary's face.

"Lula's a beautiful girl," she said, looking downward. She looked down at her watch, then away from it. At this moment, it seemed that nothing else existed besides this dog, this sun and this breeze on her face.

First, the colorful, New England-style houses came into view, as Rosemary and Lula approached the top of the slight hill. When they reached the top of the hilly path, a bright sheen seemed to wave from the water, as the river came into view. Rosemary again inhaled deeply and felt her thoughts clear, as she studied the shiny, distant water. It made Rosemary feel refreshed, as though life were worth the struggles. When they reached the end of the colorful houses, the quaint shops lined up, and the paved street had narrowed to a cobblestone road. The sidewalk still stretched the length of the narrowed cobblestones. Some of the stores were houses converted into Victorian-style shops. There were also a couple of historical buildings, one being an old post office.

Rosemary stuck her bottom lip out in a mock pout. For all her walks today, Rosemary had decided that upon reaching the town they would turn back, but it was disappointing to have so little time with Lula. The walk had to be shortened to about thirty minutes, because Sharon needed her help. Some days allowed for longer walks, but Rosemary did need to help Sharon take pictures of some new animals today. They turned around and headed back to the shelter.

Within a few hours, most of the dogs had had their half-hour of exercise. Lucas had walked four dogs and Rosemary had walked five. Jerry Lee had just been neutered, so he was only allowed in the backyard today. Honey, a collie mix, had an injured back paw, and was not able to walk, while Chuck, still anxiety-ridden, refused to leave his pen.

Lula May sat at the side door as Rosemary opened it, and they entered. As they walked down the hall, Rosemary saw that Lucas was sitting outside of Chuck's pen, talking softly to the dog. Rosemary could not distinguish the words, but the tone sounded soothing.

Lula May took a long drink of water when placed back in her pen, just beside Chuck's. Rosemary then lay down on the hard cement floor and patted her chest. Lula playfully tapped her large feet just beside Rosemary's head, then lay down herself, the dog resting its large head on Rosemary's chest. Water dripped from Lula's jowls, onto Rosemary's shirt; Rosemary felt the cold spot of drool and giggled. Lula May then rolled onto her back, her long legs seemingly dancing in the air, as she rubbed her back on the rough surface.

"Lula May," Rosemary whispered, "don't worry about finding a home: you can always come live with me." After a few more cuddles, Rosemary gave the dog a hug, then left the pen.

She stepped behind Lucas, sat cross-legged on the floor, just outside of Chuck's pen. Rosemary looked down at him. His eyes were closed. "Lucas?" she softly said.

His black eyes seemed to snap open. He quickly turned and looked up at her. "I'm just getting Chuck used to a kind voice," he said.

"I know; I heard you talking to him when I came in. Patience is the key," she said. "Look at him!"

Lucas looked back toward the dog. Chuck was resting on his mattress. His eyes were watching, alert yet calm. "We'll be buddies, friend. You watch and see," he told Chuck. He stood up and turned to Rosemary.

"Well, thank you for your hard day's work. We are done!" she said. "Share is probably taking pictures now. She takes pictures of all the animals and puts them on our website. I'm going to help hold the new rescues for her." She bit down softly on her lower lip.

Lucas followed behind her, as they walked toward the exit.

"Again, thank you for your help today, Lucas," Rosemary repeated, her back leaning against the table.

He stood in front of her. Just looking at her.

There was silence. Not even one dog whined.

The silence wasn't awkward, even though her attraction toward Lucas made her pulse quicken when he stared at her.

"Is it okay if I help out here tomorrow, too?" he asked.

"Of course, Lucas."

"I plan to help out for the unforeseeable future – that is, if you'll have me. I have a break before I begin work again; I'd like to spend my time productively."

Her breath seemed to catch in her throat. *What? The unforeseeable future?* She could handle one day of controlling her internal blather, but more than that might prove to be unmanageable. She breathed in, unevenly. "Whenever you're available. Thanks again," she said.

Hopefully, tomorrow he would be staring at her less. Now that he knew the routine, he could work on his own. It would be nice to see him in passing, as they both worked.

"See you tomorrow, Rose Petal," he said.

"Oh... Lucas?" she called, as he was halfway out the door.

He turned back. His black eyes seemingly danced with light. "Yes?"

"Don't forget, I'm making dinner for you this Sunday."

"I could never forget."

Still leaning against the table, Rosemary closed her eyes for a moment, to relax before getting back to work. But she couldn't relax; Lucas's black eyes seemed imprinted behind her closed lids.

Rosemary held squirmy cats for Sharon's camera shot – it had been a trick to release her hands quick enough for a cute picture – then her workday was complete, and she drove home.

She walked inside the door and dropped her keys on the desk, set flush with the back wall. She saw the golden Buddha statue her father had brought home for her, from one of his business trips to Asia; it sat laughing on the shelf of the white-oak surface. Rosemary picked up the statue and brought it to the couch with her. She sat there, turning the statue over, her finger outlining the wording her father had engraved on it: *"Love you Rosy, Dad."* She hugged the Buddha to her chest.

It seemed that the cushions of the couch absorbed her physical body, tired from a long day's work. A teardrop was slowly descending her cheek. She allowed the warm liquid to drain from her eyes and wet her whole face; she permitted this momentary emotional collapse. Her nose clogged and her eyes stung.

Chapter 5

Lucifer's Best Friend

Lucifer closed his eyes and slowly swallowed a sip from his cup of coffee. It felt as if a thick ribbon of silk warmed his throat. He held the cup close to his nostrils and inhaled deeply.

Waiting for Rosemary's truck to pull into its usual spot on Friday morning, he sat on the bench at the shelter property, overlooking the parking lot. His shiny, black sports car was the sole vehicle.

He had found the convertible car advantageously abandoned in an old shed, at the house he now occupied. Removal of the weatherproof cover and a thorough polish had revealed an intact vehicle. Focused energy and a couple of human lifetimes of automobile experience had helped him to reignite the engine.

The bench was set at the beginning of the walkway leading to the back door of the shelter. A trembling aspen tree hung its canopy of branches, full of glossy, green leaves, above Lucifer's head. The tall trunk reached about eighty feet into the blue sky. The powdery-white bark, scarred with black marks, could be mistaken for a birch, he mused. When he looked upward, he saw the dull underside of the roundish leaves, but when the slight breeze waved through them, they flapped like shiny, green coins fluttering in the clouds. The canopy shielded his eyes from the brightness of the morning sun, though a gentle movement at the very top allowed brief hints of vivid light. The sound of flapping leaves resembled calm waves of water. Birds' outstretched wings gracefully glided into the greenery.

It seemed that nature provided a soothing orchestra: the sound of the flute was in the tones of the notes sung by sparrows; the call of a nearby dove resembled the deep, ethereal music of the Native American flute; low-tone chirps from a couple of squirrels, perched on thick branches, sounded as though a guitar was being plucked; high-pitched sharp notes and low flats added texture to the symphony; the screechy timbre of a shifting branch resembled a violin being strung out of order; the cadence of the woodpecker's drumming inserted another component. The majestic music settled Lucifer's soul.

As he now looked down at his hands, he stretched his fingers. After examining the back of them, he flipped them over, palms up, and inspected those. The calluses and creases looked as though they had been created over a period of forty years. Being human was miraculous. To have fingers, to touch and grasp objects, never ceased to amaze him.

He had only been a human being for approximately six months, equivalent to Earth time. A dimension existed parallel to Earth, as if a piece of tracing paper on top of regular paper. In the sphere that he became human, time was calculated only through one's own perception. Yesterday, it had been one week that had passed on Earth since he had last seen Rosemary; six months in the other dimension equaled and coincided with Rosemary's one week on Earth.

Yesterday, when he had volunteered for the first time at the shelter, it had been his first experience with Rosemary as himself, being human. He had enjoyed every smell, every sound and every muscle ache.

The human birth process had depleted Lucifer's energy. It had taken far more exertion than merely projecting his image as an apparition. He had undergone an accelerated development; conception to adulthood had been completed within the comparable six-month Earth time. Each soul, having entered a fetus, normally required an adjustment period. The human body developed at a rate in which the organs, limbs and bones grew at a measured pace, and it would cause physical pain for the skin and muscles to stretch too quickly. The human brain required methodical growth, but also time to synchronize with the soul. Energy usually needed ample time to adapt to being inside the more loosely constructed form of a body, rather than the more concentrated form of an orb.

The careful pace that each soul typically entered a human fetus had been omitted for Lucifer, and he had endured the physical pain of quick growth. Mentally, he had been aware of his purpose for becoming human, throughout the entire process.

It had been a stormy night in Massachusetts; lightning had lit the dark sky in jagged streaks. The normalcy of Rosemary's life had been occurring simultaneously with Lucifer's birth from another dimension...

Lucifer and Grace had embraced. A member of the lineage, Grace had agreed to be his surrogate. The lineage was the souls who governed Hell. Grace was presently experiencing being human herself, while remembering her true identity. When she and Lucifer entered the other dimension, it was as simple as meditatively seeing the invisible wall and stepping through it. A cozy house awaited them – once something was visualized on the other plane, it appeared instantaneously.

Grace had then stood still, inhaled deeply and closed her eyes, as

95

Lucifer meditated himself into a trance. His orb then envisioned his energy merging inside of the surrogate. He imagined his condensed orb taking human shape, as it entered into the birth process. Fertilization of the egg was not required. It had felt as if a thunderbolt merged his soul into the womb of his birth mother. His orb had swiftly traveled through a swirling, translucent tunnel. The jolt had resembled the sensation of two magnets, on their way to being fastened.

Grace had willingly accepted his energy inside of her uterus, and felt the jolt of the merge, along with him. She was a soul who understood the gravity of the gift of empathy. She willingly assisted the lineage in its mission of experiencing earthly life.

Once implanted, Lucifer's embryo settled in warmth; the vibration of his mother's voice soothed him. He felt cells rapidly multiply. The heartbeat signified when his human life truly began. It was a magical development. Lucifer had no control; his soul relaxed and simply allowed the course of action. He felt his limbs, fingernails and muscles grow. He could see light and darkness as he opened his eyes. His small arms and legs moved at his free will.

The fetus grew in one week's Earth time, and his human mother experienced a quiet delivery, on the eighth day of pregnancy. A doula had assisted Grace, and laid the baby on Grace's chest.

On the first day of birth, Lucifer resembled a normal human baby, who nursed from his mother. Behind his closed eyes, he had been comforted by the sensation of the movement of her chest, as she softly hummed. Over the next few weeks of life, he had gained twenty pounds and began consuming solid foods. His first sample of oatmeal was plain, but he had enjoyed the taste of the smashed vegetables touching his lips. During the second month of babyhood, his legs began learning to walk, as he grew into a toddler. In the subsequent months, his body grew into puberty and young adulthood. This time had been spent alone in his bedroom, and had been the most physically painful growth spurt. Looking in the mirror, finally, facial hair signified that the worst of puberty was over.

In the sixth month of being human, he stood undressed in front of his mirror, a forty-year-old man. He placed his open palm on his chest and felt his beating heart. As it thumped against his hand, tears welled in his eyes, and he felt them warmly trailing down his cheeks. The brain, lungs, heart, muscles, bones and blood were covered by skin strong enough to endure a lifetime.

Before conception, he had chosen that he would take on the physical appearance of his first human life – the same appearance he had chosen to project to Rosemary, when she first saw his apparition of Lucas. Lucifer dressed in clothes Grace had set out for him: neat black jeans and a button-down shirt. He had then given her a goodbye kiss on her cheek and she enclosed a bundle of hundred-dollar bills in his hand.

Closing his eyes, he had focused his energy to infuse into the plane of Earth. Massachusetts. His body moved through an invisible margin, which looked as if a liquid wall.

Cars honking and people yelling immediately assailed Lucifer's senses.

He stood still for a moment, figuring his whereabouts. Then, breathing in, he walked to a bus stop. He took the bus to Wolfe County, then walked on foot, in the direction of the vacant house beside Rosemary's, in the dusk.

On his way, he had helped a couple on the side of the road with car trouble. The man gave Lucifer cash for his trouble, though Lucifer tried to decline it. He had passed an inviting antique store along his foot journey, where an extra set of clothes and an old-fashioned suit were a lucky find; the 1930s style of clothing appealed to his senses. He even found an antique timepiece, that he could keep in his pants pocket.

When he had reached the vacant house beside Rosemary's, it was dark outside. He inspected the home for an opening, and an old, rusted window lock allowed entry. He climbed through the window; he could have used his energy to force open the door, if it hadn't been depleted. Lucifer would be a squatter now, for a brief period. The vacant house was stocked with the basic necessities: a coffee maker, refrigerator and oven aided living a comfortable human existence. There was even a generator in the shed.

Sheets covered antique furniture. Gray dust permeated his nostrils, as he pulled the sheet off a carved, ball-and-claw side chair in the living room. He figured the other covered furniture pieces were also antiques, due to claw feet sticking out from under another long sheet.

He walked to the bedroom and found a perfectly comfortable bed. The dust produced a musty smell, but nothing a few opened windows couldn't cure.

The house would provide a suitable shelter and convenient closeness to Rosemary...

Sunday evening, he would share a meal with her. The comfort and taste of a home-cooked dinner would far surpass the bland breakfast of cereal this morning. He took another slow drink from the mug of coffee he had prepared at home. Eating food and drinking coffee had always been one of Lucifer's favorite aspects of being human, and it was a necessity for him to have nourishment, just as a good night's sleep was important. The body needed cell repair, and the brain needed a break from the perpetual consciousness of the noisy world. As his body meditated or slept, his soul would travel…

Lucifer was now a solid form, made of bones, muscles, skin, blood and organs. A spirit could occasionally appear as human, such as an apparition, but not be capable of long-term bodily functions; when Lucifer went through the birthing process, he became a complete human being – although, he could change back to his former condensed energy if meditating or sleeping. Human form was a much looser concentration of energy.

Before his present position of governing Hell, he had spent several lifetimes as a human. The experiences had been insightful and allowed for empathy. It was now his 200th year reigning, so spending time as a mortal felt foreign and draining.

Rosemary's white truck finally appeared, turning into the parking lot. It pulled into the space directly beside the black sports car. Lucifer stood, wearing the black jeans and white undershirt Grace had provided him with. He arrived at Rosemary's door and opened it for her.

A 'fifties song was playing from her radio, before she turned off the engine. Rosemary stepped down from her seat, relaxed and singing. "Hi, Lucas. Thank you," she practically sang.

A worn, brown-leather dog collar hung as a decoration from her rear-view mirror, fastened by a gold buckle; a gold charm dangled about an inch from the buckle. Rosemary saw him looking at it.

"That's Anna's collar: my red shepherd mix, who passed a few years ago. She was... my baby."

"I'm sorry you lost such a special soul."

"Thank you," Rosemary softly said.

As Lucifer held the door, a rich vanilla scent seemed to kiss the air when she moved beside him. He held the scent in his nostrils and inhaled it deeply inside. Had Rosemary always smelled like that? He detected notes of lemon. The scent increased as Rosemary pulled a nylon band from her wrist and gathered her hair in a ponytail. His nostrils seemed to gravitate close to the skin of her neck, of their own accord.

He shut her door and followed her around the structure, to the side entrance. It was a reddish brick building, with red-painted doors and red exterior shutters. The window accents framed the length of each pane. Two large pots of petunias framed either side of the front door, and potted begonias lined the cement walkway. The front entrance had a long, glass panel and the wood trim was painted red.

Lucifer again inhaled deeply, but this time closed his eyes in indulgence, as he stood behind Rosemary. She turned the key in the lock of the red, solid wood door. A distinct pomegranate scent clung to the soft waves in the waterfall of her gathered, reddish-brown hair.

Once inside, the cleaning equipment was gathered on the cart, and they each began their own job in the cat room. It already felt routine now. Both absorbed, they worked separately and quietly, except for pleasantries to the felines, although Lucifer heard Rosemary singing underneath her breath.

Lucifer enjoyed spending time with each cat. He had made friends quickly with most of them, only a few still timid. The workday seemed to hurry by. Soon, all of the cages had been cleaned.

Passing Rosemary, he watched her attempting to hold two of the four fuzzy kittens in her lap, as she sat in front of their freestanding cage, introducing a soft-bristle brush to their little bodies. A beautiful orange color rimmed the outer edges of Rosemary's aura. Lucifer had not been noticing human auras since his time as Lucas, so this sight took him by surprise. The outer edges of each person's aura changed daily, depending on one's momentary soul alignment. Rosemary now glowed in the warm orange light, as though an angel. Orange, her spiritual color, showed that Rosemary satisfied her soul's intent by being a caregiver. When she was here, performing her job, caring for animals, her spiritual mission was being satisfied, and that showed in her aura.

Lucifer pushed the shop's broom across the floor; he had told Rosemary to continue socializing the kittens while he swept. She also had to trim the cats' nails, so he would finish the cleaning chores himself. He now prepared the water-and-bleach solution for the floors. The sharp smell reached his nostrils as he moved the bucket from room to room. As he pressed the wet, cotton strings of the mop onto the tiled floor, with time his arms felt the strain of the push and pull.

Shortly, the mop rounded the bottom of one of the tall front desks. The length of the reception area allowed for two workstations and two chairs. A framed picture of Rosemary hugging a medium-sized, red dog confirmed the location of her workspace.

"Anna," Lucifer quietly called to the picture. He softly smiled, as he saw the dog leaning into Rosemary, in a loving embrace.

Lucifer finished disinfecting the lobby floor, then set the mop and bucket against the wall. A couple of racks of for-sale t-shirts, leashes and collars, all bearing the shelter logo, were set opposite the reception area. He walked to the shirts and thumbed through the different colors and sizes. He would purchase one for himself. Grace had supplied him with enough currency, until he would be able to earn his own. As he pulled an extra-large, red shirt from a hanger, he thought the expansion of styles would be favorable to customers. Maybe hoodies could be added? Jackets?

Washed with dish soap, the white undershirt he wore today, minus the button-down top, served for today's work. He looked down at his black jeans and realized he'd need a broader rotation of clothes. When he had appeared as an apparition, he wore the image of his outfit from his previous life, as Lucas: just the clothes he wore today and one other, older-style outfit hung in his closet, next to the 1930s suit. The suit pants he had worn yesterday. He had seen a few more shirts and pants at the antique store that he would purchase.

He sorted through the saleable leashes and collars sporting the shelter logo, and found there a selection of different sizes, lengths and colors.

With his new red shirt flung over his shoulder, he pushed the bucket toward the dog room. Passing the sanctuary, he stopped to look inside the window.

Rosemary was there, trimming the cats' nails. He watched her bent over a cat, lying in a basket on the floor. He wouldn't have known what Rosemary was doing, had she not explained her afternoon chores beforehand. She looked up and saw him watching her, motioning for him to come inside. He opened the door.

"Would you please help me with this kitty?" she asked. "Sunset is a little fidgety."

"Of course, I'll help." He knelt beside them on the hard floor.

Sunset was a reddish tortoiseshell cat. He gently grasped the back of her neck, as Rosemary had instructed. She assured that the scruff – the loose skin he now held – would comfort the cat; it would resemble its mother's grip, when being carried as a kitten. Adult cats, however, were heavy, and should never be carried or picked up by a human by their scruff, Rosemary explained, though it was a good technique to help restrain a stationary feline.

Rosemary whispered sweetly to Sunset, as she hunched over her. In order to extract one nail at a time, Rosemary gently pressed each toe pad separately, between her thumb and index finger. As she held Sunset's paw in place, she clipped off the curve of the claw. Lucifer curled the palm of his free hand around Sunset's soft stomach, and felt her heart thumping hard against him.

"We're done, Sunset," Rosemary told the cat, handing her a treat. "Good girl." Sunset got a kiss on the top of the head from Lucifer, before she walked away.

Rosemary looked up at Lucifer, her eyes sparkling with delight, it seemed. She eyed his shoulder. "Do you like our shirts?"

He, in turn, glanced peripherally at his shoulder, where red draped over his own white sleeve. "Yes, I love your shirts. I'd like to see even more styles and jackets."

"We'll work on that."

"I'm going to buy this one."

A sweet half-smile inched up one side of Rosemary's face. "No, you've earned that shirt; it's yours... on the house."

"Thank you, but I insist..."

"No, *I* insist," she demanded, her eyes stern.

Lucifer stayed and helped to hold a few more cats. Then, when Rosemary was finished with the squirmy ones, he left to finish disinfecting the last hallway.

He felt his own heart pump harder, as he squeezed dirty water from the last pass of the mop. The anticipation of spending time with Chuck heightened, as he pushed the bucket full of soiled water toward the utility sink.

Lucifer took one more look through the sanctuary window as he passed. Rosemary was now standing and distributing treats to all the cats.

He pushed the bucket to the deep sink, and now held it upside down to drain it. The smell of bleach wafted strongly to his nostrils, as the rush of dirty water poured into the tub. He placed the empty bucket in its spot, on the floor beside the sink, and set the damp mop inside of it.

Then he walked inside the storeroom and took a couple of dog biscuits from the shelf. Walking toward the dog room, his heart thumped and the edges of his mouth turned up. The smile felt comfortable; it felt as though he were about to see a friend. He *was*, he then thought; Chuck would fast become one of his closest companions.

"Hi, friend," he said, as he reached the front of the dog's pen. Lucifer slowly lowered to a seated position, on the cement floor in front of the door. He sat quietly.

The dog was acutely aware of Lucifer's presence. Chuck had

scurried from his bed, and now stood in his favorite corner, facing the wall. The skin under his reddish-brown fur tightened. His legs trembled. His long nose pointed to the ground as his head hung downward. Lucifer sat in place. He remained still and quiet, as he watched the frightened animal.

, After a long while of silence, Lucifer visually placed a healing golden light around the dog, and sent his focused energy through the steel gate. If an intuitive could see the exchange, it would look as though a tunnel of gold were emanating from Lucifer's eyes and traveling to the dog. The golden energy circled Chuck.

The dog now turned and looked up at Lucifer, but stayed in his corner. Chuck's brown, widened eyes began to tell a story of horror.

Lucifer concentrated as he melded his energy field with the dog. There was the sensation of an angry force; harsh vibrations. The vibrations felt as though they shattered the top of Lucifer's skull and the bottom of his feet, as if someone abruptly blasted a commercial speaker system. A reflex to want to press his hands to the sides of his head was overwhelming, but he continued to concentrate. Lucifer could smell an odor resembling rotten eggs: it was the smell of malevolence. He then saw a grayish residual energy, which played like a picture show in the dog's mind. As their energies continued to meld, the picture show persisted on a seemingly large screen. Images of a man's boot repeatedly kicking Chuck assailed the senses, like a thick, dark weight.

The abuser's face then came into focus. The face crunched into creases, as a loud, threatening voice was directed toward the animal. Lucifer felt as though he were the animal.

"No one gives a shit I lost my job!" the abuser yelled. "Just because

I'm a few hours late, you piss on the floor!" The energy of the voice seemed to resemble a dark-gray smoke that would choke the victim.

The force of each strike against the dog was felt physically, as Lucifer twisted his midsection. It felt as though Lucifer's organs were bruised and bloodied from the repeated blows. The dog's eyes clung to Lucifer's, as his story was conveyed.

Lucifer held the breath in his lungs, as he grasped the terror. He wiped his forehead, now wet from sweat. Moisture formed tears in his eyes. How could a human being contain so much rage, and direct it toward an innocent?

Lucifer mentally held the golden light around Chuck. The healing, calming light.

The horror picture show seemed as though it were abruptly sucked into oblivion. The screen went blank and then vanished. Now, only the golden tunnel connected the two energies of the dog and Lucifer. There was silence. Calm.

Time elapsed.

The side entrance door opened, and Rosemary and Lula May walked through. At least an hour must have passed since Lucifer had been connecting with Chuck. Loud barks resonated through the room, as the dogs saw their walker, Rosemary, enter. Who would be next, they must have been thinking? "Ssh," she whispered to them.

She noticed Lucifer watching her. "Hello. You were deeply concentrated on Chuck," she said; "you didn't seem to hear me or see me. I've been in and out of here a couple of times, with other dogs, today. I didn't bother you because I noticed Chuck's ears were relaxed; they weren't pinned to the sides of his head. His back muscles looked relaxed, and he was looking at you with a calm expression. I didn't want to interrupt that."

She walked inside Lula May's pen, and took the collar and leash off of the dog. "Sweet Lula," she said. She kissed the top of the St. Bernard's large head, then closed the gate to the pen.

"You are really good with him. You connect with him," Rosemary said, as she stepped behind Lucifer's seated body.

He looked up at her, from in front of Chuck's pen. "Chuck has been abused, I'm sure of it," Lucifer said. "I'm also sure that, with time, he will heal. He knows he is now in good hands. Would it be okay if I go inside the pen tomorrow? I'll just sit inside, by the door."

"Of course," she grinned. "You're cheaper than a dog trainer! Are you going to walk any dogs today? Jerry Lee still needs a walk."

"Yes," he fitted a biscuit through a slot in the slatted door, to Chuck, "I'd love to walk Jerry Lee." He then stood up.

A rich vanilla and lemon scent still embraced Rosemary's skin. She went to Lucy's enclosure and knelt inside of it; the little dog danced around her and hopped on her thighs. Lucifer went to Jerry Lee's pen and prepared him for a walk. The mixed shepherd shook its thin body with delight, as the collar slipped around his neck.

"Good boy, Jerry Lee," Lucifer said, as he ran his fingers along the dog's back. The malnourished animal's skinniness allowed Lucifer's fingers to dip deeply between each bump in his spine. He would soon gain weight, with a normal diet. "Let's go for our walk now."

They exited the building, and fresh air and sunlight encircled them. Jerry Lee lifted his nose and breathed heavily. His tail wagged up and down. After a half-hour walk, they turned back toward the shelter.

Jerry Lee seemed to know the way.

When all of the dogs were resting in their pens, content from today's exercise, Lucifer said goodbye to Chuck.

He felt sourness in the pit of his stomach, as he thought about having to say goodbye to Rosemary. When he spent time with her, nothing else mattered; he was oblivious to everything he was familiar with: the universes, the dimensions, his true identity, and the duties and obligations that his position as ruler of Hell demanded didn't exist. Only she existed.

Today, Saturday morning, Lucifer would go inside Chuck's pen; he had felt the eagerness while driving to work. His heart had thudded hard against his chest, and he had to inhale deeply to calm it.

The workday seemed to pass quickly. He felt proud to sport the red shirt with the logo today. It made him feel a part of the team.

He was now dumping blackened water from the bucket. All of the daily chores had been completed, except for the dog walking. But, first, Lucifer would visit with his new friend. Lucifer got a few treats from the storage room, then headed toward Chuck's pen.

He now stood before Chuck, outside of the enclosure. "Hi, friend," he softly greeted. "It's your buddy, Lucas."

The dog moved from the bed, to stand behind it. His back tightened, but dramatically less than yesterday, though Chuck did shiver. Lucifer lowered to the floor and sat on its cold cement surface, just on the other side of the pen door. He wanted the dog to acclimatize to him slowly, before entering Chuck's domain.

"I'm going to visit with you inside your pen today, friend."

Inhaling a deep, calming breath, Lucifer slowed his heart rate. Heat seemed to warm his face, as the golden light once again emanated from his closed eyes. The golden tunnel traveled from Lucifer to Chuck, encircling the dog.

Slowly opening his eyes, Lucifer stood and unlatched the door, with the golden tunnel still intact. Stepping inside the pen, Lucifer closed the door behind him. He descended to the floor and sat near the front of the enclosure. The dog trembled in the back corner, behind the mattress, his nose hung close to the ground.

"It's okay, friend, we'll go nice and slow."

Lucifer closed his eyes and again inhaled deeply. His heart rate slowed even more; it pumped so slowly that a passerby might think him dead. In the meditative state, he opened his eyes. He visualized the golden light around Chuck, and he infused positive energy with each slow breath. Clear, bright light, the basis for all colors, then encircled the dog with pure love, infiltrating his cells and organs. As if puffs of cloud, Lucifer mixed separate frequencies of color into the ring of light: green colors breathed in healing effects, such as harmony, balance and new beginnings; the green hue infiltrated Chuck's bones and muscles, creating rapid growth of healthy cells. Into the dog's heart organ, Lucifer exhaled red, the color of vitality and strength...

These therapeutic wavelengths, known by their hues, had an effect on body tissue. The body could be healed by applying the correct color vibrations to the chakras. Color therapy could stimulate the physical body by normalizing the cells and, in turn, the body's cells could more easily heal themselves.

He wanted the dog to have no fear of being harmed by a human. This process could not be rushed; it would take time to develop trust.

In his deep meditation, Lucifer shut out all objective life, allowing the conscious mind to become passive. His eyes still closed, he continued to breathe healing power into the light circling Chuck. Motionlessness negated the confinement of time, and they both settled in the present moment.

Lucifer focused on the slow rise and fall of his breath. He harmonized the dog's breaths with his own, and their energies slowly blended. Chuck's high heart rate slowed to match Lucifer's. It felt as though they floated together, in another dimension, through the meditation. There was no past or future. Quietness seemed to enfold them with serenity.

Time elapsed…

A faraway voice pulled Lucifer from the mediation. Bright lights seemed to suck back into Lucifer's core, as if rapid fire.

The muffled voice was Rosemary's. It appeared to echo from a tunnel behind him.

A sharp inhale seemed to bring Lucifer back to life. He felt Rosemary's presence behind him.

"You're making a little more progress each day," she said. Her voice was clear now. "Spending time with him in his pen is helping." She stood behind the closed door to the pen.

Lucifer turned and looked up at her, from his seated position. How many hours had passed? "What time is it?" he asked, attempting to sound alert, as his equilibrium regained itself.

"It's noon."

110

"I've been here almost two hours? Sorry I didn't help walk the dogs today."

"No, don't be sorry; look at Chuck," she said.

Lucifer's eyes seemed to dart of their own accord, to the corner where the dog had nervously stood. Chuck wasn't there. Lucifer fervently scanned the pen.

The dog lay peacefully on his bed, his chin rested on his front paws. Two big, brown eyes watched, brown, furry eyebrows twitching, as he looked from Lucifer to Rosemary. He wasn't trembling or cowering. Chuck was still a couple of feet away from Lucifer, but progress was definitely being made.

Lucifer felt his chest reduce with an emotional exhale. He reached into his pants pocket and pulled out a dog biscuit, which he tossed to the middle of the floor, halfway between them. Chuck sniffed at the air, but stayed in place.

Slowly rising from his seated position, Lucifer kept his gaze on the dog. Chuck's skin did tighten, but he continued to stay rested comfortably on his bed. Lucifer then backed out of the pen and locked the door. He felt his face relax, his mouth naturally curved up to form a satisfied smile. Chuck was finally beginning to think of him as a friend.

Rosemary looked at Lucifer, as he walked toward her. She was standing at the large table, near the front of the dog room. The leashes and collars of many sizes hung messily from hooks on the wall, above the table. She began to reorganize the collars, according to size. "Don't forget, dinner tomorrow night at my house… six p.m.," she said.

"I would never forget," he returned. He stopped and stood at the table directly beside Rosemary. "I look forward to seeing you tomorrow night, Rose Petal. But, would it be okay if I helped out at the shelter tomorrow morning? I'm making great progress with Chuck."

"Of course," she said. "I thought you might want a day off. We're closed to customers on Sundays."

"No, I'll still help out. This work satisfies my soul."

Rosemary's eyebrows squeezed together, in an odd configuration, but her lips formed an agreeable smile. "Have a good night, Lucas," she said.

"You, too, Rose Petal."

He could practically hear the accelerated rhythm of the blood rushing through her veins. Whenever he called her "Rose Petal", a pinkish color touched her cheeks, but Lucifer didn't want to make her feel uncomfortable. The words virtually slipped off his tongue naturally; they befitted her. She was indeed as beautiful as a rose, as delicate as a petal, and as vibrant as the soil and vine from which the flower came forth.

Before he even opened his eyes, Lucifer felt a smile pull up the corners of his mouth, as he lay on his back in bed. It was Sunday morning. Tonight he would share dinner with Rosemary, at her house. The alarm clock now read eight a.m.

Lucifer rose from the bed, nude. He pulled a pair of boxers from the dresser drawer and put them on. While asleep, his human body felt unhindered, if naked.

He prepared himself a cup of coffee. The aromatic, thick ribbon of liquid looked beautiful to him, as it poured from the carafe to his mug. He looked out of his living room window, as he took slow sips.

Lucifer watched Rosemary walk across her acre yard, to her single-cab truck. He could view the path lined with tall, green rosemary plants that led to her back door. A small vegetable garden was positioned in a sunspot, across from the willow tree. The homes were more widely spaced here, on the outskirts of town. Luckily, Lucifer's provisional dwelling was located on the east edge of the property closest to Rosemary's house, so he had a good view.

The white vehicle pulled out of the driveway and onto the road.

Last evening, Rosemary had driven off in her truck. Slightly worried, Lucifer had wondered where she was headed, but she returned home a couple of hours later, unharmed.

Inhaling a long, deep breath, Lucifer closed his eyes and rejoiced in his eagerness to be in Rosemary's presence today. Usually, being human, short, shallow breaths sustained him. Now, long, deep breaths reminded him that he was alive and human, and able to share moments with his soulmate. The same excitement of seeing Rosemary's soul in his previous lives had proven a reason to be alive. No matter her shape or shade of hair, she had always been beautiful, warm and loving.

He dressed, then walked to the antique convertible he left parked in the shed. As the public radio station softly played classical music, he headed toward the shelter. The recognition that the corners of his mouth were turned upward, without his direct intent, caused his smile to widen consciously. The anticipation of seeing Chuck today invoked joy inside him.

As he pulled into his usual spot in the parking lot, Rosemary was walking around the corner of the building. She carried an oversized animal crate. Lucifer opened his vehicle door to fresh, heated air, leaving the coolness of the air conditioning.

"Good morning, Rose Petal," he said, with a voice elevated to reach her.

Her face turned to him. It was beautiful without makeup – at least, no makeup was detectable, only natural-looking, flushed cheeks and skin-tone-colored lips, which looked as though specks of dew had kissed them. "Good morning, Lucas," she returned.

Today would be a short workday for Rosemary. With the shelter not being open to customers on Sunday, cleaning duties and dog walking would be the only chores.

The three of them – Rosemary, Lucifer and Sharon – worked in solitude, each to their unique rhythm. No direction was any longer needed for the newbie.

After having completed his share of work, Lucifer now looked forward to visiting Chuck. His hand seemed to vibrate with excited energy, as he pulled dog treats from the container in the storage room. He walked to Chuck's pen and stood in front of the entry. Then, he slowed his breaths, as he undid the latch on the door to the pen.

"Hi, friend," he said, forcibly controlling the eagerness of his tone.

He slowly lowered to the cement floor and crossed his legs, in a seated position inside the enclosure, close to the door. The dog, who had been resting on top of his mattress, did not shift or tremble as Lucifer sat still in place.

"Here you go, Chuck," he said, as he reached out his arm and placed a couple of the treats halfway between them.

The dog sniffed at the air, toward the biscuits. Then he lowered his chin back onto his front paws.

Lucifer closed his eyes and gathered positive energy, to encircle the dog. Then, in his meditative state, Lucifer slowly opened his eyes and watched.

Chuck again sniffed at the air. This time, his thin front legs, with their knobby knees, lowered to the floor, but his hips rested on the bed. He then tentatively stretched his front legs forward, on the cement; the rest of his body followed. Looking to Lucifer, before his nose pointed to the ground, at his treats, his eyes communicated a trusting hopefulness. Chuck then lay down next to the offering. His front paws curved around the kibbles and gently moved them close to his mouth. A loud crunch followed, as he crumbled one of the biscuits.

A big smile organically arose on Lucifer's face, as he witnessed Chuck unaffectedly enjoying a treat with him only a few feet away, inside the pen. The remains of one biscuit on the floor were licked clean, before Chuck looked back to Lucifer, then consumed the other treat.

It felt as though warmth moved through Lucifer's body, and the smile widened on his face. This was love. He was thankful to the flowing, loving energy that helped to heal the dog. Lucifer very slowly inched his seated body toward Chuck and extended his arm. The dog sniffed the air close to the tips of his fingers. Closing his eyes, Lucifer inhaled deeply, then again, encircling Chuck with the golden, healing light. The energy surrounding the animal melded with the dog's aura and calmed Chuck's energy fields. Lucifer breathed behind closed eyelids.

A soft wetness touched Lucifer's fingertips. He then felt a warm tingle trickle from his closed eyes. He slowly opened them. Chuck had touched his black, rubbery-looking snout to the outreached hand. Tears now trickling down his cheeks, Lucifer softly moved his fingertips across the top of the dog's long nose. Chuck stiffened his muscles and tightened his skin, but he stayed in place.

"It's okay, buddy. We're best friends," Lucifer whispered, lightly rubbing the smooth fur. This was surely the first time in years the dog had been touched with gentleness.

The rhythm of Chuck's breathing had sped up when Lucifer first moved his fingertips along the animal's nose, but now it had slowed to normal, as the closeness became more familiar.

These feelings of connection were the same that Lucifer had felt whenever he was in Rosemary's presence. He was beginning to learn that he thrived on physical contact, as well as soul-to-soul contact, no matter the form, human or animal. It was the same way Rosemary connected to all life.

"Would you like to go outside in the yard with me?" Lucifer asked.

Lucifer slowly stood and opened the door to the pen, as Chuck lay in place, watching. Lucifer gently closed the door, then walked to the front of the room and pulled a soft nylon leash from the collection of walking gear. Going back inside Chuck's pen, he knelt beside the dog, still lying in the middle of the floor. The dog stiffened its back and front legs.

"I'm going to get you ready to go outside," Lucifer said. He handed the dog another treat from his pocket, then slowly placed the slip-lead around Chuck's neck.

The dog, as expected, tensed his muscles again, but allowed the intimate contact.

"Slow and easy," Lucifer whispered. Crouching, he pulled another treat from his pocket and held it in front of the dog's nose. "Come on, buddy, let's go outside," he said, slowly inching backward, with the biscuit dangling in front for enticement. Chuck tentatively followed, the gentle pulls urging him forward.

As Lucifer backed out of the pen, he left the door open. Chuck followed.

They made it to the back door, only about a foot away from the pen. A treat was set just in front of the door. With his back to the exit, Lucifer opened the door that led to the fenced yard. He backed out slowly and Chuck followed. He set another piece of biscuit just outside the door, but the dog didn't notice it.

Furry eyebrows and eyelids twitched at the bright sunlight.

"It's okay, friend."

Lucifer led the dog to the grassy area. Chuck stood and erratically directed his attention to the noises he heard. A loud car motor drew his eyes to the nearby dirt road. His front legs shifted as a neighborhood dog's bark sounded from the opposite direction.

"You're okay, friend," Lucifer said, softly. He gently drew the leash downward, as he sat cross-legged on the grass, beside the dog.

Chuck's pointed nose dipped downward, with light tugs on the leash, as the dog was eased into a sitting position on the grass. Lucifer placed the last treat in front of the dog for the brave accomplishment. Chuck studied the biscuit, but didn't lower his head to eat it, his eyes still squinting and blinking in the daylight. He settled into his spot, then incessantly watched the closed back door.

"I'm so proud of you, Chuck," Lucifer said, as he slowly moved his fingers along the length of the dog's back.

Chuck sat still, persistently watching the building's back door. His tongue dripped as he breathed with an open mouth.

Lucifer closed his eyes and inhaled a deep breath, then breathed out golden light, to circle the dog.

He smiled when he opened his eyes; he hadn't noticed, until now, that Chuck was not trembling. His muscles were a little tight, but his breathing had slowed to a regular rate. His pink tongue circled to the top of his nose as he looked downward, then lowered his head to eat the treat that had been placed on the ground.

The two of them sat outside on the grass, in the sun. Time elapsed unnoticed as they sat there, side by side.

The door Chuck was watching opened.

Lucifer's brain hadn't registered in time that the unsecured leash lay between them, and the dog rose to his feet, then ran toward the door. He passed Rosemary and scurried into the building.

Rosemary's mouth unconsciously opened wide. "Was that…?"

"Yes, that was Chuck who went running past you." Lucifer stood. He was sure the dog had run back inside his open pen.

Rosemary held the door open and looked inside. A thin droplet of moisture gathered in the corners of her eyes as she, apparently, focused on the dog. "I'm so proud of you, Chuck," she softly told the dog. She wiped her face as she turned to Lucifer. "Thank you, Lucas."

Lucifer walked toward her and took her place, holding the door; he looked down into Rosemary's eyes as he stood close to her. "Thank you for taking Chuck in, and allowing him a chance to experience love."

He heard Rosemary inhale a shaky, deep breath, as she turned and walked toward Chuck's pen. She retrieved the nylon leash that had fallen to the floor, then closed and locked the pen door. She stood there, gazing at the dog. Lucifer joined her.

The dog had hopped onto his bed. He now lay on his stomach and watched, with furry eyebrows twitching. Though Chuck's face appeared calm, his body pressed to the mattress, signaling that he was comfortable and didn't want to move anymore tonight.

The prettiest smile parted Rosemary's lips. "Lucas, I can't believe you got him outside. I'm so happy for him."

"All knots unfold with gentleness," Lucifer said.

She turned to look up at him. "You have to do this every day now."

"It would be my honor."

Chapter 6

The Devil Returns To Hell

Lucifer stood in his living room. White sheets still covered a sofa, loveseat and television. A large bay window framed the view of Rosemary's house; the taupe curtains were split open just enough for observation.

Lucifer had not transformed back to a condensed energy since he took human form. He had wanted to keep a close watch on Rosemary's home with his human eyes.

But now attention was needed in Hell. Rosemary was safe. He would share a dinner with her tonight, but for now a brief visit to Hell, to ensure the proper second-in-command was being implemented, was vital.

Lucifer went to the bedroom. He undressed to his boxers and then lay on the bed. He quieted his emotions, controlled his mind and relaxed his physical body. He traveled deeper and deeper into a death-like trance, allowing his energy to transform and condense. He visualized the dimension beneath Earth. His orb rose from his human body on a golden cord.

The body that temporarily housed his orb lay on the bed, still breathing; his body would appear asleep to the human eye. No matter the distance, Lucifer's orb could return to the body in a millisecond, if woken.

A translucent, vaporous tunnel appeared, extending from Lucifer's glowing nucleus. His orb now swiftly traveled through the tunnel, toward his visualization.

The familiar colors and textures of the castle became clear, as Lucifer's orb appeared closer to the core of Hell. The colors swirled from outside the tunnel, as he passed through. It felt as though the tunnel flushed his orb at the same time he was strongly pulled to his destination. Lucifer felt weightless, as he now floated along the perimeters of the castle. The imposing, ornate building of Gothic architectural style was beautiful to him. It was a place of healing.

Grassy hills rolled across the land that surrounded the fortress. The countless acres of terrain rose from a mid-air plateau. Beautiful rocks and mountains dipped way below the castle's surface, in a magnificent canyon. Arched towers reached endlessly into the soaring, deep blue skies.

This particular moment, the sun and moon were both visible and captured Lucifer's focus. His energy aligned with the simplicity and calmness of nature. He took a moment to watch the grand sun dip below the hills and castle and, in a radiant array of colors, sink into the canyon, which was only viewable from a far distance, shedding an orange glow on the rocks. The warmth and brightness of the hues awakened joy inside him. Opposite the red and orange sunset, the full moon was now taking its place in the sky. Silver stars glittered from above and below, surrounding the castle. Tiny specks of silver began to gather near the canyon.

Each soul chose his own perception. Lucifer chose to see beauty.

Hell had its own sun, to awaken anticipation of new beginnings and inspire feelings of well-being. It had its own moon to inspire thoughts of beauty, transformation and action.

Each soul's overwhelming guilt, hate and resentment brought him here, and each consciousness created this space. Any object existed and originated from thought; the collective thought of Hell made it so. Each being's act of forgiveness and kindness also created the beautiful landscape and kindness here.

This special, therapeutic home could not be at risk of being overtaken by an uncaring ruler. Lucifer had long ago appointed his second-in-command, Devon, and needed to connect with him now.

As he entered the building, Lucifer traveled through the area. Soaring to the vaulted ceilings, he passed high archways made of deep-red stone and many stone fireplaces. There was not a feeling of coldness inside. Contrary to human thought, Hell embraced and comforted souls; the earth-tone colors, inspirational art and devoted school of thought here emitted warmth. The high ceilings were draped with chandeliers, lit with glowing candles. Places of worship were decorated with stained-glass windows.

Floating through the castle, he felt free. He was no longer a hindering human body. He could visualize a spot and be there, changing directions in a split second.

In the natural state, a soul was a bright, translucent nucleus with outer layers, basically an orb of energy. Lucifer's center was illumination, glowing from within. His outer aura was a soft green, with touches of blue and purple. He was not a solid; like a fluid or a gas, the colors of his aura expanded then gathered with movement.

Plunging himself lower in the castle, he floated just above the lush, velvety colors of the rugs that carpeted the floors. Exotic floor coverings, exquisite paintings and sculptures decorated the premises, for optimal expansion of thought.

Dipping up and down, as he floated along, streams, waterfalls and fountains sparkled below. Water contained healing powers. It helped temper one's mood. The streams gracefully and steadily caressed every turn and flushed impurities. Listening to the slow creek's water lazily pour over the bed of stones induced a meditative state. The waterfalls and fountains dispensed heavy rushes of water, to clean and rejuvenate one's spirit.

The castle housed a library, on the first level. The library contained collective intellectual thought. A soul could absorb the information any way he chose to obtain it; some liked learning through soundwaves, others preferred imagery. Classrooms occupied the second level. Religious and spiritual sectors were on the third floor. The fourth level contained the counseling centers. Suites for the residents reached into oblivion. The square footage of all of the levels was infinite. Voices were heard coming from a classroom above. Exquisite singing came from a church somewhere.

As he traveled about the first floor, Lucifer greeted the familiar souls and the new souls. A soul could present itself in any fashion it chose. Even though his nucleus was encircled with dominant colors of green, Lucifer could also choose to present himself as a tall structure. Most new souls here related more easily to human-looking figures, so Lucifer now morphed into a figure with dark eyes and hair, the image of Lucas. He wore a long, black cloak.

He crossed a newly arrived male energy that vibrated dark forces of negativity. A dark, drab, brownish aura circled the nucleus of the being.

"Hi, Frank," Lucifer said, projecting his human image.

A pale, white face, wet with tears, turned to Lucifer. The face looked ghostly, floating in space without a body, its bloated head attached to the orb by a thread. The spirit looked disjointed. It was Rosemary's recently deceased father.

Frank's energy put forth images using telepathy: a young girl sobbing and rubbing her eyes was his main focus. It was his last vision of Rosemary as a child, before he had permanently left the home. Another vision appeared, of a woman screaming at him. The woman was Rosemary's mother, and her reddened eyes were filled with tears.

"Frank, I know you have met with your appointed counselor, May. She is a kind soul," Lucifer said; "she will help you through this. You need to trust her."

The new souls that arrived here were usually in a state of shock, confusion and depression. As ruler of Hell, it was Lucifer's job to oversee proper procedures were in place for each soul's healing process. Numerous aides were appointed to escort Hellbound souls to this space. Once here, each new soul was assigned a specific counselor by his or her aide.

It was the ruler's job to keep order. New souls had to be welcomed; there was a transition period. Recuperation of energy, after transforming from a human, could be traumatic after a distressing Earthly experience. Each soul's time spent as a human being had to be examined, because each soul chose to come here for a reason; the new soul went through a process of pinpointing the origin of his grief with a counselor. Once this reason was pinpointed, the difficult journey of recovery began. This could probably be compared to detoxification. It could be torturous to return to the onset of the grief experienced as a human, and this step of the healing process was typically the most difficult part of one's stay here. Lucifer oversaw all the steps in each soul's recuperation process.

The course of reforming also required that each soul attend classrooms, to relearn sympathy, forgiveness, communication, spirituality and love. Teachers assigned homework, scholars and spiritualists bestowed knowledge through lectures, and clergy provided any denomination with guidance.

Hell was a counseling center, a school, and home for any soul who was consumed with grief. The healing process and its duration were different for each soul. It was a space to become restored, before re-joining the others. Once ready, the redeemed soul could re-join one of many heavenly dimensions, or reincarnate as a human form on Earth.

No demons were a part of Hell; Lucifer protected this space from any malevolence. And it was important to him to continue this path with his chosen successor. The previous ruler of Hell, Grandfather Lucious, had held his position for an equivalent of one thousand human years, but named his second-in-command for emergency replacement.

"Frank," Lucifer continued, "I promise you will get through this painful process."

The despondent soul kept replaying the image of his teary-eyed daughter.

"Frank, each soul that chooses to incarnate a human body and live on Earth does so with the plan to expand the living world, universes and one another, with his uniqueness. It should be a joyful experience, but many humans forget their soul's intentions.

"There is no such thing as sin; when a human is out of alignment with his soul, he can simply make poor decisions. They are poor decisions because they are fear-based or anger-based decisions, not in alignment with soul. Those poor decisions can bring about pain, but they are forgivable. There is never a time that any being is not loved."

Frank's seemingly detached head looked as though it bobbed along a bumpy stream. Tears still flowed from his bloodshot eyes.

"Evil does exist, but no human is innately evil," Lucifer continued. "Evil is an entity of its own, created by any negative emotion, thought or action. The constant flow of loving energy, which humans call 'God', is always available to each soul. Sometimes a soul can drift away from that flow, but it can realign with the loving energy at any time."

Lucifer reached his energy deeply into Frank's soul. A gold tunnel extended from Lucifer and circled Frank, and golden light infiltrated Frank's dark, drab, brownish aura.

"Frank, you are not a sinner," Lucifer continued. "You are not evil. You made a few poor decisions as a human, based on a disconnection with your soul and flow of loving energy."

A rush of air swept by overhead.

Lucifer looked up at the presence he'd known as Devon. Trails of yellow hovered around the outer edge of Devon's orb.

The orb, swirling, changed its image, and Devon now presented himself as a young, blond-haired man, as he stealthily moved beside Lucifer.

"Hello, Lucifer," Devon greeted.

Lucifer's energy drew back inside his core and he turned to Frank. "Frank, we will talk later." He then added: "Rosemary misses you, but she is fine. She loves you."

Lucifer looked back at Devon. "Hello, cousin. Everything has been running smoothly in your care, I trust?" he asked.

"Yes, of course, cousin."

"Good. I just wanted to make sure that all was going according to our plans. Our path of a vision, for a safe shelter for grief-stricken souls to recover, must not veer off-course. We must keep our plan of action for all new arrivals intact."

A reddish color tinted the aura of Devon's image, as his demeanor changed. Devon's blond eyebrows scrunched together, forming a deep line between them. "Your brother is angry," he growled.

"I figured Ash would still be angry about your position as second-in-command." Lucifer's voice strengthened, sternly; "You will be my successor, Devon. My brother is too unsympathetic and harsh."

"Yes, well, he—"

A swirl of grays circled an orb that suddenly rushed toward Devon and Lucifer. It suspended above them, as if a gray cloud of smoke.

The orb changed its image to a dark-haired, young man resembling Lucifer – evidently his younger brother. The projected image still hovered above them, looking downward.

"Speak of the devil," Devon said, his tone thick with dark humor. "Hello, Ash," he said dryly, only his eyes moving up to look at the figure.

"Hello, cousin," Ash returned, mockingly. He smirked with an exaggerated smile, and his eyes bulged with ridicule. He lowered to meet the two at their level. "I see my brother, Lucifer, and my cousin, Devon, are conspiring against me again."

Ash's dark eyes, still bulging with derision, looked toward Lucifer. "What business on Earth is keeping you from your duties here, brother?" he asked.

Lucifer matched Ash's glare with stern, black eyes. "I have a very involved case I'm working on now. I hope you are supporting our cousin Devon in his position, brother?"

"Of course, brother."

Silence clinched the air around them; three sets of eyes seemed to shoot daggers at one another: Ash glared at Lucifer, then at Devon, while Lucifer and Devon both glared at Ash. The pause continued.

"You have a stubborn soul, brother?" Ash asked, turning directly to face Lucifer.

"What?"

"A stubborn human soul? Not wanting to die? Not wanting to be delivered to Hell?" A grayish color darkened around the aura of Ash's image. "Is that what's keeping you, brother? A stubborn soul that doesn't want to be delivered to Hell?"

Lucifer felt his core tighten. His energy locked in place and the color red flowed through his provisional eyes. "Ash, you know that each soul chooses his own destination," he said, tempering his tone. "The aides have to be patient, and allow each Hellbound soul the time it needs to make that decision, on its own terms."

"Yes, but we facilitate a soul's descent to Hell," Ash said, with a menacing grin.

"Ash, a good ruler is sympathetic and helpful to grief-stricken new arrivals. We want each soul to recover and move on to his next journey."

"You're a romanticist, brother. I'm a realist." He spun around in mid-air and prepared to depart, then turned back, his face even with Lucifer's. "As far as I'm concerned, neither you nor Devon is fit to be ruler. I will bring that up to the lineage."

"You do that, brother," Lucifer snapped.

Ash's image moved his face closer to Lucifer's. It looked as though blood were pouring from Ash's eyes. Devon stood by.

"You both coddle the prisoners, brother," Ash continued. "The prisoners are here for a reason: they are evil. They need to be locked in a room and never seen again. They should be lashed!"

"There is no evil here, except *your* thoughts and words," Lucifer said. "You know as well as I do, Ash, that most of the souls here can recover and be freed. Each soul can be released from his own self-imprisonment. Once that happens, no walls or room in Hell can hold him. You would like to beat down the spirit of each soul, so that each one can never heal and free himself. You take advantage of your position, Ash. Our power can be used for good; you use yours to abuse. Does it make you feel strong to lash the vulnerable?"

Ash spun in mid-air and began to charge away again, but Lucifer moved in front of him.

"*Your* weakness is revealed when you attack the weak, brother," Lucifer said.

Bright-red beams extended from Lucifer's provisional eyes, and the forcefulness of the energy moved himself and Ash into an unoccupied room, where Ash was pinned to a corner.

"Thank you for the *tongue*-lashing, brother," Ash growled.

"Grandfather believes, as do I, that humans created Hell with their own energy of thought," Lucifer continued. "Everything is the energy of thought first, before it is a reality in the human world. A painting would not exist if not for a thought first. A paved road would not exist if not for a thought first. No one can truly be the jailer of the soul that created Hell. Only the Creator can be in charge of one's creation. We are only here to counsel."

"You and Grandfather believe such nonsense! You two are better suited to run a bed-and-breakfast, not Hell! *I* should be ruler when you are absent. *I* am your brother! *I* am the lineage! *I* am the most natural choice for second-in-command!"

"The lineage is the souls in line to become ruler. Devon is in the lineage, just as was his father, Heath. Each reigning ruler chooses his own second-in-command. Our cousin has the perfect temperament for the job – maybe even better than mine. Devon is my second-in-command, just as I was Grandfather's."

Lucifer calmed his energy. "Ash, all of our jobs in the lineage are to assist the broken souls that come here. We do that through compassion: compassion promotes healing. How have you forgotten that, *brother*?" The last word was spoken with disappointment.

"Our grandfather was the greatest ruler," Lucifer continued, his voice raised but measured. "He led with compassion and tenderness. Those are the things that all beings stem from. The new regimen I set in place will allow for the greatest recoveries. And I *insist* that each soul who finds his way here is treated with the utmost respect and concern. If you can't do that, *brother*, then there will be no place for you here."

"You would have me shunned from the lineage, just like our father, Nigel?" Ash said, skulking near the ceiling's corner.

"That would be the entirety of the lineage's decision, not mine alone." Lucifer's narrowed eyes continued to spark red light toward his once-blood brother.

"Nigel deserved to be removed from the lineage," he carried on; "he was abusive to our blood mother and his wife, Catherine. In our first human experience, she bore us and raised us, cooked and cleaned for us."

"You always looked upon her as a god. She was used for the sole purpose of birthing us, *brother*."

"She allowed us an extraordinary chance to experience human life, *brother*. Even though unaware at that time that she was part of the lineage, she willingly accepted the responsibility of being a mother and raising her children. Any soul deserves respect, especially one who so unselfishly sacrificed for you."

Ash flipped through the air, and the grayness of his aura scattered vapors around him as he headed away.

"Devon is ruler while I am gone! You will uphold his orders!" Lucifer shouted. He then shook out his cloak, as if to shake away the negative; he felt the red-hued energy dissipate.

He visualized his detoxification spot in the castle, and his energy was transported there. His cloak floated, as his human image descended through the levels of the castle, to his secret space, the cellar.

The walls were made of gray rocks and brick. A dirt floor absorbed the negative. A soothing dripping created a water puddle on the floor –

a reflective pool. The quiet darkness was void of anything.

Lucifer felt weightless, as his image vertically stretched and relaxed in mid-air. The rocks and dirt absorbed his negative energy and converted it to a restored balance. It felt as if heaviness were being lifted from his core in the blackness. There was no measure of time; Lucifer stayed in place until his energy felt centered.

He adjusted back to his orb, and green colors circled it...

Now gathering his vitality into images of his home on Earth, in Wolfe County, his meditative state took him there.

A swirl of translucence twirled, and he entangled and twirled with it.

The tunnel brought him to his human body.

Now hovering above his human body's chest, his core concentrated on entering, beside the beating heart. A thin, golden thread pulled the orb inside. It felt like a magnet meeting its match, as the soul reentered. Lucifer inhaled sharply, deeply, and was back inside his body.

Slowly, he opened his eyes. He was lying in his bed, dressed in his boxers.

Lucifer choppily breathed in, as he moved to a seated position, shifting his legs over the side of the mattress. He slowly stood and walked to the living room. He looked out of the large window framing Rosemary's home.

Rosemary was inside her garden, hunched over her strawberry plants. She was weeding. She wore a wide-brimmed sunhat and pink gardening gloves. Lucifer could see an orange hue circling her aura; she was obviously joyful in the garden.

Lucifer's eyelids felt swollen and weighted. As he walked back to the bedroom, each leg felt as if he had to pull it out of a block of cement, as he lifted it. Fogginess seemed to cling to his brain, thoughts were sluggish and his bones ached.

He lay back down on the bed, and felt relief from the cushioned mattress. The pillow welcomed his head and cradled his sore neck. Putting forth the concentrated energy of visualization, for his travel from one plane to another, left him feeling drained; a nap was needed to refresh his body.

He would be eager to see Rosemary and have dinner with her when he awoke.

Chapter 7

Rosemary's Dinner Guest

"No, 'Mantha!" Rosemary teasingly yelled.

The cat's brows pulled together with an intense focus, as Rosemary began to toss the newly washed bedsheet across the mattress.

Tending to her garden earlier, and doing laundry now, helped curb the nervousness of entertaining her dinner guest later this evening.

What would they talk about? Conversation had never been difficult for them, but would spending a few hours together, face to face, prove too lengthy of a time?

A large bump moved underneath the bedsheet and pulled the neatly-placed top hem downward.

"Samantha!"

Rosemary allowed the cat to play while she dressed. She pulled the stretchy fabric of her long-sleeved shirt dress over her head. The blue dress was her favorite standard for special occasions. The lacy, see-through sleeves and bottom hem made her feel girly.

This dinner was considered to be a special occasion to her, because she was preparing a home-cooked meal for the man who had practically saved her life.

She appreciated the slow and easy development of their closeness. It was possible that this friendship wouldn't develop into a romantic relationship; Lucas had never shown anything other than platonic feelings for her – although, she sensed that he cared deeply for her welfare. She would not allow herself to expect any advancement. He might not even find her attractive.

"Ugh! That is ugly!" Rosemary complained out loud. She closed her eyes. "Try to be nice to yourself. It's not that bad."

A bulge of body fat showed underneath the clingy fabric of the dress, at her belly. Though proud of her recent weight loss, a couple more shed pounds would improve her form. She sucked in her breath and stood straight, her stomach flattened.

"Jeez, 'Mantha, I won't be able to breathe all night! What us women have to put up with! I need to buy a sexy girdle from your boutique. Ha!"

Rosemary moved Samantha to a platform on the cat tree and finished making the bed.

A fully-grown, six-pound turkey baked in the oven. It would be too much food for just the two of them, but Rosemary figured she could send Lucas home with leftovers. She had followed her mother's recipe, having seasoned the bird with cinnamon and honey. Potatoes had been peeled and quartered, and now waited to be boiled in a tub of water on the oven burner. Asparagus was rinsed and snapped, resting on the cold stovetop grill. She would cook the side dishes when her guest arrived. Homemade stuffing was warming in the crock pot. Also her mother's recipe, the sweet bread had been moistened with juice from the baking turkey and seasoned with parsley; thinly-sliced, softened apples had been stirred in for added sweetness. Rosemary had also prepared a pecan pie for dessert, made from scratch. Her mother's china dishes were already in place on the dining table, along with heirloom stainless flatware.

Rosemary hoped that Lucas would appreciate the meal she had planned for him. It was only forty-five minutes until he was due to arrive.

A few details needed attention in the kitchen, so Rosemary slipped on her nice sandals and headed there.

The smell of Mama's turkey released into the air when she opened the heated oven door. Crouching, Rosemary reached her hands inside and carefully removed the two pieces of foil, which folded together in the middle, resembling a tent covering the bird. She wanted the top to brown an appetizing color. Having filled the roasting pan with about two cups of water, the bird looked moist. Whole, peeled carrots and fragrant celery stalks lined the edges of the pan. A whole onion had been cut and stuffed inside the meat, and scattered along the edges, with the other vegetables. Along with the cinnamon and honey, the top of the bird had been salted and peppered. She allowed the main dish more time to brown, pushing it back inside the oven.

Next, she pulled the pecan pie from the refrigerator, so that it could reach room temperature. As she set it on the dining table, she heard a soft knock on the front door.

"Shit!"

She looked up toward the kitchen clock; it read 5:31 p.m. He was early! A half-hour early!

Rosemary was a self-proclaimed *late person*, who appreciated her guests giving at least ten minutes of leeway in the scheduled time. Lucas was an *early person. Ugh!*

Rosemary had wanted to straighten her frizzy hair with an iron – no time for that now. She pulled her fingers through her curly strands.

Walking to the door, she felt her heart thud against her chest. She took a few deep breaths and then opened it.

There stood Lucas. He smelled good, either from aftershave or cologne. Dark, shiny eyes looked directly into hers. She looked downward and, as her gaze fell, she noticed he was holding a bag.

More importantly, he wore a suit! Lucas obviously felt as though this were a special occasion. Rosemary felt her bottom lip catch under her teeth, as she tried to conceal a giddy smile.

He was handsomely dressed in a black, two-button overcoat with white pinstripes. The lapels framed his chest, and a white handkerchief stylishly folded to a point from the chest pocket. A matching pinstripe vest and pleated pants gave a uniformly striking look. Rosemary thought the pants looked familiar; maybe he had worn them before, without the overcoat. A plain, white dress shirt underneath the vest matched the handkerchief. The black tie, with a herringbone design, formed the white collar around his neck.

Rosemary felt self-conscious, as her eyes scanned Lucas from head to toe. Her cheeks felt a little flushed as her eyes grazed his pants. She attempted to seem preoccupied with welcoming him inside, as her gaze locked a moment too long on the sexy tie.

"Come on in," she said, stepping aside.

He entered, then bent over to remove black, leather dress shoes.

"Oh, no, you don't have to take those off," she said.

"It's only polite."

Black dress socks clad his sizeable feet.

He passed, facing her. "Mmm, smells heavenly in here," he said. "Turkey?"

137

"Thank you. Yes, turkey. I only eat pasture-raised animals. I found this farm that has abattoirs right on their property. The farm humanely raises the animals and then respectfully, thoughtfully butchers them right on the same property, so the animals are never frightened by being transported to a separate butcher."

"The farm does sound very respectful to animals, just like you. Makes the meal more enjoyable." Lucas closed his eyes and inhaled deeply. "I detect a hint of cinnamon in the air?"

"Yes. Mama's recipe."

She watched him inhale again and deeply hold it in. His eyes were closed flat, with contented smoothness.

She noticed he held a burlap bag. It looked to be a gift bag, considering that a bow tied the strings together.

"Everything will be delicious," he said, opening his eyes. He reached his arm toward her and handed her the bag. "This is for you, Rose Petal."

"Thank you. You didn't have to bring anything." She undid the loops of the bow and held the long piece of orange raffia. The packaging looked romantically rustic. "How did you know orange was my favorite color?"

He only smiled, it reaching his eyes, which slanted and creased at the edges.

Rosemary moved aside tissue paper inside the bag. Her breath seemed to hold in her lungs and she felt her eyes slightly widen, as they took in the vision of two candle holders and cream-colored, tapered candles. She pulled one of the gold candle-holders out of the tissue. It was heavy, and looked expensive and antique. She hadn't expected it to be so substantial.

"Lucas, these are beautiful," she said, studying the item in her hand. "They are the most exquisite candle holders I have ever seen."

"They are hand-wrought," he said. "Twentieth century, originally from Paris. You deserve only the finest."

"Where did you find such a treasure?" They had the prettiest spiral design. She moved her fingers along the smoothness and curves.

"That's real eighteen-carat gold over bronze," he continued. His eyebrows squeezed together and formed a crease between them. "I like antique stores. I love history." He looked around her living room and eyed the old-fashioned desk, inherited from her mother. "I found the candles at the antique store in town, and thought you'd like them."

"I do. Thank you."

She glanced toward him as he spoke, and saw a thoughtful smile form on his tilted face. His skin was smooth, as though freshly shaven. The black pinpoints of his hair follicles dotted his angled chin and attractively darkened it.

"A flame dancing at the dinner table brings blessings to the lighter of the candle, and peace to the company gathered there," he said, his voice low but intense.

"That's a very nice sentiment," Rosemary said, stepping back into the living room. "Make yourself at home."

Lucas moved to the couch, where the cat perched on top. "Hello, Samantha," he greeted.

Her wide, green eyes returned his gaze, looking up at him, apparently enjoying his attention. Rosemary could tell that her usually skeptical cat had already grown fond of him, and Samantha leaned her head into his hand as he petted her. He moved his forehead down toward her, and she rubbed her own head against his.

"How is the boutique doing?" he asked the feline.

"Ha!" The spirited exclamation sounded as though Rosemary were hearing it come from another person. It felt good to express spontaneous amusement, as the loud chuckle seemed to burst from her lungs and escape through her mouth. "I don't think the boutique sells very much lingerie, because I have seen *no* profits."

She giggled as she thought about her earlier discussion with Samantha, about needing a girdle, while her fingers now skimmed the midsection of her dress.

"Maybe Ms. Samantha is saving her earnings to create a chain of Samantha's Closets," Lucas teased. Rosemary felt a gush of air release from her nose, as she exhaled another chuckle.

She walked to the dining table and placed the hand-wrought holders in the middle, then placed the taper candles into them. Lucas followed her there. He stood closely beside her.

"You look magnetic tonight," Lucas huskily murmured, with an uncharacteristic ache in his voice.

Rosemary glanced sideways and saw a smoldering look in his stare – just for a second. When she turned her head to face him, the tension in his dark eyes was gone.

"Magnetic?" she asked. She felt her eyebrows peak to an arch, and the right side of her mouth rose in question. "Is that a good thing?"

"Yes, my dear. It means you're captivating... compelling... fascinating... attractive..." The corners of his mouth moved upward, in a precarious smile. "Beautiful isn't strong enough a word to describe you," he said, in the same husky voice.

Rosemary's lips slightly parted to voice gratitude, but she was happy for the distraction, as Lucas looked downward. He reached into his pants pocket and pulled out a matchbook, which he handed to her. She ignited the red tip of the match and produced a golden flame. Touching it to one of the candles' wicks, the fire grew as two flames merged. The golden flame seemed the only light in the world, as Rosemary moved her face closely to it.

"Bless this home and everyone in it," she softly said. Her eyes turned to Lucas. "Here," she said, passing him the matches, "you light the other candle, then we both can have blessings."

Something about the way his mouth curved upward made her feel an inexplicable chill. His eyes seemed to sparkle with an inviting, yet forbidden secret. The intrigue formed goosebumps on her arms.

A muffled thud ignited a flame, as he struck the tip of the match between the cardboard book. Lucas's shoulders hunched forward, as he moved his face close to the candle. His gaze fixed on the flame that moved to the bare wick. Rosemary, too, focused on the brightness of the lit match touching the wick, producing a thick, golden flame.

The blackness of Lucas's eyes seemed to intensify as they moved close to the candlelight. "Bless this home and everyone in it," he quietly repeated. His eyes turned to her and seemed to pierce through her soul, to send more chills down her spine. Rosemary felt her eyes widen of their own accord.

"Dinner is almost ready," she said, as her inner voice chastised her overactive imagination. Her mood needed to be lightened. This was just a friendly dinner with her neighbor, nothing more.

"I have to finish the side dishes," she said.

"Can I help with anything?" Lucas asked, standing up straight.

"No, everything is done, except for the potatoes and vegetables."

"I can help with those." Lucas followed her into the kitchen.

She turned the oven burner to high, underneath the pot of potatoes; the gas flame burned hot. The stovetop grill began to heat up as the burner was turned low, for the asparagus.

"Would you like a drink?" she asked. "You can get yourself a glass of lemonade, or water, or soda pop. Or I can make a pot of coffee."

"Is the lemonade homemade?"

"Sure is. Mama's recipe." Rosemary giggled. "Mama always said: 'Add a few lemons to my sugar, please.'"

"Then I'll have that," he said.

"There is a pinch of spice in the lemonade. We'll see if you can detect which one."

"The intrigue…" he said, with the same precarious smile.

"The glasses are in that cupboard." She pointed to the top cabinet, as she seasoned the vegetables on the grill.

Turning the pepper grinder, romantic thoughts persisted. *He thinks I look captivating, compelling and attractive tonight.* Did that mean that he *was* sexually attracted to her?

Lucas opened the refrigerator and pulled out the glass pitcher. Rosemary then felt his presence as he moved closely beside her, at the stove. "For you, Rose Petal," he said, handing her a glass of lemonade.

"Thank you, Lucas," she returned. She set her drink beside her. She turned from the grill a moment, to watch Lucas take a drink from his glass.

142

He closed his eyes and his forehead tightened, as he concentrated. "Ginger?" he said, in his husky voice, with eyes still closed.

Rosemary turned her attention back to the grill and smiled. "Yes," she said. As she glanced back again, she saw his dangerously sexy smile.

"What can I do to help with dinner?" he asked, catching her glance.

ɾ Standing at the stovetop grill, she turned the asparagus. "Would you please pull the turkey from the oven," she asked, "and set it on the counter?"

"It would be my pleasure."

"Here," Rosemary said, as she turned to hand Lucas a couple of hot pads. But she misjudged her footing and stepped right on top of his thinly-clad feet, with her sandals. She felt her mouth uncontrollably open wide, along with her eyes, at the threatened plunge.

His hands gripped her waist as she felt her knees buckle, mid-fall. The entire length of her backside now collided roughly with his chest, as she was safely pinned against him.

Rosemary mindfully pressed her lips together. She felt her breath held in her throat. She felt her fingers clutched tight around the cloth hot-pads.

She moved off of his feet. "I'm so sorry!" she said, turning to face him.

He didn't blink. He didn't look affected at all. "Sweetheart, do you think your little feet could harm me?" he asked sincerely.

"They're not little."

"They are, compared to mine," he growled. "I think my big old feet can handle you, Rose Petal." A heavy exhale from his nose

143

accompanied a grin.

As he continued to hold her gaze, his smile, seemingly affectionate, widened and warmed his face. At this moment, Rosemary felt as though there were nothing she could do to offend him. She felt safe being herself.

She handed him the hot-pads. "These are what I intended to give you, when I pummeled you. You can set the turkey on the counter," she said. "There's a hotplate there."

Rosemary carefully stepped aside, as he opened the oven.

"Wow! It smells good in here!" he said.

The muscles in Rosemary's face must have still been tight, because a smile loosened her jaw. She was comfortable with Lucas, but maybe the idea of this dinner possibly being a date caused her tension. Again, she had to remind herself to settle her nerves. She should enjoy her new neighbor's company, without adding stressful presumptions. She inhaled a deep breath while he transferred the main course to the hotplate. It did smell delicious.

The potatoes had been boiling for almost twenty minutes now, and Rosemary used a fork to pierce one of the starchy vegetables, to check its tenderness. They were drained in the strainer and transferred to a red, lace-patterned bowl. Warm butter and milk were added, along with salt and pepper. She clicked the beaters into place, in the orange hand mixer her mother had given as a gift, then mashed and blended the side dish.

"That's a pretty ceramic bowl," Lucas said, coming up behind her.

She could smell his clean aftershave scent. It felt as though his warm breath moved through the fringe of her hair, on the side of her face, as he moved closer. Her imagination could have fabricated the sensation of his nearness, but her skin had heated.

"Your cookware looks old-fashioned," he said.

She turned to face him. "They were my grandmother's," she answered. "I inherited the set of cookware from my mom. And dishes. My mom liked to prepare homemade meals. And pies."

"I noticed the pecan pie on the table," he said. She felt the same movement of air from his breath warmly brush her skin. "It looks delicious," he added.

"My mother's recipe. There's a hint of lemon in her pecan pie. It was my favorite, and she made it for me whenever I had a bad day. Or a good day!"

"I can't wait to have the pleasure of sampling your mother's food."

Rosemary smiled as she looked toward the pie. It looked as though it sat up proudly in the pretty, old-fashioned pie dish. It had been many months since Rosemary had utilized all of her matching pieces of dinnerware. She had last cooked for Sharon's family many months ago. Lucas stepped back, as Rosemary reached for another bowl and placed the asparagus in it.

She quietly exhaled from her nose, as a half-smile tugged at one side of her mouth. "My mom liked to collect all the new kitchen gadgets, like automatic peppermills and all sorts of peelers," she said, as she speckled the vegetables with black pepper from the mill.

"Your mother is beautiful," he said. He looked toward the windowsill, where Rosemary kept a small, framed picture of herself and her mother, in an embrace, their arms around one another, as they posed underneath the willow tree.

Rosemary liked the way Lucas talked, as though her mom were here now, standing in this room with them. "We were best friends."

"You are beautiful – just like your mother, Rose Petal. You look like her," he said.

"Thank you." She lightly drizzled the asparagus with olive oil and added salt. "Most people think I look like my dad."

Rosemary walked to Lucas's side and gazed at the picture. "My mom turned men's heads," she said. "She had pretty, blonde, shoulder-length hair, always curled with the curling iron. She always wore make-up and dressed neatly. Her pants were always creased with an iron. And she always smelled so pretty."

Rosemary looked down at herself. "I wore a dress today, but usually… I am more… relaxed with my clothing and hair."

"I see your mother's eyes when I look at you," Lucas said, in a husky, sincere voice.

"I did get her eyes. But she was so beautiful. She was thin but shapely; petite. She had an oval face and smooth hair. I have a square face and I'm not petite."

Rosemary walked to the cupboard and pulled a couple of serving utensils from it, then started toward the dining table, with the potatoes and vegetables. "Would you like to carve the turkey?" she asked.

"I would love to."

"Thank you," Rosemary said, nodding toward the red, lace-patterned platter on the oven top.

He caught her by the arm with his hand. "Rose Petal, you are just as beautiful as your mother. Maybe in different ways, but beautiful just the same. I love your earthy, natural style."

146

She lifted one side of her mouth in a small half-smile. "Thank you."

Rosemary set the side dishes on the dining table, then returned to the kitchen, to transfer the stuffing from the crock pot to a serving dish.

Lucas easily sliced the bird with Josephine's automatic knife, and placed the pieces on the red platter. Rosemary followed him, as he took the platter to the table. He pulled out the chair for her, next to one of the place settings.

"Thank you, Lucas," she said.

"No, thank *you*, Rose Petal." Across from her, he pulled his seat back.

"Oh," she blurted, "what would you like to drink with dinner? I know you liked the lemonade, but I bought some wine." She smiled a half-smile again. "I hardly ever drink wine, unless Sharon brings it, so I didn't know what to get. I asked Sharon; she advised me a nice red wine would be good with turkey." Rosemary pushed her chair back and stood to get it. "I thought a special drink might make our first dinner together more special."

Shit! She suddenly felt her face heat. *Our first dinner? More special?*

"I just mean that you, having saved my life, deserve a special dinner," she quickly elaborated. Her choice of words had sounded desperate, as though she were hinting at a second date. Standing there, she figured she looked like a needy woman, who virtually pounced on any man that spent an evening with her.

Lucas grinned at her. A slow, sexy grin. "I'd love some wine, Rose Petal," he said. "It is our first dinner. That is a reason to celebrate."

"I'll go get it," she said. "Do you know how to open it?" After the

147

question left her lips, her palm seemed to automatically press to her forehead. "I don't—"

"Yes." His deep, sensual voice came from the other side of the table.

What a dumb question: "Do you know how to open it?" Most adults would possess such a skill; it seemed an odd question to ask her invited dinner companion. She turned and walked to the kitchen, still pressing her palm to her forehead, and inwardly cursed herself.

Rosemary pulled the bottle of wine from the cabinet and carried it in one hand, while her other hand balanced two wine glasses between two fingers. The corkscrew nestled in her palm. The glasses and wine had been purchased earlier today, at the quaint winery in town. She handed Lucas the bottle and corkscrew knife, also purchased earlier today, and set the glasses in front of him. He removed the foil on the bottle, positioned the corkscrew in the center of the cork and twisted. The cork was pulled out of the bottle with a slight pop.

Lucas held a glass by the stem as he poured the deep-red pinot noir. Rosemary stood beside him and watched the pretty, fragrant liquid color the glass. He handed her the drink and she carried it to her place across from him, taking her seat.

Over the table, he held his glass up toward her. "To a beautiful dinner and beautiful company," he said.

She clanked her wineglass to his. "And, to the man who saved my life," she added.

"Your life is definitely something to toast to," he returned.

A heat traveled through her body, to her cheeks and forehead. Maybe his toast had stirred a physical reaction, or perhaps the first sip of her drink had caused the sensation. It felt as though a stream of silk bathed her throat, as she savored the first drink of wine. The fruity taste was pleasing. She hardly ever drank wine, and was not a connoisseur, but enjoyed the festiveness it added to the dinner.

"Guests first," she said, handing him the bowl of potatoes.

"Thank you, Rose Petal." He took the side dish from her and spooned a helping onto his plate. Lucas then held the platter toward her and offered Rosemary the first serving of meat. Condiments and the remaining trimmings were passed between them.

He closed his eyes as he ate, seeming to savor the food. A husky moan rose from his throat with each taste. It was obvious that he loved her cooking. As she watched him, a small smile crept across her mouth. He opened his eyes and she quickly took a forkful of mashed potatoes, looking downward at her plate. Damn, he had seen her staring at him.

"Do you like the dinner?" she asked. Her tone was giggly.

He looked at her with sincerely-set eyes. "I would not want to be anywhere else in all the universes, except here, eating this delicious, home-cooked meal with you, Rose Petal. The meat is so tender and moist. I taste that hint of cinnamon ever so slightly. It's… pleasing… unforgettable." He rested his fork on the plate, then took a drink of wine. His eyes closed as he swallowed.

He looked at Rosemary when his eyes opened. "What did you do last night, Rose Petal?" he asked.

"Last night, Sharon invited me over to her house for a little get-together. She is so happy that I finally broke up with Mark. She's been wanting me to meet her brother's friend, Alan. Sharon showed him a picture of me, and he's been wanting to meet me." She shifted in her seat, one side of her mouth tentatively pulled upward. Her skin felt warmer as her pulse quickened.

But Lucas didn't cease his gaze; he continued to look directly at her. The expression in his eyes still appeared amiable. Rosemary hadn't meant to disclose her activities of last night, but his questions always seemed to invoke honesty from her. She had wanted to be discreet, in case Lucas had an interest in her beyond friendship. Although, maybe she *had* wished him to know that a nice, even-tempered man could find her attractive?

"Anyway, Alan is a nice person, but we were not compatible enough to date," she said.

"Do you ever have time off from the shelter?" Lucas asked. "Seven days a week is too much for you to work. You do need a social life." Last night's meeting with Alan did not seem to have conjured any jealousy in Lucas; his face and demeanor showed no reaction. Rosemary realized that she was disappointed.

"Sharon and I usually have a crew come in on Sundays. They are a husband-and-wife team. For the last couple of weeks, they have been on vacation. Share's mom will also help out, to give one of us a break. Either me, Share or her mom will stop by the shelter for the animals' dinner, if still no one is there. Or we'll arrive super early."

She held her fork vertically, the bottom resting on the side of her plate. "One day I'd like to expand the shelter. Maybe find a place with land, so we can help out livestock, too, in need of a home."

"Your heart will continually expand. It is good to find new ways to expand love." His dark eyes flashed to hers.

A few minutes of silence passed. Lucas seemed to continue savoring his meal. She watched him.

He now looked up from his plate. *Damn!* He had seen her staring at him again! He smiled at her.

"Tell me about your decision to buy only pasture-raised meat. You seem very passionate about it," he said.

"Not just pastured…" she said; "I only buy meat from one specific farm, that ships to me. They have abattoirs right on their farm.

"One day, I was driving down the freeway and saw a semi-truck hauling chickens. The poor chickens must have been scared to death. There was no coverage for them; the bed of the trailer was open, with no walls. I could see that each chicken was in an individual cage, several rows stacked on top of each other – must have been hundreds. Only their backsides were showing, because their heads must have all been pressed against the safety of the inside of the truck. Poor things must have been terrified of the noise from the freeway. I can buy pasture-raised all I want, but if the poor animals are being transported like that, what good am I doing by buying pasture-raised? So, now I buy from only one farm, no transportation involved.

"And, overcrowded, industrialized feedlots… we can do better! Large factory farms are inhumane. They are cost-effective, but inhumane. Some poor chickens' feet never touch a blade of grass. Chickens were born to peck earth; they should be allowed to express their instinctive behaviors – their God-given, instinctive behaviors. Overcrowded cows and pigs, in factory farms, can barely turn around, they are packed so tightly together, with their runny noses and eyes. It's such a poor quality of life for any animal with a beating heart.

These are living, breathing creatures we abuse. We need to care about these animals with beating hearts, because we eat them for our nourishment. We need to find a better way, like regenerative farming in a respectful manner."

Lucas intently studied her. "I'm so proud of you, Rose Petal. You investigated and found a place that is up to your standards. A place that treats animals with the respect they deserve."

One side of Rosemary's mouth turned up in a half-smile. No one had ever expressed admiration for that particular decision of hers.

"Tell me more about your mother," he asked, thoughtfully.

Animation seemed to emerge through her. She felt spirit fill her eyes, as thoughts turned to her mom. "My mom believed in *magic*. She believed there was something else out there, in this huge universe. She believed that *something else* is a loving energy, and that we all are connected and a part of it." Rosemary felt the spirit in her eyes soften, but still radiate naturally. She realized she hadn't talked about her mother to another human being in quite a while. This conversation was enjoyable.

"Your mother sounds like a very conceptual thinker – open-minded and loving."

"She is. *Was*."

"*Is*," he firmly said.

"My mom had received visits from her loved ones, after they had passed. She told me I would see her after she passed. And she *did* come to visit me after she passed." Rosemary warily looked over at Lucas. She felt anxiousness slightly lift her eyelids, and a cautious tautness stretch her lips and jaw. She was secure that Lucas would believe and appreciate her experience, but it was an unusual thing to tell a practical stranger. Gentle eyes looked back at her.

"What was your visit like?" he attentively asked.

The muscles of her face relaxed. "It was so wonderful to see her. It had been only a few days since her passing. It was such an intense meeting, it still feels like only yesterday. It was one of those moments forever ingrained in my mind and soul, like words carved in stone.

"It was in a dream that I saw her. I walked to where she was, standing in the kitchen. She told me she was proud of me, then she held me. I felt such love from her. The words didn't come from her mouth; they came... almost... telepathically. But the words surrounded me – every cell of me."

"Her love must be so great for you. It takes a soul a vast amount of energy to lower its frequency, to communicate with a human. That is an experience to carry you through every part of your life," he softly said.

"Yes, you're right! I thought of that moment with my mom, when Mark threw and broke my vase. My mama would say: 'It's just a thing. It's not things that are important; it's the love that binds all things that's important. If something breaks, the love is still there. So, I use my china!'"

Rosemary felt pressure on her bottom lip, as her teeth pressed it. "When I woke from that dream... experience..." she continued, "I felt an overwhelming sense of love from my mom, how proud she truly was of me. I still feel it today, from that one visit. That feeling always stays with me. Maybe, from where she was at the time of my dream, she knew my future? Maybe, when my mom passed and became totally enlightened, she could see the past, present and future, all at the same time? Maybe she was proud of me back then, for opening a rescue and finally leaving Mark, even though those things hadn't happened yet, then. I've had other experiences with her since, but I haven't seen her again."

"What other experiences?" Lucas asked, sincerely.

"She leaves me feathers. She told me before she passed that she would…

"Sharon and I bought the building for the shelter together, though I put up most of the money." Rosemary inhaled deeply, remembering her fear on the day she wrote the check to the real estate agent. "It was my inheritance from my mom. It was a very scary thing to do. The day we got the keys to our new building, I found a dove's feather, just in front of the door, while I was unlocking it. The feather was beautiful. I've never seen another feather in that spot, in the two years we've been there. My mother loved the sweet song of the dove."

"Always listen to your inner voice… your inner light," he said. "If your inner light told you your mom left you a loving sign, then know it as truth."

Rosemary felt her brows tightly pull together, as she concentrated on Lucas's response. "Yes, you're right. Most people would argue that I could find a feather anywhere, that finding a feather means nothing, but it's the *feeling* I get inside, the *knowing*. Feathers show up in the most meaningful places, at the most critical times.

"When I got the mail, the day after I broke up with Mark, there was a dove's feather on the front porch. I've never seen one there before," she said. "There was also a beautiful blue jay's feather on my mother's grave; it was full and bright blue, on both sides of the stem. It was set on her headstone when I visited her on my birthday, the first year of her passing. It made me smile. Of course, I keep these feathers."

"Your mom will always be involved with your life. She will help guide you. You just need to learn the way she communicates now. You need to keep trusting your inner knowing, and the messages will keep coming."

She pulled her lower lip between her teeth, then released it. A deep breath calmed the rush of emotions. "Thank you for believing my stories. You are very spiritual."

"Always have faith in your own truth, Rose Petal. Never let anyone discourage you," he firmly stated.

He took a drink of wine. His hand cradled the base of the glass, as he lifted it to his mouth. His lips looked masculine – as though they would know how to kiss a woman.

Lucas always dressed immaculately. Even at the shelter he had worn pleated pants and nice button-down shirts. His shoes had always been clean. Tonight, his clothes were even more refined. He looked like a sexy, if uptight businessman. His black hair was neat and combed back. What would it look like tousled, after a night of lovemaking?

Dark eyes returned her gaze. They seemed to pierce through her soul.

She disconnected her line of vision, as she took a sip from her wineglass. As the red liquid touched her lips and passed through her mouth, she wondered how a kiss from him would taste and feel. The wine warmed her throat as it passed. Maybe it gave her courage to be intrusive.

"Can I ask you a question?" she said, feeling her pulse suddenly quicken.

"Anything."

"Why do you call me 'Rose Petal'?"

Dark eyes seemed to sparkle hotly toward her, like black diamonds. "Your mother named you Rosemary because it meant strength to her," he began, huskily. "Your father called you Rosy because it meant love to him. I call you Rose Petal because you are *beauty* to me," he said.

She swallowed hard. A warm patch touched her cheeks. His answer bewildered her. Did he wish for a relationship beyond friendship? Did he think of this as a date?

Maybe his confidence was the only reason for his indifference concerning her social life.

"I love how natural your beauty is," he continued. His voice was slow and thick. "Everything is natural about you. The way you interact with people, animals, plants... You're confident, lighthearted, kind-hearted, warm... soft..." He took another drink of wine.

Soft?

His eyes narrowed as he focused on her. "Your hair is so beautiful tonight," he added.

"What?" She shifted in her chair, crossing her legs. "Oh, I was going to straighten it tonight," she said, pulling a strand through her fingers.

"I wouldn't change a thing, Rose Petal," he huskily said. His lips curved upward, to form a thin, sexy smile.

Rosemary didn't think of herself as ugly, but she didn't consider herself a beauty, either. His compliments made her feel as though a man could see her as a desirable woman.

Was the wine or his words causing her skin to feel flushed?

"I know this is a new loss – you don't have to talk about anything that upsets you – but would you like to tell me about your father? What kind of soul is he?" Lucas asked.

The unexpected mention of her dad seemed to shock her brain back to a harsh reality. A picture formed in her mind, of her father in the hospital bed. Moistness gathered in the corners of her eyes. She quickly wiped her face.

"I'm sorry," Lucas said, "it was thoughtless of me to—"

"No, it's okay," she started. The tension in her face loosened, as her mouth tugged to one side, in a small smile.

Rosemary inhaled deeply, to calm her thoughts. "My dad and I weren't on the best of terms when he passed," she continued. "We routinely had weekend phone calls, most of my life, but... we quit talking. About three weeks before his death, thank God, we began talking again.

"He and my mother got divorced when I was young. I had thought of him as a dependable force in my life until he left home. I was fifteen when he left us – or, rather, he was forced to leave us, because my mom couldn't accept his affair." She pulled her bottom lip inside her mouth. It tasted of wine.

Lucas studied her. He sat silent, listening, his eyes focused only on her face.

"As you can imagine, my dad didn't like my ex, Mark. I think I stayed with Mark because he was predictably unemotional about everything." She glanced into Lucas's eyes. "You see, my family could be a bit dramatic – very emotional. I liked that Mark was insensitive with me when I freaked out about something. It made me feel like everything was okay, and I was overreacting. He provided stability in my life. I could depend on him to always be unemotionally there. My mom was very emotional and my dad was gone; Mark was unemotionally there."

Lucas intently looked at her. He began to speak, with his brows pulled together. "I don't think it's insensitivity you need; I think you need someone who will take the time to listen to your concerns and be a supportive partner."

She gently bit down on her lower lip. Breaking the shared gaze, Rosemary mechanically looked downward as she considered his statement. Obviously, a quality partner should display support, but her need at the time she had met Mark was a primary one: survival. Her now-healthier soul would need an upgraded list of characteristics for a future partner. She would ponder Lucas's statement later.

"Anyway…" she continued, "my father was stern; he was raised to work hard and follow the rules." She felt her lower jaw jut forward, as the muscles in her face tightened. A heavy sigh was breathed out of her nostrils. "*His* rules; he believed everyone should follow *his* rules. He didn't realize that people are different, with different needs, experiences, skills, mindsets, desires..."

Lucas continued to focus on her. His eyes stayed steadily in line with hers.

"We butted heads about Mark," she said. "My dad wanted his daughter to be with a man who worked a traditional, full-time job. My dad didn't care if a man changed oil in a car, filed taxes or cleaned toilets, but he believed a man should be loyal to his profession." Another heavy sigh left her nostrils. "Mark is a trust-fund baby; his family owns a hotel chain. Mark bought his house with money from his trust fund. He works part-time as a real-estate agent, and loves to take clients out for dinner and drinks."

The sound of her own voice talking about her life seemed to echo in her head, as if in third-person form. It seemed as though her brain was telling her to stop boring the person opposite her. She took a deep breath.

She had kept frequent eye contact with Lucas, politely breaking the glance every so often. He had not looked away or even taken a drink since she had initiated her story about Frank.

"I know my dad just wanted the best for me," she quietly said. Her eyes lowered and she gazed at her arms, folded in her lap. "He loved me because I was his daughter. I'm not sure he liked who I am as a person.

"I loved him," she softly said. A tear trickled from the outer edge of her eyelid and she wiped it. "I respected him." Her voice cracked at the recalled vision of the day Frank brought her the Buddha statue, from his business trip. He had been casually but neatly dressed. He had talked so proudly of his automation design, which helped speed the production of parts for a manufacturing shop in Asia.

"We had gotten close again when I became an adult," she continued. "He had a gentle heart. Like I said, my dad always brought me back little gifts from his business trips, and he had roses sent to the house for every one of my birthdays that I can remember; the birthday card always read: *'Love you Rosy, Dad.'*" An unintended, short, uneven breath softened the last word. "My dad always had apple slices waiting for me when I visited him; he knew that was my favorite treat."

"Sweetheart," Lucas said directly, as he leaned forward in his chair, "I know your father likes who you are as a person; it would be impossible for him not to like you. You, like him, have a gentle, loving heart. You sacrifice your life to take care of the vulnerable. I know that, if an injured animal showed up, whether six a.m. or eleven p.m., you'd take care of it. I know you'd sell the clothes off your back to pay for any vet bill, if you had to. And, believe me, your dad sees that in you."

Lucas had truly seen all of that inside of her? She felt taken aback. "Thank… you… Lucas. And thank you for listening to my stories," Rosemary said. She reached her hands toward the back of her neck, and kneaded the sides with her fingertips.

"Your dad did the best job he knew how, as a father. Parents learn as they go, just like anything in life. The important thing is to show love… and each person shows love differently. The way Frank showed his love for you was to show that he had thought of you on his business trips: he brought you home gifts; he sent you flowers, with a special sentiment inside your card, for all your birthdays. Your father showed his love by asking about the events of your life, in your weekly phone calls. All the other stuff – the mistakes, the disagreements, the hard feelings…" he studied her face, "if your father didn't *like* you, he wouldn't have cared who you spent your time with. He didn't think Mark was good enough for you. If you forgive your dad for not loving you the way you had wished, maybe more memories of the love will resurface, because you will have opened yourself to the loving energy your mom believed in."

Her mouth relaxed, with a small smile. Her father *had* shown love, in his own way. Maybe not the way she would have preferred, but love nonetheless. She would have preferred civil conversations with her father, no matter her choice of boyfriend.

"If you forgive yourself for your unhealthy relationship with Mark, you will be able to forgive Mark. Because, forgiving oneself and others opens the flow to all goodness," Lucas added, gently.

She exhaled an intentionally heavy breath from her nose. "I will try."

Looking down at her hands, folded in her lap, she cleared her mind of her troubles, and realized the depth of her curiosity concerning her neighbor's background.

"So, tell me about yourself, Lucas," she asked, looking up at him.

He straightened in his seat. His eyebrows pulled together and formed a deep crease between them. There was a long pause. "What would you like to know?" he asked, his tone heavy.

The change in Lucas's sincere manner made Rosemary feel tentative about invasive questions, but she wasn't sharing her life without learning of his.

"How do you like it here in Massachusetts? Do you miss California? Your family... friends?"

"I like it here: a nice, calm, quaint town. My family lives all over the world. I like my friends here. I consider you my friend."

"Yes, Lucas, I consider you a very good friend, of course." She was pleased his tone became even again. "I haven't been inside your home, next door, since the old owner lived there; my mom used to take the elderly man dinners. What does it look like inside now? Is it dusty and decrepit? It sat vacant for quite a while: a couple of years. Did you buy it sight unseen, or did you look at it before buying? Did you live in Massachusetts before living in Wolfe County?"

"I did buy the house sight unseen," he answered, his voice calm, but gruff. "I had an inspector look at it for me first. The house has a lot of antiques left by the previous owner; I will keep them. There is also a lot of work to do. It is my first time living in Massachusetts."

Rosemary noticed Lucas moving his left arm. His elbow pointed out from his body, as though he had stuck his hand inside his pants pocket. He looked at her watching him. Lucas then pulled out a gold antique pocket watch. He set it on the table for her to see it.

"That's pretty," Rosemary said. "Is it a family heirloom piece?"

He put it back in his pocket and fidgeted with it a moment longer. "No, I got it at the antique store."

Rosemary's eyebrows pulled together, as she thought of her next question. She felt the tightness. "Tell me about your parents... Siblings?"

Lucas's jawline hardened. He traced the line of his mouth between his thumb and index finger. Rosemary intuitively guessed that this subject bothered him. She wondered why.

"My mother, Catherine, was a very loving, nurturing woman," he started, his tone tender: "gentle, warm, soft... She liked to give hugs."

His fingers traced upward, as a grin pulled the sides of his mouth up. "My mom would invent games, to keep us boys occupied. She was very creative and childlike."

162

Lucas had spoken of his mother in the past tense. "I'm sorry, Lucas – your mom passed, too?"

"Yes."

"Sorry," she repeated, warmly. "Boys?" she then added. "You have a brother?"

"Me and my younger brother, Ash." His fingers slid down the sides of his mouth as a small frown formed, but it smoothed when he began talking again. "My mother would read us classic books, then have us act out the scenes."

His eyes narrowed and he now looked beyond Rosemary. "Our father, Nigel, was… not a nice man. He would have been a ruler of the *worst* kind," Lucas said.

What a weird thing to say. Rosemary felt her jawline tighten and her eyelids rise slightly, but she stayed quiet. Her line of vision felt glued to Lucas's every gesture. His black eyes, staring past her, looked ominous.

He persisted staring past her as he continued: "I come from a line of treacherous men." His voice sounded thick, as though his words were quicksand and would envelop him.

Rosemary felt a chill, with the odd shift in Lucas's energy. A dark light seemed to overcome the planes of his face. His jawline became even more rigid and the bone structure of his cheeks seemed to sharpen.

"My father and brother are very negative forces," Lucas said. He glanced at Rosemary and his expression softened. "My grandfather, Lucious, is a kind soul," he said, his voice unexpectedly warm.

"Lucious?" she asked, faintly.

"Yes. I was named after him; Lucas is a derivative of Lucious. I'm

glad I was named after my grandfather. My mother, Catherine, told me stories of my grandfather. He was a farmer and gave free vegetables to the poor. He passed before I was born.

"My mother came from a modest background," he said, composed, looking at Rosemary. "I think my father wooed her with his charms, gifts and status, and she mistakenly thought his offerings tokens of love. But he was never loyal or loving to her; he was abusive... emotionally and physically..."

Lucas again looked away. It seemed that his eyes blackened into a pool of rage. "My father wanted a good woman to raise his spawn," he said, his voice thick once again.

Perspiration moistened Rosemary's underarms, upper back and chest. She felt her skin stick to her dress and her face felt clammy. Dampness accumulated underneath her hairline and on her forehead. She quietly inhaled a deep breath through her nostrils, to slow her quickened pulse. Rosemary hoped that Lucas had not noticed the onset of her unease, but thankfully he wasn't watching her. His demeanor usually seemed to have a calming effect on her, but tonight he scared her. She swallowed hard as she glanced at him. His last words had shocked her. Lucas had seemed harsh in a way that she had never before witnessed.

His narrowed eyes now appeared to stare through the walls of the house and beyond space. When a few minutes of silence had passed, Rosemary knew that he was finished talking about his family.

He closed his eyes and inhaled deeply. A slow exhale seemed to relax the muscles in his face. "I am sorry, Rose Petal," he said quietly, his eyes still closed.

He then opened his eyelids and turned to look at her. "I am sorry if my outburst frightened you. I got carried away confessing the dark side of my family. It was not a good subject for our first dinner date." He traced the line of his mouth between his index finger and thumb. "I feel comfortable with you, but I shouldn't have…"

"Don't apologize," Rosemary said. She felt the muscles of her body relax, as she breathed in a slow breath. "I asked about your life. I'm sorry about your father," she gently offered.

"Maybe that's why men who abuse women affect me so intensely," he said. He looked directly into her eyes. He had maintained his composure with his last statement.

"I am so relieved you broke up with Mark. Please follow your gut instincts in future relationships," he said. "If a man is right for you, you will know; you won't have any question. You will feel it in your soul."

Rosemary pushed her chair backward and stood. "Would you like dessert now?" she asked.

"That sounds like Heaven."

"I'll be right back. I have to get a knife for the pie."

She forcibly inhaled a deep but uneven breath, as she turned her back to him and walked to the kitchen counter. Her eyelids seemed to drop like lead, as she stood there a moment. Lucas's change of energy had scared, disappointed and saddened her. Maybe, being a man, his verbalization of the troubled relationship with his father came out harsher than that of a woman?

He had survived a difficult childhood, and Rosemary knew that wounding experiences could be damaging to one's development and perception. He obviously still had deep-rooted anger. At least

165

Rosemary now better understood the reason behind his overprotective manner toward her.

Josephine used to say: "Anyone over thirty has gone through some life. Life ain't for sissies." Rosemary glanced at the small picture on the windowsill and softly smiled, as she remembered how her mother's nose would crinkle at certain words.

The faint smile still held by the corners of her mouth, Rosemary returned to the dining table, with the clean knife and two small dessert plates. She cut into the flaky crust and handed Lucas the first piece of pie. The edges of his mouth stretched to form a long, thin smile. Gentleness had returned to his dark eyes. Lucas took a bite of his dessert, as Rosemary plated her piece.

A soft moan echoed deep in his throat, with his first taste. Closing his eyes, he held the second piece to his nostrils and inhaled, holding the nutty aroma there for a moment. Then he took his second mouthful and chewed slowly.

"I haven't had a homemade meal in two hundred years... it seems," he said. "Thank you, Rose Petal. You are an amazing cook and baker." He lightly touched his index finger to his thumb, and held his eyes closed for a second, as he said: "The touch of lemon, with the pecans and velvety brown sugar, ever so slightly cuts the sweetness and adds a touch of zest. Everything was beyond delicious," he finished, looking directly at her.

"Thank you," she returned. "You can get used to it: I love to cook, and you're only next door; you're welcome here anytime for dinner."

Hopefully, tonight's uneasiness was an isolated incident, and she wouldn't regret the extended invitation. If she wanted to be a friend to this man, who had practically saved her life, she would have to accept his tortured past. But, if he spoke of it again with such rage, she would have to withdraw her invitation.

"Thank you, Rose Petal."

After finishing dessert, Lucas leaned over the table. His face glowed just above the lit candles, as his strong-looking lips pulled together, blowing out air to distinguish the flames.

"How about an evening walk?" he asked, moving his dark eyes to Rosemary's. "Should be pretty outside. It's a full moon tonight."

"Sure," she answered. "Would you like to swing with me for a few minutes first?"

"I'd love to, Rose Petal."

She fully trusted that Lucas would never harm her. If she were honest with herself, though, after having witnessed his ominous mood, a quick chill passed through her at the thought of walking in the moonlight with him.

Rosemary glanced behind her, at the clock in the kitchen, above the oven; the teapot clock read ten p.m. They had begun dinner around six; nearly four hours had passed, and it seemed like only one. Time spent with most people usually fatigued her, but Lucas's energy satisfied her. Conversations occurred naturally, as though they were long-time friends. Even though tonight's talk was intense, time still seemed to fly by.

As they walked outside, a gust of air blew Rosemary's hair behind her. The fresh smell of the late summer breeze refreshed the heaviness of her mood.

It was dark, except for the porch light and solar lanterns that lined both sides of the driveway. As they walked to the side of the house, past the deck, the moon was low and golden. The night sky reminded Rosemary to keep a sense of awe. "Anything is possible if one just believes," her mother would say.

Rosemary and Lucas walked toward the swing, and the shadow of the enormous willow tree loomed over them. "Good evening, Audrey," Rosemary greeted it.

It had been a good release for her to talk about her mother, father and ex. She had never spoken out loud the exact feelings she believed her father had felt for her. Maybe she had been extra-sensitive, and overreacted to Lucas's temperament. After all, friends should be allowed the comfort to discuss their innermost, darkest secrets without judgment.

They both took a seat under the darkened, towering willow. The wooden swing gently swayed, as their legs moved slowly underneath it.

Crickets seemed to serenade an almost deafening song, as silence lingered between Rosemary and Lucas. The low hum of a motor sounded from a distance, near Lucas's home.

"Are you running a generator?" Rosemary asked.

"Yes. I'm having problems with electricity right now," he briefly answered.

"If you allow me to pick some apples off your apple trees, I can make a pie."

"My apples are your apples, Rose Petal. That would be wonderful."

"Fall is in the air," she said. "Will you miss the weather in California? Here—"

"You have more than made up for anything I left behind, Rose

Petal."

He slowed the sway of the swing, as he stilled his legs, then stood. "Let's go for a little walk now," he said.

Rosemary stood. *What an odd thing for him to say.* He barely knew her. How could she take the place of nice weather?

Lucas cradled her elbow in his palm, as they began the walk. They crossed a rutted section of her gravel driveway, behind her truck. Upon reaching the dirt road, he released the warmth of his touch. She missed it.

"I never tire of looking up at a full moon," Lucas said, gazing toward the golden sphere in the dark sky.

Rosemary squinted her eyes, attempting to find a falling star.

"What will you wish for tonight, Rose Petal?"

"How did you know?"

He only smiled, as he held her gaze.

"Peace. A peaceful love," she breathed. "I want to be able to trust my inner... *light*, as you call it... again. I need to take care of myself now."

"That is a wonderful wish, Rose Petal."

Lucas stopped walking. They had just stepped off her long driveway. Two golden lanterns glowed with simulated fire, just beside them.

Rosemary turned to look at him. Unhurriedly, he moved one leg forward, then the other, stepping closely in front of her. Peripherally, she watched his hands move to either side of her face. She felt warm, as her heart pulsated and blood rushed under her skin. The palms of his hands heated her cheeks, as he caressed her.

169

He looked down at her, holding her gaze. It seemed that he thrust into her soul and examined it; she felt dissected by him. The scrutiny caused her to feel understood by a man. He saw everything she was and still cared for her.

"Please, Rose Petal, always trust your inner light," he huskily whispered, his breath caressing her lips. His fixed stare slowly descended to them, black eyes focused on her mouth. Even in the dark, she could sense the intensity. A sheen showed the desire in his eyes. Rosemary felt pressure on her bottom lip, as she distractedly folded it under her top teeth.

She then relaxed, as the reach of his fingers began to extend and move through her hairline. The tips of his fingers gently massaged her head, as they moved deeper through the strands of her hair. She felt gentle tugs, as he entangled with her curls. Gripping sections at the back of her head, his palms flattened against her.

His forehead leaned downward, almost touching hers. He closed his eyes. He seemed to inhale her scent deep into his nostrils. While arching his face, his mouth lowered close to hers. His lips were almost brushing hers. Again, he closed his eyes and breathed in. She felt his warm breath on her lips again, as he exhaled.

Rosemary closed her eyes. Her lips felt swollen with need.

Please, kiss me! her body practically begged. *Oh, god, please kiss me!* Breaths hitched in her throat.

"Rose Petal, *promise me* that you will always trust and listen to your inner light?" he roughly asked. His deep voice seemed to hum through her bones.

She opened her eyes. His mouth was just above hers. He opened his black eyes. "I will," she said, faintly.

"Good." As he spoke, his voice seemed to swelter with need... and restraint. Her eyes focused on his eyes... his mouth....

She hadn't seen his hands release their hold on the sides of her head, but she now felt the removal of his warm embrace. Lucas took a step backward, away from her.

"I'd better get you home." His voice seemed to wispily materialize from the darkness.

He headed toward the front door of her house, and she followed beside him. She looked up at his face, but he only focused ahead. Again, he fidgeted with the timepiece in his pocket.

Rosemary knew that tears would appear when Lucas left her alone. He had almost kissed her. What had stopped him? He had told her to trust her inner light. She had promised herself to be bold.

They now reached her doorstep.

Rosemary looked directly into Lucas's dark eyes, seemingly with no desire left smoldering in them; his gaze looked composed. Kind, but composed.

"What happened back there?" she asked. Her voice was collected, but a little spiciness had been candidly injected.

Lucas's eyes narrowed, as his eyebrows pulled together. "I'm sorry," he said. "I got carried away. You are not ready for a relationship, and I cannot..." His voice tapered to a brittle stillness.

"Goodnight, Rose Petal. Thank you for the dinner," he said respectfully.

Lucas's black eyes looked tortured, as he then added: "Please forgive me?"

Chapter 8

Lucifer's Poem

After Lucifer had left Rosemary, he walked next door to the vacant house. His stomach felt full. It was a comfortable sensation.

He had almost kissed her tonight.

If he had permitted himself the pleasure of the feel of her mouth, the taste of her breath and the experience of her human form, he would have to become Earthbound. It would be emotionally impossible to leave her if he allowed himself that intimacy.

Her soul had chosen the main characters intended for this life's journey. A life plan, including family and friends, was already in place for her deliberate experiences. He was not a part of that equation.

Running his fingers through the black hair on the top of his head, he breathed out a heavy gush of air. Staying human was wearing on him.

His body had yearned for closeness to Rosemary's.

He had been too exposed tonight.

Entrusting her with intimate details of his past human life had been an irresponsible action. Learning anything about his historic or current existence could only cause her harm. Emotional harm.

The original Lucifer, the angel, appointed a group of beings to rule Hell. Grandfather Lucious was the leader of the beings. Once the beings overtook governing Hell, Grandfather assumed the name Lucifer, as the ruler of Hell. It was established that each subsequent ruler would assume the name Lucifer when he was chosen as successor.

Although there were two Lucifers before him, and there would be a line of Lucifers after him, he now held the title.

Lucifer felt his eyelids close tight, as he now thought about what the name Lucifer meant to most human beings, like Rosemary.

Lucifer lit a candle to soothe himself. He shed his clothes and lay in bed, with only a sheet covering his skin. As he gently but intently closed his eyes this time, he intended a peaceful rest.

Unconsciousness came, but voices from the past disrupted his sleep…

"Lucas," his first human mother, Catherine, called from his dream.

Catherine had been a loving energy in his first human experience. After her human death, she had become once again cognizant that she was a member of the lineage of Hell, just as her children and husband had been.

"Lucas," she playfully called again.

This time, Lucifer saw her face clearly in his dream. She was beautiful. At home, her long, brown hair lay loosely down her gown-covered back.

In his dream, Lucifer was Lucas, a young boy hiding in a game of hide-and-seek. He was peeking out from under his bed as his mother rounded the corner.

"Where is my gentleman and scholar?" she sang.

Lucifer's grandfather, the previous ruler, had established an innovative practice. Potential candidates for successor as ruler of Hell would inhabit Earth as humans. Their souls would enter a human womb and develop, like any other soul. Each soul, lineage or not, chose its parents with an agreement from all beforehand. Grandfather experimented with humanizing Hell by spending time as a mortal himself. He gained such indispensible knowledge that the new practice was launched. Grandfather wanted each hopeful to experience firsthand the tribulations and sufferings the soul of a human encounters. Empathetic rulers would understand human affliction, and be able to better facilitate the healing process for souls seeking refuge at the castle. A bloodline was developed for such an endeavor; Grandfather Lucious and Clara were the head of the lineage. Their blood children were Catherine and Grace; Daniel and Melanie sired Nigel and Heath. Lucas, Ash and Devon were the grandchildren of Lucious.

Being the head of the benevolent beings, Grandfather Lucious had volunteered himself as the human grandfather of the first lineage to inhabit Earth, along with his counterpart, Clara.

Once human, each hopeful successor was allowed to forget his or her true identity, like most any human. Each member of the lineage was encouraged to live out his or her life in a conventional manner, experiencing a human birth and death. Once the death occurred, each hopeful successor was encouraged to experience other lives, until one's reign in Hell. Lucifer's first blood-father and brother had been competing for the position alongside him.

Lucifer now heard his grandfather's voice in his dream. The voice seemed to fill the dark space underneath the bed, and vibrate through the young boy's body. Though the youngster's grandfather had passed before his birth, he sensed it was his elder's presence.

"I am an old soul, Lucas, and you are a young soul, a kind soul, perfect to one day be my successor. You are now human, and will experience the sufferings the soul of a human encounters," Grandfather

Lucious's booming voice said.

"I don't want to be human," the young boy whispered in the dark.

"You must," Grandfather said; "it is the only way to obtain empathy."

Young Lucas considered his grandfather a compassionate soul, by his mother's accounts. After Lucas's human death, Grandfather had declared him the second-in-command and eventual successor. With Grandfather's retirement, the second-in-command would assume the ruler's name, Lucifer, and position as ruler of Hell.

In his current dream, Lucifer watched young Lucas slam his back against the wooden floor underneath his bed. The child scrunched his eyelids closed and tightly pressed his palms to either side of his head, over his ears. Tears quietly streamed down the boy's face, as he hid in the dark.

Nigel had roughly grabbed Catherine by the back of her hair.

"It is time for dinner, *not games*!" Nigel wailed.

Lucifer's eyes seemed to now fly open. His lungs seemed to gasp for air, as his heart pumped quickly. He rested the palm of his hand on his chest, slowly inhaling deep breaths.

During Lucifer's first human experience, he had remained unaware of his soul's purpose throughout Lucas's birth and human death. Lucas had fallen in love and married Margaret, which had been Rosemary's soul. Not until he returned to his condensed form had he remembered his true identity, as a member of the lineage.

The memory of being named Grandfather's forthcoming heir had been remembered during his subsequent human lifetimes. He hadn't wished to interfere with Margaret's soul's journey, so he chose instead to play a passive role in her following lives.

Only the happiness and expansion of her soul mattered to him. His concern for her well-being far outweighed any romantic passion. He had always watched over her from a distance.

This time, her life's mission had been threatened by Mark.

Mark had not intentionally set out to harm Rosemary, but his negative thoughts and actions would have eventually endangered her.

Lucifer's soul had always been connected to Rosemary's, in an unexplainable way. His senses told him when she needed his guidance. His energy had been pulled to hers as though a magnet.

He again felt his heart thump, under his bones.

This mission of watching Rosemary needed to conclude quickly; he was becoming more accustomed to being human every day. He was becoming more aware of his physical senses. A raise in his body temperature always occurred with Rosemary nearby. A deep breath of air, filling his lungs, was necessary to slow his increased heart rate.

Anxiousness was not a sensation a soul commonly experienced. This *human* creation, anxiety, caused lightheadedness to now overwhelm Lucifer's body. It felt as though one more thought might detonate his brain. Lucifer needed sleep.

Lucifer opened his eyes. Daylight filtered into the bedroom, as bright triangles on the lower wall and floor. The candle he lit on his bedside table last night had been burned down to a small mound of melted wax.

He did not feel rested from his fitful slumber, but Lucifer would still go to the shelter this morning. Rosemary might have confusing emotions concerning their intimate moment last night. Lucifer had to reestablish the root of their friendship.

Time with her was limited. His objective now was to empower Rosemary to trust her inner wisdom.

It was eight a.m. He got out of bed and performed his morning ritual, of preparing a pot of coffee and surveying the house outside his living room window. Rosemary usually left for work at about 8:30 a.m., arriving there about 8:45 a.m.

Taking long drinks, he stood in his briefs and inspected the usual areas of Rosemary's home. The house windows were shut and covered, and the yard was still, except for small critters moving about. The white pickup truck was parked in its usual spot, in the gravel driveway.

He stood and watched. It was meditative to gaze into Rosemary's yard, which was full of nature and color. Bees hummed around the flowering vegetable vines in her garden. Chipmunks seemed to enjoy playfully chasing one another. Crows honked out calls. Leaves of nearby oak trees fluttered with the birds' landings. And butterflies floated through it all.

The back door of Rosemary's house opened. She walked down her path, lined with green herbs and pink splashes of flowers. She held a large scooper. She tossed large, shelled nuts onto the feeding table and grass near the willow tree. After filling the bird feeder with seeds, she returned the scooper inside the house.

Shortly, the back door reopened and, this time, she walked directly to her truck.

Lucifer rushed to dress and headed for the convertible. He wanted to arrive at the shelter early this morning; a conversation needed to be had with Rosemary, before work.

Lucifer sped toward Wolfe Rescue, but slowed his car as traffic stood still in front of him – "traffic" being a few delayed vehicles on the dirt road.

He curved his head out of his low, driver-side window to see the obstruction… and laughed out loud.

There was a large, beige car directly in front of him, a black pickup in front of the beige car, and Rosemary's white pickup at the very front. Rosemary appeared to be waddling across the dirt road, as she ushered a slow-moving, large snapping turtle across. Her truck was parked sideways, so that it would block traffic both ways.

Lucifer heard laughter come from the vehicle in front of him, and saw a wave come from the red truck stopped in the opposite lane.

However, he felt an angry energy from inside a blue S.U.V., that sharply stopped just behind the red truck. The man inside the S.U.V. honked his horn and yelled words of disgust out of the window. Lucifer felt his heart pound and jaws tighten, because Rosemary was the target of this abuse. It took every ounce of his strength to wait calmly. If that man set a foot out of his vehicle, Lucifer would not stay seated in his.

Rosemary only fleetingly looked the offending man's way. Thankfully, the man's anger was quickly diluted by the goodness of the patient, kind-hearted group of people he was stuck behind, as the humane group continued offering support to Rosemary.

Once the creature was safely delivered inside the thin woods, traffic moved and Lucifer followed Rosemary to the Wolfe Rescue parking lot. The white truck pulled into its usual space, the black sports car alongside it.

Lucifer felt his heart beat faster underneath his shirt, as he walked to the driver's side of the pickup. Rosemary's door opened and he held it for her. The sunlight cast a gold sparkle, as it shone on the buckle of Anna's collar. Rosemary stepped down from her elevated seat and stood in front of Lucifer, her back turned to him, as she pulled her purse from the passenger side.

"Good morning, Rose Petal," he said. "Human integrity is alive and well. I was at the end of the traffic jam, as you protected the turtle's crossing."

"Why did the turtle cross the road?" she asked him, emphatically.

"Why… why?" he responded, soberly. He knew by the tightness of her face that this wasn't a joke.

"To lay her eggs," she answered, with a touch of moisture in her eyes. "They have just as much right to reproduce as humans," she cried. "Every single being is just trying their best to survive and raise their own little family. Why can't some humans know that?"

Her forehead creased in a deep line, as she softly said: "I have taken too many hurt turtles to be humanely euthanized, because they are struck down by speeding vehicles on a dirt backroad, and left there to suffer a long, painful death. A lot of the time, a cracked shell can be mended if a kind person takes the turtle to a wildlife rehabber." She wiped tears from her cheek, under her right eye. "Did you know, even if the turtle has to be humanely euthanized, the eggs can still be harvested?" She breathed out her lips to release tension.

"I just wish people cared," she said. "Accidents happen. I, too, have unfortunately hit wildlife while driving *under* the speed limit. But

179

I care, and check to make sure the animal is not suffering." Her face scrunched up in childlike disappointment. "A snapping turtle can live for thirty years and a painted turtle can live for fifty years, if people would slow down and watch for them! Why would a human being not care if they injure a fellow creature? We all share this Earth together, and humans have no more right to be here than anyone else!"

"Because some people forget they have a soul," Lucifer softly answered.

Rosemary inhaled a hard breath, and her face scrunched again in an innocent frown. She looked into his eyes. "Sometimes I hate humans! Life gets overwhelming caring for hurt animals, due to humans' neglect and malice. Sometimes the things I see make it such a painful world for me to cope with." Tears now moistened both of her cheeks.

He had never seen Rosemary angry. This wasn't bitter anger; it was rightful, matter-of-fact anger. He knew she wouldn't hold a grudge against anyone who was devoted to betterment.

"When I see an abused dog," she continued, "like Chuck... beaten... When I stop to move a turtle across the road, and see that its shell is cracked... and it is bleeding... and still moving its limbs... red blood dripping from them... alive and suffering...! How can a human being see a fellow creature of this Earth bleeding and not care?"

"Some humans forget they have a soul. They are disconnected from soul," Lucifer reiterated. "When each human being remembers his own soul and the soul of every other creature, and the loving energy that flows through each and every cell of each and every living thing, then there will be a raised level of love and consciousness throughout the universes." He physically softened his expression, to try to show his empathy for Rosemary's trauma. "Please don't focus on the disconnected. Only focus on the love."

Rosemary's moistened face looked toward his eyes with trust.

"Will you sit with me for a minute?" he softly asked. "I want to talk about last night."

The pupils of her eyes enlarged, as they usually did while looking at him. It seemed that she still felt emotion for him, which caused his lungs to release a sigh of relief. She didn't verbally answer, though followed him to the bench. They took their seats on the wooden slats, beside one another.

He looked into her eyes, searching for her gentle core. "I messed up last night, Rose Petal. I am sorry. You are so special to me. I never want to lose your friendship," he said. "I am sorry I made you feel uncomfortable. I took advantage of our friendship. I want you to take time for yourself now."

Her pupils dilated a little bit more. "I appreciate our friendship," she said. Her eyelids lowered as she glanced down. "What about the *almost* kiss?" she softly asked.

"You are not ready for a relationship," he said, gently. "I am sorry for the *almost* kiss; I got too carried away."

He moved his hand to her face and gently lifted her still-moistened chin. "Always listen to your inner light. Your soul *always* knows the answer to any question."

Sharon's little vehicle pulled into the space beside the white truck.

"I *am* ready," Rosemary firmly said, as she stood. She walked toward the side entrance, and Lucifer followed.

"You forgot your leftovers last night," she curtly said.

"Can I pick them up tonight?"

"Yes."

Sharon met them at the door, as Rosemary turned the key in the lock.

"Hi, Lucas," Sharon greeted cheerily, as they waited for the door to open.

"Good morning, Sharon," Lucifer politely replied. "Rosemary is the best home-cook I have ever known."

Sharon concurred.

Lucifer had soon completed his chores at the shelter.

Rosemary had quietly worked alongside him. She was cordial, but not her usual, sociable self.

The corners of his mouth slowly rose to a small smile, as he now headed toward the storage room. He stuck a few dog biscuits in his pants pocket and then walked to Chuck's pen.

The time spent between the two had created an extraordinary bond, beyond Lucifer's expectations.

"Hi, friend," Lucifer melodically greeted, as he opened the door to the pen and set a treat on the floor.

Chuck's head perked upward from his slumber. His tongue wrapped the side of his mouth. He did not tremble or look away. The dog slowly stretched his legs, then his body, from the mattress, then Chuck went to the treat and sat beside it. He took it inside his mouth, and a crunching sound was heard as it was eaten.

Lucifer met the dog in the middle of the floor, and sat down beside him. "How 'bout we go outside again? Get some fresh air? It's a nice day."

Lucifer slowly stood. He retrieved the slip lead, then placed the soft leash around the dog's neck. He gently pulled forward on the leash and the dog followed, picking up treats along the way.

Once outside, they both sat on the grass. Chuck sporadically looked toward the door he had just exited, but didn't watch it as intently as he had yesterday.

An hour passed while sitting outside; Lucifer pulled the watch from his pocket. For him, time was infinite, so a clock was necessary.

Rosemary brought out a regular leather collar and leash, to put on Chuck. It was placed on him without too much resistance; only a small flinch from the dog indicated a successful feat.

"Want to stretch your legs?" Lucifer asked Chuck. Lucifer felt stiffness in his long limbs as he stood. "Heel," he firmly said. He had learned to use that word to begin a walk from Rosemary.

He walked the pup the length of the fenced yard. Lucifer didn't think Chuck ready for the commotion of neighborhood streets just yet; a quiet stroll in a controlled environment would be nice practice. The pup did seem comfortable with the collar; there was no pulling on the leash.

"Good boy." Lucifer looked down at the reddish-brown dog. Chuck walked with his nose in the air, sniffing the freshness. He was still timid and quick to wince at any unfamiliar noise, but he now trusted another soul.

*

It was Friday morning.

Again, Lucifer followed directly behind the white pickup truck, en route to the shelter.

This time he drove slower, like Rosemary, partly because he drove right behind her, but also because he had learned, from her, that it was a good idea to be prepared for crossing wildlife, especially on a dirt road.

Red lights flashed from the back end of the white truck. Lucifer pressed down quickly on his brakes.

Then he chuckled. A group of wild turkeys leisurely crossed in front of Rosemary's vehicle.

Rosemary exited her truck and stood on the opposite side of the road, to alert oncoming traffic.

Lucifer felt pressure in his chest, as he inhaled a quick, sharp breath. A large, blue truck halted just in front of Rosemary, as she shielded the turkeys' passageway.

Having arrived at the shelter, after the turkeys' safe road crossing, Lucifer made quick work of cleaning cat pens, sweeping and mopping.

His heart now palpitated with anticipation, as he walked toward Chuck's pen. Today they would go for a walk into town. For the past three days, the dog had tolerated a standard collar and leash, while walking in the fenced yard; Chuck now seemed to enjoy his outdoor breaks.

Lucifer reached the pen, collar and leash in hand, and stood for a moment as he gazed at the dog. Lucifer's soul felt full, and a nourishing, innate smile seemed to extend from his soul. Chuck lay on his bed. As he looked up at Lucifer, the dog peacefully tilted his head. He stretched his front legs. His tail slightly wagged, as his body

184

stretched up from the mattress.

Moisture accumulated in Lucifer's eyes, as he opened the pen door and sat down beside his friend. They met in the middle of the pen, where Lucifer unhurriedly smoothed his hand along Chuck's back and gave him a treat. The dog received another treat after he allowed the collar to be placed around his neck. Lucifer bent toward the top of Chuck's head and kissed the smooth, brown fur.

The pup had gained a couple of pounds. He was fuller in the stomach area and his ribs were less pronounced.

Goosebumps formed and tingled on Lucifer's arms, as the dog leaned into his chest for closeness. More tears formed in Lucifer's eyes as the closeness lingered. Lucifer petted the soft fur on the side of Chuck's face, and kissed the top of his head again.

"Come on, friend. We can do this."

Lucifer stood. He figured he'd better get going, or he'd likely become a lump of soggy tears. He exited the pen and led the dog outside. This time, they exited the side door, not the back door that opened to the fenced yard. Bright, hot sunlight, practically blinding, greeted them. The door closed behind them and they stood still. Chuck's eyes squinted.

"We'll have fun," Lucifer playfully assured the pup.

As they started out, walking the cement parking lot, Chuck's long nose pointed to the bright sky of the early afternoon. The tip of his nose looked rubbery as it twitched, seemingly stretching for smells. The reddish tint of his fur glistened in the daylight.

"We are going on an adventure, friend."

They slowly trekked the length of the dirt road, about a mile.

Luckily, no vehicles passed. It was a quiet walk thus far.

Whiffs of pine scent wafted in the air, as they passed evergreens and towering deciduous trees, which lined the sidewalk leading into town, a few blocks east.

The late summer day brought hotness from the sun, but cool breezes and the shady trees gave gentle relief.

Brightly painted, New England-style houses framed the long, rolling street on either side now. Most of the homes were two stories high, with brightly-colored doorways. The doors were flanked with scrolled columns, in the vibrant colors of pink, green, blue and yellow; they looked like gems. Some of the century-old homes had added wraparound decks, with inviting-looking porch swings.

Lucifer looked down at Chuck. Only a couple of vehicles had driven by them, and the dog seemed to handle the light traffic well.

Very few people were bustling around town as they reached it. Quaint shops now lined either side of the narrow, cobblestone street. The small, one-room post office was located at the edge of town. The court was opposite the post office. A couple of family-owned restaurants and colorfully decorated boutiques greeted hopeful customers along the way. The Italian restaurant looked appetizing, with a red awning and flowers out front. Good smells encircled the building, enticing patrons.

A child squealed with laughter, exiting the ice-cream shop. The fur around Chuck's shoulders creased, as his muscles tensed.

"You're fine," Lucifer assured, decisively.

Chuck looked up at Lucifer, then continued the pace.

Lucifer kept the dog on the inside of the walkway, farthest from the street. They had walked almost a half-hour at this point.

A bench was set near the flower store; yellow roses and Queen Anne's lace were showcased in glass vases, in the large bay window of the store. It was the last shop in the long stretch of buildings, on the south side of the road. The river could be seen in the distance. It looked calm and beautiful. Lucifer led the dog toward the empty seat.

"Let's take a break," he said, as they reached the bench. Lucifer sat down and Chuck lay on the grass, in front of the seat.

The side of the flower shop exterior was painted with daisies. Grassland extended from it, opening into a public parking lot full of available spaces and meters.

The antique store where Lucifer had bought the hand-wrought candle holders was across the street from them. An old-fashioned dresser, with period dresses and a floor-length mirror, was showcased in its window.

Lucifer inhaled a deep breath of fresh air. It filled his lungs and he held it there for a moment. He slowly breathed out. Feeling the air fill him, then dissipate, was a reminder that human life was precious.

Chuck seemed to be relaxed. His chin lay on his outstretched front paws. A sparrow glided to the grass just in front of them, and the dog's eyebrows twitched as he took notice of the bird. It pecked at the ground.

Bird watching was mesmerizing for humans, too. Lucifer watched its little body, with brown feathers, methodically move with the breeze at its back. The bird was a being the humans could study and learn from. This sparrow was only considering the present moment. It was simply concerned with looking for a worm. There was no thought of the past or future. It was not remembering the morning storm that had soaked its body and blown its nest from the tree. The bird was simply doing the present moment's necessary work. It was acquiring this afternoon's food.

Tiny bugs buzzed in the air above the bird, near the decorative potted flowers; they seemed to enjoy the warm weather. The bees, ladybugs and gnats also weren't thinking of the past or future; only the present moment of the sunny day. If a gnat's last second on Earth were to come now, it would have enjoyed life until the last second.

If a human being were only to consider the present moment and not be concerned with anything except one's current endeavor, there would be nothing to distract from one's continual connection to the flow of well-being.

Chuck watched as the bird continued to search the soil beneath the grass.

Soft voices came from the other side of the cobblestones. Lucifer looked up. An older woman and a child held hands, as they walked across the street. The elder looked down adoringly at the young girl, and quietly gave instructions. The child looked up at her apparent grandmother, holding her hand with awe, listening. They both softly exchanged giggles.

There was great knowledge to learn from one another. It was irresponsible to discard another's life experience and viewpoint, no matter her age. The old could learn from the young to preserve fresh outlooks, have positive expectancy and recapture enthusiasm. To listen without judgment. To trust, expect agreeable results, laugh out loud and scream with delight. The young could learn from the old to savor the moment and move without haste. To watch a sunset, enjoy one's breakfast, pause to talk with a passerby, breathe slowly and focus wholeheartedly.

Being human was a chance to experience Earth with eyes, fingers and ears. It was miraculous.

Most humans have forgotten to take the time to feel a gentle spring rain tickle the skin on their faces, or to listen to the haunting sound of a train at night, or to see the brilliant yellow field of dandelions. The human experience would be an amazing journey if one took the time to relish his surroundings, and find joy in watching a bird peck at the ground. To slow down, listen, watch, center energy, dive into exhilaration, relax into comfort, smile, laugh, touch, feel and be open to new ideas would be Lucifer's suggestion, to any being who wanted soul alignment.

A spiraling depth of waves speckled the light-blue sky with flecks of brown, as a flock of sparrows seemed to dance in cadence, mid-air. In graceful succession, they gathered on branches of the nearby tree and, now, spotted the greenness with their rich brown colors. Lucifer closed his eyes and virtually cradled the soft, melodic chirps in his ears. He symbolically captured the varying bronze, downy feathers in his mind's eye.

A human's Earth age is actually only as old as the lives his soul has experienced. There is always room for expansion. In this human experience, Lucifer would appreciate these small, simple, magical moments.

*

Lucifer opened his eyes to a muted light in his bedroom's east window. It was close to sundown.

Hunger must have woken him, because he felt almost a rawness in his stomach, and it grumbled with noises. Having fallen asleep for a nap without lunch, he now was hungry for dinner.

He'd like to try one of the eateries in town.

Maybe Rosemary would join him? Today, she had been her usual friendly self at the shelter.

Lucifer got out of bed and walked to the kitchen, to prepare coffee. He stood with only boxers covering his midsection. There was something so extraordinary and comfortable about being unclothed. He wanted to experience his body in its natural form, without hindrance.

Setting the coffee cup on the table, he pulled on his pair of black jeans, then the red t-shirt over his head, as he looked out the living room window. The sun was hovering just above the tree line, on this Friday evening.

There was no movement in Rosemary's yard. The white pickup truck was parked in its usual spot.

Lucifer smiled as he gazed at the bunches of rosemary lining the back-door walkway. A second row of pink begonias added a splash of color. Clusters of tall lavender plants circled the two spruces in the backyard.

He took his last drink of coffee, then headed outside. He walked to Rosemary's back door.

As he lifted his hand, his heart's rhythm sped up. He knocked.

He waited. His breaths quickened so much that he had to slow them with deep breathing.

It worried him that she might no longer consider him a close friend. He may have generated too much confusion and distrust in their relationship.

"Who is it?" she called, from the other side of the closed door.

"Lucas," he answered, his voice raised. His breath hitched in his throat for a moment, as he wondered her reaction. He mindlessly reached for the timepiece in his pants pocket and held it. Lucifer had lost his ability to hear Rosemary's thoughts. It was a frustration, yet a relief; it meant that she was healing and centered, in peace.

The door opened. Rosemary looked stunning in a pair of casual shorts.

"Hello, Lucas," she said, shielding her eyes from the bright rays of the late-day sunset. "Come on in."

She smiled as her eyes scanned the shelter's logo on the front of his t-shirt. "Looks good on you." She stepped aside.

"Yes, I'd like a sweater for winter. Hoodie? Jacket? Maybe you could add those to your line of logo shirts?" He walked inside and removed his new tennis shoes.

A thick, zesty aroma filled the house.

Darn! She has already started dinner for herself.

"I was hoping to take you out for dinner tonight," he said, "but it smells like you already cooked for yourself."

"I made stew for Mrs. Travis, our neighbor. Her husband is in the hospital."

"How nice of you."

"I was just going to steal a little bit of her stew for myself, for dinner tonight."

191

"I would like to try the Italian restaurant in town. Would you, please, allow me to take you out for dinner?" he asked.

"Thank you, but I was planning on doing some housework," she said, looking toward a laundry basket on her couch, filled with towels.

"It'd be good for you to relax and have dinner with me." He crossed his arms in front of him. "We have some important things to talk about."

Rosemary turned to look at him. Her eyebrows pulled together. "Oh?"

"Yes." The tips of his fingers pressed together, to form a teepee shape, and he held his chin with it. "Why don't you deliver Mrs. Travis her thoughtfully-made, delicious stew, then we can take a nice drive into town? It should be a very pleasant evening. The weather is gorgeous. It cooled off a bit this evening." He smiled and added: "We can put the top down…"

Her bottom lip pressed underneath her top teeth, as she considered. Her glance shifted from the unfolded towels to the bottle of all-purpose cleaner on the desk.

"I'm really excited to try the Italian restaurant. Please?" he pleaded. He touched his stomach. "I'm starving." He attempted to keep his tone sweetly needy.

"Okay," she breathed out, parting her lips. "I have to go change clothes. I'll be back."

As Rosemary went to her bedroom, Lucifer relaxed. He exhaled a heavy breath he hadn't been aware of restraining.

Helping his body ease into its normal state, he deeply, slowly inhaled. He closed his eyes, as scents delicately invaded his senses –

scents that his nostrils hadn't distinguished until now. The rich, vanilla aroma of a lit candle drew his eyes to the table in front of the couch. An orange flame appeared still atop the wick. The clean smell of newly-washed fabric lingered on the towels in the laundry basket. A slight pine odor wafted from the cleaning supplies on the desk, behind the couch.

The beef stew had been the first fragrance his nostrils had recognized, but now settled pleasantly in the background. The smells of her home were comforting. Easy. Peaceful.

One scent he had immediately discerned, the moment he passed the doorway, was Rosemary's skin: the sweet vanilla and fresh lemon perfume. Lucifer felt a rigidness creep through practically every muscle and bone of his body, as his olfactory glands memorized the smell of her. It was as though he could feel the blood in his body, hastily flowing through every vein.

He had been consumed with the need to protect her, but now romantic thoughts were beginning to percolate.

His prolonged stay on Earth would only complicate matters. He needed to leave. The longer he was human, the stronger his Earthly needs would become. Love would develop into a desire for physical closeness.

Lucifer would be just as dangerous to Rosemary's emotional state as Mark.

The excuse Lucifer had given himself to remain here was no longer credible. The mission of protecting Rosemary was complete. His job was done here. Mark had been eradicated from her life and was no longer a threat.

Lucifer had then told himself that he wished to see her confident, trusting her inner light. If he were honest, though, he felt confident she was now at that point.

It would be cruel of Lucifer to subject this beautiful girl to his truth. The longer he stayed, the more likely his truth would be revealed.

He would say goodbye to Chuck this coming week, and spend every possible remaining minute with Rosemary. Relishing a few more precious moments, and making a couple more treasured memories, might satisfy him for eternity.

Tears began to pool behind his closed eyes.

His reason for existence, for all of infinity, now walked into the room and stood before him. It was Rosemary.

As he wiped his closed eyes, he feigned itchiness. He then looked again.

Lucifer felt his eyelids separate, then widen. His lips parted as his bottom jaw loosened. Rosemary wore a floral sundress. Her revealed skin looked soft and creamy.

He loved her. Everything she was, he loved.

As his pulse quickened even faster, his body warmed.

He couldn't leave her.

But he must.

"I'm ready," she said.

She walked past him, to the coffee table in front of the couch. Her lips rounded together, as she blew on the flame of the candle to extinguish it. A glow seemed to embrace her mouth and face, as she bent close to the wick. A loose, reddish-brown strand of her hair curled around her hand as she gathered it behind her, so as not to singe it.

The gauzy material of her dress appeared to kiss her skin, especially where the bottom hem danced around her thighs. An outline of her slip showed slightly through the light fabric. The radiance of her soul was mirrored through her beautiful, feminine body. The dress skimmed the shape of her hips, and virtually sent an electrifying reaction through his bones, as she walked to the kitchen.

He followed.

"I'll carry that," he said, and took the crock pot from her.

"Don't worry," she said, following his eyes, "these sandals are very comfortable for walking." She bent over to fix the straps.

Rosemary took the pot back from him, as he tied his sneakers. He still had a limited supply of attire and footwear: one pair of dress shoes, one suit, one pair of tennis shoes, one pair of work jeans, one pair of dress jeans and a couple of shirts. He lived simply. His needs were met.

Most any necessity could be visualized and then appear tangible: money, clothes… He had thought of sneakers, and the next day saw his size at a garage sale. A stranded man with engine trouble had generously given Lucifer money for his on-the-spot mechanical help. And Grace had tucked a few hundred dollars into his shirt pocket, when they had hugged goodbye. A man's mind created his own reality. Each person chose the picture of his life. Focused visualization could manifest anything.

Rosemary transferred the pot back to Lucifer, as she closed and locked the door.

She delivered the greatly appreciated dinner to Mrs. Travis, while Lucifer pulled the convertible out of the shed. They would welcome the nice weather. He lowered the roof.

Fresh air pleased his senses as they drove to town. He drove extra slow, to enjoy the scenery, but Rosemary giggled as her hair blew all around her – seductively, as if in slow motion. The sensual piano-and-clarinet piece playing on the radio provided a comfortable break in conversation, for the ride.

When they reached town, Lucifer parked in the public parking lot, then opened the door for his passenger. Lucifer reached into his front pocket and pulled out a few quarters, which he slipped into the slot on the meter in front of his vehicle – then also the expired parking meter beside his.

"That's nice of you," Rosemary said.

"If not for acts of kindness, human integrity is threatened," he returned.

She looked up at him. Her eyes widened and she smiled. "Like attracts like," she said.

"Right you are."

Walking toward the restaurant, he took the outside of the walkway, nearest the traffic.

The cobblestone street, lined with shops, was active at early evening. Streetlamps illuminated the warm tones of the stones. Children passed in the street on bikes; laughter followed behind them. A couple, holding hands, moved aside to the grass, as Lucifer and Rosemary neared them. The town seemed an appealing gathering place for families. Chairs were now being spread across the courtyard lawn, in preparation for tonight's outdoor concert.

Instinctively, Lucifer lightly put his arm around Rosemary's lower back, as he led her across the cobblestone. Looking downward, he saw her pretty, lacy sandals and painted toenails.

As his glance moved upward, it lingered on her shapely, bare legs. It was an exceptional sight, which took him by surprise each time. Only at their last shared dinner had she worn a dress – though, she looked beautiful whether attending a fancy dinner or working in jeans and sneakers.

The setting sun shone golden rays through the tops of the maples, planted on the side of the restaurant they neared. Birds flittered, seemingly giddily, gathering on the branches with the last songs of the day.

The good smells Lucifer had gotten a whiff of this afternoon were still present outside the door. This time he inhaled deeply. The scents were an appetizer for the senses. The small, brick building looked cozy. The bricks were a warm, red color, with red awning above the entry.

"This restaurant has been in the same family since I have been a kid. They have great food," Rosemary said, as Lucifer held open the door for her.

They walked inside, to a strong garlic aroma. Each table had a red flower in a vase. The atmosphere was vibrant, with patrons eating, talking and laughing. The waiting staff was bustling. It was noisy but stimulating. Lucifer watched a dessert tray pass. The hostess walked them to a table, and Lucifer pulled Rosemary's chair out for her.

The menu was concise, with only two pages, not including the wine section. Lucifer was in the mood for homemade lasagna, and placed his order after Rosemary. She had chosen the mushroom ravioli.

After taking a drink of her water, and setting her glass down, she looked across the table at him. She held his gaze.

"I know we met under the worst of circumstances, but I've gotten to know you; you are an amazing person," she said, then smiled. "You are so kind-hearted. So patient. The way you are with Chuck..."

"Just because someone is good with a dog doesn't mean they are a good person," he interrupted.

"I disagree with that statement: anyone who treats a dog as good as you do is *most definitely* a good person." Her eyebrows scrunched together. "Why would you say such a thing?"

The waitress reached in front of Lucifer and set his cold salad dish down, then Rosemary's. He was relieved by the distraction.

"Animals are the best judges of character," she continued. "You even said that!"

"Tell me about your first boyfriend," he asked.

"What?" Her brows pulled together again. "Why would you want to know that?"

"I just want to know you. What shaped your life?"

"Hmm..." She tapped her fingertips across her lips. "Johnny Starr – he was my first boyfriend."

"Was he nice?"

"Not really. He cheated on me."

"How old were you?"

"I was seventeen."

"Have you ever been with a man who treated you with love, trust and respect?"

A loud gush of air came from her mouth. "Jeez!" Her forehead scrunched in angry wrinkles.

"I just want the truth," he said.

She tapped her lips again. "Not really. I've only known one good man, besides you: he is Sharon's fiancé." Pursing her lips, she looked downward. "There was one nice guy I dated, but I broke up with him," she said, sheepishly. "I was stupid and in my early twenties." One side of her mouth turned up into a half-smile. "It seems I have always worked hard to save my bad relationships."

"You should never have to *work* to make someone treat you with love. You need to know that you deserve to be happy," he said, with intent. "A soul enters into a human body for the sole purpose of experiencing joy, and expanding her soul and the world with joy. Everything you study, labor over and pursue should be for the sole purpose of creating joy in your life. You came here with the sole purpose to enjoy life, Rose Petal. Each soul does."

She breathed heavily in through her nose. "That's pretty deep, Lucas." She looked sincerely into his gaze. "You are very spiritual. I like that. Maybe I could learn something from you," she lightheartedly said.

Then she admitted: "I think maybe I was more intent on proving my father wrong than making myself happy."

"How is that?"

Rosemary took a forkful of lettuce. Lucifer followed suit.

"I wanted my dad to be proud of me, but he just criticized me. I wanted him to see that I could make a relationship *work*, despite his and my mother's example." She pulled in her lower lip and pressed it.

She took another bite of her salad, then continued: "Instead of finding a nice guy for myself, and someone my father would approve of, I cheated myself."

"Your father *was* proud of you, Rose Petal," Lucifer began. "That's why he wanted a good man for you. He thought you *deserved* a good man."

Rosemary sat still. The light in her eyes seemed to soften. She took the last bite of her salad.

Lucifer waited for her eyes to rise to his. "Rosemary…" he called.

"Yes?" She held his gaze now.

"No need to ask for directions,

The way is hidden inside your soul.

Just follow your inner light,

And that will guide you home," he recited in cadence.

Her whole face seemed to suddenly flatten of any expression. She then looked to force a smile.

"It's a poem that I want you to remember. Always trust your inner light, Rose Petal."

"I will. Did you write that poem?"

"I wrote it with you in mind. It means that you don't need to ask others' opinions; you *know* the answers."

Rosemary looked up at the waitress as she approached. Their entrées arrived with an orgasmic aroma.

Lucifer's body seemed to liquefy with pleasure as he tasted the handmade pasta. It practically melted in his mouth, with flavors of ricotta cheese and tomatoes. He cleaned his palate with a drink of ice-cold water.

"Tell me when you first got interested in animals. Did you grow up with pets?" he asked.

Rosemary dipped a piece of bread into a decadent olive oil mixture. She seemed to also enjoy the sublime experience of this food, as she closed her eyes after a taste.

She told him about the rescue dogs and cats her mother had provided a home for, and how Rosemary had learned the respectful treatment of animals from her. Lucifer listened. Her voice soothed him, as if a piano in classical music. The highs and lows of her tone seemed to strike chords deep in his body. It felt as if the low hum of a violin vibrated inside him, as the sounds of her voice slipped through his ear canal. His energy fields felt in sync with hers. He felt his hyper senses calm to match hers, and he now felt more centered within his body and soul.

Sharing this intimate evening with Rosemary, being this close to her, was a contentment he couldn't explain. It was a comfort, as if they were siblings born of the same womb. It seemed impossible to leave her. How could he?

"Will you be at the shelter tomorrow morning?" she asked.

"Yes."

"Good. Chuck is so attached to you. You are the only one he feels comfortable walking with right now."

It seemed that only five minutes had passed since they arrived at the restaurant, but one-and-a-half hours later he was setting the cash for the bill inside the money holder, for the waitress.

He walked to where Rosemary sat, and pulled her chair aside as she stood.

"Thank you so much, Lucas," she said, turning to him.

"No, thank you."

They walked outside to a darkened world. A quiet world.

"Look!" she said, pointing toward a shop on the opposite side. His gaze followed the direction of her extended finger. She was pointing at Samantha's Closet boutique.

"Samantha must be home waiting for me now; her boutique looks closed for the evening. I would be surprised if that place gets any business; *I* never see any money."

A chuckle rose from his chest and flowed from his lips. It felt nourishing.

"Now that you mention it, whenever I come to town I never see any customers in there," he said. "Maybe the lingerie boutique is a cover for an underground catnip business!"

A childlike giggle made her face blush in the darkness, below the tall streetlamp.

"Hey," she said, "I have a favorite place, just around the block. I'd like to show you. It's where I go sometimes, when I'm in town with a dog, for a little peace."

He wrapped the crook of his arm around her, as they crossed the cobblestone. They walked from the lit town road to a darkened trail. Rosemary took his hand in hers as she led the way.

The dark trail led to a park. Evenly-spaced light-poles revealed the gravel parking lot, and the wooden sign that read: *"Wolfe County Nature Center"*.

"There are dirt paths here that are fun to walk the dogs on," Rosemary said, "when there is a little extra time."

She tightly gripped his hand as she laced her fingers through his.

202

She drew him into blackness, past the lot. "Watch your step," she whispered.

It was so quiet that any sound was magnified. Their footsteps were audible as they walked along soft earth.

She released his hand but cradled his elbow, as they rose up a few stairs. It was dark, but Lucifer's eyes had soon adjusted, and he could view outlines of thick woods bordering a long, wooden bridge. He slid his hand along the thick, blocked railing of the ascending stairs. Black water could be seen just below. The intermittent, deep croaks of frogs began an evening song. Crickets synchronized their steady flow of high-pitched chirps.

Rosemary stood close beside him, on the bridge.

"This spot always soothes my soul," she quietly said, as the length of her arm and shoulder pressed against his. A gentle breeze moved her perfume to his nostrils. "This is my thinking place – besides the swing under my willow."

"It is quiet. Still. Good for the soul," he said.

Looking into her eyes as they stood outside her front door, Lucifer sensed the hopefulness from Rosemary for a goodnight kiss. Her pupils were dilated, her skin had flushed. She smiled a small, tentative smile.

"Sweet dreams," she softly said.

Lucifer gently took her hand and kissed the back side of it. He then quietly backed down the steps of her porch. "And sweet dreams to you, Rose Petal," he returned.

Her pupils contracted. The fresh, pink color of her cheeks appeared to fade. Her smile departed, for a restrained pout.

Chapter 9

Rosemary's Questions

Rosemary woke before her alarm clock sounded. Her eyes hadn't opened yet, though. She lay in bed concentrating on last night's dream, trying to remember every detail of it before opening her eyes. She had smelled her mother's perfume and heard her laughter.

A smile followed her memory.

Dreams of her father hadn't occurred thus far, but maybe, when her grief subsided, she would get visits from him.

Upon opening her eyes, brightness filtered through the bedroom curtains. It was 7:15 a.m., on Saturday.

Last night she had shared dinner with Lucas. He had been candid about his concern for her lack of intuitiveness. His poem described the need to trust one's inner feelings.

His poem – he had written it with her in mind. Did he feel she wasn't connected to her spirituality?

She *had* rejected her own inner voice in defiance. A little focus in that area would only be beneficial. She wondered if Lucas couldn't be attracted to a woman he considered unspiritual. He felt a need to prolong their *platonic* friendship. His patience was attractive, yet frustrating.

Last night he hadn't kissed her goodnight, yet again. Was the reason his concern for her readiness, or did he in fact have no romantic interest?

She bit down on her lower lip. It saddened her to think that he would never want more.

Rosemary considered getting dressed and walking to his house. She had to return large crates to the shelter today. Maybe he would be willing to help load them into her pickup. She would take him out for breakfast before work, at the cute little diner in town. Loading crates was a task she had performed solo many times, but thought it would be a good excuse to spend extra time with him.

She liked Lucas. He was attentive. He listened and responded sympathetically. Deep concern for her was shown in his actions. Lucas focused on her when they were together, and offered thoughtful advice.

Her mother would say: "Listen to what they say, but pay most attention to what they *do*."

Rosemary appreciated that Lucas was taking his time forming a friendship with her. It was comfortable talking about her family and personal issues. She had never felt judged by him. She felt she could do or say anything, and he'd accept her.

He resembled a brother. She wanted more.

After coffee, then brushing her teeth, Rosemary dressed in her most attractive work attire: the raglan top and form-fitting jeans.

A couple of handfuls of nuts were tossed to the squirrels and chipmunks. The birds were chirping, the blue jays' piercing calls alerting one another that the peanuts had been placed on the feeding table, which was set underneath the hanging feeders. One blue jay swooped right by Rosemary, calling out as it plucked a single nut.

Standing outside, watching the wildlife and looking toward Lucas's home, Rosemary made a decision: she wouldn't allow herself any more time to contemplate inviting him to breakfast. Her legs and feet had seemed to deliver her directly to his front door, anyway. She now stood on his porch. She knocked. A shallow, shaky breath moved to her lungs.

He should be awake now; it was almost eight a.m. He usually arrived at the shelter at the same time as she.

After waiting for a few seconds, she boldly knocked again.

His car was parked in the opened shed. Maybe he was in the shower?

She peripherally glanced into the wide, bay front window. Not seeing any movement, she turned her head and looked more closely.

Plastic coverings and white sheets topped most of the living room furniture.

For an unexplainable reason, she felt her stomach churn. Something felt odd about the look of his house.

Lucas was admittedly slowly renovating the home, but it looked vacant of any comfort.

Maybe it was just this room that was devoid of life?

"Is that you, sweet Rosemary?" a familiar voice called from the gravel road.

A sharp breath caught at the bottom of Rosemary's throat. She felt her eyes widen.

How embarrassing! To be seen peeking through a window!

Rosemary recognized it to be Mrs. Travis before turning around. She turned and greeted: "Hi, Mrs. Travis." The edges of her mouth formed a rigid smile. Seeing her neighbor's miniature poodle relaxed the tightness. The two were obviously about town for their morning exercise.

"What a glorious morning," Mrs. Travis said, as she stopped right in front of Lucas's house. The little, white dog sat by her owner's side. "Thank you, sweet Rosemary, for the delicious stew. I enjoyed it. You were a lifesaver last night; you provided my nourishment."

Thankfully, Mrs. Travis seemed oblivious to Rosemary's spying. "I'm so glad you liked it. How is Mr. Travis doing?"

"He is recovering well. He has a new hip." She looked down at the dog and smiled. "I am going up to the hospital after our walk. Thank you, again, for having recommended my little Sissy to me last year, when she arrived at the shelter. She's been such a comfort to me while I've been home alone."

Rosemary smiled, looking at the dog. "Hi, Sissy."

"Are you watching Gino's house for him?" Mrs. Travis asked, nonchalantly.

"What?"

"Gino Mollini – are you watching his house?" The woman's face brightened with a smile that bared her teeth. "I heard from the mailman that Gino bought this house from the bank, and he will be moving back here after his brother recovers from surgery, in Florida."

"Gino Mollini moved out of Wolfe County a long time ago."

"I know," Mrs. Travis said, still smiling; "it'll be nice to have the old-timer back. He used to live on the next street over. Didn't you used to go to school with his son, Michael?"

"Yes." Rosemary felt her eyebrows tightly pull together. "Gino bought this house?"

"Yes. I thought you knew that." Mrs. Travis's expression was still soft, free from judgment. Her arm flailed as she held the dog's leash. "You were standing there, at the doorstep; I figured you were watching the house for Gino. Maybe getting his mail?"

Rosemary felt her brows pull tighter as she searched her neighbor's face.

"Are you sure *this* is the house Gino bought? Because I thought Lucas Brownwood bought it," Rosemary said.

"Who? I don't know any Lucas." Mrs. Travis shook her head. "No, this is Gino Mollini's house. He should be moving back after winter, in springtime."

The older woman looked down at her dog. "Ready, Sissy?" she asked the poodle. She then smiled at Rosemary, as she began walking. "Time to get to the hospital. Thank you again, sweet Rosemary. We will have you over for dinner again soon."

"That will be nice."

"Your mother was beautiful. You resemble her."

"Thank you, Mrs. Travis."

"Bye, now."

When the neighbor passed, Rosemary's eyes searched the front of the house and mailbox for any evidence. Her eyes landed on a magazine in the mailbox, next to Lucas's front door; the large item stuck out of the container and forced the top of the box slightly open. After another glance toward Mrs. Travis confirmed that the woman's back still faced her, Rosemary pulled the mail from the box. A few small envelopes and ad flyers fell out with the magazine; they scattered to the ground and Rosemary hurriedly picked them up. She now held the evidence. Her heart pounded fast against her chest, as she searched for the address labels on the mail.

"Mr. Gino Mollini," the first envelope read.

Rosemary shuffled through the other small envelopes and flyers, dropping some. *Shit!* She bent down to pick them up again. One by one, she went through each piece of mail. It was all addressed to Gino Mollini. Even the junk mail.

Her breaths came short and quick.

Rosemary curled the magazine back around the other correspondence and put it back in the mailbox.

She felt nauseous. The queasiness in her stomach rose to her throat, with a burning sensation. Her short, choppy breaths became audible.

Was Mrs. Travis mistaken? She had to be. Maybe Lucas had rented the home from Gino.

Lucas had practically saved Rosemary's life. He had been a neighbor walking by when he heard her scream. He claimed he had been slowly renovating this house.

Her hand seemingly moved of its own accord, to hold her chest, as she walked down the stairs.

Clutching to the thought that there was an honest mistake on Mrs. Travis's part, she loaded her truck bed with crates. Maybe Lucas was friends with Gino. She would talk to Lucas at work.

Lucas arrived late to the shelter today; Rosemary was already cleaning cat cages when he got there. He walked into the cat room with his usual steady gait. With her back turned, she could tell it was him who came into the room.

"Hi, Rose Petal," his deep voice greeted. "Sorry I'm late today. I had a couple of things I had to do this morning."

He opened a cage a few rows over and began cleaning it. "I can't wait to walk Chuck into town again today," he said.

"He'll like that," she flatly returned, as she continued to face the cage. "Did you have to run errands this morning?"

"Errands?" he asked, inattentively.

"You said you had things you had to do this morning. Errands? Did you use your car for your errands?"

"Oh... yes," he simply said.

Her eyes tightened shut as she still faced the cage.

After walking the dogs today, she would initiate a frank discussion. She couldn't continue working alongside him another day without clearing up this matter. Rosemary pulled her bottom lip inside her mouth, as she turned to look at Lucas.

"I need to talk with you for a minute after dog walking, before you leave today," she said, her tone even.

He turned to look at her. "Of course, Rose Petal. Is everything okay?"

"Yes. I just need to ask you a couple of questions."

He smiled at her, then continued to sweet-talk Angel.

She and Lucas were in sync with a routine, and quickly completed chores. He was soon walking Chuck, and Rosemary was on her last walk of the day.

Her heart thumped hard under her chest, as she and Lula walked the gravel road back toward the shelter. They neared the side door.

Rosemary's breath quickened, as she returned Lula May to her pen.

Rosemary lay on Lula's mattress, and the dog climbed up and joined her. Turning to her side, she gently petted the length of Lula's back. Moisture threatened to escape Rosemary's eyes, but she pressed them closed and wiped them. She was going to confront Lucas as soon as he returned with Chuck.

Depending on his answer, it might be the last time she was ever again to see him.

As she sat upright and slipped Lula's collar from her neck, Lucas walked inside the door and passed by, with Chuck.

"What a nice day," he said, as he briskly walked the dog to the pen. "Chuck and I had a wonderful time in town today," he continued. "We walked a little in that park you showed me last night."

She mechanically unlatched the door to Lula's pen and walked to the front table, where she set the leash and collar. Then she walked to Chuck's pen. Standing there, she watched Lucas. He was bent over from the waist, kissing the dog on the top of the head.

"I have a couple of questions. Can we talk now?" Rosemary said.

Lucas stood and turned to look at her, attentively. "I will help in any way I can."

"What was it that you had to do this morning?" she asked. "I went to your house today, before work." Her pulse sped as she studied his face. Breaths seemed to get caught in her throat. *Please have a logical answer.* The churning in her stomach instinctively told her he would not have one. "Where were you this morning?"

He smiled. His face looked relaxed. "Oh, I just had a few errands."

He walked out of the pen and locked it behind him. He stood directly in front of Rosemary. She felt the body heat radiating from him.

"Your car was there, but you didn't answer the door," she said.

"Maybe I was in the shower when you came over?" he casually said.

Rosemary felt goosebumps rise on her skin. It felt prickly.

Lucas's eyes searched Rosemary's. His eyebrows rose as he took in a sharp breath. He knew something was wrong.

She was confused as to why her attraction was still just as strong toward him. Being in his presence now, being this close to him, emotions seemed to attack her from every direction. She wanted to scream at him: *"How could you tell such a lie, you impostor?!"* She knew intuitively the given answer of his whereabouts had been untruthful, yet she wanted him to explain away the obvious.

Deep inside of her, she knew she wouldn't allow herself to continue a relationship with a liar.

This man could be even more dangerous than her ex.

Thoughts seemed to swamp her mind so fast that everything became a blur. Her heart thumped even harder against her chest, and she felt as though she would faint.

"Do you own the house next door to me?" she firmly asked.

"Yes."

Short breaths now came so quickly that she couldn't grasp onto one of them. They exited as quickly as they entered.

"Lucas, I talked to Mrs. Travis this morning. She claimed a man by the name of Gino Mollini owns that house," Rosemary said. "Do you know Gino Mollini?" The words didn't seem to come from her. She felt weak.

He stood still, silent. His eyes continued to look into hers.

Lucas tensely stuck his hand in his left pants pocket. He fidgeted for a moment, then took his hand back out and roughly wiped his face. His eyes looked sad, as though moisture was building in them.

"I was there this morning – at your house. Mrs. Travis told me it wasn't your house," she said.

Lucas seemed to now stare right through Rosemary. He swallowed hard. Water filled his eyes.

"Are you friends with Gino? Do you just rent it?" she practically begged. This time, a loud, quick breath audibly slipped from her lips.

"No," he said in a raspy whisper.

He turned from her and looked over at Chuck.

The dog's eyes moved upward and watched serenely, as Lucas reopened the gate. He walked to Chuck and crouched down, to once again kiss the top of the pup's head. Lucas's lips lingered on the reddish fur. He seemed to deeply inhale the scent of the fur. Tears trickled down Lucas's chiseled face, to the edge of his jaw.

It felt as though a bucket of ice water poured through Rosemary's entire body. The quickness of her pulse seemed to push the coldness into every vein, every cell in her bloodstream. She heard pounding in her ears.

When Lucas stood, he wiped his face free of the wetness from his eyes. Then he exited the pen and secured the door.

Rosemary remained motionless, right in front of him.

"Rose Petal, it was a pleasure to meet you," he said, gently. "Knowing you has been the best part of my existence."

"So, you—" she started.

"Yes, Mrs. Travis is correct. Sorry, Rose Petal."

He walked out of the building.

She watched him, all the way down the walkway and out the door.

Her breaths became audible as she gasped. Warm liquid wet her eyelashes and traveled down her cheeks. She placed a hand on her chest, as though it could slow down her accelerated heartbeat.

Rosemary walked to the table near the side door and forcefully pushed her palms down on it. She could have screamed, but didn't want to scare the animals.

Chapter 10

Rose Petal's Letter

Rosemary felt a nudge on her shoulder. She turned her head to Sharon.

Sharon signaled with glowering eyes, to a seemingly aggravated customer.

"Excuse me," the customer said, looking directly at Rosemary.

"Sorry, how can I help you?" she said to the lady, standing by a cat cage.

Rosemary had struggled today to keep her mind on the present. Sharon had to alert her, several times, to irritated customers who needed assistance.

Lucas had left her standing dumbfounded earlier this afternoon. He hadn't defended his original story. He was a con artist. A squatter. Maybe even an escapee from a high-security psychiatric hospital or prison.

She feared her rational thinking abilities had been derailed from her brain. What kind of idiot was she?

Sadness superseded her emotions of fear and anger. She had felt an inexpressible closeness to Lucas, and now felt loss.

Had she gone crazy? She had possibly been attracted to a dangerous person.

Have I been falling in love with a dangerous psychopath?

How could he have fooled her so easily? Rosemary thought that she had learned the lesson from Mark, to no longer involve herself in harmful relationships. At least she had always known Mark's negativities; she felt more violated by Lucas, because she had believed him to be a man of honor. She had felt safe with him. Though, Rosemary had recently endured her father's death and a volatile breakup; those events must have incapacitated her lucid judgment. How else could she explain her attraction to Lucas?

At the end of the workday, her legs seemed barely able to carry her to the truck. On the drive home, she wondered if Lucas would still be living in the house next door.

Shivers trickled down her arms and back. Should she call the police? Her hands were visibly trembling as she pulled into her driveway.

Looking toward Lucas's house, she saw no movement; it looked vacant. Though, that gave her no comfort, because his house always looked vacant. The pounding of her heart felt as though it traveled to her throat and head.

The early evening light comforted her somewhat, though she walked quicker than usual from her vehicle to the back door. Her hands still shook as she unlocked it.

Somewhere deep inside her soul, she knew that Lucas would never hurt her – he had saved her life, after all – but still her whole body trembled.

She hadn't told her best friend about Lucas's fictitious life. Now, she wished she had. At least Sharon would have led the police to her killer, if Rosemary were found dead. Her mind seemed incapable of discounting such deranged scenarios.

It had been too difficult to think of the unimaginable at work today;

home would be a better place for Rosemary to allow herself to collapse in her bed and cry. She preferred to lose control in privacy.

Once inside her house, she locked the door and ensured all the windows were secure. The drapes were drawn. Her cell phone was set on the nightstand as she got into bed.

Rosemary shed the workday clothing, to her underwear. As she removed her clothes, she mentally concentrated on removing the panicked energy of today's events from her mind. Having felt nauseous and lightheaded, her body needed repose. She would allow tears, frustration and anger, but the fear needed de-escalation.

She tucked the flat sheet all around her legs. Pulling at the bottom edge of the material, she released the sheet from under the mattress and folded it under her toes. She carefully edged her body downward as she lay flat on her back, so as not to disturb her self-made cocoon. Her arms rested close to her sides, just under the comforter.

The soft, orange glow from the nightstand lamp provided a feeling of security. She was warm. The cool sheet that enveloped her was layered with the comforter. She felt softness and warmth all around her.

Samantha's weighty steps pressed onto Rosemary's chest, as the cat settled herself. The extra shield was appreciated, as the cat's soft but heavy body provided even more warmth, and the vibrations of purring.

The curtains blocked most of the light left in the late-day sky. It was too early for bedtime, but a nap was a necessity right now. Maybe, if she were unconscious for a couple of hours, when she woke her mindset would be improved. She closed her eyes.

Her face muscles were relaxed. She felt cozy and safe. A warm line of wetness traveled from the corners of her eyes to the pillow; it was a gentle release. It felt cleansing to allow the tears. Soon they intensified, with a heavier flow. Both sides of her face became wet, as the tears rolled down her chin and throat; she felt the wetness reach her ears. After struggling through the day, she now allowed herself this grieving time.

She was crying for Lucas. She was crying for her mom. She was crying for her dad and their recent strained communication. Lucas's kind words regarding her parents had practically meant the world to Rosemary. "You are beautiful, just like your mother, Rose Petal. You look like her," he had said. "Sweetheart, I know your father likes who you are as a person. It would be impossible for him not to like you," he had said.

Rosemary opened her eyes.

"I wish you were here, Mama," she said softly, out loud; "I could use your advice. I could use a hug."

Josephine had known a turbulent relationship with her husband. They had gotten divorced, yet neither one of them remarried. In their most vulnerable moments, each parent had confessed separately to their daughter that, even after the turbulence and divorce, they were still one another's true love.

Frank and Josephine had known each other since high school, and got married after graduation. Dad had pursued college and become an engineer; Mom was a homemaker. Rosemary's childhood had been obliviously pleasant – except for Josephine's bouts of depression and her dad's frustration – until the day her mother learned of Frank's infidelity and kicked him out of their home.

Rosemary could still visualize herself as the fifteen-year-old girl who stood by her mother's side, the day her father confessed.

"Josephine, please," he had begged, "I didn't know what to do; some days you don't lift your head off the pillow. You and Rosy are my life."

"Leave this house now and never show your face here again!" Josephine had demanded.

Neither Frank nor Josephine had been taught proper marriage skills by their parents. Frank had not been shown affection as a child and, as a result, neglected his wife. Josephine had suffered from a long-term blood disorder and depression, which altered her good-humored personality into that of a woman with intermittent outbursts of rage.

Rosemary's contact with her father had become limited when the divorce was finalized, after her sixteenth birthday. Her parents remained uncommunicative until her adult years.

Josephine occasionally dated other men, but did not pursue any serious relationship, even though she had idealized romantic love. Rosemary had attended the local college while residing with her mother.

Rosemary now struggled for breath as the tears continued; she was forced to breathe through her mouth, as her nose was clogged. The itchiness of the wetness on her face drew a hand from under the covers, and she wiped her face and nose.

As an adult, she now realized that the manner in which her grandparents had reared their children orchestrated to some degree the framework for Rosemary's family life. If only her parents had been given better examples.

"I forgive you, Dad," she said out loud. "You did your best. Then you did better when you learned better, and tried to teach me better."

After her mother's passing, Rosemary and her father had begun to repair their estranged relationship. He had supported her through the process of funeral arrangements. She had realized that her father always loved her mother; he had always thought her beautiful, intelligent and passionate. The regretful affair that had ended the marriage with his one true love sentenced him to a life of self-inflicted penance, and Frank had looked old. Miserable. Tired. Rosemary had found herself enjoying sharing his memories of her mother as a young adult – as a young mother.

Still laboring for breath through her mouth, Rosemary had to move Samantha from her as she now sat upright. She pulled a tissue from inside the drawer of the bedside table; her face felt soaked as she wrapped the tissue around her nose. Her eyes were sore and heavy.

"I miss you, Dad," she said out loud.

It seemed impossible that any moisture was left in her body, but a thin line of tears continued down both sides of her cheeks.

Frank had explained to her that, although he had learned the importance of showing respect, affection and love to a spouse, it was too late for him to implement. He had wanted a better life for his daughter. The truth was, he didn't approve of her relationship with Mark because of the lack of affection. Sitting in her bed right now, she could practically hear her father's voice…

"I want a better life for you, Rosy. It's the little things," her father had told her. "I wasn't physically affectionate enough with your mother, but I used to bring home her favorite magazines when we were first married. She would pour me a glass of milk when I got home from work."

He had looked downward and pulled his brows together, with his forefinger and thumb, when he said: "We stopped doing those things. We stopped doing the little things – the actions of love." He had moved his dim eyes to hers. "When your mother and I dated, the love and friendship flowed easily, but a marriage does take work. You need to tend to your marriage like you would a garden: weed out old, hurt feelings, let the small things go, but bring light to the things that really bother you, in a nice way.

"A wife likes to be kissed and hugged. I see myself in Mark, that way; I didn't do enough of that. Plus, a husband should applaud his wife. Encourage her."

He had then placed a warm hand on the side of his daughter's face. "It's too late for me, Rosy, but for you there's still time. I'm sorry my actions ruined our home," he had grimly uttered.

"I forgive you, Dad," Rosemary now repeated, out loud. It felt good to release those words, although she wished she would have told her father in person. She was proud of him, for having the bravery to admit his mistakes and make amends to his daughter.

Tears soaked her eyelashes, and her nose clogged again from the drainage. Not able to breathe freely again, she took more tissue from the drawer.

Exhausted mentally and physically, she scooted back down in bed and lay her head beside Samantha, on the pillow. The feeling of pleasurable sedation soothed her. A foggy dizziness cleared her thoughts.

Sleep came fast.

Her eyes remained closed, as Rosemary took a mental account of her surroundings. Quietness enveloped her.

There was only one familiar sound: Samantha purred above her head. A slight movement and a suction sound assured her that the cat was cleaning itself.

Upon opening her eyes, the darkness in her bedroom confirmed it to be evening, although the curtains were drawn. Looking at the alarm clock on the nightstand, it read nine p.m.

Rosemary now took notice of her own body. Her muscles were relaxed and the swelling of her eyelids had diminished; they felt lighter. Her nasal passage was clear of residual drainage; she could breathe freely.

Her mind felt rested. It seemed that either her brain had temporarily ceased the grief, or a pleasant numbness shielded her.

Rosemary petted Samantha, then got out of bed and wrapped her robe around her bare skin. She walked to the kitchen; a cup of lemonade would satisfy her thirst. She poured a small glass and drank until she finished it.

The ingredients were stocked for the construction of a hearty ham sandwich. First, though, while there was still a faint light in the sky, she would retrieve the mail; it had been forgotten when she arrived home from work, earlier today.

The long nap seemed to have dulled her senses, but a brisk wariness moved through her body, as she turned the knob and opened her door to the outside.

It appeared harmless beyond her doorstep. The sun was setting. A look toward her willow showed that the squirrels, chipmunks and birds were almost all in bed.

Her eyes briefly glanced toward *his* house.

Nothing looked different.

An approximately three-foot-tall cardboard package was set underneath her mailbox, and it drew her attention to the porch's cement floor.

She pulled envelopes from the mailbox, attached to the house siding beside the front door, and set them on top of the package on the ground. Her name and house number were handwritten on the package, but no return address. Rosemary bent down and lifted the cardboard box. It was a substantial weight. Maybe canned food? Her neighbors would occasionally leave supplies and food for the shelter on her doorstep.

She walked as quickly as possible to the dining table, set the package on it, then hurried back to lock the front door.

Sorting through the envelopes, she piled the first three together, to be thrown into the garbage. Only the last piece of mail would be retained – it was the electric bill.

She walked to the kitchen and threw out the useless correspondence, then pulled a utility knife from the drawer packed with miscellaneous items. Returning to the dining table, she began to open the anonymous box. Careful not to slice into its contents, she lifted the cardboard flaps of the parcel as she slid the knife along the center tape. The ends of the package opened easily, as she slipped the knife along its taped edges. Rosemary pressed all the flaps back. Packing paper covered the contents; she removed several pieces of the thin sheets and set them on the table.

There was one last layer; underneath it was the outline of a tall, single object. She lifted the final piece of paper.

Her heart felt as though it crashed against her ribcage. She felt the pressure of her breath held in place at the base of her throat.

Her mother's vase!

She had thought she would never again see the heirloom piece intact, with physical eyes.

Releasing slow, uneven breaths, she touched her fingertips to the thick, cool glass of the rim and pulled it from the box, onto the table. Her breathing continued irregularly, as she stood and stared at the object as though it were alien.

As she scrutinized it, there were obvious spots where it had been glued back together, like a collage, but the blemishes were only visible up close; standing a little farther away, the spots weren't noticeable. The main essence of the vase was still there.

It did feel to have the same aura, from all the generations of women who had admired it, but, for some reason, looked as though it now contained even more strength and spirit. Rosemary felt that it matched her very own soul, which had been patched back together itself, it seemed.

When Rosemary pulled the vase from the box, she noticed an envelope lining the bottom. She inhaled a long breath, to try to slow the rapid beating inside her chest. Only one person had been inside her home and known that the jagged pieces were stored in the garbage bag, in the dining room cupboard. Only one person understood the sacred meaning of those broken pieces of glass.

A tremble visibly tugged her hand, as she reached for the envelope. She turned it over in her palm. It read, *"Rose Petal"*, in black ink across the front. Shivers vibrated at the crown of her head, and moved down her neck and shoulders.

Slipping her forefinger under the length of the sealed flap, to open the envelope, Rosemary felt for the chair behind her and lowered into it. The force of her heartbeat felt as though it rose to her throat and temples, as blood pulsated through her veins. She slid the letter from the opening, feeling the pressure of her teeth against her lower lip. She placed the envelope on the table, then unfolded the ruled white paper.

Handwritten in black ink, the note read:

"Dearest Rose Petal,

Please don't be angry with me for reassembling your vase. It was one small way I wanted to show my gratitude to you, for your graciousness in befriending me.

The very best part of my existence has been experiencing you as a friend. Please know I do care about you, and I am sorry if I caused you any harm. I have parts of my life that I can not explain, and would not want to burden you with.

You have nothing to fear from me. By the time you read this, I will have left Wolfe County.

Please, remember this poem:

'No need to ask for directions,

'The way is hidden inside your soul.
'Just follow your inner light,
And that will guide you home.'

Love you for eternity,
Lucas."

Tears slipped from the corners of her eyes and down her cheeks.

Lucas had left her life as swiftly as he had entered it. And his involvement in her world would remain a mystery.

Rosemary believed that everything happened for a reason, and there were no coincidences. Maybe Lucas had been sent for the single reason of helping rid her of Mark.

Nonetheless, she would fall asleep tonight, seeing in her mind those farewell words, in black ink and Lucas's handwriting: *"Love you for eternity, Lucas."*

It was an unusually cool morning. A chilliness brushed Rosemary's bare arms, as she walked down her back porch steps. It looked almost gray outside.

She walked toward the willow, and replenished the feeding table with bird seed and nuts. She glanced toward Lucas's home. It was still quiet.

Last night she had read Lucas's note, in which he wrote that he had left town. Had he gone back to California? Was his previous home truly on the west coast, or was that a lie, too? There were so many things she did not know about him. He had never discussed his work or friends.

Somehow, Rosemary felt that she would benefit from saying goodbye to the house she once believed to be Lucas's. Her emotions might get closure from a ceremonial farewell to a physical entity – the house – that she related to him.

The crisp scent of pine pleasantly refreshed her nostrils, as she walked across her yard to the gravel driveway. A surge of anxiety caused her breaths to quicken, as she walked the dirt road toward his gravel drive. *This will be good for me. Be brave.*

A crow called out.

It was seven a.m. and the neighborhood was quiet, except for the crow. The sun shone bright, white rays through the trees, now breaking through the grayness of the sky.

She had walked this path with Lucas. Looking up at the stars that night, she had wished for a peaceful love. Maybe with him...? Now, as she neared his house, it looked lifeless.

From her distance, she looked into the small shed's windows. The old convertible was still parked inside. It had never been Lucas's car. This had never been his home. But it was as close to him as she would ever again get.

Rosemary deeply inhaled, as she lifted her foot up the first step to his porch. She felt emotionally awkward as she continued up the brief stairway, holding onto the iron railing. Indeed, most people would consider this an odd thing to do.

Upon reaching the front door, she looked inside the large bay window. White sheets still draped the furniture. Reflecting dust particles seemed to sparkle in the living-room air, from the rays of sunlight shining into the space.

"Goodbye, Lucas," she whispered. "I hope you are okay." She closed her eyes. "I love you."

The last words exited her mouth freely and unexpectedly.

She *had* loved him. It had felt as though they were long-lost friends. They had shared a level of comfort that allowed her to confide her grief to him. He had offered attention, advice and support. She had enjoyed his company. Lucas had showed kindness to her and the animals at the shelter. That's what Rosemary would choose to remember about her time spent with him.

A pastel color flickered from the ground near the front door, in her peripheral vision, as she turned toward the steps.

It was a feather: a dove's feather. It hadn't been there when she had first arrived... had it? As she knelt and picked it up, she noticed the birds had begun chirping. Gingerly, she held the shaft of the feather between her fingers. Inhaling deeply, gazing at it, a calmness overcame her. The feather resembled Lucas: clean, pure, loving... It reminded her of the man she had once thought Lucas to be. She carried the feather to her house.

When Rosemary walked through the living room, to the kitchen, it seemed that a refreshing peace had washed through the space. She felt safe. She set the dove feather on the windowsill above the sink, next to the small china bowl filled with feathers from her mother.

Looking in the bedroom mirror, Rosemary smiled. Her wound had completely healed; only a tiny scar remained, the same pigment as her complexion. That would fade, too.

Samantha ran underneath the fresh bedsheet Rosemary then attempted to neatly fit. Rosemary giggled as the cat hunkered down, a lump in the middle of the bed.

Rosemary occupied her attention with Lula's enjoyment of the late summer air. The dog looked as though she smiled on the sunlit afternoon walk. Her tail wagged. The dog's pace increased along with Rosemary's, as their walk turned into an interval jog.

It felt as though Rosemary ran into the sun, as its rays shone on her and Lula. With the run, the rush of wind pushed Rosemary's hair back, out of her face.

A smile and an audible laugh surprised her, as they emerged from her. Her soul was free and joyful when coupled with animals'. She knew that she would slowly heal from her losses if she concentrated on her soul's calling.

Work today had been a nice distraction from the recent events in her life. A couple of new puppies had needed baths, and Rosemary and Sharon enjoyed the lighthearted moment, filled with giggles, as bubbles of soap covered both of them.

As Rosemary had cleaned Angel's pen today, she noticed that the cat seemed less resistant to her presence. She hadn't been close to Angel before Lucas began volunteering here, then he had requested time with the cat. Now, Angel hadn't hissed or swiped at her hand as she reached inside today.

It had been difficult to explain Lucas's absence this Sunday morning. Sharon deserved to know the truth, but Rosemary had fabricated a story of work-related relocation for him. A large time allotment would be needed for the true explanation. Although a nice distraction, the increased workload had been noticed without the extra help.

Now standing in front of Chuck's pen, Rosemary gazed at him. Chuck was asleep on his bed. Rosemary unlatched the door and his big, sweet, brown eyes looked up at her, with a calm expression on his face. She opened the door and walked inside.

Chuck stayed still as she sat beside his bed, on the floor. The large, brown pupils of his eyes moved down toward her, and his brows creased together.

"Hi, Chuck," Rosemary cooed. She slowly moved her gaze toward the dog, but didn't look directly into Chuck's eyes for more than a moment, so as not to threaten him.

"Lucas says hello," she told him. "He misses you. He loves you." Rosemary smiled. There was good in Lucas. She had been attracted to that goodness.

The dog no longer trembled. She slowly reached her arm toward him, and he took a treat from her hand.

Able to easily put a slip-lead around his neck, she walked Chuck outside to the yard. Tomorrow, she would use the collar Lucas had. Due to Chuck having never walked outside of the fenced-in area with anyone except Lucas, Rosemary thought that she would take things slowly with the dog. Maybe he would be ready to walk outside of the yard with her in a few days.

Chuck looked up at her with his big, brown eyes, as they stood just outside the door.

"We'll go for a walk to town, as soon as you get used to me," she told him. For now, they took a walk around the yard.

They then sat side-by-side on the grass, staring at the back door. Both wished Lucas were about to walk through it.

Chapter 11

Rosemary's Rescue

A couple of volunteers worked at the shelter for the next fourteen days, to fulfill their mandatory community service. It was helpful to have extra people to sweep and mop, but Lucas's natural abilities with the animals were missed by Rosemary and Sharon.

Sharon had family health concerns at the moment, with her aunt, so Rosemary hadn't, as of yet, found an appropriate time to discuss Lucas. She still briefly explained his absence as business-related.

Rosemary had taken Chuck on several walks into town this past week. She was grateful for the time and patience Lucas had devoted to the dog. She now walked by the flower shop in town, with Chuck. Looking down at him, she noticed his reddish fur was looking shinier and thicker with his new diet, though he still had a narrow rear and knobby knees, which added cuteness to his appearance.

Taking a seat on the bench, she popped up a collapsible dog bowl and filled it with bottled water. Chuck moved his brown eyes to look up at her, his chin resting on his paws, then the dog took a few drinks when she set the bowl beside him. He then stretched out his front legs and rested his chin back on them. His eyebrows twitched as he watched the birds on the grass, across from him.

Sadness seemed to persist in Rosemary's soul. She knew it wasn't for her father or Mark. It was for Lucas.

The grief she felt for her father was laced with guilt; their bond should not have been strained due to her immaturity. The loss of her relationship with Mark only left a sense of peace inside of her. This sadness she now felt was a pure and simple longing for Lucas to walk into the shelter, with his smile and contagious optimism. She wished for his non-judgmental opinion. His wise words of encouragement. His company.

Rosemary lowered her body to the grass in front of the bench. Chuck immediately began to stand.

"Ssh, it's okay," she gently said, "I'm just going to sit down here with you."

She rested her palm on the back of the dog, and he eased back down beside her. Slowly, she glided her hand along the length of Chuck's spine. It felt comforting to be close to a loved one of Lucas's.

"Let's go to the bridge," she said.

Rosemary stood, then led Chuck past the town, past the field, to the park and onto the bridge, where they stood above the water. She watched the ripples.

The day's work was finished. Rosemary collected her purse and her light, button-down sweater, then turned off the lights in the dog room.

She was closing the shelter later than usual, this Monday evening. Sharon had already left a couple of hours prior, and Rosemary had rearranged some supplies in the storage room. A peaceful feeling overcame Rosemary when she was alone in the building. It was quiet. The cats were asleep in their beds and the dogs were asleep on theirs.

She locked the deadbolt from the outside, then headed to her truck.

It was almost nine p.m.; Samantha would be waiting on her meal of canned food and Rambo on his serving of worms. Rosemary would prepare herself a sandwich and watch a recorded soap opera. First, though, she'd make a quick trip to the small grocery store just south of town, which closed at ten p.m.

The pink underbody lights automatically turned on when the vehicle's engine started, and brightened the empty parking lot.

The evenings were cool this time of year. Fresh gusts of air swirled through the cab, as she traveled with opened windows.

Rosemary savored the quiet of the low-traffic dirt road, from the shelter into town. It was a pleasant drive on her way to the food store. She enjoyed the ability to drive slowly, without the pressure of traffic behind her. This pace would allow her adequate reaction time for a passing animal; opossums, raccoons, skunks and deer were all active early evening.

When driving, in the past springtime, she had seen an obviously recently-dead opossum, on the side of the dirt road. Rosemary had immediately pulled over to check on the poor critter, and to see if there were babies still inside the pouch. Although Mama had passed from the impact, Rosemary had indeed noticed movement coming from the belly area. Thankfully, five babies were able to be nursed back to health by Rosemary's wildlife rehabilitator acquaintance. It was a great sight to witness: the five opossums returning to the wild that fall.

People forget that they are behind the wheel of a deadly machine – as Rosemary was taught in driver's education. She would always be on the lookout for anything in the road.

Her eyes now visually stayed focused in front of her, but mentally she felt a thousand miles away. She contemplated if she should organize the other side of the storage room tomorrow. When she got home, she would call Sharon to ask how her aunt was doing.

Where is Lucas right now...?

Did Rosemary need eggs for breakfast tomorrow? She should probably buy some, to be safe, along with potato chips, bread and peanut butter. Living alone, most dinners were sandwiches: egg salad, peanut butter and tuna. Tonight would be peanut butter with strawberry jam, made fresh from her garden.

A black, compact car pulled out in front of her, a half-mile up the road. It slowed down for a minute, then continued, the vehicle randomly making sudden jolting stops.

Rosemary got close enough to see the novelty license plate: *"2Hott"*.

When the car sped up again, Rosemary decided to keep her distance.

It was now swerving on the dirt road, practically crossing from the far right of the road, near the ditch, to the far left lane.

She reached for her cell phone. Rosemary didn't want to cause any problems for this person, but they could cause harm to an innocent passerby. It was also a possibility that the person needed help, due to illness. She stilled her vehicle and dialed the police, reporting the location and plate number of the car.

It was dusk, but Rosemary could still observe fairly clearly, when the black car stopped in the center of the road ahead; it came to a standstill this time. A tree line edged both sides of the path. Rosemary stopped her truck and watched.

An object was thrown from the passenger side window. Rosemary couldn't see exactly what the object was, but the little thing was moving as it was tossed outside. As it fell into the ditch, it looked to be a small animal. The vehicle then sped swiftly away. It had been near the middle of the tree-line, next to the speed-limit sign, when the object was thrown. Rosemary mentally marked the spot.

She pressed the gas pedal to reach that point, slowed down and pulled over to the side. She parked her truck and gently opened the door. The perpetrator was now out of sight. It was quiet as she stepped down onto the gravel road. Rosemary slowly walked alongside the ditch; she didn't want the sound of the scattering rocks to scare the animal.

"Hello, pumpkin," she softly called.

A whimper cried out. The sound came from the right side of the road, just ahead of Rosemary.

"It's okay, pumpkin," she said. "Where are you?"

She didn't hear the animal again, but continued walking toward the area the sound had originally come from.

Her heart seemed to pound directly against her chest. Terrified of what she might see, but too worried about an injured creature suffering alone, she stopped beside the speed-limit sign and searched. She looked in the ditch and toward the tree line. "Where are you, pumpkin?"

Rosemary persisted in checking the area where she thought she had heard the whimper. Not another sound guided her. Everything was quiet and still. *The car stopped here.* The animal had to be near the sign, unless it ran off past the tree line.

Rosemary slowly lowered herself into a seated position on top of the ditch, in front of the sign. Maybe the scared animal would be less threatened if she took a seated position. "I'm here for you, pumpkin," she softly called out.

A slight movement was detected in her peripheral vision. She turned her head and looked toward the movement.

The little dog had smooth, brown fur and blended with the clumpy, dark dirt in the ditch. Its front paw had shifted out of place. Two brown eyes looked as big as saucers, as they stared up at Rosemary. The skin on the dog rippled as its body trembled.

"Hi, pumpkin," she softly said. "I won't hurt you."

The Chihuahua's body shook vigorously, as Rosemary stood. The dog cowered, but stayed in place and kept its eyes on Rosemary, as she walked toward it. Its right front leg looked broken, because the pup tried to scurry but couldn't put any weight on it. Its left front leg was covered in blood. Both of his injured front limbs scraped the earth, with no agility.

Rosemary wished she had a towel to wrap the scared animal in, for security and safety. She took off the light sweater she was wearing over her t-shirt. Her feet sunk into clumps of dirt, as they descended the slanted mound, toward the dog. She crouched just in front of it. The little pup's big eyes looked up, as it continued to shake.

"It's okay." Slowly, Rosemary reached her fingertips to the dog's nose. It took a couple of quick sniffs of her, then turned its head. Its skin rippled from the top of its smooth shoulders, down the length of its back.

Opening the sweater, Rosemary swiftly gathered the dog in it, so that neither of them had much reaction time; the frightened animal could bite her, and Rosemary did not want to emit fear of that possibility. She held the dog against her upper body, as she walked up the slight hill of the ditch. The pup's little head bounced, and Rosemary tried to cradle it closer to her. A few short, sharp yelps were muffled into Rosemary's chest, as the little pup wedged its nose against her.

The moderate pace brought them to the truck, where Rosemary opened the driver's-side door and set the dog on the passenger seat. She had felt it trembling in her arms, and it now shook vehemently in the cab. Rosemary took in a deliberately long breath; the dog was safely in the car.

Rosemary took her seat and shut the door, but kept on the interior light. A quick observation confirmed the injured animal to be male. It was underweight; its spine poked through the fur immensely. The dog was probably infested with fleas, due to patches of missing fur and, most likely, dehydrated and anemic. Its paw pads looked pale under the cab light; a further examination would probably find pale gums. Veterinarian attention was needed immediately.

The left front leg was bleeding from a puncture wound. The fur was stained red, but it was easy to pinpoint the puncture. Rosemary pressed her fingertip to the lesion and held it there for a few moments. When she pulled her finger away and checked the blood flow, the gush did look a lot slower now. She tightly wrapped a sleeve of her sweater around the lesion. She would have continued pressing her finger there, but she had to drive.

As she looked across at the pup, he continued trembling, his head bobbing from the tremors. He was surely in pain from his broken leg.

"It's okay now, pumpkin. You will feel better soon."

Rosemary called the emergency veterinarian clinic stored in her contact list. Their number had been programmed into her cell phone since the opening of the shelter. It was just south of town. She headed there now. The doctor who usually treated the shelter animals would not be in attendance at this hour, but all staff at the Wolfe Animal Hospital were proficient.

The pup stared straight ahead toward the glove compartment, as its head bobbed.

Rosemary glanced into the rear-view mirror, where Anna's collar hung. *How could someone do such a thing to this little soul?* "The motherfucker," she said, under her breath. "What kind of disgusting piece of shit would do this?" She slowly inhaled another deep breath.

When they arrived in the hospital parking lot, Rosemary secured the dog against her chest and carried it inside the building. She held the Chihuahua close, as she walked to the front desk. She could feel the pup's heart pumping fast against its little body.

The room was rather crowded, with several families and their pets. Wolfe Animal Hospital had reasonable prices and good care, so it was most always busy with patients, who traveled from far distances.

The receptionist, Karen, looked up and saw Rosemary with the dog.

"Hi, Rosemary," she said. "Nice to see you again. But sorry it's under these circumstances."

The receptionist took a pen, and filled in Rosemary's name and arrival time on the sign-in sheet.

"Do you know the dog's name," she gently asked, "or did you give the dog a name yet?" Her voice was hard to hear over the noisy bustle of the clinic.

"Fred," Rosemary answered. She had been considering an official name.

"Thank you for having called ahead," Karen said. "I'll let them know you're here with the emergency."

"Thank you, Karen."

The receptionist called for a technician, and he promptly arrived to take the injured animal directly to the doctor. Blood loss was considered a priority in the emergency room. The man in white scrubs took the dog from Rosemary's arms, with a warm blanket, then disappeared through the door to the examining rooms. Rosemary stood still near the desk, looking blankly at the closed door.

"Fred is a funny name for a dog," Karen said, as she giggled. "Cute."

Karen had been a receptionist for the veterinary hospital since Rosemary first began her business with them. Rosemary considered her a casual friend.

"How did you come up with that name? Fred?" the receptionist asked.

"One of me and my mom's favorite old, classic movies; I decided to name the pup Fred after the lead character."

"I can't believe anyone would do that! To throw an animal out of a car!" Karen said.

"I know. It breaks my heart."

"The police will have to be notified."

Rosemary took a form from the front desk to fill out, and sat on the wooden bench, nearest the door to the examination areas.

241

A few people in the waiting room responded with questions about the emergency. Rosemary answered with vague details, partly due to tiredness, but mainly discretion related to legal issues.

Whenever a technician opened the door to the waiting area, the seated families looked toward the white lab coat, hoping it would be their pet's turn to see a doctor. Each minute that passed seemed an hour.

"For Fred?" the woman in white scrubs called out, from the open door. Rosemary stood.

The woman began talking to her, right in the doorway. "Dr. Pillsbury did a quick exam. The right front leg will need fracture repair. She will do the surgery tonight," she said. "I'm going to take Fred back to the lab now: Dr. Pillsbury wants a blood test. Then we will get a few x-rays and she may want an ultrasound. We will look at his broken leg and organs, to see if there is internal bleeding. We'll come get you when all that is done. At that time, we'll have a price summary prepared for the surgery."

The technician handed Rosemary back her sweater, which had been wrapped around the dog's leg. Rosemary then watched the back of the woman's white scrubs disappear through the closed door.

"Rosemary?" the receptionist called.

She walked to the front desk with her finished paperwork.

"Did you call the police?" Karen asked.

"Yes, but I have to call them back," she returned, with a low-as-possible, discreet volume. "I initially called 9-1-1, because the car was swerving; I gave them the plate number. But they don't know about the animal cruelty yet."

242

"I can call them for you, after the surgery. Just give me the information – the plate number."

"That would be great. Thank you."

"Will Fred be taken to the shelter, and available for adoption soon?"

"No, I'm keeping him at my house."

"Oh, you're adopting him?"

"Yes." A sigh left her nose. "Assuming the dog wasn't stolen from a responsible owner. You guys will check for a microchip?"

"Oh, we will."

As a new patient opened the door and walked to the desk, Rosemary took back her seat. She folded her bloodstained sweater in her lap. She looked down at her empty arms, which had carried and held Fred. The blood had seeped through to her shirt and stained patches of her skin.

What kind of deranged, weak human being could do such a thing? No real man would attack the vulnerable. She would love to throw that asshole out of a moving vehicle, at 55mph!

She inhaled a slow, deep breath. *Now, now – follow your inner light... and that will guide you home,* she repeated inside her head, several times, to align back with *her soul.* She would have to gather positive energy, for Fred's sake. *Only focus on the love.*

Rosemary had basically fallen in love with the dog, the moment she first saw its eyes look up at her. Even through the animal's traumatic experience, it still accepted help from Rosemary; its lips were never curled back, and teeth never bared in defense. The little soul still trusted a human being to care for it. Some souls feel an immediate connection, and are comfortable with one another, Rosemary felt.

She sat in the waiting room with all the other anxious families, hoping to hear news soon. Staring straight ahead of her, into oblivion, she wondered how Fred was reacting to the tests.

His home would be with her now.

Chapter 12

The Devil's Tricks

Lucifer's throat had felt swollen and sore, after screeching the most horrifying scream he's sure anyone could have ever heard.

He screamed so hard that he fell to his knees, on the wooden frame of the bridge.

His mouth had been open wide, his face wet. His jaws ached from the duration of the outcry. His chest hurt from the pressure, and his lungs felt like raw slabs of meat.

Even his hands had ached, from gripping the posts of the bridge he knelt on.

Tears had squeezed from his eyes, as the guttural misery was released from his human body.

The birds had scattered. The insects had scurried. Leaves on the trees had fluttered away, from the expulsion of his spent energy. He was surprised the water below the bridge hadn't parted.

He was kneeling on the wooden slats of Rosemary's favorite bridge, in the park; she had always gone there for solace. Holding the bridge, he had sobbed onto it.

Having looked up at a canopy of surrounding branches, with oval, green leaves, that framed his upward view, he saw what Rosemary would see in her suffering. He did not want her to suffer any more than need be. He had stayed too long with her, out of selfishness. It was time to go.

After his release, he had returned to the house next to Rosemary's, and Lucifer's human body had lay still on the bed – even now his body lay there. If Rosemary were to walk into the bedroom, she would see Lucas's motionless body. But the heart still beat, though faintly. The lungs still allowed breaths, though inaudibly. His body rested in a death-like state, though his soul would be able to return to it in a millisecond.

His soul had now returned to Hell.

He was no longer tethered to the physical pain, but the consciousness of his core still retained the ache of experiencing human loss.

His soul presently found refuge in the cellar of the castle. No visitors, no bright lights, no noise. Only darkness and silence.

The monotone-gray colors of the bricks and rocks of the walls were soothing. The arches of the ceiling provided comfort. Gray cement stairs wound upward from the dirt floor. There was a bright light at the top of the stairs, near the door, unnoticed unless from the doorstep. Ornate statues in monochromatic colors decorated the brick walls, and sconces held lit candles, which glowed.

Lucifer considered this his personal detoxification room. No visitors bothered him unless there was an urgent matter. There was only the pleasant sound of water dripping from the ceiling, to a puddle on the dirt floor.

Lucifer needed recuperation time, from the trauma of his human experience. He had slipped into a deep meditation the moment he arrived back in Hell, and did not know if he would ever again regain his former self.

His glowing orb's green aura was now lined with a misty gray color, reflecting his soul's somberness. The orb hung near a back wall, in a dark corner. The seclusion of the space matched the loneliness of his soul.

His stomach had churned when he witnessed the look of disgust for him on Rosemary's face. She had thought him a liar. Now, in her eyes, he was the *devil*.

After he had left her standing in front of Chuck's pen, he had then driven the convertible to the park. There, he had released the outcry of grief so unimaginable, even to his own comprehension. He then drove the car back to its place in the shed.

He had handwritten Rosemary's letter. He had already been working on mending her broken vase, days before, and after finishing the note he placed it in the box, along with the vase. He placed the box on her porch.

Having lay in his bed, the glowing orb housed in Lucifer's human body had then risen, with its thin, golden cord attached. Through meditation, the translucent tunnel materialized from Lucifer's orb and stretched to his soul's desired location. His soul entered the tunnel, traveling through a translucent swirl that transported him to his home.

He had arrived in the core of all universes: Hell.

In need of isolation, he hadn't greeted a soul upon his arrival. Directly, he locked himself in his refuge.

Infinity could be as miserable to a discontented being as measured time was to a human soul not at peace. Had it been two hours in human time, or two years? Lucifer had no perception of his duration in the cellar.

"Lucifer, my cousin," Devon's voice telepathically called to him.

Yellow ribbons of color trailed Devon's orb, resembling the tentacles of a jellyfish, as he moved to be beside Lucifer. When Devon's soul had settled in place, the yellow, gauzy color circled his orb. Devon's image then transformed, to present himself as the young, blond male of his first human experience.

"My cousin," Devon continued, "Hell needs its ruler. You have had a sufficient period of recovery; you must re-join the castle. Your family needs you. Your students need you."

"My students?" Lucifer asked.

"Yes, there have been many new souls who have arrived, and are in desperate need of counsel."

"I can't help anyone. I am struggling myself."

"You heal yourself by helping others, cousin."

Devon gazed at Lucifer's aura. "Cousin..." Devon began, "there is grayness all around you. This isn't a productive way to exist."

Lucifer changed his image to that of Lucas, knowing that the projected face expressed sadness.

"Did you ever have a true love, Devon?" Lucifer asked.

"True love?"

"Something that made you strive to be honorable... accountable?" Lucifer used the image of his face to show his tears. "What if that something were taken from your existence? Should you still strive to achieve goodness?"

"One strives for goodness because that is all he knows to do. There should only be love, in any situation. Cousin, you have always realized integrity; this healing center is successful because of your attentiveness."

"I need a while longer here," Lucifer said.

"Lucifer, whatever your experience was on Earth, it did not change the core of your soul."

"Devon…"

"Yes?"

"You are the lineage's bloodline, like me. You are my blood; you are my uncle's son. Our grandfather is a kind soul, and he was a good ruler. Your father is noble, but my own father was rightfully eliminated from the lineage: Nigel was disrespectful and malicious. Ash is like Nigel, and he must never be ruler. The next ruler must be from our bloodline and, as you know, I have chosen you. You must take over for me, if I never recover."

"You will recover, cousin."

"Devon…"

"Yes, cousin?"

"I wish *you* had been my blood brother."

"We are brothers by choice, Lucifer."

"That we are."

Devon evaporated through the walls of Lucifer's refuge, after his last words.

Lucifer's soul, immersed in grief, hung as an immobile orb, in deep meditation. Had it been two days, human time, or two years since Devon's visit?

A strong wind abruptly entered the cellar and woke Lucifer from his stupor. The flames of the candles in the sconces flickered, then extinguished, as something swift and furious invaded the cellar.

Lucifer lost his bearings. It felt as if a fist of bad energy punched him in his core, as a red ball of gases tore through his aura and fragmented the gray color. Horrific sounds, like nails screeching on a chalkboard, assaulted Lucifer's energy. Colors of brownish-red flashed all around him. The murky, threatening hues infiltrated his space and then encircled his own soul.

He heard a deep, male voice. It was unfamiliar to him.

"I'm going to kill that girl!" the voice rumbled.

It sounded as though it came from speakers surrounding him. The whole room echoed the words. "I'll find her!" the man yelled.

It felt as if a freight train plummeted through Lucifer's soul. This evil struck him so hard that he shook.

"I'm going to kill that girl!" rang through the cellar again. The words continued to pierce the dark room, loud and clear.

A soul's cry of death proclamation was not unusual, but *this* chilling voice threatened another life.

Lucifer's aura ricocheted off the four corners of the room. His essence felt as if it were distorted ripples, bouncing from ceiling to floor and wall to wall, as though the ripples were produced by an amplifier.

Lucifer transformed his image to that of Lucas.

"Rosemary!" Lucifer suddenly cried out.

Someone was threatening Rosemary's life! Lucifer felt it in his soul.

This malevolent force was not Mark.

Like a movie on a big screen, Lucifer telepathically watched scenes take place...

It was sundown. Rosemary was driving along the dirt road, her truck lights shining into the back of the car in front of her.

Lucifer felt the energy of the man who drove the car. This person was irritated by the lights shining through his back window.

As both vehicles continued down the dirt road, Lucifer could see inside the car. There were cigarette butts all over the floor of the vehicle, pill bottles and beer cans. The man's emotions seemed to be altered by recreational drugs. His anger elevated easily, as the truck headlights bounced along the ruts and flickered behind him.

Lucifer concentrated, allowing his energy to merge with this man's. The colors of brownish-red that he had seen and sensed represented the level of hatred which consumed this person's state of mind. Lucifer's energy now morphed into this human being. He felt the man's temples twitch, as his jawline tightened. His eyes narrowed, as he looked into the rear-view mirror. It was as though Lucifer saw his own reflection, as the man's face crossed the mirror.

The scene then showed the car speeding up, distancing itself from the truck behind it. There was then an eerie calmness.

An intended malice, so disturbing, caused the smell of rotten eggs to permeate the cellar. It sent ripples of unease through Lucifer's core. If he were human, he would have surely vomited. Something horrific was about to take place in the telepathic movie. Lucifer did not want to watch the next scene, but Rosemary's life depended on it.

The man pressed on the brakes and cursed, because he had to place the vehicle in park. He then reached over to the backseat floor and yanked up a small, trembling dog. The strength of his hands around the little creature nearly squeezed the life from it. The dog was then thrown out of the passenger-side window, its little body hitting the window frame on the way out. It never made a sound; it only trembled.

In another scene, the same man slammed his fists against a metal wall. Spit spewed from his mouth, as he shouted: "I'm going to kill that girl! I'll find her!"

Were the scenes past, present or future?

Lucifer abruptly changed to his condensed energy.

An iridescent, swirling tunnel formed from Lucifer's core, and he felt his soul swiftly enter it. He did not know where Rosemary was at this present moment; he only knew that, if he concentrated and visualized her energy, his soul would be delivered to hers like a magnet.

His core centered its concentration on her, willing himself to her location.

A surge of fear, of what condition he might find her physical body and emotional state in, caused the meditation process to erratically reconstruct his energy. He felt disjointed as he traveled. It felt like a brick firmly dropped when he was pinned to Earth.

His energy had been drawn to Rosemary's bedroom.

She was in her bed, asleep.

Safe.

His orb hovered over her.

Green colors returned to circle his soul. Although his natural energy realigned, there was still an urgency that seemed to pulsate through him.

To physically watch over her, his human body was a necessity, so his core now visualized Lucas. He hovered over the chest of his human form and the golden cord connected to his soul, guiding him back into the body. It again housed his core energy. He was Lucas again.

He felt his backside resting on the bed, in the same position he had left it. Bone structure, internal organs, cells and blood flow made up his solid form. Lucifer felt his heart beating, fast; pressing a palm to his bare skin, he welcomed the magic of a heartbeat.

Lucifer opened his eyes. He looked up at the white ceiling of the bedroom. The ceiling spun as he slowly rose to an upright position. His chest tightened as his breath came shallow. He pressed a pillow to his upper body and squeezed his eyelids closed, as he lowered one leg to the floor, from his high mattress seat; a sharp pain accompanied the movement. The ache seemed to stab him in the lower back, as his other leg lowered to the rug in front of the bed. Inhaling a deep breath, while pressing the pillow to his chest, his core trembled and his legs shook, as he slowly stood and put weight on his feet. He continued to hold the pillow tightly, as though it absorbed some of the pain. Dizziness made him feel weak as he stood. The room spun as he attempted to keep the wall in focus.

It was vital to get to Rosemary's house.

The ache in his back and the pressure in his core faded, the longer he stood in place. He placed the clutched pillow on the bed and breathed freely, his chest expanding.

Lucifer slowly pulled his t-shirt over his head; his stiff muscles caused his shoulders to lock momentarily, as his arms moved above his head. Stepping into his pants proved an easier task, but he felt his jaws clinch in a grimace, as he bent to tie his shoes.

He shuffled one foot, then the other, in a forward motion, and made it to the front door. Holding tightly onto the rail, he hobbled down the stairs.

A portion of the bright moon was revealed through a break in the opaque passing clouds. The night air seemed to enliven his body with some energy.

An owl softly called out, as Lucifer reached Rosemary's yard. In the darkness, he slid his hands along each of her windowsills. He found a loose frame and pried it open.

His soul, even though now housed in a human body, could use its energy to force open the door, but his energy was weakened at the moment, due to transformation. Anyhow, Lucifer thought it magical and pleasurable to actually use his human body.

Her kitchen window allowed a small gap, and he widened the space to fit his body. Gently forcing the window frame upward, he managed to lift both legs over the sill. He moved aside the small picture frame and the bowl of feathers, so his whole body was able to slide through. He rolled onto the counter and stumbled to the kitchen floor.

It felt as though his heart pumped up through his throat and temples, as he headed toward Rosemary's bedroom. A quick assessment of the darkened living room proved that she had not moved to there. The whole house was dark. His legs felt stiff, but manageable, as he opened the closed door to her bedroom.

A swift release of stored breath reduced the pressure in his chest, as his human eyes fell upon her.

There she lay, safe in her bed. Alive. Unharmed. Her chest was methodically rising and falling.

Lucifer felt his pulse slow. It felt as if every muscle in his body eased into a pool of liquid; the blood moved smoothly through his veins. His energy now felt centered inside his body. He exhaled another heavy breath, as he further adjusted to his human form.

Samantha looked at him, perched on top of the pillow. She then closed her eyes and curled her tail around her.

Lucifer would not leave Rosemary until he figured out who was threatening her life. That man would be neutralized.

Lucifer watched Rosemary sleep.

Her eyes rolled beneath their lids.

"No!" she called out.

He did not wake her. He was in no rush for the moment she woke and found him standing guard.

"No!" she cried again.

Still asleep, Rosemary turned to her side, facing toward Lucifer.

"No!" she called out, yet again.

Her eyes suddenly opened.

The bedside lamp illuminated the room with a muted clarity.

She first took in the vision of his jean-clad legs...

Lucifer watched Rosemary's gaze move slowly upward.

Breathing in a sharp breath, her hand instinctively covered her chest. It sounded like an inward scream.

The blackness of her pupils enlarged, as she became aware a man was present in her bedroom. She backed up to the headboard of her bed and sat up, pulling her legs in front of her body. She wrapped her arms around them. Her quickened breaths became audible, as she abruptly moved her line of vision to the man's face.

The initial rush of fear seemed to subside when she looked at a familiar face. The muscles around her jawline and throat relaxed.

Her brain then seemed to relive her last encounter with Lucifer, when she realized his lie. She now looked up at him as though he were a stranger, meaning to do her harm.

"I won't hurt you," he gently said. "I'm here to protect you, Rose Petal."

In one swift movement forward, she made an attempt to grab the cell phone on the nightstand. Her hand trembled as she reached it, and it fell to the floor. She scooted herself back to the headboard and planted her backside against it. Her body shook and she again brought her knees up to her chest, hugging her legs to calm herself.

"How did you get in here? What do you want?" she asked. Her trembling voice wavered between unbridled fear and forced self-control. Her eyelids quivered, as if she were watching a horror film.

"Rose Petal, I have no time to be delicate about this..." he smoothed his forefinger and thumb along his jawline: "you are in danger."

She bit down on her lower lip, and tears filled her eyes.

"Not from me; I am here to protect you. I will not allow that danger to come to you."

Tears quietly slipped down Rosemary's cheeks. Her breathing was still audible and uneven. Her arms wrapped around her held her body's trembles. The expression of terror on her face was frozen. Immobilized.

"I came back here to protect you. Someone... has threatened your life," Lucifer said. "What has happened?"

"What?"

"Has anyone threatened you?"

"No!" The word came out angrily.

"I heard an unfamiliar man's voice. 'I'm going to kill that girl,' the man said."

Rosemary hugged herself tighter. She resembled a wilted flower, as her chin slumped to her chest, her eyes pressed closed.

"That man will not touch you; don't worry. That's why I am here. I'm not leaving your side until I find out who this is. I will neutralize this man."

Rosemary opened her eyes and looked hesitantly at Lucifer.

"That's crazy! Leave now!" she shouted.

It then seemed that she gained a gust of energy: all at once, she scurried off the bed and scratched her fingernails across the grain of the wood floor, as she retrieved her cell phone, just under the nightstand. Regaining her balance, at the edge of the mattress, she leaned against it. She moved her fingers over the keypad of her phone. "I'm calling the police," she said.

"Don't do that." He kept his distance, so as not to frighten her further.

Lucifer did not want Rosemary left alone for a second. He was given the vision to save her life. The police could be evaded if summoned here, but any moment not focused on Rosemary could be of great cost. He needed to nullify distractions.

"Who are you? What do you want from me?" she asked Lucifer, looking up at him for a brief moment. "I'm calling the police now."

"I will tell you who I am." He held up his hands, palms facing her, in submission. "Please?"

She didn't seem to blink, keeping her eyes alert and now focused on him.

"Rosemary, your life is in danger. I am the only one who can help you. You will be okay. I'm here to protect you."

She had already dialed 911 on the keypad of her phone; now she was moving her index finger toward the call icon. It paused just over the top of the green phone symbol.

"Who are you?" she asked.

He moved his hands to each side of his head and moved his fingers through his hair. "Rosemary, your mother taught you to believe in magic. I am magic of the worst kind."

Her eyes widened. Her finger began to move.

"Rosemary, wait! Please, don't," he said. "I will tell you who I am, but that will also put you in harm's way, because you will know things you shouldn't have to know. I am sorry." He held his jawline between his forefinger and thumb, then lowered his arms to each side. "Rosemary, my real name is Lucifer. I am the devil."

She involuntarily took in a choppy breath, with another seemingly inward scream. Her face wet from tears and reddened, her finger moved downward, toward the call icon.

Lucifer had no choice; he had to prove his identity. He felt tightness between his eyebrows as he pulled them together, in deep concentration. He mentally focused his vision on the cell phone that Rosemary held in her hand, and encircled the phone with a golden light, which then turned bright red.

Red represented the color of movement to him, and he picked up the phone with his circle of concentrated hue, lifting it from her hands. It swiftly moved through the air, and he set it on the nightstand with a clink.

Rosemary's eyes had followed the cell phone and now stared at it, as it was set in place. Her lips parted. Her chest visibly rose and fell, in rapid palpitations, pushing air through her open mouth. She had not seen the phone encircled with color, but she witnessed its movement.

But Lucifer's red eyes had been seen.

"I saw you following a compact black car in your truck," Lucifer said, sounding more impatient than he intended. "You were on the dirt road. I saw a small dog thrown out of the passenger-side window of the car in front of you."

Her eyes looked from the phone to Lucifer, back and forth.

"During my vision, I heard a man's voice threaten your life," he continued. "Could the man who drove the car have followed you home?"

"Were *you* following me?" she asked.

"No. I was in Hell. In the castle. Locked in the cellar."

Rosemary looked to now be holding her breath.

"Breathe, Rose Petal," he said. "Could that man have followed you home?"

"What kind of tricks are these?"

"Tricks?"

"You moved my phone. You read my mind."

"I didn't read your mind." He shook his head. "I can hear the negative thoughts of a human soul when he is about to pass... but... not

259

usually a healthy person's thoughts. I am connected to you. I heard your thoughts when I first recognized you, but..." he shook his head again, "I haven't been connected to you in that way... hearing your thoughts... since you've... healed. That man has a death wish, so I read his mind. I saw with my inner vision everything that happened; everything played for me like a movie."

Tears filled her eyes again.

"My soul is connected to yours," he said. "You are in immense danger, so my energy was drawn to you."

He took in a deep breath. "I'm sorry I frightened you with the phone. It is imperative that you understand who I am – now!"

Her eyes seemed to now be pinned open, with shock. "You're a telepath, a psychokinetic... You can hear thoughts, move things – that doesn't mean you're the devil..." the words came unsteadily from her mouth, "...are you?"

She lowered her eyelids, then looked back at Lucifer. "Do you need help? I can get you help."

"I hear only the dark thoughts of humans – humans that are about to pass. I only heard your negative thoughts when you grieved; never before had I ever heard a healthy human's thoughts. I heard that man's thoughts, not yours.

"I can manipulate energy. I can change from my human form to a condensed energy... I am the ruler of Hell."

He inhaled a deep breath, then spoke firmly. "Understand this, Rosemary: I am the devil. My name is Lucifer."

Rosemary moved her eyes to his face, but looked downward uneasily as he matched her gaze. Her chest again rose and fell, in rapid movements.

"I am very sane, Rose Petal," he assured.

He needed to secure her belief, quickly. What would be the least daunting way to prove his truth?

"Rosemary, please look at me," he asked.

She begrudgingly moved her chin upward and looked at him.

He searched into her eyes and connected with her soul. His eyes glowed red, as his energy passed through him to her. A gold, threadlike channel linked their souls. The link between them forced her immersion.

"Rose Petal, I mean you no harm. You are safe." The words were telepathically transmitted, through the channel of connected energies.

Rosemary did not blink, her lips slightly parted. A thin line of tears slid down her cheeks. "I hear you…" she said softly, "but your lips are not moving." She blinked incessantly. "Your voice is filling my head."

"This is the truth," he said telepathically.

"Your eyes are glowing red," she said, as the thin line of tears continued down her face. "How can this be happening?"

"The red is only the movement of my energy," his soul conveyed to hers. "It's only what your mother taught you, sweetheart: she taught you to believe in oneness, afterlife, soul…"

The gold channel dematerialized, as he withdrew his stream of energy connection with her; it felt as though it were sucked back inside him with a straw, as all of his essence returned inside his body. His eyes returned to black.

"I don't mean to be harsh," he said, verbally, "but we have little time. Tell me about the incident with this man, please. Every detail you can remember. If you haven't crossed this man yet, you will – trust me. I was warned an evil act would cross your path."

Rosemary scooted back to the headboard and hugged her bent knees. She looked at the alarm clock on the nightstand: it read six a.m.

"It was yesterday," she began, in a hoarse voice, and swallowed hard. "I was driving, after work, to the little grocery store. I had worked late, so it was about nine p.m. A black car pulled out in front of me, about a half mile ahead. I caught up to it enough to see the license plate. The person was driving erratically, so I called the police."

"What information did you give the police?" he asked.

"The car license plate and location. I thought there was a chance that the person could be sick – maybe experiencing a sudden ailment – or under the influence of alcohol, or drugs."

"Did you give the police any information about you? Could this man have got your address from the police report?"

"No, I gave no information about myself to the police; just my phone number. They never called."

Her eyes were now dry, but her face still remained moistened, and she wiped her nose and cheeks. She glanced up at Lucifer for a moment, but then gazed past him – into mid-air, it seemed – as she continued with her story.

"The car sped up a couple of times. Then it slowed down and stopped in the middle of the road." She pressed the palms of her hands over her closed eyes. "That's when the dog was thrown from the window."

Lucifer wished he could comfort Rosemary, but if he set one foot closer to her, she would surely recoil. He closed his eyes after her last statement and inhaled deeply, attempting to keep his emotions intact.

"Did the driver of the car see you?" Lucifer asked, with a soft voice.

"No."

Her eyes reopened and again looked past him. "I got out to look for the animal," she began, her voice dry. "I was so scared to see it hurt. I wasn't sure what I would find: what kind of animal was it; what condition would it be in?"

"You weren't followed home?"

"No, I sat in the emergency room for hours before heading home."

"Could the veterinary office have given that man any information?" he asked.

"No. This is the man you think wants to kill me?" she asked. A touch of anger underlined her words with exaggerated pronunciation.

"Yes. In my vision, I saw the face of the man driving the car. I heard his voice yelling the threats. We will have to get his name. There must be a police report available."

"You need to leave now," Rosemary said, sternly.

"I'm not going anywhere – except wherever you go."

She exhaled an exaggerated, sharp breath. "You need to get out of my room; I need to get dressed. I am going to go to the veterinarian hospital to check on Fred before work. He will have to stay there today; he had surgery late last night. I am going to get a doctor's report and visit him. Maybe I will be able to bring him home tomorrow."

"You named the dog Fred?"

"Yes, after a character in my favorite movie."

"That's unique." Lucifer felt his facial muscles loosen, as he smiled.

He then pressed his chin between his forefinger and thumb. "What day is it? How long have I been gone, in human time?" he asked.

"You left about two weeks ago – Saturday. Today is Tuesday; it has been sixteen days since I've seen you."

She loosely puckered her lips, in thought. "You're coming to the shelter with me, too?"

"Yes."

"I know Chuck will be happy to see you. He's missed you. He's reverted to being more withdrawn since you left."

"I missed that dog only second to you."

Her eyebrows arched as they pulled tightly together. "You need to leave now," she repeated.

"I'll be right outside your bedroom door," Lucifer said, as he walked out. When he left the room and closed the door behind him, he heard her lock it.

His human heart felt as if it sank, as he listened to muffled sobs; it sounded as though Rosemary's breaths kept hitching in her throat. She was *crying*.

He closed his eyes and inhaled deeply, as he stood, leaning his back against the wall opposite her bedroom. A stinging sensation began at the top of his throbbing head, and slowly traveled down his sore neck and shoulders, to his lower back, legs and feet. His truth had altered her reality. Lucifer dropped his head and rubbed his temples.

Twenty minutes had passed since Rosemary locked her bedroom door. Lucifer lightly knocked on it.

He stood and waited, facing the door.

His hand reached for the timepiece inside his left pocket. He smoothed it between his thumb and index finger. He put the timepiece back and ran his fingers through his hair.

There was a window in her room. Had she possibly fled? With the current threat to her life, being alone outside of the home was a danger.

"Rose Petal?" he called.

There was no answer.

Feeling a sudden panic, as his heart thumped fast, he hurried to the couch. He lay on it, his back cushioned against the padded material. Lucifer closed his eyes and deeply inhaled, then slowly exhaled, lulling his human brain into a meditative state. His breathing slowed and his heart rate slowed. Thoughts became nonexistent.

Focused energy placed a gold light around his core, and he altered into a condensed form. His soul rose from his human body, casting a golden glow. The orb had a green aura, with a thin, golden thread attached. His essence concentrated on the inside of Rosemary's bedroom. He visualized her.

Rosemary's pupils grew full, when she watched his glowing orb materialize only inches in front of her. Sitting on the edge of her bed, she clutched its frame. Her eyes seemed unable to close or move from the orb. She fanned out her fingers as she covered her open eyes, still peeking through.

One sudden inward breath moved her chest in a forceful compression. Her mouth opened with another inward scream, that seemed as though her rational mind cried out with every cell in her body.

Though distraught, she was physically present and uninjured.

His energy drew her bedroom door open…

His soul now centered above his human body. His luminosity faded into its chest, as he nestled back inside.

Weak and tired, Lucifer's face scrunched, as his body slowly moved to an upright position on the couch. It had taken a great deal of strength to make his orb visible, having to lower his soul's vibrations to match those of a human. He now stood on legs, though it felt as though he pulled them through quicksand with each step, as they staggered to Rosemary's bedside.

Rosemary's widened eyes stared at him. Her skin was pale. She sat still, her fingers gripping the edge of the bed, her knuckles practically white.

"You are…" she began, weakly. Her voice was trembling.

"Yes… I am Lucifer, the devil. You saw my soul. I am back in human form now."

Having taken so much energy to manipulate his form, his breathing was still labored; he now inhaled deep, uneven breaths.

Rosemary sat on her bed, dressed in her usual, everyday work clothes, but there was nothing usual about her day, on this particular Tuesday. Her fixed eyes were still wide with stark clarity and fear.

"There was a bright, clear orb… your soul… floating in the mid-air… in my bedroom," she shakily said. "Then, you… now, you…" She extended her arm and pointed her finger at him. "It seemed to happen instantaneously, that you… you appeared, like magic."

"It was never my intention for you to learn about my world. In fact, that was my biggest fear. I never wanted to frighten you," he said.

"You can move through doors?" she whispered.

She seemed to hold her breath again. Except for red-rimmed eyes, her skin was still pale and her lips were pasty.

"Breathe, Rosemary," he told her, calmly and firmly. "I don't move through doors as a human, but I can transform my energy; I can change from being my soul, inside a human form, to condensed energy. Condensed energy is unbounded.

"You can do the same, Rose Petal. A soul's energy can manipulate physical objects, even if housed inside a human body. The energy of my soul could have manipulated the door open while inside my body, but maybe you actually *seeing* my soul… further confirms my truth to you. You need to realize the gravity of the situation."

"You said that man wants to kill me?" Rosemary asked. Lucifer heard her swallow hard.

"He will never lay one finger on you, Rose Petal. That is why I am here. I will not allow him to harm you in any way."

"You said your soul is connected to mine?" she asked. "Why? Why are you connected to *me*?"

"Don't worry, you are a positive energy… a good soul. I just meant… That's a story for another day, sweetheart. Just know that there is nothing to worry about. I will be by your side at all times. And then, after this is all over, I will leave. When that man is neutralized, I will leave."

The swollen lids and red rims of her eyes looked as though her soul were aching through them. The paleness of her skin made her appear ill. She was sleep-deprived and overwhelmed.

"Rosemary, think… Do you know how that man would know you? Did you have any contact with him?" Lucifer asked.

"No, I had no contact with him. He would not have seen my license plate. He was never behind my truck. Like I said earlier, he could not have followed me home; I spent hours at the vet."

"Can we get on your laptop and look for a picture of him?"

"Yes."

"My energy melded with his in my vision. I could meditate and be drawn to him, but it would take less energy if I knew where he was. I want this done as quickly as possible."

She moved to her feet and stiffly walked to the desk in the living room. Lucifer followed. Rosemary pulled out the chair tucked into the office space and turned on her computer. Lucifer stood beside her and crouched over the bright screen.

"Can you search yesterday's local arrests?" he asked.

"Yes."

Rosemary scanned through the community newspaper and found the leading news stories. Her index finger moved down each line, to keep her place on the screen.

She paused right next to the small picture of a man's face. It was boxed next to a short paragraph. She skimmed the story, then turned back to look at Lucifer's face. His jaw clenched and his eyes fiercely stared at the screen in front of him. The muscles of his stomach tightened, as he took in a long breath and held it. His fingers firmly gripped the edge of the desk, as he leaned further forward to look at the screen. The clash of his teeth locking together sounded in his ears, as his teeth clenched tighter.

He was peering into the eyes of the man who had threatened Rosemary's life and attempted to murder a defenseless animal. Lucifer wished he could reach inside the computer and pull out the man by his neck.

"That's him, Rosemary," he said. "That's the man I saw in my vision."

She deeply inhaled a shaky breath, as she now studied the picture.

The article stated that the man, named Louis Koratz, was picked up on drug charges, and was being held for a handful of warrants. He had been pulled over by police last night, due to a reckless driving tip-off.

Rosemary sharply breathed in another gulp of air, as her index finger stopped next to the last line. It read: *"Koratz might be facing animal abuse charges, in addition to his four warrants. Jail time will be inevitable."*

Biting down on her lower lip, Rosemary turned to Lucifer. "This is the man who wants to kill me?" she said.

"This man will never lay a finger on you; I will make sure of that," he said, firmly. "I will protect you with all of my existence." He continued to focus on the man's expressionless eyes in the picture. They looked blank, as if no soul were connected to them.

"This is good news," he said: "Koratz is in jail. He's confined and I can easily get to him."

Her lips slightly parted, as she looked from the screen to Lucifer. "What are you going to do to him?"

"I just want to convince this unhinged, misaligned man that it's in his best interests to forget you exist. I can be persuasive."

Sensations of a gravitational pull toward a departing, Hellbound soul, and the grim inner voice of that essence, had always been a natural occurrence for Lucifer. Countless anonymous souls had cried out for aid. Only one time before, though, had Lucifer experienced a vision as graphic as the one he had received of Koratz. The two visions had both involved loved ones.

In his first vision, he had been Lucas. Fists repeatedly punching bruised skin and ribs had played like a film-strip through his mind. A migraine headache had pummeled his brain with the occurrence of his first vision. Nausea had overcome him and he had felt faint.

There was a certain knowledge that the images had been given to him, in warning of the abuse of a beloved. When the face of his mother had been revealed, it felt as if the blood had drained from Lucas's own body.

Being human at the time of his first vision, and unaware of his true identity, the vision had frightened him. Despite thinking his experience was a hallucination, or insanity, he nonetheless traveled, in darkness, to his parents' home. Lucas's horse had been pushed to the limit, as he continued leg pressure on the mare, until the parents' windmill was in sight.

When he had physically arrived at the actual scene, he looked down at his mother's seemingly lifeless body, lying on the wooden floor beside the woodstove. The silk material of the top of her square-neckline dress had been dampened red, from her hemorrhaging flesh. The skin of her bare neck and forearms, where her full, loose sleeves ended, was discolored black and blue. She was unresponsive, her expression emotionless. Her jaw hung loose, as if broken. Tears seemed to burn trails down Lucas's face, as he gently moved a blood-soaked clump of brown hair from hers. He sharply inhaled each breath, unsure if life still existed inside his mother. Holding an ear to her chest, he listened for breath, watched for movement.

It had felt like a long train of connecting cars sounding their horns, as they passed through his heart. Chaos dizzied his emotions. Holding his mother's hand, as he knelt beside her, he had wondered if it would be the last time he was afforded the privilege of that chance.

Loose strands of her brown hair had fallen from the disheveled bun, as he gently lifted her head and carried her outside. As he had lifted the back of her head, warm blood dripped into his hand. He wasn't sure if it had come from underneath her hairline, her ears, her nose or her mouth; she was bleeding from several orifices.

Lucas had thought that he would faint from the terror, but he secured his mother on his mare, in front of him, and got her to the town doctor's home. The doctor found a weak pulse, but told Lucas that his mother probably wouldn't survive.

That day, the gift of his vision had saved Catherine's life. Her body had begun to mend, amid an elongated bed-rest.

But, recovery from a broken jaw and collarbone was secondary to recuperating from the abuse and loss of a husband.

Nigel had been found dead from natural causes, the night Lucas rushed his mother to the doctor's home – or so Lucas had thought at the time. The truth had been revealed to Lucas after his own human death: his blood-father's soul had been plucked from human existence by the lineage. Grandfather and the lineage had elected to nullify Nigel's family connection and his opportunity to become ruler. His soul had been immediately removed from Earth, after the violent act of harming his wife. The body appeared to have suffered a heart attack. His soul, even now, remained in seclusion, its energy connected with nothing.

"Are you an angel?" Rosemary asked, her voice delivering Lucifer from the dark reminiscence.

He shook his head slightly, as though clearing his mind for the present. She seemed to be searching the blackness of his eyes, hoping to find the answer she wished for. He held her gaze. "I am no angel," he said, his voice thick with wryness. "The original Lucifer was an angel. I am Lucifer the Third."

Rosemary's eyebrows pulled tightly together, and she pressed her lower lip between her teeth. Silent, she waited.

He backed up to the couch and leaned against it, facing her chair.

"There were two Lucifers before me. The title 'Lucifer' is given to the current ruler, for the duration of his reign. Each reigning ruler of Hell chooses his successor. My grandfather chose me to follow his reign."

"Your grandfather? The one you told me about?"

"Yes. I was human and I did have a human grandfather; he was my first human mother's father. He was my blood grandfather and the ruler of Hell. I told you that he is a kind soul; we are likeminded, so to speak. He chose me on account of my understanding of human life.

"Grandfather reigned as ruler of Hell for approximately one thousand years, Earth time. I am in the infancy of my reign, so to speak; I have only held the title of 'ruler of Hell' for about two hundred Earth years, so far. Grandfather believes that all guardians of Hell should experience human suffering."

Rosemary's shoulders hunched forward, as her upper body endured a tremble.

He softened his tone and continued: "Hell is a sacred castle, a place of healing.

272

"The original Lucifer appointed a lineage of benevolent beings to be the guardians of Hell. He chose one of those beings to become his successor, and allowed each subsequent ruler to choose his own successor.

"I'm sorry if this is all too much for you to handle." Lucifer tipped his head down and moved his fingers through the hair at the crown of his head. He then looked back up at Rosemary.

Her eyelids moved downward, as she unconsciously gazed past him. An audible breath was released from her fallen chest.

She turned back toward the computer screen and looked at the clock in the lower right corner. "I have to go now!" she said.

"I'm coming with you," Lucifer returned, his tone unyielding.

"I'll make a pot of coffee, and we can take some with us."

Her movements seemed robotic, as she prepared the coffee and then poured some into a Thermos. She offered Lucifer a Thermos and he filled it. Rosemary was quiet, as she fed both the fish and cat breakfast, then kissed Samantha's head, before heading outside to the truck. She walked at an accelerated pace, and Lucifer felt his heart pump as he followed behind her.

He opened her door for her, once she had unlocked it, then walked to the passenger side, taking his place beside her in the cab.

"Breathe, Rose Petal," he said. "Everything will be okay. Fred will be okay, and everything else will be, too."

She looked over at him. "What should I call you?"

"Call me?"

"Your name?"

"Call me Lucas. That is my true human name."

273

For the time being, he then thought to himself. Once his job as a human was complete, he would return, as a condensed form, to Hell. Soon enough, his duties as ruler would recommence. He would resume his position as Lucifer.

Chapter 13

Helen's Great-Great-Great-Granddaughter

Rosemary inhaled a long, deep breath as she settled behind the steering wheel of the truck. After turning the key, the engine hummed. The tires rolled across the gravel driveway, on the way to town.

Fred would recuperate, but he would need his caretaker fully conscious and attentive. He would adapt to Rosemary and his new home.

Koratz was in jail.

Rosemary swallowed hard as she now considered the man who sat beside her in the cab. He was so close. She could touch him if she chose. She peripherally glanced his way.

He was a man. His body consisted of flesh, blood, bones and everything else that forms a human being, yet he was the ruler of Hell. He had almost kissed her at one time.

A prickle crept up the skin of her neck.

She felt as though she were having an out-of-body experience. Her brain did not feel connected to her head. It was an unsteady sensation, as though she might faint from an emotional overload.

As she looked down at her hands on the steering wheel, they did not seem to be connected to her physical body, either, even though they gripped the leather object so tightly.

Life ain't for sissies, she thought to herself.

She inhaled another deep breath and shakily held it for a moment.

I am Helen's great-great-great-granddaughter! The anthem only sounded within her own mind. *I can handle anything!* she internally added. Helen had once intimidated a pack of threatening wolves. Rosemary could do the equivalent.

What if there was no devil? What if there were no evil? What if there was no torturous Hell? There would be nothing to hate, and there would be nothing to fear.

Deliberately, she returned her thoughts to Fred. He might need special equipment for his recovery. A lifting harness or sling would most likely be needed to help him stand. He would probably be released tomorrow morning. Fred would need continuous supervision, and to be confined in a dog carrier at the shelter, for the duration of Rosemary's workday. She would introduce the dog to his new home that evening. Hopefully, Samantha would be tolerant.

It would be a good idea to purchase another cat tree for Samantha, to put in the living room. It would allow her a place to put her scent, to claim as only hers.

Would Lucas insist on staying the night with them?

The Wolfe Animal Hospital sign now came into view, about a quarter-mile ahead; there was a large road sign with a paw print.

Rosemary would revisit her mindset around the reality of Lucas when she got home that night. She and Samantha would lock themselves in her bedroom, and there she would allow her thoughts to flow freely.

Later today, work would be a distraction. Right now, to get through the day, she would have to focus on absorbing the veterinarian's report.

After filling in the sign-in sheet, a technician had placed Rosemary and Lucas in an exam room, then put the dog in Rosemary's arms. Fred's thin body now trembled; he didn't know Rosemary. She petted the smooth fur on top of his petite head, through the protective, cone-shaped gear wrapped around his neck. Two widened, brown eyes looked like saucers, as they peered through the Elizabethan collar. His right front leg was wrapped in a white cast, and his left front leg was covered in a couple of layers of gauze and blue elastic bandage. When the technician had delivered the dog to the exam room, Fred had been wrapped in a warm towel. The towel now loosened as he fidgeted.

Lucas sat beside Rosemary, as she held Fred in her lap, on the bench. The stainless-steel examination table protruded from the side wall. The room smelled of antiseptic.

This would be only a brief visit with the dog. The technician would return Fred to his enclosure in the hospital, after the veterinarian visited them to explain yesterday's procedure and postoperative care.

"Hello, Rosemary," Dr. Greene said, the robust veterinarian entering the room through the door that opened to the clinic lab area. He held two large X-rays.

"Hi, Dr. Greene."

The doctor was dressed in a white lab coat, with buttons that fastened over his protruding stomach. He wore thick, black glasses. "How's the shelter doing?" he asked.

"Good," Rosemary said. She trusted this older veterinarian. He had treated the animals at her shelter for the last two years.

"This little guy sure is lucky to have found you!" the doctor said.

"I am just thankful I was at the right place at the right time, and I found him."

"Are you keeping him for yourself? I know you don't have a dog."

"Yes, I'm keeping the little guy," Rosemary said, smiling. "I already named him Fred."

The doctor chuckled. "Well, Fred sure is cute, and that's a cute name."

"Dr. Greene," Rosemary said, "this is my friend, Lucas." She transferred her glance between the two men.

"Hello, Lucas. Nice to meet you," Dr. Greene said. He shifted the X-rays to his left hand and reached out his right to Lucas. "Always nice to meet a friend of Rosemary's."

"Nice to meet you, Dr. Greene," Lucas returned, as they shook hands.

"Let's take a look at these," the doctor said. He lifted one x-ray up to the lightbox.

Lucas now reached for Rosemary's hand. He held her palm against his, securing his hold by lacing his fingers through hers. They rested their cupped hands on the bench between them. Her other hand gently petted the length of the pup's back. A natural smile formed, pulling up the sides of her mouth. She felt warm and safe inside.

The doctor cleared his throat, as he fastened the black X-ray to the wall-mounted lightbox with the top clip. He turned and looked at Lucas. "We're still old-fashioned here," the doctor said, and chuckled; "we have *those* computers, but I find this way easier than us all hunching over a little computer screen."

Lucas chuckled, then said, "I prefer old-fashioned, Doctor."

Dr. Greene turned on the light switch to the viewing area, and shapes were backlit on the black film.

"This was his right front leg before the operation," Dr. Greene said, tracing the splintered, crooked, slender shape with his index finger. He then exchanged that x-ray for the other. "This is his leg after the operation." He traced a straight, slender shape. "This is the radius. You can see the nuts and bolts, so to speak," he lightheartedly said, outlining the obvious new hardware inside the dog's leg.

Dr. Greene heavily exhaled through his nose, as he turned from the x-ray to Rosemary. "We call what he had a 'closed' fracture, because the skin above the broken bone was still intact; no bone was exposed. His surgery went well last night. Dr. Pillsbury did the surgery – she is the best surgeon on staff; she did a great job. Dr. Pillsbury had to repair the bone with pins, plates and screws, which internally set and stabilized the fractured bone. We have him on antibiotics and pain medication.

"We did, of course, blood work before the surgery, and found no underlying medical condition, although he was slightly anemic – likely partly due to his blood loss from injury, but also because he had a bad case of fleas. We bandaged the mild lesion on his left leg and gave him flea medicine. He also got intravenous fluids before and after surgery, for dehydration; he probably hadn't had access to fresh water for a while. Luckily, he didn't have any internal bleeding or any damage to organs."

He looked down at Fred and pointed to the dog's left front leg. "You can probably change the dressing yourself, but you know you can always bring him back in, a couple of days after his release, to have a tech do it."

Rosemary glanced over at Lucas, who sat there intently watching and listening to the vet. He still held her hand.

"You poor little guy. What an awful ordeal this guy went through," Dr. Greene said, looking down at the Chihuahua. "I understand you witnessed this little guy being thrown from a vehicle, Rosemary?" he asked, now looking at her.

"Yes. It was the worst thing I've ever witnessed."

"Well, he's in good hands now." The doctor's chest rose as he inhaled a deep breath, and it fell as he exhaled heavily through his nose. "Did you hear the story of this little guy?"

"Story?" Rosemary asked.

"Karen called the police after the surgery. They wanted to know the extent of the dog's injuries, for the animal abuse charge. They caught the man who did this; he will serve time. The man was jailed the moment they got him – which was last night, of course. He had several warrants, and was driving while high on street drugs. He had stolen his ex-girlfriend's car."

"Oh, my gosh," Rosemary said.

She and Lucifer listened intently, as Dr. Greene leaned his back against the exam table. "The dog had been this man's mother's pet," he continued. "The mother died a few weeks ago, and apparently the man didn't want the dog. That S.O.B.!" He quickly centered his focus on Rosemary. "Excuse my language."

"I agree," she said.

"Anyone who would do something like that to a defenseless animal deserves jail," the doctor said. "Why didn't he take the dog to your shelter, if he didn't want it?"

"You are right, Dr. Greene: he deserves a stiff jail sentence," Lucas said.

"Yes," Dr. Greene agreed.

"Could this office have given out any information on Rosemary to anyone? Her name? Her address? Her phone?" Lucas asked.

Rosemary watched the doctor's eyebrows arch at the questions. Was he irritated by them?

"No," the doctor said. "You mean for the police report?"

"Yes. Or would any information be given out, regarding Rosemary, to anyone who might have called with questions about the incident?" Lucifer asked.

"No, of course not."

"We just can't believe all of this," Rosemary quickly interjected.

She released Lucas's hand and stood there, holding the dog. "Thank you so much, Dr. Greene, for all of your care. And the staff's." She didn't look at Lucas, but peripherally saw that he still sat. "When can I take him home?" she asked the doctor, looking down at the dog.

"Probably tomorrow," Dr. Greene said. "He's been stable, and he did eat a little for us today. We'll continue to monitor him overnight. Everything will mend with time. You saved his life," he told Rosemary. "Enjoy the little guy."

"I will."

"I'll send a technician to come get him." The doctor petted the dog, then exited the room.

When the door was shut, Rosemary turned to give Lucas an irritated expression. She squeezed her eyebrows together, as tightly as she could, as she looked down at him.

He looked up at her, his expression innocent. *"What?"* he began. "I have to ask and make sure—"

The door opened. The technician came in and took the dog from Rosemary's arms.

"Any questions?" the young girl said.

"Should I use a lifting harness or sling to help him to stand?" Rosemary asked.

"Sure, you could try one. Try a pet store or online store. For this little guy, you could try using a folded towel, too.

"When you take him home, the tech will go over all medications and home care with you, and set up the follow-up appointment. He'll also need to have follow-up x-rays, to make sure the break is stabilized and healing."

"Sorry I'm late!" Rosemary called to Sharon, as she opened the side door to the dog room, at the shelter. "I was at Wolfe Animal Hospital, checking on Fred." Lucas walked into the room beside Rosemary.

Sharon had been sweeping a front pen and halted the broom, amid a brush.

"Look who's back," Rosemary said.

"What...?" Sharon's face seemed to flatten with no expression, then brighten with surprise. Her eyes seemed to light up as she smiled.

"We've missed you, Lucas," she said. "Rosemary didn't tell me you were back." Sharon directed a mock scowl at her best friend.

"I'm just as surprised as you," Rosemary returned. "He got back early."

"I'm glad I'm back," Lucas said. "I've missed Chuck only second to you both. I have to go see him now."

"Oh," Sharon chirped, "Rosemary said you had some business to take care of – in California?" She squinted.

"Yes. I finished my project, and this town seemed to beckon me," he said.

"Or *someone* seemed to beckon you?" Sharon returned, with a wink aimed at Rosemary.

"Okay," Rosemary interjected.

Lucas headed to Chuck, walking past the women as they talked.

"How is Fred doing, after his operation?" Sharon asked Rosemary.

"He is doing well."

"Rose," Sharon whispered, after he had left them, "Lucas really likes you. He came back here for you, you know. You need to be honest with him if you're not ready for a relationship. He is so serious about his feelings for you. But I don't think you are as serious about him, and you need to tell him."

Why did Sharon have the impression Rosemary wasn't as serious about her relationship with Lucas as he was about her? Maybe because Rosemary felt a need to protect Lucas's secrets, which disallowed full disclosure of her attraction to him.

Sharon resumed sweeping, and Rosemary walked to Chuck's pen. She stood behind Lucas.

Chuck had risen from his mattress and stood in front of the gate, as Lucas opened the door. A hum seemed to vibrate from the dog's long nose; Rosemary heard that same sound come from the pens when Lucas had first spoken today, greeting Sharon. It had been unclear which dog had responded in that manner, because Rosemary had never before heard that unique whimper.

"I've never heard Chuck do that before," she told Lucas. Lucas smiled back at her.

As he now closed the pen door behind him, the dog seemed to skip on its two front legs, shifting its weight from right to left repeatedly.

Lucas directly descended to his knees. Level with Chuck, Lucas wrapped his arms snugly around him, and held the back of the dog's head against his neck in a hug. Chuck continued to moan with happiness. A long whine was unleashed, as the dog pushed its nose upward and closer. Rosemary could see from a side view that Lucas's eyes were pressed shut, as the dog rested his brown, furry chin on Lucas's shoulder and pulled tightly against his neck. Lucas wiped his moistened face.

Pressure built up in Rosemary's own eyes, and she wiped the dampness from them. A small smile naturally formed across her face. Chuck had developed closeness with a human!

It was an intimate reunion between the man and dog, and Rosemary wanted to give them privacy, so she turned and walked away. She had arrived late this morning, and needed to tend to her work.

Soon after she began her duties, Lucas followed suit, cleaning cat cages alongside her. She then moved to the cat sanctuary, while he finished the enclosures. Rosemary now began sweeping the cat sanctuary, while Lucas swept the lobby floor. The morning chores were easily accomplished, in little time. Lucas's help lightened the workload.

She was in a separate room from him. Only a door with a long window separated them, but it was *some* breathing room. A little private time was nice; it had allowed her to focus only on the repetitive actions of sweeping the floor. Lucas had kept close to Rosemary today. He had told her he wouldn't leave her side until Koratz had been neutralized. But the man *was* in jail.

Rosemary finished sweeping, and now mopped the sanctuary. The slight, clean bleach scent caused a couple of cats to sneeze.

"Bless you!" Rosemary said to each one.

Rosemary had completed filling a large garbage bag, after cleaning litter boxes and sweeping inside the sanctuary; it now was set against the closed door. Done with the room, she now grabbed hold of the heavy, black bag and opened the door to the lobby. Her body tilted to one side, as she made her way to the front door of the shelter. It was still locked to the public, but Rosemary would temporarily open it, to take out the garbage to the bin. She set the large garbage bag on the floor, leaning it against the wall, then turned the latch to unlock the deadbolt.

A large hand covered the top of hers.

"Rose Petal," the deep voice called, from just behind her. She could feel his breath moving through the side of her hair. Her eyelids closed, as she exhaled loudly through her nose.

"This is serious," Lucas's gruff but calm voice said. "It is why I am here. Please don't go outside by yourself."

She felt the warmth of his skin, as he cupped the back of her hand and laced his fingers between hers. He determinedly lowered her hand.

Rosemary turned around and, just as determinedly, looked into Lucas's dark eyes. "I am safe now. Koratz is in jail," she quietly, but tenaciously, said. Her brows pulled tightly together. "You know it was

Koratz who threatened me, and he's in jail."

"Yes, but I have to neutralize his harmful mindset." He then pulled his brows tight, to narrow his focus on her. "I am not taking any chances when it comes to your safety. I won't feel that you are completely safe until I am soul to soul with him, and have defused his anger against you." Lucas shook his head, then said: "I thought I sensed another person in the car with him."

"I am not going to stop living my life. I have to walk dogs!"

"I will follow behind you."

The ceiling came into view, as her eyes rolled upward in frustration.

Lucas's strong lips curved in a smile. His black eyes appeared to dance with mischievous pleasure.

"It will only be for a day or two," he growled, sexily. "I will walk a dog at the same time as you, and I will be a good distance behind you, if you prefer."

Rosemary's vision narrowed, as her face scrunched. "So, you'll be the overprotective bodyguard who lurks behind me, staring at my backside?"

Lucas only held his smile, with those strong lips, his black eyes matching her stare. "There are benefits to my job," he growled.

Rosemary rolled her eyes again.

"Okay," she breathed out, "I am going to walk Lucy now."

Lucas hauled the garbage bag to the dumpster, then joined Rosemary in the dog room.

Rosemary was kneeling beside Lucy, as he walked toward Chuck's pen. She fitted the collar around the little dog's neck.

"Has Lucy got a home?" Lucas asked.

She followed his gaze to the top of Lucy's enclosure, where a red *"Adopted"* sign was slipped inside the clear plastic binder that contained the presentation page.

"Yes! Her new family is taking her tonight. She will make the perfect, sweet lapdog. A cuddle bunny." A little moisture formed in Rosemary's eyes. "This will be our last walk." As she said those words, her voice seemed to crack with dryness. Then she and Lucy exited the pen, for the last time together.

Meeting at the side door, the four headed toward town, for an afternoon walk. Lucas and Chuck followed Rosemary and Lucy at a distance.

How long had a smile been fixed on her face? Her jawline and cheekbones felt loose, in an easy grin. Rosemary had not consciously formed the smile.

Her whole body relaxed in the sunlight and easy breezes. Wind pushed her hair behind her, as she now ran on the soft, grassy earth alongside Lula May. She now purposely pulled the corners of her mouth up further.

Colorful houses swirled by, in her peripheral vision, as her feet met the strip of grass next to the sidewalk that led to town.

Lucas and his dog, Jerry Lee, followed far behind them. Rosemary hadn't looked back since she passed the dirt road. This would be Rosemary's and Lucas's last dog walk of the day.

It had been stressful, being back at work the first day after learning of Koratz. Lucas had acted as if her shadow. Running with Lula felt like a sweet escape.

When Rosemary and Lula May reached the post office, at the edge of town, Rosemary slowed their pace to a fast walk.

Good smells wafted from the ice cream shop, as they passed its opened door. An adult held open the entryway for a child, who passed through holding a waffle cone filled with chocolate ice cream. Rosemary now approached the flower shop, where she headed toward the bench. Lula would appreciate a break. As Rosemary took a seat, she looked down the sidewalk and saw Lucas and his dog drawing near.

Jerry Lee panted as Lucas slowed the gait. Rosemary giggled quietly. It looked as though Lucas panted a little himself; he still breathed heavily as he now took a seat beside Rosemary. Jerry Lee's tongue curled around the top of his long nose and licked drool from his upper lip. He lay down on the grass in front of the bench.

Rosemary slid her hand along the soft fur of Lula's back, as the dog sat beside her on the end of the bench. "Lie down, pumpkin," she told the dog.

Lucas looked at Rosemary. His face was flushed. Perspiration speckled his temples. It was a warm day, so Rosemary's shirt felt damp on her skin, but her body had recovered quickly from running; she was used to running daily with the bigger dogs, especially Lula.

"That was some good exercise," Lucas said. "You know, my body isn't up to par just yet. We did our best to keep up with you. We ran a little, too," he said, gazing down at Jerry Lee. "I think good old Jerry Lee slowed us down a bit," Lucas teased.

Rosemary giggled. "Ha!"

Lucas pulled a thick strap from his shoulder and carefully

unscrewed the attached, round, plastic container. He held it level, but water splashed as he removed the lid and set the water carafe on the ground. Jerry Lee took a few gulps from the portable bowl, then Lula May.

"It is late morning and Samantha is still not at work," Lucas said, nodding toward the end of the street. "Is that cat still asleep on your pillow?" The mock seriousness in his tone would have convinced a passerby.

A hearty chuckle seemed to rise from Rosemary's chest and release from her mouth on its own, without any direction from her brain. She felt her face relax, as the edge of her mouth pulled up in another easy smile. There was an inexplicable familiarity between them. "Oh, my gosh, that cat is lazy! No work at all. The shop looks dark and empty!"

Rosemary closed her eyes and felt the air on her cheeks, smelling it through her nostrils. When she opened her eyes, she turned to look at Lucas. Her top teeth flattened her bottom lip, as she considered asking him a question. She straightened her back along the boards of the bench.

"What is Hell like?" she asked, as casually as she could manage. A tinge of fear for his answer made her want to look away, but her head remained turned toward him, as though stuck in that position.

He rested his forearms on his thighs and leaned toward her. "Rosemary, is this something you really want to know?"

She didn't answer. She held his gaze, but the silence informed her there would be no reply until she verbally confirmed her interest.

She closed her eyes again and inhaled, deeply. Upon opening her eyes, she unflinchingly looked into his dark pupils. "Yes, I'd like to know," she said.

He held her attentive gaze. "Hell is a place of healing," he began. "It is a castle; the castle provides a home for troubled souls. A soul chooses to descend to Hell because of embedded negative emotions that soul experienced during his human lifetime. Detoxification takes place in Hell, and each soul is appointed a counselor.

"The law of nature won't allow negative energy into the afterlife, which is what humans call 'Heaven'. Like a magnet, all energies are pulled to positive or negative. Positive energies are pulled to the afterlife and negative energies are pulled to Hell. Once a soul is healed and once again connected to the loving energy, it can move on to the afterlife."

He exhaled a heavy breath and lowered his eyes. "Unfortunately, some souls are wounded so badly..." He solemnly shook his head.

Lucas looked back into her eyes. "I never give up trying to help a negative energy attract love, by letting go of hate," he assured. "When the negativity is lifted from the core, the soul will no longer be drawn to Hell. It will become buoyant... light. Each and every soul has a choice to free itself from Hell, by learning to reconnect with oneness, the flow of loving energy."

"Have you personally nurtured and healed a soul, and helped it return to the afterlife? Do you remember a specific soul that you helped?" she asked.

"I remember every soul that we've cared for in the castle. I personally greet each new arrival. I also help choose a counselor for each new arrival. I learn each soul's hardships, in its past human life. I incorporate meditation and self-healing classes, and group counseling sessions. I watch each soul progress and heal, then move on. It is my greatest joy to see *love* return to a depressed soul. The energy field of that soul becomes buoyant, like a kite. The color of the aura brightens. It is a joyous occasion for me to witness."

"That is amazing work that you do. You heal."

"It is not work. It is compassion. Like what you do, Rose Petal."

"What does Hell look like?" she asked.

"It is everything the human mind can imagine – in fact, *human thought* created Hell. I think most humans want a place for redemption, not punishment. In reality, Hell is a place of love. But, if a soul views himself as ugly, he will view Hell as ugly, just as he viewed Earth as ugly. No matter where a negative soul dwells – in a human body or in Hell – negativity will draw more negativity.

"When a soul begins to heal herself, and sees herself more clearly, as a loving being, then Hell becomes a counseling center, church, library and study. Hell has all the beauty a soul is *willing* to *see*. When one sees himself as beautiful, then he will have the ability to see everything as beautiful."

"How do you see Hell?" she asked.

"I see the moon, stars, sun and canyons. I see the beautiful architecture of the castle. I see the rich hues inside the castle. I see the waterfalls, sculptures, art, classrooms, libraries, places of worship and luxurious meditation rooms. There are educators, clergy, counselors and inspirational speakers; all those generous beings volunteer their knowledge."

"So, if a human dies and the soul leaves Earth with *any* negative emotion, it goes to Hell?" she asked.

291

"No," he replied, "I'm not talking about a soul that has a couple of negative emotions every now and then; I'm talking about a soul that is *consumed* with negativity. Total consumption."

"Do you believe in evil? Can a human be evil? Like Koratz?" Rosemary asked. Her eyes lowered and she inhaled a shaky breath through her nose. "Are there demons?" Rosemary breathed in sharply, as she attempted a smooth breath.

She watched a half-smile form on Lucas's face.

"I can honestly say that I don't know the answer to the last part of your question," he said. "I've never seen a demon, because my energy is positive and I don't attract demons to me. Hell does not attract demons because it is a place of healing, not evil.

"I do believe that there is evil. Evil is caused by a soul that is unaligned with oneness, the flow of loving energy. Loving energy flows freely and abundantly through every living thing, every being, every cell... everything. If a soul is disconnected from that wealth, it can create evil."

Rosemary looked toward him, but broke her glance periodically, for reprieve. He held his gaze directly on her. She could sense that he watched for a signal to end this conversation when it became too overwhelming for her.

"A human is not innately evil," he continued. "A man can *create* evil, when he is disconnected from the loving energy, *oneness*. The loving energy 'oneness' is what humans call 'God'."

"Why does a human disconnect from the loving energy, God?" she asked.

"Such turmoil can occur when a human forgets he has a soul. He forgets he is not just skin, blood and bones. The soul has great experience and knowledge, but the human mind can teach the soul new things. The human mind can also block the connection to a soul that is always free-flowing. A baby is a soul newly integrated into human life. It is innocent and excited about life, but also vulnerable to danger, at the hands of unaligned parents and society.

"The soul always knows the truth. Love and oneness is everyone's connection. Once human, if not properly nurtured, the human brain can become unaligned with that love and oneness. Evil originates when a particular society, specific family, or forgetfulness of the loving energy corrupts a human mind and, therefore, a soul. If spiritual growth and connection are stunted when a soul occupies a human body, that *soul* will be neglected. One's inner voice or light is her soul. When the inner light is quieted, negative experiences can occur because human emotions of fear and anger are likely to take over. Any type of negative emotion can draw any type of negative circumstance into a human's life.

"That's how evil is created. If a human relies only on his negative emotions, and not his inner light – a fear of minorities, for example – it will cause that human to create a world of fear-based evil. That's how hate crimes originate."

He studied her gaze. "This is all very intense. We should take a break from this discussion."

"I'm okay." She pulled her bottom lip under her front teeth.

"I do understand what you're saying," she began. "I do believe that most evil is created by unaligned souls... negative humans, but I also think that *sometimes* negative things can happen because of a cosmic upset. Some things we can't understand. Illogical, mysterious things might occur because the stars become out of alignment, so to speak."

Her lips puckered as she searched for the right words. There were none. "Sometimes, I believe there are freaks of nature."

She looked Lucas's way and scrunched her face. "One time, we had this cat at the shelter. We named her Bandit, because she was white with black circles around her eyes. She was pregnant when we took her in. She seemed happy in her private room, and she gave birth to four kittens. It was a normal delivery; everything looked okay; the kittens looked healthy; the mama cat looked healthy; she was nursing the kittens. We had Dr. Greene check everyone out, and mama and babies were kept in the private room. We left the shelter for the night, and when we came back in the morning, the kittens were gone."

Lucas's eyes were glued to her face. "What happened?" he asked.

"Mama must have... eaten her newborns."

Lucas's lower jaw actually dropped, opening his closed mouth. "What happened to the mama cat?" he asked.

"Bandit was okay. We waited a few days, then got her spayed. She had always been very loving toward us, and we did find her a good home; a couple fell in love with her. They heard her whole story: a neighbor had witnessed poor Bandit being tossed in the air between two big dogs; the neighbor intervened and brought the traumatized cat to our shelter. Maybe that incident caused internal injuries to her babies.

"Sometimes bad things happen, and we can't explain them," she continued. "What was it that caused Bandit to do that? Maybe the kittens *were* injured, and only she knew? Maybe Bandit was distressed to deliver her kittens in the shelter, even though she had been with us for a month before? Maybe her brain just misfired? I do agree with you that negative things do happen as a result of negative thoughts, and negative things can happen when a person is out of alignment with their soul. But, once in a blue moon, I think unexplainable things happen for no good reason."

He pulled his brows tight. "Like, the full moon's gravitational pull has an effect on a person's emotions?" he asked.

"Yes. Also, I think that, when bad things happen, it's *how* one reacts to them that defines that person's character."

"I've noticed that the way *you* react to anything is with love," he said. "You realize that each of your actions makes an impact on the world." His dark eyes focused on her. "I've seen you pick up garbage from the sidewalk when you walk dogs; that action impacts the world with love. I've seen you help a turtle across the busy road, and a spider out of harm's way."

"And *you* fill overdue parking meters," she said, smiling.

Her mouth formed a pucker, as she lightly nibbled on the inside of her cheek. "What are you really going to do to Koratz?"

He closed his eyes and let out a slow breath, then opened them. "Don't worry, I will not hurt Koratz. I will communicate with him on a soul level. We will come to an agreement."

"Like you did with Mark?" she asked.

"Yes. Telepathically, I will ingrain exactness. It will be embedded into his being that harming you in any way is not an option. Sometimes the human mind is too rigid to comprehend, but the soul always understands."

"Let's go to the bridge," Rosemary suggested.

295

"Sure." Lucas's tone was relaxed.

They each stood up, Lucifer more slowly, due to his sore muscles.

It seemed that a heavy weight had nearly crushed Rosemary. Their conversation had brought up feelings of a hurtful subject, and it felt as though a hundred-pound dumbbell rested on top of her head and fell through her, to her feet. Her heartbeat felt as though it thumped hard in her chest. She was about to confess a chilling secret.

Why?

Maybe she should leave it settled inside the safe confines of her own awareness. The secret had never before left her lips – except under entrustment of her best friend.

She trusted that Lucas would sympathize with her guilt. He surely wouldn't judge her.

They casually walked, side by side, with each dog on the outside of them. The sun shone and warmed them, as they passed the gravel lot of the park. Walking up the stairs to the bridge, Rosemary felt her heart thud. Her breaths came short and fast.

"What is it, Rose Petal?" Lucas asked, concernedly looking at her. His arm draped around her back as they stood beside one another.

She looked down into the clear water. Stones and sand were the bed for the small waterfall at the crown of the stream. Rosemary tightened her grip on the top of the leash and she looked down at Lula. The dog seemed to smile up at her, and its fluffy tail calmly shifted positions across the planks. The tightness in Rosemary's fingers was alleviated, as she loosened her grip on the lead.

"I had a miscarriage," she said, while looking into the water. "When I found out I was pregnant, I wasn't happy; I didn't want the baby." She still didn't look at Lucas, but she sensed his eyes upon her. "Will I go to Hell?"

His arm, still around her, hugged her back tighter. "Sweetheart..." he said, "of course not."

"But..." she turned to him now; there was gentleness in his eyes, "I considered..." she couldn't bear to finish her thought out loud. "I didn't want a baby at that particular time in my life. I didn't wish the baby any harm... I was just... terrified. My life was a complete mess at the time. I was in an abusive relationship... I had no money coming in..."

"You did nothing from a place of hate. Maybe you had fearful thoughts; maybe you hadn't thought yourself ready to raise a child – those were thoughts of fear, not hate."

Still looking into his eyes, there was no look of shock in his expression, only attentiveness. Rosemary backed away, breaking his embrace.

"But fear is a negative emotion," she quietly said.

"Fear is a *human* emotion, sweetheart." His eyes held sincerity, as his forehead creased deeper. "I never said a human shouldn't experience negative emotion – being observant of one's negative emotions is mature and responsible – it's just best not to let negativity *consume* a life. When a human pays attention to her emotions, and consciously decides to deal with a negative emotion maturely, that is healthy. Maybe she will decide to sit and cry for a day, a week, a month, with the sadness? Then maybe she will ask for help from a counselor or friend? Then maybe she will focus on the positive things in her life, more than the negative? Human life should be about experiencing, learning, growing, forgiving... loving."

Rosemary moved her eyes from his again, as moisture built in them. "It happened with Mark. Maybe I stayed with him after because I felt I didn't deserve better."

"You deserve everything good, Rose Petal."

"I can't have children now; they found cysts and... there were... complications. I would have liked to have had children in the future, but now I can't." A small smile eased the tightness of her mouth. "I wanted *that* baby with *another* man – a man who loved me and would be a good father. I wish that baby could come back to me."

"I'm sorry." Lucas's full face looked at her; she saw it in her peripheral vision. "Forgiveness is a gift you give to yourself and, in turn, others. You need to forgive yourself, in order to continue accomplishing good deeds. Only with an open heart can you fully participate in life. It wouldn't be fair to those you care for, if you weren't wholeheartedly available."

She slowly moved her eyes back to his. "Thank you for listening. I don't know why I told you... that. I feel I can tell you anything."

She took in a deep breath, through her nose. "Of course, Sharon knew about the miscarriage, but I never confessed my true, deepest feelings about it to her. I thought maybe I was being punished for not being happy when I first found out."

Lucas brought his hand to the side of her face and touched the edge of her chin. He feathered his fingers through the side of her hair, then reached for her left hand. She gripped the leash with her right hand, and Lucas now held her left.

"Please don't feel that you are being punished for something you did wrong," he said. "God does not operate like that. God only loves. God does not punish. God does not forgive; God doesn't have to forgive, because God never gets angry. God is a constant, ever-flowing, loving energy. That is all."

"I was brought up to believe that God looks down at us, protects us, loves us, but also judges us. My mom was spiritual, but I also went to church as a child."

"God does protect you and love you – He is a combination of all the goodness watching over you – but He never judges. And He doesn't look down at you. He is inside of you and all around you, every second. He is all goodness, every truth and every piece of love. A part of God is your guardian angels, loved ones, spirit guides, animal guides, and everything else that is loving energy. This loving energy is always with you, watching over you, guiding you and loving you."

"Thank you, Lucas." Her cheeks felt a trickle of wetness, from the accumulated moisture in her eyes. She released his hand and wiped her face.

There had been a relief with her confession to him, and comfort from his words. Though, she still couldn't help but wonder if he now thought her less respectable.

His eyes darkened with warmth, as they continued to hold onto hers. "You are the most loving soul.

"It is very brave for any soul to enter into a human body; a soul is vulnerable inside a human body. When a soul enters into a human, it agrees to take the risk of being vulnerable, because humans make mistakes. The human mind is not always rational; a human mind is swayed by emotions. Fear, for example, can override a soul's intuitiveness. Humans need to allow for leniency. Human life is multifaceted, and a clear answer is not always available at the time one needs it. In hindsight, mistakes can be very painful.

"Forgiveness will strengthen the soul. Great knowledge is gained from personal mistakes. Empathy, in turn, is instilled for others who falter. It is through the act of forgiveness that one strengthens her soul. A soul enters a human body to strengthen itself, become more enlightened, and to experience joy from having learned these lessons of forgiveness.

"Remember, mistakes we learn from are precious. A soul enters a human body fully aware that mistakes will be made. It does this to strengthen its core with grace, acceptance and love. Once forgiveness is an integral part of a human's core, pure joy can be a part of every experience. Being human means you get to experience all emotions, sensations and events. You figure out what you like most and then attract more of that into your life."

He then brought his hand toward her chin and dipped it downward. Slowly, he brought his lips close to her forehead. Softness touched her skin, as he kissed her there. She gently closed her eyes.

"Sweetheart, you are the sweetest soul I have ever known," his husky voice breathed, just above her head.

Her mouth relaxed with another small smile, which felt as if it arose naturally on her face. She let out a gush of air, from her mouth and nose.

Lucas returned the crook of his arm around her back, as they watched the water below the bridge.

300

*

It was a quiet ride home from work; Lucas must have sensed Rosemary's need for silence. She had acquired a headache near the end of the day.

Still absorbing all of the information, and events over the last forty-eight hours, her physical body required solitude and rest. Maybe if she locked herself in a still room for the night, her anxiety would subside. Her stomach gargled and ached with inflammation, and her hands and feet seemed to vibrate with nervousness.

Arriving home, Rosemary and Lucas made sandwiches, and mindlessly watched a program on television. She then excused herself to her bedroom.

She now lay in her bed with Samantha.

The bedside lamp brightened the area with security and the door was locked – though she knew this offered a false sense of protection against Lucas.

Lucifer, her rational brain corrected, in a harsh whisper.

It seemed that she were floating among many different emotions for him: love, trust, fear, anger... A wet trail of tears slipped down her face, to the hollow of her throat.

Could everything about Lucas be true? Was he really the devil?

She was Helen's great-great-great-granddaughter... Would Helen be better prepared than herself to deal with the devil? Rosemary called on the strong woman to impart strength her way.

Tomorrow morning, she would have Fred as a pleasant distraction. Hopefully, she would be able to keep her mind occupied with other things, until Lucas left this town. This Earth. Once he was gone, she could collapse in her home and lose all control of her contained emotions and physical tension. Everything would eventually return to normal.

But, a startling and persistent truth resided deep in her soul…

She did not want Lucas to leave.

Chapter 14

Rosemary's Orange Aura

It felt as though Rosemary had experienced a deep sleep last night, during her five hours of unconsciousness. She woke to feel rested, as though she had slept for a full eight hours.

Having lingered in bed upon waking, she mentally prepared for the day. It would be the day she introduced a new pet into the home. Caring for Fred would consume most of her time, and she hoped that Samantha would be tolerant of him.

Rosemary cuddled with Samantha, as she waited for the clock to reach 6:30 a.m., at which time she rose to dress and prepare a pot of coffee. Normally she would have set the alarm for eight a.m., but had to rearrange her schedule, to pick up Fred from the hospital.

When she opened her bedroom door, dressed in work clothes, Samantha ran ahead of her and jumped on top of the couch.

Lucas was seated on the sofa. He greeted the cat with an affectionate bump of his forehead, when Samantha offered the top of her head. Lucas had slept on the living-room couch last night, though Rosemary had offered him a bedroom upstairs.

She noticed the aroma of coffee the moment she stepped outside her room. When she walked into the kitchen, Lucas accompanied her and poured her a mug of the fresh brew.

Rosemary filled a Thermos with more coffee, after consuming her first cup, then drove to the veterinary hospital.

She found herself grateful that Lucas now sat by her side, as they waited for the technician to bring Fred into the examination room. They sat close on the small bench. The room was quiet. An empty, clean table was fastened to the wall, just in front of their view.

Rosemary thought to herself, as they waited, that her father's illness and passing had been experiences she had dealt with mostly alone; Mark had given no emotional support. Sharon had offered her friendship, but Rosemary had felt isolated in the most intimate ways. In her bed at night, she had cried. At the hospital, her father's bedside had been an intimidating setting, but he had depended on her visits. She had experienced anxiety as she had driven, unaccompanied, back and forth to the hospital.

She had now grown weary of dealing with daunting circumstances by herself. Any moment now, the technician was about to come into the room and explain post-operative care. It was a relief to have Lucas listen, ask questions and be concerned alongside her. His presence was as comforting as a partner's would be. Rosemary knew that he cared about the dog as much as herself; he had already demonstrated his love for all animals.

Her relationship with Lucas felt so intimate. She trusted him. He had always shown concern for her well-being, understood her true nature and respected her uniqueness. He understood her in ways no one else ever had. There was almost an obsessive quality in how she rethought her misjudgments, and he always directed her contemplation toward the positive. She even felt as though he had known and loved her mother and father, because he showed such interest in them. Unlike anyone else, he recognized her bond to them, and that her deep-rooted beliefs and customs were derived from them. He continually aided her through her grief, by offering objective points of view. He reminded her that Frank's love for his daughter was what had guided his concerns for her.

Rosemary loved Lucas.

Oh, my god.

This relationship with Lucas would not endure. He was the devil! He would be returning to Hell. These were all bizarre realities.

The devil! Hell!

She *loved* the devil. She had a *relationship* with the devil.

No! she hollered, inside her own head. It was a man named Lucas who now sat by her side. *Lucas's* calm demeanor eased her anxiety. *Lucas's* attentiveness made her feel safe.

Rosemary had promised herself to be bold. She looked for Lucas's hands: they were folded in his lap. She reached for his left hand and laced her fingers through his. She felt no resistance from him.

They sat in quietness, waiting. Rosemary was *happily* waiting.

The door in front of Rosemary opened, as she expectantly stared at it. A technician in blue scrubs walked into the room. She cradled Fred in a blanket, and also held a small bag.

"Hello," the woman said. "We will miss Fred here, but we are happy he has recovered so quickly." She bent forward and handed the dog to Rosemary.

Rosemary was very conscious of having to release Lucas's hand.

The technician then set the small, white paper bag on the examination table. "All of Fred's medicines are in here," she said. She opened the bag and pulled a pill container from it. "These are appetite stimulants: you give one tablet every three days."

She pulled a thin syringe from the bag. "These are pre-filled with pain medicine. There are five of these. You give him one a day, orally. This tastes bad, so try to aim the medicine on the side of his mouth, past his tastebuds."

"Okay," Rosemary said. "If he's eating okay, I can discontinue the appetite stimulants?" She stated it as a question.

"Yes." The technician leaned her back against the sink, near the front of the room. "Fred has had an antibiotic injection that will last two weeks, so no oral antibiotics are needed."

"Great."

It felt as though sweet, soothing energy passed through Rosemary's body. The thigh of her right leg felt warm through her jeans; Lucas had placed his hand there. A small smile relaxed her face. He gently squeezed her thigh, then rubbed the inside of his hand along the length of it.

"You'll do good, Rose Petal," he said. "Fred's a lucky guy."

Rosemary turned toward Lucas and saw him smile at her. The easiness of his facial expression calmed her even more. "I hope he lets me tend to him. I hope he learns to trust me."

"There is not an animal on Earth that would not fall in love with you, Rose Petal."

His overt affection caused her to feel slightly awkward, but it also gave her a feeling of security. She glanced over at the technician. "Do I change his leg dressing?"

"We will do that in three or four days. They'll make your checkup appointment for you at the desk."

"Okay." She mentally searched her internal checklist; "I guess that's all my questions."

"Call us if you think of any more," the woman said. "My name is Heidi – ask for me or Dr. Greene."

"Thank you."

Rosemary placed Fred in the crate she had brought with her.

The woman left the room and the three of them – Rosemary, Fred and Lucas – headed outside after setting up the checkup, as if a little family.

Lucas carried the crate into the shelter. He set it on the floor, next to the chair behind Rosemary's desk. Rosemary followed him.

"I have a favor to ask you," she said.

"Of course. Anything, Rose Petal."

"Would you be willing to sit with Fred this morning, while I do chores? I'd hate to leave him all alone in a strange place. He'll need bathroom breaks, and food and water breaks."

"Of course! I'd be happy to do that, Rose Petal. But why don't *you* spend time with your new dog, while *I* do the chores?"

She pulled in her bottom lip, underneath her top teeth. His answer pleased her. "You'd do that for me?"

Lucas had been bent over, looking at Fred through the crate's door. He now stood and turned toward her. "Of course. I've grown to love the shelter and doing chores here. I like spending time with the animals; I've missed them." He smiled and his black eyes seemed to shine at her. "It'll be good for you and Fred to spend time together."

She stepped in front of Lucas and reached her arms around his shoulders. Then she hugged him. "Thank you," she said.

It felt good that he was receptive and tightened his arms around her lower back. His breath warmed her neck and, as his chest pressed against her, she felt his heartbeat quicken. Were his eyes closed, along with hers? Was it desire?

The sound of the side door opening was followed by energetic barking, and Lucas released his hold.

Sharon began cleaning her section and Lucas his.

It was quiet. The front of the building was free of any work-related noise; there was only an occasional bark from the back dog-room. Lucas would eventually begin sweeping and mopping the entire building, after cleaning cages and the cat sanctuary. For now, Rosemary was relieved to have this private time with her new dog.

She lowered to the plush rug and sat beside his crate. The raised platform was bordered by a paneled wall that concealed the two workstations. They were snug in the private cubbyhole. She opened the door to the crate and reached inside, to pet Fred. He moved his head backward, at the movement of her hand reaching toward him. She untied the string of the protective collar and removed it from around his neck; as long as he was being watched and discouraged from licking his bandages, the riddance of the restraining collar would allow comfort. He tentatively stretched his front legs, as his half-closed eyelids opened wide. A pink tongue curled over the top of his mouth.

"Are you thirsty, Fred?" Rosemary asked.

She set the water and food bowls at the opening of the crate. The dog tried to shift his weight to his wrapped front paws, so Rosemary lifted the water bowl to his mouth and he took a couple of drinks. The dog's little body trembled, as he then turned his head from the bowl.

Rosemary moved the dishes and rounded her body, to lie on her side around the front of the enclosure. She folded her arm underneath her head, which was positioned right in front of Fred.

As he looked at her, the dog rested his little, brown chin on top of his wrapped front legs. His tiny head quivered, but his eyes began to intermittently close.

Rosemary shut her eyes. She planned to only close them for a moment...

Warmth touched her shoulder.

Rosemary opened her eyes and saw Fred asleep, in front of her. She lifted her head and turned to see Lucas crouching over her, his still hand placed on her.

"Oh, shoot! I must have fallen asleep. I didn't put Fred's collar back on him!" she cried, in a soft voice.

"It's okay, no harm was done," Lucas said.

"I was going to sweep and mop the front now," he softly added; "everything else is done." He swept her bangs from her forehead. "Is it okay if I start in here? I hate to wake Fred."

"That's fine. It has to be done. Thank you, Lucas."

The bristles of the broom brushed the floor and woke the dog.

Rosemary offered the pup food again. This time, thankfully, he did eat a small can of wet food. Rosemary then gently pulled Fred from his crate, to give him a bathroom break.

Lucas took a rest from sweeping and followed them outside, as Rosemary carried Fred to the fenced yard. She wrapped a thin sling under the pup's chest and pulled the two ends up toward her, over his shoulders. While she supported his front end, he managed to relieve himself; the urine flowed steady, with normal color. The stool was loosely formed, but Rosemary had requested that the new dog be treated with a dewormer, as a precaution, and she wasn't alarmed to see that the medicine had affected the output.

"Good boy, Fred," she said.

The pooper-scooper would have to be retrieved from the small shed at the back of the yard; from a distance, she examined the entire lawn and noticed a few more spots that needed to be picked up, from this morning's outdoor breaks. After replacing Fred in his crate, she would tackle that chore.

Lucas rested his body against the fence, overlooking the few neighbors that distantly bordered the yard. Rosemary sat on the lawn, beside Fred. He lay on his stomach, his chin rested on his front paws. His eyebrows arched as he despondently looked around the grassy enclosure.

"Everything will be okay now, Fred. We'll be a family: you, me, 'Mantha and Rambo, and maybe someday you'll have another sister." Rosemary barely whispered the last part of the sentence. A picture of Lula May was added to her mind's family portrait. A fenced-in area at home would have to be considered, but for now Fred's emergency care took the forefront of her mind. Samantha would have time to adjust to one dog... then another. It would definitely take some time for the dog and cat to become companions, but positive energy could make anything possible. Samantha did not prefer to share her space with other cats, but hopefully a dog would prove acceptable.

A small, sympathetic smile pulled at the edges of Rosemary's face. Fred's eyebrows continued to twitch, as he observed new surroundings.

It must be a scary experience for him to be separated from his previous owner, the criminal's mother, while going through the healing process from his injuries. Hopefully, his previous owner had treated the dog with care.

"Hey, Rose Petal," Lucas called, "does that cat look okay?"

Looking up, Rosemary followed Lucas's gaze. She saw a small-framed, black cat walking along the outside perimeter of the yard. The cat's back hunched up, as its head lowered and bobbed above the grass. It was vomiting.

"The cat looks sick," she called back to Lucas.

"Let's get you inside," she told Fred, as she moved to her knees and picked up the dog.

"I'm going to get a crate for the cat, see if we can get it," she told Lucas, as he walked to her. "Maybe it's lost. Maybe a stray. But it's sick."

She opened the back door and quickly walked the middle path, through the dog pens. She carried Fred to his crate and placed him in it, with his collar on, then hurried to the stockroom. Lifting up on her toes, she pulled a small crate from the top shelf. Rosemary then opened the back door, holding it ajar as she leaned back against it, and searched the fence line, where the cat had been.

The cat hadn't moved from her spot. She looked to still be sick, her head suspended just above the grass.

Lucas had moved from his spot, though. Rosemary's eyes followed the fence and saw him steadily walking toward the stray. The cat didn't notice Lucas approaching, as she now pulled at the front bib of her fur with her mouth. Her head appeared to snap up and down. Lucas rounded the corner of the fence line, to where she was, and scooped her up from behind.

The animal twisted in his arms, but he gently secured her behind his locked clutch. He soothingly grasped the back of her neck while he supported the weight of her body.

"Sorry, I didn't want the sick cat to get away," Lucas said, as he neared Rosemary.

She felt the energy and warmth from his body across her chest, as his tall figure stepped directly in front of her and entered the back door.

"Take her to the quarantine room," Rosemary said.

She followed him through the walkway. A couple of dogs yelped but, thankfully, most did not notice the cat. "Good job," she said to Lucas.

They both entered the quarantine room. The cat now more vigorously writhed in his arms, and he set her on the tiled floor.

The cat settled when released. It looked up at them. Rosemary knelt next to it, and slowly moved the tips of her fingers in front of the cat's nose. It sniffed, then purred and rubbed its head against the touch.

Chunks of fur were missing all over its body. Small blisters had formed on the bare spots. Slowly feeling the length of the cat's spine, it felt bony; Rosemary's fingers dipped in and out of the hollows. If her eyes had been closed, she would have felt as though her fingers were sliding along an educational plastic spine.

The cat's belly looked full and low on the sides. She allowed her distended tummy to be physically examined; small movement was felt. It could possibly be gas. Or, most likely, babies.

"Good girl, Mama," Rosemary said.

"Mama?" Lucas asked.

"She looks pregnant." Rosemary looked up at Lucas. "She's friendly; this is a stray cat, not a feral. We will be able to find her a home."

The cat allowed Rosemary to fold back the tips of her ears and look inside, then feel along the tail. "She probably has ear mites: the ears look dirty inside," she told Lucas. "That's itchy. We need a litter box in here, a food and water bowl, and a blanket for a bed."

Rosemary gave the cat a pet on its head, then stood. "I've seen other cats with bloated stomachs, from worms and allergies. We'll have Dr. Greene look at her during his already scheduled upcoming visit, but I'm almost positive there's kittens in there. She definitely has flea allergies, though; that's why she has patches of missing fur, and blisters all over her poor little body. You can see the flea dust all over her; it looks like black pepper when you part her fur. We will give Mama a flea treatment that's safe for her pregnancy.

"There is oral medication that can kill the fleas instantly," she continued, "but you can't give that kind of medicine if the cat is pregnant. We have topical flea treatment in the stockroom, with all the medical stuff. I'll weigh her to get the correct dosage."

As Rosemary looked down, she saw the cat scratching her blisters.

"She is suffering, so I'd like to be extra diligent, and use a certain type of dish detergent to kill those fleas instantly. The topical detergent is safe for a pregnant animal." She looked at Lucas. "Will you help me?"

"Of course, Rose Petal."

"Usually, I would wait and let her acclimatize to being here before causing stress, but this poor girl has sores all over. The sores are painful and itchy."

"Let's get started," he said, as he knelt next to Mama and petted her. She pressed her head against his legs.

"We can treat her in here, where it's quiet. I'll go get the stuff."

Rosemary left Lucas with Mama, and prepared a bowl of warm water in the deep sink. She added about three tablespoons of detergent and mixed with a spoon, until bubbly. Then she headed back to the quarantine room with the bowl, soap, a flea comb, a washcloth, a paper towel, a small food bowl and a can of food. Her heart thudded against her chest; how would Mama react to the treatment?

She opened the door to see Lucas sitting on the floor, with the cat in his lap. Mama was stretching her front legs and seemingly kneading the air, as he petted her. Kneeling beside the two, Rosemary set down the supplies. She saw flea dirt circling the teats, as the cat continued to stretch on her side. Mama cat's nipples did look swollen, as if she were pregnant.

"Fleas are very hard to kill if they jump on you," Rosemary said sternly, and she felt her face scrunch. "You have to smash them against your fingernail if they jump off of her." Rosemary scrunched her face tighter. "They are gross."

Lucas picked up Mama and turned her onto her feet, on the tiled floor. Rosemary set a dish of food in front of the cat and Mama started eating. Hopefully, the distraction of food would last for the duration of treatment. Rosemary moistened the washcloth in the bowl filled with detergent. Slowly, Rosemary placed the cloth on the cat and gently rubbed, to dampen the fur. Mama turned to look up, but continued to eat as Lucas put more food in the bowl. When Mama was evenly wet, Rosemary squeezed a little more dish soap onto her fingers, then massaged the cat's body to produce lather. Rosemary then dipped the flea comb into the solution and started brushing through the fur. The comb had very finely spaced teeth, that were able to collect the fleas, eggs and flea dirt.

A flea jumped onto her hand.

"Eww!" A hushed shriek came from her lips. She dropped the comb and sliced the small, black bug with her fingernail, against the back of her hand. "I never get used to that!" she said.

Lucas picked up the comb and followed her procedure: dipping it into the solution then moving it through the fur. "I'll do this part," he said.

"Thank you, Lucas."

Little, black, dead bugs collected in the comb, which was wiped clean after each use, with the paper towel. Lucas unhurriedly combed through the entirety of Mama's body. She shook her limbs as he lightly brushed them. He continued until the swipes showed no more signs of any bugs.

"I'll go get a towel, to dry her," Rosemary said.

She got two cloths from the laundry room, and dampened one in running water from the deep sink. It would help to get some of the suds out of Mama's fur.

After drying the cat, Lucas helped Rosemary apply the topical flea medicine. They then furnished the space with a litter box, a water bowl and a bed.

They both now stood over the cat and watched her lick her paws, on her bed. Mama curled her head into her stomach as she cleaned herself; the towel-lined basket was the perfect fit. A larger box would be needed when the babies came.

"If she is pregnant, then that's one lucky mama and lucky babies, to have found you," Lucas said.

"Mama is sweet; she will find herself a good home. And the kittens should go pretty fast, once weaned. Right now, we only have four kittens, in the cage in the cat room. Babies are the first to be adopted," Rosemary said.

"I'm sure she'll have beautiful babies. She's a beautiful girl," Lucas quietly assured.

"Yes. Believe it or not, some people still believe the old wives' tale that black cats are bad luck, or evil."

He shook his head and ran a hand through his hair.

Rosemary left the cat a portion of dry food. "Okay, Mama, we'll check on you in a little bit," she said. She turned off the overhead lights, and the nightlight cast a soft glow on the room.

Mama was still cleaning herself as they left.

"I will finish sweeping and mopping, then walk Chuck," Lucas said, as they closed the door.

"Okay. I'll walk Lula when you walk Chuck."

Lucas completed the chores then headed toward the front table, to pick out a leash and collar for Chuck. Rosemary followed him to the dog room.

"Would you mind walking all the dogs, except for Lula?" Rosemary asked.

"Of course, I will."

"I feel like getting out for a little bit; I'll walk Lula for a half hour. Then I'll check on Fred and Mama." She looked down the walkway. "That will leave you with seven dogs to walk today. Do you think you can handle that?"

"Yes."

"Ronnie is the new black Lab we've got in. He just got neutered, so no walk for him. A quick bathroom break outside will be good."

"Okay."

"Thank you, Lucas."

"Rose Petal?" he said.

"Yes?"

"I noticed that Lucy is gone. So, her new family did adopt her last night?"

"Yes, after we left. Sharon stayed late to accommodate them."

"How wonderful for Lucy."

"It is wonderful! Her new family will do a great job of taking care of her. They have to feed her a special diet for diabetic dogs. They are an older couple, and have so much love to give her." An unintentional snort exhaled from her nose. "When the adoption was approved, they showed us pictures of items they had already purchased for Lucy: she has a pink dog bed, and matching pink food and water bowls. They promised to send pictures of Lucy settled in her new home."

"I see why you do this: it's good for the soul. It keeps the memory

317

fresh in your mind, every day, that you are connected to soul. To the animals." Lucas gazed intently at Rosemary. "You know, Rosemary, right now – and, whenever you're at work, or out in your garden – your aura glows orange," he said.

Rosemary softly smiled. "Orange is my favorite color," she said. "It's the color of warmth, to me."

"Orange is your spiritual color. It shows that you are satisfying your soul's intent by being a caregiver."

After retrieving the walking gear, Lucas went to Chuck's pen. He bent over and fastened the collar and leash on the pup, as Rosemary stood just outside, watching.

"Do you eat and drink just to go through the motions?" Rosemary suddenly asked. It was a question she had pondered, but she was almost stunned that it had come vocally from her mouth. "Or do you really need nourishment?" she continued, quietly.

He rose to his six-foot stature and turned to her. "You're asking if I need food?" A deep chuckle came from Lucas, as his head tipped back.

Rosemary felt her facial muscles flatten. Her eyes widened. *Was that an insulting question?*

Lucas seemed to lightheartedly smile at her. "I'm *not* a vampire. I am in human form now," he said, "and I am human. My energy is channeled inside this complete physical form. I have all human needs. Yes, I need food."

"It's just…" Rosemary began, quietly, "back when we first met… I noticed… you didn't drink your coffee. You smelled it. You seemed to enjoy smelling it, but you didn't drink it. I forgot 'til now."

"Oh, yes," Lucas said, sincerity appearing to replace his amusement, "when we first met, I was only an apparition, not human. My soul projected itself to you as human."

Rosemary stood silent. She felt her hands grasp the metal of the gate she stood in front of.

"That's a discussion for another day," Lucas said.

Rosemary inhaled a deep breath, as Lucas studied her.

"Breathe, Rose Petal," he worriedly said.

"I feel like pizza for dinner," she casually said, still gripping the gate. "I assume you will be at my house tonight? Do you like pizza?"

His eyebrows pulled tightly together, forming a deep crease between them. "I love pizza."

Rosemary pulled the sides of her mouth into a small smile.

"I am a pizza connoisseur," he added. "Pizza is my favorite food when I am human. I tasted pizza pie when it first became popular, in the eighteen-hundreds. I have had pizza in Italy, in Chicago, in Boston, in Philadelphia... I've tasted pizza from California to New York to New Jersey to Detroit. From Brazil to Australia!"

"Pizza for dinner, then," she curtly affirmed.

Chapter 15

Lucas's Last Meal

Lucifer crouched in front of Fred's crate and opened the door. He coaxed the dog to scoot to the front of the enclosure, then picked him up and untied the protective collar around Fred's neck. He fed him, then carried him outside for a bathroom break in Rosemary's yard.

It was a cool evening, maybe only sixty degrees. Fall would be soon approaching, which had always been Lucifer's favorite season on Earth. A raw acid twisted in the pit of his stomach. He would not experience fall as Lucas.

He would manage Koratz in jail tomorrow morning, then make one last visit to the shelter. Hell would be his subsequent destination.

In Lucifer's mind, he now visualized kissing the top of Chuck's soft head. He pressed his eyes tightly, to stop the built moisture from escaping. It would be near impossible to kiss Chuck, knowing it would be the last time.

Could it be possible to stay human, after completing his mission to protect Rosemary?

Just as quickly as the question formed, it was answered. It would not be fair to rob her of a normal life one second longer than need be. He had been selfish. Knowing that Koratz was locked in jail, Lucifer had chosen to steal a few precious moments from Rosemary.

Catching a cool wisp of air in his lungs, he held it there. This would be the last crisp intake of a breeze he would experience. He looked up at the sky. It was dark shades of blue, with sparkles of light, spanning the entire length of his view.

Every detail of tonight would be imprinted on every part of his being. Tonight would be the last time he tasted a meal as Lucas. It would be his last evening with Rosemary.

He again closed his eyes, then picked up Fred and headed back inside the house.

Mmm... vanilla, lemon and pomegranate... The smells of Rosemary's home pleased his nostrils, as soon as he opened the door and stepped inside with the dog. He secured the protective collar around Fred's neck, then placed him back inside the crate.

The pomegranate scent wafted strongly from the bathroom. It clung to the moistened air, from the recently-used shower. Lucifer closed his eyes as he committed the smell to memory. It was present not only in Rosemary's home; no matter how far she traveled, she carried the fragrance with her. It was always enfolded in the strands of her hair.

A sweet vanilla perfume lingered in her bedroom. He imagined her moving the small glass bottle across her body, and the mist spraying the skin of her neck and wrists. The cologne blended with her natural oils as she went about her daily business. The smell of her skin had always intensified with exertion at work. Her favorite refreshment was lemonade. Every few days, she sliced open and squeezed fresh lemons into a pitcher. He had watched her hand fold around the yellow fruit and the juice dripping from it. The tanginess, combined with the sweetness of the sugar, induced a tickle at the back of his throat, as he swallowed the drink after holding it under his nostrils.

There was usually a vanilla candle in the house, lit with a dancing flame, whenever she was there. Whenever he had bent over to remove his shoes, near the living-room desk, a cedar scent, lush and earthy, lingered from the drawer liners.

The bouquet of pungent coffee always filled the kitchen in the morning.

These smells would forever represent home to him. Peace. He wished he could secure them in a treasure locket, to open whenever he needed remembrance of soul.

The clear, plastic guard flattened under Fred's chin, as he lay down in the crate. Lucifer was fast becoming aware of the dog's mannerisms. He crouched just outside the enclosure and watched. The pup's small mouth opened and his dark-pink tongue extended with a yawn, his chin resting on his wrapped front legs. Fred stretched out his legs in front of him and shifted his hips. It was nap-time.

Across the room, Rambo appeared to shimmy his long, fancy fins, as he glided to the top of the water. He was requesting dinner. Lucifer picked a couple of live, black worms, from the container in the fridge, and dropped them in the tank. He watched the treat being snagged with exquisite precision.

"Thank you for feeding Rambo. And thank you for taking Fred outside," Lucifer heard, coming from behind. He turned around and saw Rosemary before him. From midsection down, she was clad in smooth cotton pants that hugged her curves and were tied at the ankle.

She leaned over at the waist and the fullness of her breasts heaved forward, in two soft-looking mounds, with the gravity; she wore a spaghetti-strap shirt. She was small-framed, but her upper body revealed a sexy ampleness, as she gathered her cascading hair.

322

Standing there, she pulled her hair through a nylon band and piled it into a bun. The fleshiness of her upper body shifted, as her arms lifted.

He watched every detail of her.

He was virtually immobilized.

Lucifer inhaled a very deep breath, very slowly, as he memorized every scent of her.

That was a mistake. Her scent was intoxicating. It seemed to awaken every part of his human body.

Her eyes looked at him.

"Where... would you like to order pizza from?" he asked, barely managing to choke out his words. "Or are we going somewhere?"

She fixed her eyes to his. A playful flicker seemed to brighten them, teasing him; he had never seen such mischief in her expression. Her mouth formed a slight smile, as one corner of it turned upward. He was bewitched by her.

"Oh, we're not going out," she said, "*and* we're not *ordering* a pizza."

He studied her. He knew that his face appeared blank. What was she planning?

"We are going to put your pizza-connoisseur skills to the test," she said, teasingly. A full smile pulled both sides of her mouth upward. "We are going to make our own pizza pie!"

"We are going to *make* pizza?"

"Yes. I haven't in such a long time," she said. "We have all the ingredients we need: we have homemade sauce and veggies from my garden."

"This will be the first time I made my own pizza," he admitted. "I

323

sure love to eat it, but never made it before."

"Let's get started," she said, "I am hungry! But we need some music to cook to."

She started to play a 'fifties C.D., in the record-player stereo system.

Lucifer followed behind her as she walked into the adjoining dining room, toward the kitchen. Rosemary paused beside the dining table.

"Thank you for fixing my mother's and grandmother's vase," she said, her voice low and thoughtful. She momentarily turned to look back at him. Then she reached out, and her fingers lightly traced the thick rim of the stained glass, as she gazed into it. Cattails now filled the stained glass.

"My mama loved cattail plants. She would get a new bunch every August, shuck them and place them in this vase," Rosemary said. "Thank you again. Makes me feel close to my mom, seeing these."

"You are more than welcome," he said. "I fixed it for your mother and grandmother, as well."

"It means more to me than you will ever know. It feels like you also played a part in repairing *my soul*," she said, still gazing at the vase.

"You mended your own soul, Rose Petal. When you forgave yourself and others, and reopened your heart to love, healthiness flowed freely."

Rosemary's expression went unseen, as she started into the kitchen. He followed. She reached the refrigerator and turned to face him.

Her eyes were free of anxiety. They looked brightened, with varying hues of reflective browns. The rims were of a healthy tone, and the skin surrounding them looked smooth. Lucifer had never seen her smile so big. The smile seemed to reach her eyes and bring life to them.

She tucked a few loose strands of hair behind her ears. "Would you like something to drink, before we get started?" she asked.

"You know I will have a glass of your lemonade," he said. "I'll get our drinks." He put Rambo's food container back inside the refrigerator, washed his hands, then pulled two glasses from the cupboard.

She held her smile. "Thank you." She turned and gathered some utensils from the drawers, into a large, red bowl.

The lemon halves gathered under the lid of the pitcher, as Lucifer poured. He added a couple of ice cubes and handed Rosemary the first glass of refreshment.

"Thank you," she said. She took a long drink, then set it on the counter.

He poured his glass. The ice clanked as he gently swirled the drink. He closed his eyes, then held the glass under his nostrils and inhaled deeply; slowly, he drew in the concentrated lemon scent and slightly sweet aroma. Pressing the glass to his mouth, the cold liquid passed his lips. A tanginess and sweetness tickled the skin of his inner mouth; he held it there for a moment. The tastebuds at the back of his tongue became immersed with flavor, and the coolness of the drink coated his throat as he swallowed it.

Rosemary set the large, red bowl, containing all the needed supplies, on the kitchen counter. Among the gadgets were the same rolling pin her mother had used and a new pizza cutter.

Already waiting on the counter was a basket heaped full of an array of colorful vegetables, freshly picked from the garden today, after work. The basket was fragrant with the earthy scents of the peppers, onions and tomatoes. Rosemary tossed a large, red tomato to Lucifer. His sluggish reflexes from transformation were improving, because he caught it.

Obviously, tonight was going to be playful...

Jars of garlic powder and crushed red pepper flakes were gathered from the spice rack. Rosemary now pulled a block of mozzarella and a wedge of cheddar cheese from the fridge.

"I went grocery shopping a few days ago, and was going to make myself a gourmet grilled cheese sandwich," she said, giggling. "But, then, everything happened..." She stood back and looked at the provisions. "So, here we are, making pizza tonight." One corner of her mouth pulled up. "You never know what tomorrow will bring."

The kitchen counter was long, but narrow. A canister of flour and a jar of tomato sauce were placed near the sink. The items stretched from the faucet to the end of the six-foot-long surface. The wooden cutting board seemed to be eagerly awaiting the juices of tomatoes, the seeds of peppers and the skins of onions, to be shed atop it.

"Someday, I'd like to add an island in this kitchen, for more counter space," Rosemary said.

She crouched in front of the oven and pulled a cookie sheet from its bottom drawer. She handed the silver baking sheet to Lucifer. "Would you please get the bacon from the crisper and put a few slices on here?" she asked.

"Of course."

As she turned the dial, to preheat the oven to 350 degrees, a clean, meaty smell, from the raw slices of bacon, assured freshness as Lucifer pulled them from the package.

"What do you like on your pizza?" Rosemary asked, as she sunk a knife into a purple onion, pulling it through to make two halves.

"I like everything," he said; "everything you have here."

"I forgot…" she started, as she began to slice one half of the onion, "I have leftover ham in the crisper, too. It's only been in there a few days."

"Sounds good to me."

Rosemary measured the flour and poured it into the red stoneware bowl, now emptied of the supplies. Baking powder, salt, garlic powder, olive oil and milk were combined and mixed with a wooden spoon, until the dry ingredients were moistened.

Rosemary turned to Lucifer. "Wash your hands," she said.

He moved to the sink, poured dish soap into his palms and lathered them. He stepped beside her as he dried himself with a dishcloth. She set the bowl directly in front of him.

"Just dig in and knead, until a soft dough forms," she said. "It's easier if you just dig in there with your hands; they are the best tools."

His eyes narrowed in concentration, as he looked into the red, lace-patterned bowl. Lumpy globs of nothing, it seemed, caked the bottom. Rosemary smiled and he smiled back at her, relaxing his face.

"Hold on," he said. Lucifer walked to the cupboard, just outside the kitchen, in the dining room. He remembered having seen a few aprons hanging on pegs in the closet, and thought he'd continue to set the mood for a lighthearted evening.

With his back turned to Rosemary, he slipped on one of the aprons and tied it around his back.

"What are you doing over there?" she called.

Lucifer turned around.

Two bright-yellow sunflowers appeared to be strategically placed in the exact location of his chest. A pink, checkered pattern decorated the bottom. Due to his physique, the hem landed just below his waist. He watched Rosemary's mouth open wide in a smile. She grasped just above each of her knees as she bent over laughing.

Seeing her this happy, he wished he had a wig and lipstick, as well.

"I'll have to put one on, too," Rosemary said. "You can't be the only ridiculous-looking person."

Rosemary walked to the dining-room cupboard, bustled a moment then turned to face Lucifer. Her lips puckered as she patted her bun, in her owl-themed apron. Two brown, feathered eyes were now strategically placed over her chest. "Now we're ready to get cooking," she said.

Lucifer smiled widely, as he watched her walk toward him. She stood beside him at the counter, as he lowered his hands inside the bowl. As the mixture squished between his fingers, it felt satisfying. It was a primal feeling, making one's own food. He closed his eyes and smelled the spices, smoothing the ingredients into a pliable shape. The glob was being sculpted into something.

After a soft ball was formed, Rosemary set a round baking pan on the counter, next to him. "Good job," she said. "You can now spread the dough out on this."

Lucifer dabbed a small amount of caked dough onto Rosemary's cheek. Her mouth opened wide in surprise. She laughed out loud.

She then took his hands and turned his palms upward. She slowly poured olive oil onto them, and rubbed the oil onto his gooey, dough-covered skin. "That'll help it not stick," she said. Then Rosemary dipped her index finger into the pool of olive oil in his palms, and dabbed the oil onto his closed lips. She softly giggled.

He took in a slow, deep breath of air through his nostrils. His chest protruded with the intake. He slowly rubbed his lips together.

Lucifer oiled the soft ball of dough with his palms, then plopped it onto the baking sheet. He now used the rolling pin that Rosemary had handed him. She momentarily stopped him from rolling, and dusted the pin and dough with a little flour.

Lucifer impulsively dabbed his index finger into a patch of the flour, on the pizza dough, then lightly moved that finger down the center of Rosemary's nose. The whites of her eyes showed with the surprise. Her mouth then opened wide with another laugh.

Lucifer went back to rolling out the dough. The tool rotated under his palms, in different directions, spreading the clump over the circumference of the round pan. It was meditational to gently manipulate the substance, created by hand, into circular form.

He felt warmth, as Rosemary took the pin from him and placed her hands on top of his, attempting to teach him her crust-pinching method. She turned her body to his, standing so close. He had bits of dried dough on the back of his hands, and her skin seemed to merge with his, to create a gooey, tantalizing mess. She then moved her hands underneath his, and tried to better demonstrate how to pinch up the edges of the pie.

Every inch of his body became aware and rigid from the impact of her touch, her warmth.

She flattened her hand under his, and asked him to flatten his on top of hers. "Ha!" she exclaimed. "You have bigger ones!"

Just as quickly as she had moved beside him, and placed her hands under his, she removed them and left his side. She had flittered about as though a butterfly, and now stood near the sink, as she stirred red tomato sauce with a wooden spoon.

He continued to pinch a thick crust between his fingers, all around the edge of the pizza pie. He turned the pan as he moved his hands around the flat dough.

Having shaped the soft dough between his fingers, while watching Rosemary rhythmically slice vegetables, had been a sensual experience. Side by side, silently in sync with one another, while preparing a meal, he felt as if part of an intimate couple.

"That looks great!" Rosemary said, as she came up behind him. As a final touch, she sprinkled a little more garlic powder and red pepper flakes on the bare crust. "You can add the sauce now," she said. "It's homemade; Sharon and I canned it ourselves, at her house."

"That's impressive. Certainly another talent of yours," he said.

She pivoted her body weight on her right toes, in a playful movement. "What's impressive?"

"That you canned tomato sauce."

"Oh. Share taught me."

The wooden spoon stuck out from the top of the jar Rosemary held. She spooned out a dollop of the chunky sauce, then brought it close to Lucifer's lips. He tasted, closing his eyes at the immediate rush of flavor. A ripe tomato seemed to burst in his mouth, with a soft crunch and sweetened garlic; a touch of sugar curbed the saltiness. All the spices seemed to flirt with his tastebuds. Onions and peppers supplied a spicy aftertaste.

"*Good?* Do you like it?" Rosemary asked.

He opened his eyes to her gaze, focused on him. "'Like' is not the word I would use."

She studied him.

His eyes narrowed. "*Worship.* 'Worship' is the word I would use. I *worship* your homemade tomato sauce."

A heavy sigh, turned chuckle, relaxed her face. Her arm crossed her chest and her hand rested upon it.

"I'm not kidding, Rose Petal: the sauce is unbelievable. You have many talents; cooking is one of them. I can't wait to taste the pizza, with all the trimmings."

"Thank you, Lucas."

She handed him the jar of red sauce. Lucifer slowly poured the thick mixture in the center of the dough, so as not to splatter. The spicy aroma of garlic and tomatoes drizzled out, and he spread it to all the edges with the back of the spoon. The pie was now covered, up to the crust, with the homemade, red topping.

He watched Rosemary then crumble a wedge of cheese atop the pie. It looked as if delicate snow were falling from the sky, onto the blank canvas. Their hands crossed and their skin touched as, together, they spread the toppings over the cheese. As Rosemary added the last of the vegetables, Lucifer tore the cooked slices of bacon and ham, and placed them.

Rosemary opened the heated oven's door and transferred the pan to

331

the middle shelf. The timer was set.

"I hate to take off this sexy apron. It really outlines my manly chest," Lucifer teased.

"Well, my owl's eyes definitely help to add a little padding for me!" she said.

"You don't need any help when you are perfection, my dear," he returned.

Rosemary hung the aprons back in the cupboard. She then switched from the music on her C.D. to the classical radio station.

Samantha lay on the couch cushion, just above Fred's crate on the floor. She purred in a soft, golden ball. Rambo slept in the base of a plant. It was heartening to look across to the living room and see the creatures that Rosemary loved, peacefully resting.

Lucifer knew where Rosemary kept the matches, and pulled them from the kitchen drawer. At the dining table, Lucifer reflexively curved his fingers around the wick, as he lit one of the candles in its hand-wrought holder. "Bless this home and everyone in it," he whispered.

He asked Rosemary to light the second one. The flame appeared to dance in a quick back-and-forth movement, until it settled into a slow waltz. "Bless this home and everyone in it," she said.

The scent of vanilla and sweet lemon swirled through the air and followed her, like fairy dust, as she walked back to the kitchen. He followed.

She pulled two stoneware plates from the cabinet. Walking back to the dining room, she set the plates across from one another. Lucifer set napkins, silverware and wine glasses beside each dish.

"Oh, we're having wine tonight?" Rosemary asked.

"Like you said, a special drink will make the dinner feel more special."

A small grin pulled the side of her mouth up. "The first dinner we shared together seems like a lifetime ago."

Lucifer pulled out the chair for her. She moved in front of him and took her seat. The smell of vanilla drew his attention to the bare patch of skin on the back of her neck. A few strands of hair had gracefully fallen from her bun. He sat down in his chair, on the opposite side of the table. They would await the timer to ring on the oven.

Still with a little lemonade left in his glass, Lucifer lifted it to his lips.

"Can you stay human?" Rosemary asked. "Do you *have* to go back to…?"

His chest tightened as he held his breath. The drink was held in his mouth for a moment, before a hard swallow released it down his throat. "Hell?"

She nodded her head.

"Yes, I have to go back to Hell. The castle needs its ruler, to welcome and watch over the gathered souls. The castle is my home."

Her eyes seemed to watch his words forming in mid-air. She looked toward him, but also off into space. Her playful mood tonight had dissipated to sadness, it seemed. Her bottom lip flattened over her teeth.

"I would miss you if you left," she said.

She had spoken those words carelessly, as though he weren't the devil. Her eyes lowered and darkened. Her shoulders rolled forward, and her upper body hunched over in the chair.

"Rose Petal, I want you to live the ordinary human life that your soul planned for you," he said, gently. "I don't want to meddle in your life any more than I already have."

"Is that why you don't want to stay human? Because human life is *ordinary*?"

"Living an ordinary human life is *extraordinary*, Rose Petal. It is the most exquisite experience a soul can partake in. In the human body, a soul can create, expand and experience. The journey of engaging Earth, through a human experience, constructs a collective expansion of consciousness for all."

"Do you really believe that? You are so much more advanced than any human I know. You can do magic. What's it like to be able to do magic?" she asked. She was overlooking the uniqueness of each level of being. "You can move things. You can—"

"Rose Petal, you perform magic every day. Humans are magical. You pick up a pencil and write a letter. Don't you think that is magical? It's magic every time you walk to the door... breathe... The soul gets to experience different aspects of being.

"The life you have created for yourself is magical. And you create a better life for other creatures, by taking them off the streets and out of abusive homes. You clean for them, feed them and care for them. Your human body is strong, and able to perform such duties. Don't you think that is magical?"

Rosemary intently listened to him, watched him.

"It is magical to see a bird in flight with human eyes," he continued. "It is magical to touch an animal's soft fur with fingertips. To listen to the breeze with ears, and to smell the scents of home when one walks through the door." He recollected his favorite experiences, which would be greatly missed. A pull of sadness seemed to bellow deep in the pit of his stomach, and tears began to build at the corners of his eyes. He held them back, but was sure his gaze glistened with the touch of moisture. "It's magical to be able to see Earth's beautiful trees through human eyes, and touch their bark with fingertips." He felt a smile lift the corners of his mouth. Just thinking about his journey here, in this body, was sentimental.

"When you explain it like *that*…" She pulled her bottom lip into her mouth and pressed her top teeth down. A few moments passed.

"So, you like being human?" she asked.

"Yes."

"*Could* you stay here, if you wanted? What would happen to you if you stayed? Would you grow old and die, like everyone else?"

"No one dies. Humans grow old and then their energy transforms. But, yes, if I stayed human, I would grow old and transform."

"Would you still have your powers, if you stayed human?"

"The longer I stayed human, the weaker my ability to transport would eventually become. It takes so much energy to move from one plane to another, to change from one form to another. If I were to stay human, I would become more comfortable and settle into that existence."

The bell for the oven timer rang.

Lucifer pushed back his chair and walked to Rosemary's side of the table. She stood as he reached her.

"Saved by the bell," she teased.

He pulled the pizza from the heated oven and set it on hot-pads, on the counter. The cheese was gooey and needed to cool for a bit, before being sliced.

Rosemary's eyebrows arched. "All I have is the red wine from our last dinner."

"That will work," he said.

"What is death like?"

"It's nothing to fear; souls go there all the time. Each soul already knows the afterworld. 'Death' is a word created by humans; it is not a fact. Like I said earlier, no one dies; one only transforms energy. In a human death, the soul breaks out of the cocoon like a butterfly. It carries with it all the knowledge from that life, and previous lives that particular soul might have had. One never loses their autonomy. A free soul has personal likes and dislikes, like it did when encapsulated in a human body."

"I'll pour us the wine, but can you please open the bottle?" Rosemary said. She handed Lucifer the bottle and he pulled the cork from it. He handed it back to Rosemary, then followed her into the dining room. The red liquid smoothly painted the side of the glass as she poured. She handed him the first glass, then filled herself one.

"Rosemary," he continued, "when one is experiencing a human life, he should have fun, enjoy it, revel in it – create, love, expand. But one should never be afraid to return to the afterlife, for he is already there, already a part of it. Remember the visit from your mother, after she passed?"

"Yes."

"Did you use your human mouth to communicate?"

"No, I just *knew* what she told me."

"Did you need your human arms to embrace her?"

"No, but I felt embraced."

"That's because energy is energy, no matter the form. Love is love, no matter the form. A soul doesn't need human flesh to feel love. Or spoken words to communicate.

"Like the experience with your mother, humans are constantly in touch with Heaven and other dimensions, so there's nothing to fear from death or the afterworld, because a human's soul visits the afterworld on a regular basis. Each soul has an ongoing, intimate relationship with that world – only, most human minds can't comprehend it."

"So, you're saying that I visited Heaven when seeing my mother?" Rosemary asked. Her eyes were focused and alert, yet there was hesitation to hear the answer.

"Your mother may have come to *you* for a visit; maybe your soul didn't travel to her. But, having any communication with Heaven is part of visiting it. Even when a human is awake, he experiences the afterworld on a daily basis. Whenever one looks into an infant's eyes, or a mother's eyes, or a lover's eyes, that feeling is a soul-to-soul connection. It's Heaven. One is constantly connected to Heaven – the afterworld. The way one connects in the human body with that infant, mother or lover is exactly how it will be in the afterworld. One doesn't feel his body when looking into the eyes of a loved one; he simply feels a connection."

They moved to the kitchen, and Rosemary began slicing the pie with the pizza cutter. As the silver disc cut through the crust, it became pasted with chunky, red sauce and gooey cheese.

Moving the round blade back and forth, she did not speak; a small break in the discussion was needed. Lucifer had given an abundance of information to be absorbed. Even though Rosemary was a spiritual being, and open-minded, any human would have uncertainties concerning their thoughts about the afterlife.

Rosemary carried the pan of sliced pizza to the dining table, and set it on hot-pads. Lucifer pulled out the chair for her and she took her seat. He sat opposite her, across the table. Moist, warm cheese clung to the metal spatula, as he slid it under a slice of pizza; the cheese clung to the pan like a stretched accordion as he plated it. He passed the first piece to Rosemary, then served himself.

"To Fred," she said, as she lifted her glass of wine toward him.

"To Fred."

She clanked her china against his, producing a high-pitched chime.

After taking a sip of wine, Rosemary asked: "So, you're saying – sort of – that humans are in touch with Heaven and not aware of it?"

"Exactly," he said. "Why not? Before becoming Earthbound, the soul of each human was a part of Heaven; that's where you all came from. Why would you shut it out completely, until you cross over? Why would you think you're separate from Heaven? You are in touch with Heaven every time you see a butterfly, or smile, or feel connected to something greater than yourself. That's Heaven. That connection is Heaven."

Lucifer took his first bite of pizza. The conversation was thought-provoking, but his body seemed incapable of waiting a second longer to taste the homemade dinner. The crust folded as he lifted the wedge, the toppings and cheese gathering in the middle. His nostrils held the aroma. With the first taste, the tangy sauce rolled across his tongue, then bathed his whole mouth with tickles of spicy garlic and peppers. Gooey, thick cheese melted on his tongue, and warmed the skin of the inside of his mouth. Onions and bacon added a burst of flavor, as they lightly crunched between his teeth. He must have had an orgasmic expression on his face, because Rosemary watched him with a grin.

He finished his slice and they both took another piece.

"What is Heaven like?" she asked, a smirk lifting one side of her mouth. "Do you know?"

"Don't be surprised, but I do know what Heaven is like."

Rosemary lowered her mouth to meet the end of the wedge of pizza she held, but her eyes were on Lucifer.

"Heaven is not one specific place," he said; "it's actually everywhere – anywhere that positive energies gather. Like I said, humans visit Heaven, or the afterlife, regularly, without even noticing. Humans are always connected to it; it's that loving energy that flows through every being. Sure, in the afterlife certain groups of positive energies might congregate in a particular place, but that doesn't mean that Heaven can't also be right here on Earth, among living human beings. Anywhere positive, compatible souls meet is Heaven, even if those souls are in human bodies. Heaven is in everything joyful. It's a peaceful state of being. Why would humans think they *weren't* a part of it? Anytime a joyful laugh is shared, or a connection is felt with another being, or one experiences a visit from a deceased loved one, like you did, that is Heaven. Anytime one sees that butterfly, or looks into that lover's eyes, those are glimpses into Heaven."

"Tell me more," she said. "What does Heaven *look* like?"

"It looks like anything joyful. Souls can gather at a baseball game or concert, in any dimension or on Earth. A soul can meditate alone, in a beautiful, vast garden. My mother, Catherine, likes to cook in her kitchen. My grandfather likes to devour her meals." He took a drink of wine, for a pause. "Obviously, a soul inside a human body gets to experience the physical senses in a palpable, substantial way, but energy in the afterlife can still participate in a favorite activity, for a moment.

"When a soul chooses a human body, a life, a career and a family on Earth, the same energy that comprised that soul before becoming human will always be a part of that human," he said. "That's why no one should be afraid to go through a human death. The energy that was one's soul, before becoming human and continued when inside the human body, goes to the afterlife upon the human death. The energy you were before becoming human is still a part of you now, only you're in human form: same energy, same you, same autonomy, same energy for eternity. No matter how many human forms one may take, always the same energy."

Rosemary reached for a third piece of pizza, and so did he. "So, when I saw you as an orb, in front of me on my bed, and when I'm looking at you now... it's... you? Same energy?" she confirmed.

"Yes, same soul. When you saw my orb in your bedroom, I was a soul without a human body. Now, I am that same soul *with* a human body."

He reached into the pan with his fork and scraped out a spot of stuck cheese; vegetables adhered to it. "It takes a lot of energy to reveal an orb to human eyes. I chose to show myself to you, and that utilized a

340

lot of energy on my part. If a human is open to seeing the spiritual side of life, then more will be revealed to her, more easily.

"The soul is an energy that can't be captured or crushed," he continued. "That energy is a part of the afterlife. A part of Heaven is inside every human. It's impossible to be separate from it – forgotten... but not separate.

"What is peace? Joy? You can't see it. You can't put a box around it. It is energy. It is your connection to Heaven. Heaven is inside you. It's your soul. You're not *going* there when you die; you're *already* there."

Rosemary's face seemed to lock in place. She pressed down on her lower lip as she drew it between her teeth.

"Please, Rose Petal, remember to always spend time with your plants, your animals. Feel the peace and joy they bring you. That peace and joy is your connection to Heaven; whenever your soul is at peace, you are connected to Heaven. I always want that for you, Rose Petal."

"What if I were to tell you that I'd like you to stay?" she asked in a low voice. "Here, with me?"

"You shouldn't say that." He cleared his throat. "You wouldn't if you knew what I have done."

Rosemary pushed her chair back and picked up the pizza tray. Only two pieces were left on it. She walked to the kitchen without looking at him.

"Rose Petal," he called after her. He pushed aside his chair and followed her into the adjoining room. He raked his fingers through the top of his hair.

341

"You said that you were connected to me. Why?" she asked, determinedly. Her back was turned to him, as she wrapped the leftovers and placed them in the refrigerator. Her hand dramatically rested on the long, narrow handle of the fridge's door. Her upper back moved as she took in a deep breath.

She then turned to look at him, her eyes narrowed with thought. "You once said your soul was connected to mine. Why? I would like an answer this time."

"That's a story for another day."

"How many days do we have?" she asked, angrily. "I deserve an answer."

"I don't think you are ready to hear those details right now, Rose Petal."

"Yes. Right now," she demanded in a smooth, but firm voice.

His body became rigid, not offering any physical response or movement. He then slowly reached inside his left pocket.

Rosemary's fingers directly circled his wrist and pulled his hand from his pocket. His fingers were folded over his palm, as Rosemary lifted it face up and lightly pulled them back. She removed the gold timepiece from his palm and set it on the kitchen counter.

"I have the right to know, and I want to know," she continued, looking straight into his eyes.

Lucifer exhaled heavily through his nose. He closed his eyes as his brows arched. "I have always loved you, Rose Petal," he began. Another gush of air exhaled from his nose; the release seemed to purge him of any breath in his lungs. He looked at Rosemary now. "Yes, my soul has always been connected to yours. You are my equal. My sister.

My wife. My lover. My friend. The goodness to my essence. You are all things to me."

"What does that mean? My sister? My wife?"

"I don't want to scare you."

"Too late." Her eyes held his, tentatively but steadily. She would not accept his avoidance.

He smoothly closed his eyes and forced another slow, long breath from his nostrils. As his eyelids remained shut, he visualized the first time he had ever connected with Rosemary's soul. He now felt a small smile emerge, as the past resurfaced...

Rosemary's name had been Margaret. It had been the late 1600s. Margaret was a farmer's daughter.

Lucifer's name was Lucas, and he had just arrived at the small frontier town. He watched this young woman exit the general store, with her arms full of packages. She had worn a working-class-woman's dress, and an orange ribbon around her wrist. Lucas introduced himself to the young woman, and helped her carry her packages to her carriage and load them.

She had been a determined female, in this harsh environment. Her face was smudged with a spot of dust, as her blue eyes tipped up to him. She smiled at him underneath the wide brim of her hat. Margaret wore white gloves, fingertips stained from mud. She reached out her hand to shake his.

Her smile and touch seemed to awaken life in his soul. From that day forward, she had been his virtual lifeline.

After leaving his first interaction with Margaret, he had never before felt so lighthearted. He found himself smiling for no good reason. He felt that she had made him healthy and whole. She was everything he would ever need or want. Her smile seemed to fill his heart with peace. Margaret had been the first and only love of his existence.

Lucas loved his mother, but Margaret had been the first woman he loved healthfully. Catherine had been attentive to her children but, due to her turbulent relationship with her husband, she suffered from depression. Lucas had concerns for her well-being.

Margaret was an independent female. She lived with her family when he met her, but her liberated spirit not settling for a loveless marriage intrigued him. He had been attracted to her joyfulness. She loved the farm animals and cared for them; her favorite cows had all been given names. A smile had always been on her face as she worked the farm, a song always sung under her breath. When Lucas had arrived at Margaret's family farm on horseback, after their first introduction, he found Margaret in the cow pasture, pouring water from a bucket over a cow's back, to cool it, while singing to it...

He now opened his eyes and narrowed his line of vision, straight into Rosemary's hesitant gaze. He would begin the story of their intertwined souls.

"In my first human life, I met you." Tears filled his eyes and he quickly wiped them. "I am sorry, I never would have... I took your innocence. I was in line to become the next Lucifer at that time, and I inserted myself into your... existence." He bowed his forehead and held it, his hands shielding his eyes from her horrified expression.

He felt Rosemary's hands cup the back of his, and she moved them away from his face. When he opened his eyes, he saw only love in hers. "I don't blame you... for anything..." She released his hands.

"Please," she said, softly. "Please continue."

"You were a farmer's daughter in the sixteen-hundreds," he began again. "Your name was Margaret. You were a determined young woman who worked hard on the farm. You loved all the farm animals. You sang to the cows as you bathed them."

Rosemary smiled softly. "I *bathed* cows?" she said.

"Yes, your family's cows were precious to you," Lucifer said. "You taught me unconditional love, no matter the form. I have strived ever since to match your compassion.

"I fell deeply in love with you and made you my wife," he continued, his tone contrite. "We had a little farm of our own.

"I would not have involved you in my life had I remembered, during my first human experience, that I belonged to the lineage of Hell. In my first human experience, I had forgotten about soul. Enduring human suffering was part of my training, to become ruler of Hell. As I previously told you, my grandfather believed it necessary to actually inhabit Earth with a family, and undergo tribulations. He believed in empathic leadership."

Lucifer was unaware of feeling any emotion at this moment, but a single tear rolled down his face. He felt the wet trail.

"You were as beautiful then as you are now. We shared a nice life together. We had two children; you were a doting mother. I died a human death, then watched over you."

Lucifer looked at Rosemary, to check her reaction. Her eyes revealed emotion, but she was still attentive, so he continued the story...

"When I died my first human death, I then remembered the truth about soul, and who I was. And, every subsequent human life I experienced thereafter, I remembered about soul and my true identity, while experiencing the human lives. I did not want to complicate your subsequent lives, so I distanced myself from you, though I watched over you. We were close, but not intimate. Once, I was your brother; once, your friend," he carefully said.

He studied Rosemary's expression. Her eyes tipped up to his, just as they had the first time, when she was Margaret. There was no fear shown behind the brown and green flecks in them; there was only calmness – or, maybe, relief.

"Always watching over you, but never wanting to intrude upon your personal experience," he firmly added.

"I have always felt comfortable with you – trusted you... even though... there were things that didn't add up," she softly said. Her bottom lip pulled underneath her front teeth for a moment. "I do feel... you feel like home to me. This makes sense, what you're saying.

"You say we had children...? I was a... good mother? "You have to tell me..."

He thoughtfully nodded. He then intently looked into the brown and green flecks of her eyes, slightly glistening with moisture. "I will always love you, Rose Petal," he said. "In this lifetime of yours, we were not meant to cross paths." He ran his hand through the top of his hair. "I intruded upon your experience. I am sorry."

"How do you know *I* didn't write you into my story, this lifetime?"

"What?" He felt his eyebrows pull tightly together.

"My mother believed each soul wrote her own story, before being born. Like, who her parents would be, what she would look like, and

346

which family and friends would surround her." Rosemary did not look away. "What if *I* decided to have you in my life?"

The muscles of Lucifer's whole face tightened. "You would never have written me into your life, Rosemary," he said, flatly.

"It's *my* life, my story to write. How do you know?"

"First of all, no soul would write the devil into her life. Secondly, I had no intentions of ever being human again," he said, almost angrily. "Both parties have to agree to share their lives together. You can't just write me into your experience; I would have had to agree."

Her face became sullen. The skin surrounding her eyes looked worn. A glare shadowed her irises, framed by red rims. Was it fear? Anger? Failure to grasp reality?

"You have always been my one true love, Rose Petal," he said, tenderly. "My only love. But I love you enough to allow you an existence free from—"

"The truth?" she inserted. "Free from the truth?"

"No! Free from *trauma*. Trauma from knowing things you shouldn't know."

"The truth doesn't cause trauma," she quietly, but determinedly, said. "One's *reaction* to the truth causes trauma."

His heart thumped hard against his chest. As he watched Rosemary, he could practically feel his vessels swelling, with the acceleration of blood pumping through them. She looked faint.

"Breathe, Rose Petal," he said, restlessly.

"I handled everything else; I can handle this," she said. Her voice sounded tired; it cracked near the end of her statement. She cleared her throat.

347

"The way I see it, my life story is fluid. I believe I have the power to change my intended life journey as I go. Why wouldn't each human have the power to change direction, or the people in their life? Maybe we discover new preferences or become open to different experiences? I believe we are fluid. Sure, I do believe that we each have a general plan, and people in place for each of our human experiences, but I also believe that there are no rigidly set rules when we are human. We can change our minds." She defiantly looked at him directly. Her voice had become stronger.

"You said that we are the same energy when human as when not human," she seemed to bellow now, "so, why wouldn't it be possible to make changes to the life plan, no matter our form? You said we never lose our autonomy."

She exhaled a heavy breath as she walked past him. "I'm going to rest in my room for a while." She went to the living room and picked up Samantha from the couch. Cradling the cat, she didn't look at Lucifer as she made her way to her bedroom. She reappeared to collect the crate, with Fred inside, then closed the bedroom door behind them.

Lucifer lightly knocked on her door. "Would you allow me to let Fred outside? He would probably like to—" he began, through the closed door.

"Yes," came a soft voice, through the wooden barrier.

Lucifer entered the private domain and saw the opened crate on the bed, the little dog lying on Rosemary's chest. Samantha lay on the pillow above Rosemary's head. The dog's two front legs stretched forward in tandem, as Lucifer approached.

"Come on, Fred," he said, in a low voice, "I'll take you out." He picked up the dog and headed outside.

When they returned inside, Lucifer found that Rosemary's bedroom door was again closed, so he sat on the sofa, resting Fred right beside him. He scratched the dog's neck, underneath the protective collar.

Lucifer closed his eyes, and felt the air fill and empty from his lungs.

He sat there, still, for an hour. It seemed an eternity since Rosemary had confined herself.

Her bedroom door slightly creaked, as it finally opened. But it seemed that a ghost had unlocked it, because only vacant space showed through; Rosemary did not appear.

Lucifer carried Fred with him, as he walked to the opened door. Samantha sat on the pillow, beside Rosemary's seated body, as Lucifer looked toward the bed. He set the dog next to them. Rosemary's back leaned against the corner wall, her knees pulled up to her chest.

"You can sit on the bed," she said, sounding rested. "I would like to talk more."

He took a seat on the edge.

"You moved my phone, mid-air," she said, just above a whisper. "That is very different from anything I can do."

"But it is not." He forced a deep intake of air that extended his chest. He raked his fingers through his hair. Maybe re-examining their past discussion would relieve her of the avalanche of new information. "Me generating an energetic force to move your phone is not that different from you picking up your phone with your hand. As a human, you *think* about picking up your phone, then your brain sends the signals through your body, to move your arm, your hand and your fingers… then you pick up your phone. You think nothing of it, but it's also magic to be human, and to have that mind and body communication and interaction. You can pick up objects and feel them."

Her chest now moved with a slow inhalation. Color had returned to her cheeks. Her eyes looked rested and the rims were less red. The skin around her eyes was brighter and firmer.

"Rosemary, it *is* magical," he continued. "The primary motor cortex generates neural impulses that control the execution of movement, which allows you to pick up your phone. Signals from the primary motor cortex activate skeletal muscles on the opposite side of the body; the posterior parietal cortex transforms visual information into motor commands, so the posterior parietal cortex determines how to steer your arm toward the phone. The premotor cortex is involved in the sensory guidance of movement, and prepares the body's muscles for the exact movements they will make; it helps you control your arm movement toward the small object."

She looked at him, but didn't seem to be fully processing the information. Her eyes did not focus on him; they only foggily gazed his way.

"Don't you think all of that is magic?" he asked. "The way the human mind and body are designed to work together? And then, how the soul interacts with the mechanics?"

"Yes," she said. "You have made me think differently about being human, and the magic of it."

"Good."

"*Hell, devil…* those are names placed on the unknown. They are names given to label fear. It is not the truth," Rosemary said. His focus narrowed directly on her eyes.

Her line of vision moved toward the corner ceiling, her concentration like a laser cutting a hole. "People fear the unknown; it is usually considered negative or scary. People fear what they consider negative, scary, ugly… *dark*. But, sometimes, darkness can be a place of healing – just like Hell."

Her eyes now turned to him. "I was healed in my darkness. My darkness was my grief at losing my father, during our turbulent relationship. My darkness was my relationship with Mark. Maybe the troubled relationship with my father, since childhood, had attracted Mark into my life. Having Mark in my life was negative, and brought further negative emotions and experiences.

"*You* helped me heal," she said, now looking directly into Lucifer's eyes. "You taught me that positive attracts positive. You taught me to forgive. You taught me to examine the darkness."

"Yes," he said, "any constant negative feeling will attract a negative response. Dark periods are times for reflection. In darkness, one is forced to go within; when one is alone in darkness, she is forced to look deep within and find the courage to look for answers, give forgiveness, and contemplate purity of thoughts and heart. It can be scary to look at all the corners of one's mind, so to speak; sometimes there may be angers and hurts that are unexamined. Some people may be uncomfortable in the dark, because their own soul is unfamiliar to them. Some people are afraid to listen to their inner light."

He thoughtfully smiled at Rosemary. "Even though one may be afraid to examine the darkness and find the answers, the answers are already known to the soul," he finished.

"Yes," she agreed, "I have always known that Mark was the wrong man, but I did go against my inner light, my soul. By my free will, I kept Mark in my life. Everything inside me was practically screaming: 'Leave him!'"

"Go to sleep now, Rose Petal. You need some sleep," Lucifer said.

"How are you so sure my soul didn't know that you would be a part of my human experience in this life? You said you wanted to spare me the trauma of learning about your world, but maybe *you* weren't the one to find *me*? Maybe my soul did write you into this life experience? Maybe that's why you *just happened* to find me? Or, you think you found me... but what if I summoned you?"

A laugh rose from deep in Lucifer's stomach, up his throat and out through his lips. His head tilted back, his mouth opened wide with the laughter. The sound was ominous as it parted from him.

"You don't know everything," Rosemary said, defiantly. "Each soul has its own independent right to make its own choices!"

"No soul would choose to be friends with the devil."

"I would," Rosemary said. Her face did not show any sign of wavering, her expression resolute. "I did, when I was Margaret!"

"Goodnight, Rose Petal," he said, forcing an even tone into his voice.

"I'm not tired now."

"I am."

He walked toward the door and did not turn to look at her. "Peaceful dreams," he said, as he closed her door.

Hopefully, sleep would come fast for him. He did not want to lie awake and think about tomorrow.

He opened his eyes to darkness.

The surface on which his back lay was soft, but narrow. Lucifer pulled his arms and legs closer to his torso, as his right side slid to the edge of the couch.

Rubbing his fingertips across his forehead, he pressed his temples. He squeezed his eyes shut, as he contemplated the order of today's tasks. A visit to the local jail would be his first mission. Afterward, he would find the courage to sever his human connection to Rosemary.

Lucifer's fingertips smoothed his closed eyelids outward. He couldn't allow his thoughts to extend beyond this very moment. The process of neutralizing Rosemary's threat depended on his utmost concentration.

He lay still and listened for any movements in the dark house.

Judging by the darkness, it was probably four or five a.m. Rosemary was obviously still asleep in her room.

Lowering one foot to the floor, then the other, Lucifer stood and walked to Rosemary's room. Her door was closed and he quietly opened it. He stood before her as she slept.

Fred was asleep in the crate, beside Rosemary. Samantha's tail was curled around herself, while she slept on the pillow above Fred's crate. The alarm clock on the nightstand read five a.m.

Lucifer went back to the couch and lay there, on his back.

Slowing his heart rate, Lucifer breathed in and out, with intention. His chest rose and fell, in measured rhythm.

In his meditative state, he no longer felt his human body…

His inner vision focused on Koratz's face.

A golden light glowed over Lucifer's body, as his soul rose from his chest…

Chapter 16

The Two-Headed Snake Inside Lucifer

Koratz was asleep on his cot. Lucifer hovered over the prisoner.

Speaking telepathically to Koratz's soul, Lucifer demanded its alertness.

A beam of red extended – a vaporous tunnel – from Lucifer's orb to the man's soul, inside his body.

Koratz opened his eyes. His pupils enlarged. His mouth opened, with no sound.

The bright, translucent orb above soothed the man's brain immediately back to slumbering unconsciousness. Koratz's eyes closed.

The prisoner's glowing soul now ascended from his body; it was lined with a grayish aura. It stayed connected to the body with a golden cord. Lucifer circled the man's body and aura with the same red beam of light, connecting the two souls.

The souls communicated in another dimension. If anyone looked into the cell, they would not be visible to the untrained human eye.

As their spirit connection locked, Lucifer showed the man telepathic visions of what would become of him if he did not realign with the loving energy. The visions resembled movie screens, allowing the man a look into his future. One screen presented Koratz slamming down the prison phone, because his brother would not accept his call. Another screen showed an older Koratz, with gray hair, being beaten in a maximum security prison. The third movie displayed Koratz's long self-imprisonment in Hell, in which his negative core has attracted an experience of isolation in a dark cell. All three movies played for Koratz simultaneously.

Lucifer only hoped that the disclosure would direct this human to reconnect with the goodness of soul.

Then the movie screens blackened.

Koratz's Earthly experience had been derailed at an early age, due to his father's abuse. The combative approach to life was modeled by the father and passed to the son. It was a result of disconnect.

Lucifer displayed for Koratz the reason behind his disconnection to the flow of loving energy: one screen now showed wounding scenes of Koratz's childhood, being scolded and beaten by his father. In the scene, the young boy cried: "Daddy, I will never be like you!" Hopefully, the revelation would help Koratz's soul heal.

The movie screen blackened.

Lucifer then showed Koratz the act of Rosemary caring for Fred. The scene of Rosemary presented her surrounded by a thick, golden light, glowing all around her body protectively. Rosemary was hugging and kissing the dog. Gold light also surrounded Fred. The light surrounding Rosemary then turned so bright as to blind and repel Koratz. It established Rosemary was a positive being, who did not draw negative.

"Your energies do not match. You must leave her be," Lucifer communicated, on a soul level.

At this point in his human existence, there was no magnetism to the positive for Koratz; his essence must separate itself from incompatible energies. By universal law, it would be improbable that he would be afforded significant interaction with Rosemary, but her life was too precious to leave any opening for a chance meeting with this man. In case of a possible cosmic upset, or a mysterious happening that caused misaligned stars, a rigid command was embedded in this man, on a soul level, that he would no longer have a desire to engage Rosemary.

Lucifer focused the last of his force on permeating a gold light, surrounding Koratz with healing energy. The light extended from Lucifer's orb to Koratz's, and circled Koratz's soul and human body.

The message of recovery had been spiritually received, but it would require active work, on a human cellular degree. Koratz's human brain would probably never remember this meeting, but deep in his subconscious would remain a distaste for destruction. Koratz's soul was now housed back inside the chest of his human body, which lay on the cot.

As Lucifer began to withdraw his focused energy, foggy voices and blurred figures came into his awareness, from beneath his orb. Lucifer's energy, now firmly back in his core, discerned that two men in dark uniforms, with holsters on their hips, had gathered and now stood over Koratz. The voices and figures were clear now, as they shook Koratz's body and moved his face from side to side. One of the men felt for a pulse, as he held two fingers against the prisoner's throat.

"I feel a pulse," he said.

"Koratz! Wake up!" the other guard shouted.

He would wake, Lucifer knew. Hopefully, the encounter with Koratz's soul would kindle an innate yearning within the man for redemption.

Lucifer's energy now concentrated on Rosemary.

The iridescent tunnel extended from his core...

Rosemary's face was envisioned, as Lucifer's vaporous orb was magnetically pulled into the channel, toward her. He equated the sensation to a rollercoaster. There was no thought during the travel, only course of action. The swirling, translucent tunnel propelled him through space to the determined destination.

The soft skin of Rosemary's face hazily came into view. Her eyes were closed in slumber. The feathering of her smooth, reddish-brown locks, perfectly disorderly, framed her forehead and cheeks.

There she was. Asleep in her bed. Peacefully. Lucifer's orb hovered above her.

His energy now prepared for the conversion to Lucas's body. His essence envisioned his human body, and he was directly transported there. The golden cord pulled the illuminated soul inside.

The human chest soon rose and fell, in a hard compression. Leaving his eyes closed, his energy adjusted to the human form. He mentally registered feeling in his fingertips and toes. Breaths became more evenly distributed by his lungs. He opened his eyes.

Sluggishly, he stood. Heavy breathing now laboriously moved his chest, as he budged his legs in forward motion. A cool wetness dripped from his forehead, yet his skin felt heated beneath it. It felt as though he pulled his arm from cement, as he lifted it to wipe his forehead.

He walked to Rosemary's room and stood before her. He now viewed her with human eyes.

The alarm clock on the nightstand still read five a.m.

Time did not exist.

Only on Earth, worldly components and humans aged physically. Afterlife and other dimensions were infinite.

Lucifer quietly exited the room and lay back down on the couch. Transforming had taken its toll. He closed his eyes.

He heard light footsteps move toward him. A heavy breath of air exited his lungs, as a weight rested atop his chest. Two front paws pressed onto him. His stomach then felt the impact of Samantha's back legs as she settled in place, with the bulk of her concentrated on his chest. The weightiness of her warmth covered him like a cozy blanket, as she curled her soft body. It was comforting. He took slow breaths in and out, listening to her purrs. She calmed his physiological makeup.

The strong aroma of brewed coffee slowly coaxed Lucifer into wakefulness. His nostrils flared as he deeply inhaled the house's morning scent.

He lifted and turned his head to see Rosemary. She was in the kitchen, pouring steaming, dark liquid into a mug. She wore snug, faded-blue work jeans. The t-shirt she wore must have been favored work clothing, because he had seen her in it a couple of other times: an orange logo shirt from the shelter; it curved around her chest and clung to her taut midsection, flaring slightly over her stomach.

He sat upright and watched her. Rosemary's movements were graceful, as she flittered about the kitchen. Her fingers appeared to curl around the coffee-pot handle, as if each one were a separate butterfly, approaching its perch. Pretty, pink nail polish decorated the tips of her fingers; she must have painted them this morning, while Lucifer slept.

She looked bright and attractive, with her orange shirt, pink nails and cherry-colored lips. Rosemary placed the pot back onto its platform.

Femininity graced all of her body movements, whenever she relaxed in the carefree environment of her kitchen or garden. At the shelter, her body performed with focused feminine strength. Lucifer admired the softness and warmth of a woman's body. The shape of the female form stirred a reaction inside him, as it would any other man. There was such beauty in the curves of Rosemary's chest and hips. There was sensuality in the reddish halo that appeared to kiss the long strands of her golden-brown hair, which glided around her shoulders.

She had a welcoming air about her: mothering, loving... She spoke so affectionately to the animals and plants that Lucifer found himself wanting to be around her, craving her sweet voice and gentle touch.

As he continued to watch her, Rosemary turned her body toward him. Her eyes now met his. He swallowed hard. His throat felt dry. There was tightness in his chest, as he held his breath. A bright gold seemed to sparkle in her eyes as she caught his stare. A smile pulled at one edge of her mouth.

"Good morning," she said, as she walked toward him with the mug.

He quickly folded the blanket, strewn on the couch, and placed it on the armrest, as Rosemary handed him the mug.

"Thank you," he said. "Isn't this yours?"

"I already had a cup. You can have this one."

He patted the cushion beside him; "Have a seat." She sat down.

"Fred's doing good," she said. "The first day of having him here, his little body shook when I opened his crate; he doesn't shake anymore. Maybe he is feeling more comfortable here."

Lucifer looked toward the open crate at the foot of the couch. It was empty. The little dog lay on the rug in front of the coffee table.

"I see the pup is beginning to make himself at home," Lucifer said.

"You were sound asleep when I let him out this morning," Rosemary said. "He hasn't tried to walk, so I let him lie on the rug."

"He is a lucky pup, to have been adopted into this family," Lucifer said.

Samantha studied Fred from atop the couch. Her slow, blinking eyelids showed her tolerance. Her tail curved around her body, and the tip only occasionally flicked. Attentive yet relaxed, her ears only twitched at louder sounds.

"My 'Mantha was sound asleep on your chest when I got up to let Fred out," Rosemary said. "You two looked cozy. She must have snuck out of my room when I used the bathroom last night."

"Yes, Samantha kept me company."

Lucifer took a drink of coffee. The warm liquid filled his mouth and coated his throat. It seemed to rouse his alertness. He set the mug on the table and carefully held Rosemary's gaze.

"Koratz is taken care of. You have nothing to worry about now. You are safe, Rose Petal," he said.

She tightly pulled her brows together. "You saw him? When?"

"Early this morning I met with the man." Lucifer felt his shoulder muscles relax, voicing those words. There was such relief knowing that he had completed his mission of protecting Rosemary. "I communicated with Koratz, soul to soul. He knows to leave you alone."

"Thank you," she quietly said. "So, everything went how you

361

expected?" A short pause followed each word.

"Yes," he again held her gaze, "everything went according to plan. Koratz is neutralized." He picked up the mug and took another slow drink of coffee.

"How much longer do we have?" Rosemary quietly but firmly asked.

"What?" Lucifer set his mug back down on the table.

"You have always said that you would leave after neutralizing Koratz."

A heavy breath was exhaled from his mouth. "I will leave today."

"Would you stay?" she asked. Moisture began to glisten in her eyes. "Here? With me? I need you. Chuck needs you. The shelter needs you. Will you stay?"

"You shouldn't ask that. You wouldn't if you knew what I have done."

"You are not the devil, Lucas; you are just Lucas to me," she said, resolutely. "There is no such thing as the devil. 'Devil' is just a word humans created, to label their fear. You are a healer. You are a good soul, who heals others. Your soul is pure."

"Rosemary—" he began.

"Please, let me continue. Some people consider me odd," she said, "that I'd rather share my time with animals and plants and trees, but you've always appreciated that in me. You've healed me, in some ways, just by listening to me, and talking with me about my family. You helped me look at some dark places in my heart and examine that darkness. I feel it allowed a healing light to shine through. You came into my life…"

She softly trailed off. As he looked toward her, she lifted her hand and rested it gently on the side of his face.

"...and you altered my whole view of the world. Of being human. You made me fall in love with you," Rosemary said.

She pressed her shoulder against him, as she leaned her upper body into his. Her hand felt warm, still caressing his face. As though she were *his* ruler, her caress compelled him into submission. He turned his face further into her touch. He wished he could articulate a proper objection.

"You can't come into my life, do all that and then just leave," she demanded.

Lucifer did not like the urges her touch on his skin encouraged, but it felt comforting to allow her control. Moisture beaded on his forehead. He knew he was not going to resist.

It seemed that human desires overtook his ability to maintain self-control. Perspiration also accumulated across his shoulder blades and up the back of his neck. It felt like his blood became molten and slowly flowed underneath his skin, heating every inch. His heart was pumping fast. It felt as if a freight train barreled through him, racing underneath his shirt, threatening to crack through his chest.

As he looked into her affectionate gaze, her other hand moved to the other side of his face, and she now held him securely on either side. He felt safe being held by her. He only focused on her gaze. Her soul. The sensation of touch was intensified as he stilled his mind.

Lucifer felt as though he were her puppet, as she pressed her fingertips into his skin and tipped his face down, closer to hers. Her fingers seemed to dig deep into his skull. It felt as though her fingertips now reached under his skin, gripping his cheeks and jawbone, as she pulled him even closer. His eyes closed.

An incredible softness crushed his mouth, as Rosemary's lips pressed against his.

His chest rose and fell quickly, pushing the air from his nostrils. It felt like venom coursed through his entire body and immobilized him. Otherworldly sensations were being felt, it seemed, as her mouth pressed onto his, with an ethereal pressure. He deeply inhaled the rich scent of vanilla and lemon, she leaning in so close.

The fleshiness of her lips slowly gathered, then flattened along the line of his slightly opened mouth. The softness of her lips smoothed out across the entire length of his. She held the position, as if savoring the sensation herself. Their lips touching, barely open, only a small hint of her breath passed through to him.

A moist heaviness more fully parted his lips, as her mouth added slow pressure to his. He was immersed in the warm, sweet rush of her breath. It flowed inside him, like a stimulating summer sun.

He wanted to possess a part of her essence inside him, so she would be with him always.

As they sat so close, Rosemary hugged her upper body against him. Her arms moved around his neck, pulling him into her, as she pressed herself onto him. Her feminine shape fit on top of his chest, as her body weight pushed both of them against the arm of the couch.

His mouth slowly began to move underneath hers. Her breaths came even faster and harder inside of him. It felt as if a forbidden snake had entered his body and moved his arms, when each hand held either side of Rosemary's face. His fingertips pressed onto the smoothness of her skin.

Gently coaxing, her mouth opened wider, and his tongue slowly moved along hers, in long, sensual caresses. Two acquainted energies became one, once again, as their breaths merged together. Lucifer relaxed in the comfort and ease of the familiarity. Wetness moistened his fingertips, as they seemingly melded into Rosemary's skin.

He pulled back to look at her, her face just above his. She looked into his eyes, her own watery. His thumbs gently wiped her tears as he held her face.

"Please don't stop," she softly begged. "I love you."

He closed his eyelids, to stop his own tears from building. Lucifer then opened his watery eyes.

"Rose Petal, you are my life. You are anything and everything good that is a part of my existence. I love you for eternity."

She closed her eyes and he moved his hands to her hairline, on either side of her face. His fingers entangled her strands. He had a desire to feel a strand of her hair underneath his nose. Straightening a long curl between his fingers, he smoothed it all around his nose and lips. He deeply inhaled the lush fragrance and felt the silkiness on his skin.

Tingles seemed to disperse embers, then sparks of fire, throughout his core. His whole body became rigid, alert. It felt like every cell inside him was awakening with a new, vivid color.

His chin tipped up to her, and he placed a deliberate kiss on her forehead; he closed his eyes as his lips lingered there. He breathed in her scent. Continuing to inhale deeply, his mouth lightly stroked the delicate skin of her face, as he moved downward to her cheekbone. He kissed along the hollow. His lips lowered to the edge of her jaw and kissed the length of it, while gently turning her head.

He skimmed his fingertips along the sides of her neck, to the nape of her hairline. Strands of her hair fell all around his face, as her chest rested on top of him. His mouth followed the direction of his hands; he slowly moistened her throat with kisses, while he massaged the back of her head with gentle tugs of her curls.

Lucifer moved his legs up on the couch, to lie flat. Rosemary lay on top of him, her legs nestled between his. The softness of her upper body pressed into him.

His whole physique felt hard, responsive. Every muscle contracted, as Rosemary's midsection snugly fit against him.

Not able to wait a second longer, he took possession of her mouth again. Her warm breath once again entered him, as she welcomed his breath inside her. Moans rose from inside her chest and throat, as his tongue circled hers. His tongue curled like the forbidden snake's head.

It then seemed that another snake slithered up his spine – this one a two-headed snake. One of its heads curled around a blood vessel in his veins, and expanded each one to a pulsating balloon, so swollen that each would soon burst.

The other head of the serpent was icy cold, and soon wrapped around his beating heart, nearly shocking it into awareness. The mouth of the snake then spewed numbing-cold serum into every recess of his sluggish brain.

Stop! You are stealing her innocence!

It seemed that the cry from within him screamed at the unrestrained snake, that had seemingly overtaken his human body.

His legs fitfully loosened their clasp on Rosemary's, nestled snugly between them. Rosemary's soft hair fell from his opened hands, as he moved his arms from around the back of her head.

He took one last breath, with her inside of him, then his mouth slowly withdrew from hers.

He quickly wiped a warm, wet trail that etched the sides of his face and jawline.

Lucifer grasped the sides of Rosemary's waist and moved her aside. He sat upright and distanced himself.

Rosemary sat up beside him. Obviously confused, her facial muscles scrunched, and her lips remained slightly open in question.

"I know your work is important at the castle," she said. "I understand that you need to get back there."

She didn't look at him as she stood, and walked toward her bedroom.

"I would love nothing more than to stay here with you, Rose Petal," he called after her. Fresh tears filled his eyes. "You will not want me to stay after you know what I have done. I could never stay without telling you first. It would be dishonest."

She turned to him. "What are you talking about? What have you done?"

Tears pooled in the corners of his eyes, and escaped in two virtual rivers down both sides of his face. "I delivered your father to Hell."

Her lips formed an open circle. They stayed rounded, as she stood in place. She did not speak. The sufficient gravity of words, it seemed, could not be formed in her traumatized mind. Water began to pool underneath her bottom eyelids. The shiny tears sparkled, as they filled

367

to her irises and spilled out.

He had underestimated the amount of hurt he supposed he would witness in her, and misjudged the magnitude of the shame that would afflict him. His hand quivered, as he raised it to wipe his face.

"Leave now!" she said, firmly. Her voice was stronger than her shaky stance. "I can't believe I fell for your sham."

Her face scrunched tightly. "You told me that you were drawn to me." Rosemary chuckled, in distress. "You probably made all that stuff up about us... being married before. You weren't drawn to *me*; you were drawn to my father, and I just happened to be there. He thought he deserved Hell and you merrily took him. Get out!"

Darkness shielded Lucifer from the difficult moment, as he shut his eyes. He listened to his breaths slowly, shakily inhaling and exhaling. Then he reopened his eyes.

"Rosemary, I am sorry. I could not have divulged the information about your father when we first met. I have always loved you. You are my *only* love. And, yes, we *were* married. I lost track of you on purpose, *because* I love you. I did not want you to be subjected to the dark side of being."

He wanted to walk to her and hold her. He wanted to touch her face in a thoughtful caress, but he kept his distance.

"You know that no one is forced to Hell," he continued; "each soul chooses one's own destination. It wasn't up to me; your father chose to go there. It was where his energy was drawn. I helped your father acclimatize to the human death process."

"Leave!" she screamed.

"I will go, Rosemary, but not until we talk calmly about this. I don't want to leave you when you're distressed."

"Leave now, or I will call the police."

"I will be next door," he said, calmly. "I will wait there until you are ready to talk."

His voice a low rasp, he then added: "Rosemary, my darling... all you have to do is tell me to stay. Now that you know the complete truth, all you have to do is tell me to stay, and I will stay."

She turned and went to her bedroom.

Chapter 17

Rosemary's Void

Rosemary shut and locked her bedroom door. She lay, fully dressed, on top of the comforter.

She listened for the front door to open, then shut upon Lucas's exit. When she heard his departure, she removed her clothing and changed into a tank top and pajama pants. She then went to the living room to get Fred. Leaving him in his crate next to her, she lay on her back in bed, hoping to get a quick nap before leaving for work.

A slow trail of tears made their way across her cheeks, to the pillow.

Her father had thought his soul deserved Hell?

The ingrained sound of Frank's impatient voice now rattled through her mind. He had continually warned her of Mark's lack of affection. It had felt like a struggle to spend enjoyable time with her father.

She then remembered the look on her mother's swollen face, the day her father had admitted his infidelity. Josephine's cheeks were bright red and moistened from continuous crying. Frank had begged for forgiveness.

He had apparently regarded the total of his human life awful enough to have gravitated to the negative of Hell.

Her father had learned from his mistakes, and wanted his daughter's life to be enriched by his experiences. There was atonement observed in his act of helping plan Josephine's funeral. In Rosemary's opinion, he had redeemed himself *before* he had died; his soul should have been

370

released from any negativity.

Unconsciousness for just a few minutes would benefit Rosemary's state of mind. She closed her eyes. Tears still trickled from under her lids. She slowly breathed in, allowing her stomach to protrude with the air.

Behind shut eyes, she pictured a blank, white space. Not attaching her brain to anyone, she visualized the random thoughts that bombarded her, floating across the ceiling of the white space.

A welcoming void seemed to swathe her…

Rosemary's eyes opened slowly, to a sense of rebalanced emotions. As she turned her head on the pillow, it remained wet; the tears and rest had allowed a release. She felt her soul and body had healed a bit.

She inhaled sharply, as she considered the time spent napping, and looked toward the alarm clock; it proved she had slept for twenty minutes. It felt longer. The time was now 9:45 a.m., and Lucas had left her home this morning, at about nine.

Actually, Lucas was kicked out this morning.

If she left right now, there would still be time to get to the shelter and complete most of her chores, before customers arrived at eleven a.m. She had texted Sharon, before her nap, to say that she'd be an hour late into work this morning.

Glancing at her cell phone on the nightstand, it notified a missed call. She picked it up and opened a text from Sharon. It read: *"Hey BFF, Lucas is here and is doing chores. He said you weren't feeling well today. Don't worry about coming in today. We got things covered. Talk later, Share."*

The dog's covered legs tapping against the crate was fast becoming a familiar sound.

"Okay, Fred," Rosemary said, "I'll let you outside now."

Rosemary opened the small door of the crate and carried the dog out to the yard. It would be a joyous day when Fred's cast was removed, and he no longer required the constraint of the enclosure. When they returned to the living room, after the bathroom break, Samantha watched from atop the arm of the couch, to observe the dog eat his breakfast. The cat's ears rotated toward the sound of her own dry food being poured into her dish, which was set on the plant table, in front of the moon plant in the kitchen. The cat jumped off the couch, and gave Fred a sideways glance as she passed him.

Rambo swam up to the top of the water as Rosemary approached the tank. He had already known her for a year, because she was the one who fed the fish whenever Frank traveled out of town for business.

It was about a half-hour trip to her father's home. He lived on a lake, and Rosemary considered it a mini-vacation for her and Samantha to stay at her father's while he was gone. His house was modern. His kitchen had always been stocked with Rosemary's favorite snacks; only when staying at her father's home would she eat chocolate-peanut-butter ice cream, frozen waffles, frozen pizza and microwave popcorn. A movie would be watched over the electric fireplace, with a view of the lake outside.

The sneaky memories that stole her focus as she fed Rambo caused an onset of anxiety. She would never again feed Rambo in that house. She would never again be greeted on his doorstep with a hug, by her father. She had to sell her father's home. Even though Rosemary appreciated the modern design of the lakehouse, her soul seemed to thrive more with land and trees. Sharon had promised to help her with Frank's estate.

With the sudden anxiety, and having to mentally digest all of the supernatural information Rosemary had received over the past few days, it would probably be beneficial to stay home today.

The morning ritual of drinking a cup of coffee while applying her facial moisturizer and sunscreen had been Rosemary's routine for years. A homemade egg sandwich, prepared the prior night, was typically consumed on the ride to work, due to time restraint. She preferred to watch her recorded soap opera and read at night. Usually, she set her morning alarm for just enough time to prepare coffee and dress for work.

A hearty breakfast was usually reserved for Sundays. The shelter was closed to the public on that particular day of the week, and allowed a later arrival. Rosemary's lips pressed together, as she thought of cooking scrambled eggs and bacon for herself now.

She eyed the dog, lying still on the carpet, by the couch, so she left him there while she went to her bedroom.

It was a little chilly in the house. She got her long robe, hung from a peg on the closet door, and slipped her arms into the lengthy, cozy sleeves. She snugly tied the cloth belt around her waist. It felt like her mother giving her a hug. Josephine had given her the robe as a Christmas gift.

Last night's and this morning's clothes had been tossed onto the floor, beside the closet. Usually Rosemary was fairly neat but, when stressed by a busy schedule, a little clutter around the house didn't bother her.

She put on her pink, fluffy socks. They corroborated with today's easy schedule, as she now stood at the oven and arranged the cold strips of red meat in a pan.

Samantha's golden face looked up at Rosemary from the floor, as the bacon sizzled and splattered when Rosemary flipped it.

"You'll get a little," she told the cat, "but you have to save some for Fred, too, now."

She prepared the scrambled eggs and toast, and plated the breakfast. The cat followed her to the couch and settled on the armrest. Rosemary turned on the television to a morning talk show and ate her food. She tore a small piece of meat each for Samantha and Fred.

Rosemary enjoyed the relaxing morning, but missed all the animals at the shelter, and her regular walk with Lula May. She also wondered how the new mama cat was doing. Surely Lucas would give extra attention to both Lula and Mama for her.

She set the empty plate on the coffee table. Fred's head did not move, but his brown eyes looked up at her.

"Hi, pumpkin," she said. "Come lie with me."

Gently cradling the dog, she moved him to the couch. She lay on her back and positioned him between the back cushion and her torso. His front legs and head rested on her stomach, while his back end was supported by the bulky blanket draped over her.

A little wet lick kissed the back of Rosemary's hand. She looked downward. It felt as though her whole body bubbled with a warm stream of joyfulness, as Fred continued to gently lick her hand. She closed her eyes and felt the sweet closeness, listening to the voices from the television.

She was covered with the very same blanket Lucas had used when he had lay on her couch. She rested her head on the same pillow.

Tomorrow would return to normalcy. Today would be a day of rest.

This day she napped, cuddled with Fred, ate comfort food, watched television, napped, cuddled with Fred, read a book, ate, watched television and slept.

Friday morning, Rosemary woke to the heaviness and warmth of Samantha on her chest. It was comforting. Her eyes still closed, she reached for the cat's head and petted it.

The house was quiet. Only deep purrs vibrated from Samantha.

Rosemary smiled at the thought of exercising with Lula today. Breathing in fresh air and basking in the late morning sun would be therapeutic. She opened her eyes and widened her smile at Samantha.

The clock on the nightstand read 8:31 a.m. Typically, Rosemary woke about a half-hour earlier on a weekday, but had indulged in a few minutes of extra rest this morning. She reached for her phone, with Samantha still on her chest.

The screen indicated an unread text. She opened the message. It read: *"Rose! Lucas is here doing chores. He said you need another day off. He said you still weren't feeling well. You better call me! Love, Share."*

As Rosemary forcefully sat upright, Samantha jumped off of her and then the bed. Rosemary felt her eyebrows scrunch together. She would not stay away from work today. It was not Lucas's place to direct her life!

She would not miss out on a walk with Lula today, no matter how uncomfortable it might be if Lucas were at the shelter. Plus, she wanted to check on the new mama cat. She would text Sharon in about an hour, to ask if Lucas was still there. Rosemary did not wish to see him but, even if he were still there, that would not deter her from working.

She admitted that she would benefit from a more leisurely morning, not rushing right to work. Although her physical body now felt fully primed to shed energy, her brain would benefit from a gradual return to busyness.

"I know, Samantha. I'll get it now," Rosemary told the cat, while she headed for the kitchen.

The cat rested on the armrest of the sofa. Her golden, rounded face was lifted to Rosemary, and a delicate meow came from it. Breakfast had been requested.

Fred was fed in the living room, and Samantha always ate in the kitchen. Rosemary would still have to get used to plucking worms for Rambo's meal every morning. Directly after breakfast, Fred would have a bathroom break.

When Rosemary opened the front door to the outside world, the freshness of it tantalized her senses. The smells, sounds and sights excited her even more for a walk with Lula.

After another day's hearty breakfast for herself, Rosemary dressed in her work clothes. She felt most beautiful in a t-shirt, jeans and sneakers. Her frizzy, curly hair hung loose from underneath a ball cap.

Only moisturizer, sunscreen, and an S.P.F. lip balm were applied to her face. She took a nutritional meal bar from the cupboard and a reusable water bottle from the fridge.

Looking down at her phone now, she saw that Sharon had just texted a reply to her, stating that Lucas had left the shelter for the day. Even if he hadn't, Rosemary had already gotten ready to leave for work.

The early-afternoon sun cast a soft, yellowish light. Walking out of her back door and onto the porch, she glanced toward her neighbor's house. Supposedly, Lucas would be occupying the vacant place now. Rosemary continued sideways looks as she made her way to her vehicle. The thumping of her heart increased as she hurried her stride.

The glimpses provided no sign of the shiny, black sports car in the neighbor's driveway or shed. The house looked dark and quiet. Was Lucas there? Would he eventually contact her? Or would he only respond if she initiated contact?

Maybe Lucas had returned to Hell? The thought caused sadness. She already missed him.

How could she be in love with the man who took her father... to...?

She needed time to grasp those facts but, for now, she forced her thoughts toward an emotionally uplifting walk with Lula. Determinedly, her mind would be occupied only with the present moment, when she opened the door to the shelter.

Pulling into the parking lot, she saw Sharon's car was parked in its usual spot. An unfamiliar truck was parked alongside it. A look inside the long front window showed a young woman cradling a cat. Rosemary walked around to the side of the building, not wanting to disturb the customer. Upon unlocking and opening the door, a smile emerged from deep within her at the sound of the dogs' soft whimpers, in delight at her appearance.

"Hi, pups," she said, only glancing down the row, not wanting eye contact to generate louder barks.

They had been let outside in the yard for a bathroom break and fed, and they greeted her with restraint, compared to an early-morning opening.

She put her keys inside her purse, as she walked to the storage-room closet. She stashed her purse there, then took a handful of dog treats from a container on the shelf, and placed them in her pants pocket. On her way out of the room, she enfolded a few cat treats in her palm.

"Hello, Mama," she greeted, as she opened the door to the quarantine room. The nightlight provided a soft, comforting glow.

The black cat lay in her blanket-filled basket. Her fluffy tail curled around her protruded stomach; her bony back contrasted the fullness. Mama looked up at Rosemary and softly meowed. The cat then yawned, and her long, pink tongue was bared as it rolled out. Rosemary knelt next to the cat and gently petted the length of its curled back. She then set the treats inside the basket.

"Share texted me that you've been eating good, Mama," Rosemary quietly said. Smiling, gazing at the cat munching on her treats, Rosemary then backed out of the room.

A cheerful hum came from her throat and vibrated out of her nostrils, as she started back to the dog room. The song appeared to emerge on its own, letting her know that she was okay.

Now, in front of the row of pens, her eyes searched. Her heart felt as though it flipped with anticipation, but anxiety slowly seemed to grasp its hand around her throat and choke it.

Rosemary quit humming.

Something sorrowful in her soul seemed to sink through her bones. Thinking back to her entrance, there had not been her most-loved, distinctive yowl amongst the group. That unique sound had always been present, whenever Rosemary approached the pens. Peering toward Lula's enclosure, she saw that the mattress was not in its usual spot.

Rosemary's gait increased. The heightened heart rate caused breaths to rush through her chest. She looked for the water bowl, or a toy. Did Sharon rearrange things? With each stride closer, Rosemary saw an empty pen. There were no bowls, toys, carpet or bed. No dog was occupying that particular space.

Rosemary curled her fingers around the cold steel of the gate, as she looked at the bare cement floor. Her breaths continued to come shallow.

A rigorous checklist had to be confirmed before any adoption: there were vet background checks, inspections for fenced yards, and checks for past animal cruelty offenses.

Rosemary now peered inside each pen, going down the rows one pen at a time.

A volunteer must be walking Lula. But there were no extra vehicles in the lot. Only hers, Sharon's and that one customer's. Maybe the volunteer who was on a walk with the dog had ridden a bike to the shelter? There hadn't been a bike stored in the lot.

Sharon must be in the middle of cleaning the pen. Maybe the dog had a bathroom accident on the floor. Lula is outside, in the fenced yard...?

Rosemary hurriedly walked the middle aisle toward the back door, and opened it. The yard was empty. Her hand instinctively grasped her chest. It rested over her heart as she examined the empty yard.

Moisture built in her eyes and spilled from the corners; it wetted her eyelashes as she blinked. She shut the door.

Rosemary audibly exhaled the restrained breath in her chest, as her back pressed against the cold steel of the closed door. Looking down the rows of enclosures, the dogs returned her blank stare.

Chuck glanced up at her.

"Hi, pumpkin," she softly said.

The trail of wetness quietly continued from her eyes, down each side of her face. She rubbed her forehead. A small headache was beginning to form. Rosemary wiped her cheeks and her fingertips dampened. She swept them across her jeans.

There were questions for Sharon. Using the bottom of her shirt, Rosemary dried her dripping nose.

"Share!"

Sharon had been going about her busy workday, and had just entered the dog room, reaching for a collar and leash. She looked down the pen area to see Rosemary.

"*Rose?* What are you doing here?" Sharon asked. She studied Rosemary from a distance, down the walkway. "You look like you don't feel good. My goodness, Rose, are you okay?" Sharon walked down the aisle, toward her friend.

Rosemary again rubbed her forehead. "I thought it would be good for me to come for a visit, but I guess it was too much," she replied.

Sharon reached her friend and gave Rosemary a hug. "What's wrong, Rose?" she asked, her arms still tight around her friend. "Are you sick? Lucas said you were just run down... exhausted. He thought you might need a little extra time off, with everything you've been through lately: losing your dad and that ordeal with Fred. I agree a few days off would be good for you. You do look awful."

Sharon released her embrace and stood back, to again study Rosemary. "Your face is all red. Your eyes are pink. Do you have a fever?" Sharon asked, feeling her friend's forehead. "Have you been crying, Rose?"

"No, I'm just tired. I have been through a lot."

"Lucas seemed really worried about you. How close *are* you two? I know you had dinner together – you said it was just a neighborly gesture – but he seems to really care about you."

"He's just my neighbor. He acts like an overprotective brother."

"Good. He's a little intense—"

"Where is Lula May?" Rosemary interrupted.

"I was going to tell you tonight, when we talked. It's the best news!" Sharon smiled. "Remember that couple that had wanted Jerry Lee, but lost out to the first applicants who applied for him?"

"Yes." Rosemary's stomach seemed to spin with bile and she felt nauseous. She gripped her arms around her waist as she stood in place.

"We already had all their information; their veterinarian had verified past pet records; a fenced-in yard was confirmed; they were already approved for adoption. They decided they would take Lula!"

A swift rush of lightheadedness weighed Rosemary down. It felt as though a hammer pounded downward from the top of her head, through the inside of her chest, down her spine and legs. Could she withstand this news?

"But they said they preferred a smaller dog," Rosemary managed, "not a St. Bernard."

"Well, they decided to take Lula. They got her last evening." Sharon's eyes narrowed, as she studied Rosemary. "I'm sorry, Rose; I know Lula was your favorite. You'll miss her.

"I think you need some more sleep. Please go home and sleep. Take care of yourself. Everything is good here. Lucas said he'd be here tomorrow, so if you still aren't feeling well—"

"Good, I might need one more day off tomorrow."

"Promise you'll go home and take care of yourself? I'll call you tonight. I'll even stop by to check on you."

"Thank you, but I'll be okay. I just need sleep." Rosemary then added: "You're dealing with a lot now, too. How is your aunt doing? You said you've been driving your mom to see Aunt Sybil."

"Aunt Sybil is feeling much better. Thank goodness her pneumonia is finally clearing up. So, you'll stay home tomorrow and get some extra rest? I don't need you getting sick on me, too. You'd better call me if you need anything!"

"I will. You sure you'll be okay without me?"

"Yes, Lucas will be here. You know he does a great job. He'll walk dogs tomorrow. Today he just had time to clean, but tomorrow he said he will stay longer and do walks."

Sharon quickly hugged her friend again, then left the building, with a dog, for an afternoon walk – a job Rosemary should be doing right now. With Rosemary on the fritz and no replacement, Sharon closed the lobby temporarily while she exercised the pups.

Rosemary walked to Lula's pen and went inside. She descended to her knees on the hard floor. Her eyes felt swollen; the lids were thick and heavy. She closed them and felt her chest shudder with shaky intakes of breath. *No tears.* Her face still. Her mind dull. It felt as though she were standing at the edge of a cliff, looking down.

Chuck looked at Rosemary from the pen beside her. Turning and seeing his brown eyes and gentle face caused the tears to form in her eyes. He would miss Lucas as much as she would miss Lula May. Rosemary now felt as though her spirit was freed, and she floated down that cliff.

She sobbed right there. As if a child. Or was this a nervous breakdown?

The sobs came so fast and hard that her nose clogged, and she couldn't breathe through it. The discharge from her nose mixed with the saturation of the tears that edged her chin.

Every article of Lula's was now absent from the pen. Her favorite plush teddy was not waiting on the bed. There was no reminder, not even a tuft of loose fur on the floor. Only pictures would remain of Lula.

In Rosemary's mind's eye, she could see herself now bending to the dog's neck and attaching a leash to the collar. A kiss on the thickly-furred head had been the standard before heading outside for the walk.

Rosemary audibly pulled in a gulp of air.

It was quiet in the dog room now; only constrained whines from a few pups could be heard. Most napped on their mattresses, having eaten breakfast. Romeo, the new dog beside Lula's pen, drank from his water bowl. Each lap of liquid from his tongue sounded loud amid the stillness.

It should have been conveyed to Sharon that Rosemary would adopt Lula herself, after Fred had healed and settled into his new home. No customer had expressed interest in adopting the large dog, so Rosemary had not felt pressured to explain her long-term plan. Maybe she hadn't explained her plan out loud because there was uncertainty in her decision, but now the decisiveness had become perfectly clear. Rosemary loved Lula May, and had wanted to take her home. Her anguish over losing the dog would be explained at a later date to Sharon; it was too embarrassing now to admit, even to herself, the negligence of not claiming Lula as her own.

Rosemary rose from her knees and gathered her purse from the closet, then walked to the door. It would not be a joyful return here. Tomorrow would be too soon to resume work.

Rosemary stepped outside. As she opened her truck door, she felt moisture rebuild behind her lashes. She inhaled deeply, started the ignition and drove from the parking lot.

The thought of opening home's front door, and seeing Samantha, Fred and Rambo, gave her some relief from her sadness.

After arriving home and caring for the animals, Rosemary locked herself in the bedroom. She pulled the cord that lowered the blinds, and there was darkness and privacy from the outside world. Blackness. Its calm would shield her.

Everything she had learned and experienced the last few weeks would slowly be absorbed by her brain and soul. She would begin that process underneath the covers of her bed. Tomorrow morning would arrive without her seeing the first of the daylight; she set no alarm.

Now dressed in pajamas, she positioned herself on her side on the mattress, facing Fred's crate. Her nose was still slightly clogged, and it was easier to breathe if not on her back. Safely tucked underneath the sheets and comforter, the world seemed to disappear as she closed her eyes. Samantha took her place on the neighboring pillow.

Nothingness. Rosemary's thoughts became emptied from her brain. The self-preservation instinct overtook her body.

The void was welcomed.

A full night's sleep last evening had been nourishing. It had given Rosemary a renewed will to live a faith-based life.

The universe had arranged a family for Lula. Rosemary had to trust God's plan.

The days ahead would be most productively spent caring for the dogs and cats without families, that made their way into the shelter. That would be tomorrow's focus. Today Rosemary would grieve for many things. Especially Lula.

She attended to Samantha, Fred and Rambo, then lay back down in bed and pulled the covers up to her chin. The room was still darkened from the closed blinds. Sleep came easily. Her mind and body were worn.

Sadness would consume her emotions if she allowed her thoughts to center on seeing Lula's empty pen today.

Sharon had texted Rosemary earlier this morning, to inform her that Lucas was there and Rosemary's presence was not necessary. Rosemary had glanced at her phone during a wakeful moment, before falling back asleep.

"Good morning, pumpkin," she now whispered to Samantha. "Mom is finally going to get out of the house today. I will take your brother to get his bandages changed, and then Mom is going back to work."

The cat studied Rosemary's face, as if to try to understand the words. Lying on her side, Rosemary viewed the pair of wide-set, green eyeballs looking back at her from atop the adjacent pillow. A darkened-orange crease folded between the feline's eyes.

The new daily regimen of feeding Samantha, Rambo and Fred, and giving medicine and a bathroom break to the pup, was a reminder that life would always be enfolded with joyfulness. Rosemary would continuously share her home with animals, and the shelter would always accept a new stray.

Life had to go on.

Being Sunday, and the shelter being closed to customers, it would be a nice, quiet day. First, though, a trip to Wolfe Animal Hospital.

At 11:30 a.m., Rosemary had just returned home from the brief visit to the animal hospital. The veterinarian technician had made quick work of taking X-rays and redoing Fred's bandages.

Rosemary changed into her sports bra and logo t-shirt, then prepared coffee and poured it into a Thermos. A bottled water and protein bar were put in her purse.

After carrying Fred inside, after a bathroom break, and securing him in his crate, Rosemary now walked to her truck. It seemed that her eyes looked toward her neighbor's house of their own accord. Today there was no anxiety. Her energy felt zapped from her body, and there didn't seem to be anything left to fear.

Surely Lucas had vacated the shelter by now. Was he home? She stepped into her vehicle, wondering if he watched her from a window.

She drove to the shelter and pulled into the parking lot. She did not see the black sports car; only Sharon's little car, placed in its usual spot.

Upon her late-day arrival, opening the door to the dog room provoked only subdued barks and whines. One voice was missing, and the void caused Rosemary to hold a sharp breath, as though shielding the hurt. Her chest tightened as her breath appeared captured there. She held onto the edge of the table, near the side door. A thin strip of tears edged her cheeks, as she walked toward the storage room, to put her purse in the closet.

Now standing inside the storage room, she wiped her face and breathed out freely; she had held it until now. She had survived the first part: walking into the shelter.

As she went into the cat room, the floor looked shiny and there was a hint of bleach in the air. The room was clean. Most of the cats were sleeping or licking their paws, apparently after a nice breakfast.

Rosemary walked toward the reception area, where Sharon was facing the lit computer screen in front of her. Her fingers were moving over the keyboard.

"Share!" Rosemary called.

With a cheerful expression, Sharon turned back toward Rosemary's voice. "Hi, Rose!"

Though Sharon's eyes seemed to light up at the sight of her friend, Rosemary felt as though Sharon now scanned her body, from head to toe, in scrutiny.

"How are you feeling today?" Sharon asked. "You look tired. The rims of your eyes are still pink and your face is still blotchy."

"*Thanks*, Share," Rosemary teased.

"I thought you'd stay home for one more day – especially it being Sunday."

"I feel better." Rosemary walked to her desk space and slouched in her chair.

"*Are* you okay? What is it?" Sharon prodded with concern.

Rosemary had reflexively folded her bottom lip under her teeth. She then bowed her head and pressed her temples between her thumb and forefinger. Sharon breathed heavily, obviously continuing to carefully examine her friend.

"I wanted Lula," Rosemary said, her head still hung.

"What?"

She looked back up at her friend, then lowered her glance again with a loud exhale. "I wanted to take Lula home after Fred healed."

"Oh, Rose, you should have told me."

She looked back at Sharon. "I know. Maybe I was a little embarrassed… taking home another animal from our shelter. The crazy hoarder."

"Nothing to be embarrassed about. You shared a special connection with Lula." She giggled. "And I took three kittens from here. I'm the crazy cat lady, not you." Her smile lightened the mood.

"I just thought it was meant to be, and nothing would change that," said Rosemary. "No one had come in looking for a big dog."

Sharon's eyes seemed to soften, as they narrowed on her. "I'm sorry."

"There's nothing for you to be sorry for. I should have told you."

"I know you loved her. Are you going to be okay?"

"Yes, I will. She went to a good home. The universe arranged a family for Lula. I have to trust God's plan." Rosemary felt the heaviness of her swollen eyes.

Sharon got up and hugged her, then smiled. "I have something that might cheer you up a little: Lucas cleaned. He got here around eight a.m. I was here early. I asked him yesterday if he could get here early today."

Rosemary listened.

"Lucas did walk most of the dogs before he left today," Sharon said. She then smiled bigger. "Just Shelby and the two new beagles still need a walk."

"Beagles?" Rosemary pulled her brows tight.

"They're in Lula's pen." Sharon jutted her bottom lip in a grimace. "Sorry."

Another heavy breath exited Rosemary's lungs. "Life goes on," she said. "More animals need homes."

She closed her eyes as she concentrated. "*When* did you get the beagles?"

Sharon took Rosemary's hands and pulled her from her seat. "This morning, at eight a.m. That's the reason I was here early. I opened up, let Lucas in to clean, got two crates and headed to animal control, in Bravetown. The poor pups were on the euthanasia schedule for next week. Two females. Louise called me."

"She's always good about calling us, if there's an animal on the euthanasia list."

"She told me the beagles have already been quarantined there, thankfully, since Mama Cat is in our quarantine room. I would have told you about the beagles, but I wanted to surprise you."

A small grin pulled one edge of Rosemary's mouth. "Thank you for doing that by yourself today."

"Oh, and Dr. Greene already had a scheduled visit here this morning, for booster shots, so he was able to check out the beagles this morning. They got treated for tapeworms, even though Dr. Greene didn't find evidence of them, because they had fleas. And they got their first round of vaccinations. He said they looked to be about three years old. Go say hello to them, Rose. We have to name them."

"Okay. I'll check on Mama Cat, too."

"Yes, he also gave Mama an exam, and said she looks healthy. He drew blood and will call us with the results."

Rosemary began walking toward the cat room, and Sharon went back to her computer.

"Rose?" Sharon said.

"Yes?" Rosemary turned.

"I'm having a little dinner this evening. Since you're feeling better, I want you to come. I will invite Marten, Bob and Tracy... and Alan."

"So, it's a couples' dinner? You and your fiancé; your brother and his wife; and Alan and... me?"

"It's *just* Sunday dinner. Come! Six-thirty."

"Okay, I'll be there."

Rosemary started back toward Mama Cat's room.

"Alan does like you," Sharon called to Rosemary.

She once more turned back to her friend. "Did he tell you that?" She still felt no romantic feelings toward him, Rosemary mused to herself, but it would be nice to hear if he found *her* attractive.

"Yes, he did. He told me he considers you sweet. And pretty. He was over at my house with Bob the other day."

Rosemary contorted her mouth to a pucker on one side. "Your *brother* knows? You know I'm not interested in dating right now."

"I know, but it won't hurt to practice flirting. You're so bad at it, Rose. Practice on Alan."

Rosemary felt her mouth open, as though on its own, in surprise. She felt the ache in her eyes, still worn, as they widened. *"Share!"*

"Who knows? Maybe you'll change your mind about him?"

"I'll come to dinner tonight, as long as you realize that I have no plans of dating Alan."

"Just come. Six-thirty!"

At least there was something on Rosemary's mind now, besides grief.

Tenderness seemed to caress her insides, as Rosemary opened the door and watched over Mama Cat sleeping. A soft meow inadvertently came from the cat, as she yawned from her bed. Rosemary would spend some time with Mama later. Now, she closed the door to the quarantine room and headed toward the dogs.

She felt herself holding her breath as she neared the pens. Her lungs felt full; her chest felt tight; the air gushed out from her nose. She pressed her hand over her chest. Over her heart.

Lula's pen. It was going to be in plain sight, when she turned the corner into the room. Her eyes would open wide to confront the grief. She would look directly at the space that once contained her... *love.* Sadness would be inevitable. She again filled her lungs with air, and held it there.

She looked. There it was: Lula's pen. The air again gushed from her nose.

As she tensely peered in that direction, a small smile gently pulled up the corners of her mouth. The area didn't look cold and empty, like it had before the new pups arrived; a clean mattress, with sheets, was set in the middle of the floor. Two bowls had been placed at the foot of the bed. A few toys were strewn across the cement floor.

Two younger pups, with floppy ears, slept cuddled together, atop a layer of newspaper near the front of the pen.

She walked to the enclosure. The introduction sheet pinned to the gate was void of any information. Sharon and Rosemary would create the new presentation page together. She slowly lifted the latch and opened the door. Both pups' eyes opened wide, as their heads jolted upward.

"It's okay. Hi, girls," she said, gently.

Slowly, she lowered to a seated position on the floor. The two girls walked onto her lap and sniffed her clothes. She moved both hands along each one's sleek head and back. One of them licked her bare arm, and the other stuck its nose up to her face. A giggle came from within and passed her lips.

Rosemary laced her fingers together, behind her head, and lay on her back on the hard cement floor. The two pups stepped over her stomach, walked toward her head and nuzzled either side of her. The breath from their noses tickled her neck.

A full-voiced chuckle proved her resiliency. Lula May would be missed in the days to come, but the new pups would be a reminder that life should always be lived with appreciation.

She lay there for a few moments, to relish the new life in Lula's pen. She felt the girls' smooth fur, as she wrapped her arms around each one, resting the palm of her hand on each soft belly.

Rosemary finally sat back up, then stood and walked from their pen to the front of the room. Reaching above the table, she picked out two leashes. She'd walk the beagles together.

It had been emotionally beneficial for Rosemary to visit the shelter. Now home, pulling back into her driveway, she glanced toward her neighbor's house. As always, it looked vacant and dark. No sign of Lucas.

Walking to her front porch, she saw a small package sticking out of her mailbox. Forgotten mail of yesterday. Rosemary pulled the small box, and a few envelopes, from the mailbox, and opened the front door. She set the package and other pieces of correspondence on the desk.

She heard a soft whimper, as she walked through the living room. Rosemary smiled; the dog was beginning to respond with a sense of normalcy.

"Hi, pumpkin," she said to the pup.

She escorted Fred outside. Upon their return, Rosemary set the dog on his favorite spot on the carpet, with a treat and water, then she sat at the desk. The shine of the golden Buddha caught the attention of her peripheral vision.

Rosemary relaxed at the desk chair, her body practically collapsing into it. Her forearms and head rested on the smooth wood, as her torso bent forward. There seemed to be nothing left inside her to form tears, but her face scrunched anyway, as if trying to squeeze something from her eyes.

It was Sunday, and her father had always called her on her cell phone, at around six p.m., on this day. They would talk about each other's plans for the coming days. He would ask about her work and she would inquire about his.

Samantha jumped onto the top of the desk, as Rosemary stayed in place, shifting only her head to look at the cat.

"Hi, Samantha. What am I going to do, 'Mantha?'"

Rosemary closed her eyes. The rhythm of her breaths slowly moved through her bent torso. Her mind wandered to memories of her father's hospital stay – and his burial.

Opening the mail would be a good distraction. With a deep inhalation, she rose to an upright seated position and reached for the white envelopes: one bill and two credit card offers.

She lifted the small box and noted its weight: about two pounds. Her face pinched together in a tight scowl, after having inspected the address label; shutting her eyes seemed to reduce the uneasiness. There was no postage; no return house number. Just her name, handwritten in thick, black ink, in the same print that had topped the box her mother's vase was returned in.

Her chest tightened with a held breath, as she tore the sealed cover.

Chapter 18

Rosemary's Story

Rosemary pulled loose, white tissue paper from the beige box. It felt as though a ticking time bomb awaited her, as she felt her heart thud against her chest. Paper tore as she grabbed at it, until her fingertips landed upon the main content: a thick, padded object. She grasped it and pulled it from the packaging. There was a note and a small plastic container in the package; she left those for now.

The thick, padded item she held was covered and taped with the same white tissue it had been topped with. She opened the drawer of the desk that contained the scissors. Securing one end of the object with a firm hold, she cut through the clear band of tape.

Upon removal of the covering, a medium-sized statue was revealed. It was a figurine of St. Francis of Assisi. It looked antique and was about eight inches tall. The wood felt cool and smooth in her hands, as she turned it to its end. A sticker on the bottom read: *"Anri, Made in Italy. Hand-carved olive wood."* Moving the piece in her palms, she saw swirling colors of tan and brown.

The saint's palms were uplifted, and a dove was perched on each one. At St. Francis's feet, a wolf looked up at him with adoring eyes. The sculptor of this piece had carved an emotional face for St. Francis; the deep-set eyes seemed to have a life of their own, and appeared to smile down at the wolf. The subject did not stare blankly ahead, like other statues Rosemary had seen, in yards; this one looked to have been given loving energy, which seemed happy to be once again released in her hands, as she gazed at it. St. Francis was smiling with gentleness, his mouth slightly curved upward, as if caught in a moment of joy.

Breathing out a heavy breath, Rosemary set the statue on the desk, and reached for the note she had seen at the bottom of the package. She unfolded the paper and began to read the handwritten letter, with the penmanship she had become accustomed to. It read:

"Dearest Rose Petal,

Please accept this little gift. Do not think of it as a reminder of me. Think of it as a reminder of how I see you.

St. Francis is a gentle, loving soul. That is how I see you.

I'm sure you know his story. He cared for the poor and sick. He talked to the birds and thought of all creatures as his brothers and sisters, just as you. Your soul is loving, generous, compassionate and welcoming, to any passerby in need.

Rose Petal, I want you to know that your father is no longer in Hell. He recovered from his trauma on Earth, when he heard you talk to him after he had passed. He heard your words. He heard you forgive him. Your words were medicine to him. He has forgiven himself, and freed his soul to join the loving flow of energy.

Please, someday find it in your heart to forgive me.

I love you always.

I will return to the castle if I do not hear from you in the

next couple of days. I will not interfere in your life anymore.
Please live a good life and take care of yourself. Know that
you are so special. You are a positive energy on Earth and
elsewhere.

Love you for eternity,
Lucas."

Rosemary closed her eyes, still holding the note between her fingers. She supposed tears would form, if any moisture had been left to materialize them. Upon opening her eyes, she opened the desk drawer. She set the letter inside, on top of the last one she had saved from Lucas, along with the pretty, orange raffia bow.

She now pulled out the small, plastic container from the box. She undid the lid.

Slices of an apple were inside. It was probably a Granny Smith, from the tree in Lucas's front yard. A comfort only he would understand. She smiled.

Bending downward from her seated position, Rosemary untied her tennis shoes and pulled them from her feet.

Holding the container of apple slices, Rosemary walked to her bedroom feeling as though a zombie had overtaken her body. As she moved, she did not feel as though it were her own brain that commanded movement. Sitting on the side of her mattress, she ate her treat. The fruit was a little discolored, but the tart crunch was satisfying.

Unconsciousness, even if only for a few minutes, always seemed to refresh her mind. She needed a feeling of rebalance before preparing herself for Sharon's dinner.

Rosemary undressed to her underwear. She climbed onto her bed and underneath the comforter.

Her body stretched, lying on her back, feeling at ease as her mind awakened. She opened her eyes and turned her head toward the alarm clock: it read five p.m.; a quick shower would be achievable before it was time to head to Sharon's. Rosemary's bare body, except for a bra and panties, felt chilled when she pulled the comforter off her. Hugging herself, her arms folded beneath her chest for warmth, she walked to the bathroom.

Warm water reduced the chilliness, as it cascaded over her shoulders and swathed her back and breasts. She couldn't allow her mind to wander to thoughts of Lucas. Not now. She wanted one relaxing evening.

Even though she had never felt attraction toward Alan, it was refreshing to feel her life was normal, and she was preparing for an ordinary couples' date.

Her fingers massaged her head with cleanser. Suds spilled down her chest and stomach.

She would apply mascara, eyeliner and lipstick tonight. Her mom's favorite gold necklace and the matching bracelet were always hung in the jewelry box Rosemary had given her as a Mother's Day gift; tonight they would also be worn. Josephine didn't believe in things not being used.

Broken china or lost items meant a life well lived.

Rosemary considered clothing ideas for tonight's dinner. A dress? She had not worn a dress since the evening she went to the Italian restaurant, with Lucas.

She stepped out of the shower and put on makeup, wrapped in the robe her mother had bought for her. When wearing the plush, white housecoat, Rosemary felt close to her mom's spirit. Josephine believed a woman should care for herself, and wear things that made her feel special.

Sitting at her mother's vanity, Rosemary tinted her eyelashes black and her lips red. A mist of vanilla scent was applied across her wrists, upon removal of the robe. Pulling the red, flowery spaghetti-strap dress over her head, she smiled. Josephine had purchased the sundress for her daughter, during a fun day shopping together.

After a quick bathroom break for Fred, Rosemary headed to her truck. She felt feminine as she walked. Her dress flowed; her jewelry shone.

Is Lucas watching?

Quickly altering her attention, she thought of Alan. She knew in her heart that this comfort of carefree romanticism would be momentary, but it was a moment she needed. Tomorrow would undoubtedly prove to be another day of impossible decisions.

Could she *truly* forgive Lucas – *Lucifer* – for delivering her father to Hell? Would Lucas *genuinely* enjoy a human life with her if he did decide to stay?

Had he already left Earth? Did she already lose him?

It still looked quiet and dark at her neighbor's, as she drove onto the road. She looked through the passenger window of her truck. The

400

thought that Lucas was already gone was fleeting; next door always looked vacant.

He had written that he would wait for her response, for a couple of days.

"Can I help you with anything?" Rosemary asked, as she followed Sharon into the kitchen. Rosemary had been the first to arrive at Sharon's house tonight. Now, Marten, Bob and Tracy were gathered in the living room.

"No. I have everything ready." Sharon opened the oven door. "I am taking out the lasagna now." Sharon always prepared Rosemary a meatless portion of food, knowing her friend was particular about the meat she consumed.

A tangy aroma filled Rosemary's nostrils. "That smells divine, Share," she said.

"Thank you." She pulled the two bubbling-hot trays of pasta from the oven, and set them on a hot-plate on the counter. Turning to her friend, she smiled. "Are you nervous, Rose?"

"About what?"

"About Alan being here tonight?"

Rosemary exhaled sharply from her nose. "No, I'm not nervous about Alan. He's nice…"

"Oh?" Sharon studied her friend's face.

"What do you think about Lucas, Share?"

Sharon's pupils seemed to grow bigger. Her lips changed from a smile to a flat line.

"Do you like him?" Rosemary pressed.

"I do like him, Rose…" Sharon began, with a sharp edge to her tone. "Do *you* like him? Are you thinking of dating him?"

"I do like him. We shared a couple of dinners as friends, as you know, and we have had long conversations. He has helped me sort out some of my grief."

"If you start a relationship with him, I will support it. He seems like a good guy. I'm just not sure he'd be good for you. He seems to be distant at times, and at other times very intense."

"He is definitely… an introvert. But, when we're alone, during our personal interactions, he's very warm toward me. And he *loves* animals."

"Sounds like you are making excuses for him, Rose."

"What do you mean?"

She heavily exhaled. "Well, like with Mark: you explained him as unemotional. He was *uncaring*!"

Why did Rosemary's heart begin to thud hard against her chest? "Yes, but that's not what I'm doing here. I'm not making excuses—"

"Yes, you are," Sharon interrupted.

Rosemary's pulse continued to mount, with air moving faster through her lungs, and she felt her heart flutter. The skin on her face felt heated; she was sure it must be flushed.

"You make excuses for the negative attributes of men you care for," Sharon continued.

"Being an introvert isn't negative, Share. I am an introvert myself."

Sharon looked directly into her friend's eyes. "You *really* have feelings for Lucas?"

Rosemary moved her line of vision to the floor. She then moved a firm glance back to Sharon. "I guess I do have feelings for him, and I want to know what my best friend thinks of him."

The lines of Sharon's face softened. "Like I said, I do like him, Rose. If you choose to date him, I will accept him, of course. He does seem too intense for you, though. He is very serious. Solemn, almost. I picture you with someone more lighthearted. Someone you can laugh with."

Rosemary pulled her bottom lip between her teeth and pressed, as she listened. Her father had given sound but totally disregarded advice regarding her relationship with Mark. Maybe she should heed her best friend's opinion, though a pang in her heart throbbed.

As Rosemary set the stack of plates on the table in the dining room, Alan walked into the house. She arranged each dish on its placemat. As she watched Alan talking to Sharon's brother, there was no feeling of awe. She respected Alan as a person, but he didn't cause her to feel any wonder, or expansion of thought. Their last conversation never confronted her stubbornness, fears or doubt; they had discussed his recent vacation. And they hadn't *laughed* – not wholeheartedly.

Alan took off his jacket and hung it on a hook near the door. Rosemary watched. As he greeted everyone gathered at the house, his eyes did not seem to light up with joy as they met hers. It was the same look for everyone. He smiled, but it was the same smile for everyone. There was nothing special for Rosemary; no distinctive hint that he thought her any different from anyone else. That was fine; she had no private romantic feelings for him.

She loved another man.

Lucas met her gaze with intensity. Warmth. Love.

With all of Sharon's guests taking their seats at the table, the loudness of voices filled the room. The main course was soon being passed around. Alan sat in the chair beside Rosemary, but he spoke to Bob.

An authentic, quiet smile seemed to rise from Rosemary's chest to her mouth. She had figured out a small part of her life: she loved Lucas. No matter whether he had already disappeared from Earth, or would remain human, Rosemary loved him.

The people gathered here were nice, but her intimacy with Lucas was on a deeper level. Her relationship with him felt comfortable and safe. His soul felt to her as though she had found home.

Rosemary tasted the lasagna and garlic bread. It was good. She laughed at Marten's jokes and truly enjoyed the lighthearted company. Dirty plates and glasses askew, the guests sat and noisily talked.

When dinner was consumed, she decided to excuse herself. Rosemary walked to Sharon's seat.

"I'm going to get going now, Share," Rosemary said to Sharon, bending to meet her ear.

"Don't be mad at me," Sharon said, covering her mouth for privacy. She stood and gave Rosemary a tight goodbye hug. "I love you."

"I love you. I'm not mad; I asked for your honest opinion," she returned. "I'll be at the shelter super early."

"Thank you."

As she walked to her truck and drove home, the poem Lucas had once shared with Rosemary seemed to speak inside her mind:

"No need to ask for directions,
The way is hidden inside your soul.
Just follow your inner light,
And that will guide you home."

She had memorized it.

Whether or not he agreed, Rosemary *knew* she had written Lucas into her story. It was her self-scripted life. Maybe she had arranged this reality before she had been born? In the universe, maybe her soul had wanted to once again meet Lucas's? Or maybe she had just now reworked him into her life? Nonetheless, this existence was her personal creation and choice.

Rosemary didn't need to ask for directions. Her own soul revealed the answer to her question about Lucas. When she closed her eyes and pictured herself trapped in an elevator, Lucas would be the one she wanted to be trapped with. He injected calmness, humor and comfort into any situation. That would make him a good partner for her.

Sharon gave sound advice. As a couple, Rosemary and Lucas would do well to loosen up now and then, laugh, go sightseeing, flirt and add romance.

The lesson learned from Lula was to never be silent about the desires of one's inner light – especially not to oneself.

The lesson taught Rosemary that she did not need to worry about others' opinions, or reactions to her decisions; only her happiness mattered. It didn't matter if someone else thought her foolish; she needed to live with her decisions, so her decisions had to make her happy. She would now think of herself, and take actions that best supported her.

"Lucas, I love you," Rosemary said out loud, alone in her truck.

In Lucas's presence, Rosemary felt free to do or say anything. He accepted her, even appreciated her. He taught her. He listened. They talked or didn't have to talk. They loved together. He cared for the shelter animals as much as she did. She taught him. She felt it an honor to know him. He was a very loving person. He was protective and nurturing. Lucas was smart, and he was spiritual, like she was. *They laughed...* some.

He was patient and easygoing. She mused that he hadn't griped when she had stepped on his toes, or when she took time to change clothes. He had never belittled her thoughts or fears. Only her joy from her job and hobbies mattered to him. He never criticized her personal choices or preferences.

Rosemary knew that Lucas felt his position as ruler of Hell would have a negative impact on her. Emotionally? Physically? She wasn't clear *how* he felt his honorable mission in this universe would be harmful to her Earthly existence. Lucas had performed his duties in Hell and on Earth with thoughtfulness and love. Countless souls had been uplifted and healed by his positive energy.

He wasn't *the devil*. That was a label. He was a fellow soul.

Would he truly be willing to give up his position and leave his beloved castle?

When she pulled into her driveway, late dusk, Rosemary searched for any sign that Lucas may be at the neighboring house. Even now, there were no lights or activity in the property. Standing outside her truck, she pondered walking to his house as she shut her vehicle's door.

Eeriness accompanied the darkness, and drew her eyes in several directions with each sound, as she slowly walked toward his front porch. Her feet landed on the soft grass across his yard. A hard, thin object snapped underneath her left foot, and she reflexively pressed the palms of her hands to her chest. Looking down, she saw a harmless twig.

Upon reaching the porch, she stepped up the three steps, then lightly knocked on the door. "Lucas?"

He did not answer. Several minutes passed. Still no movement in the house.

The slightly-opened curtains of the bay window exposed a speck of orange glow from inside. A nightlight was probably plugged in, in the living room.

She turned around on his porch, and watched a nighttime breeze ripple through the leaves of his tall oak and apple trees. Waiting, she watched a bat fly above her own porch light. She felt herself tremble. An owl softly hooted.

The new reality of negative forces, and their counter-positive ones, caused consideration of the direction of her thoughts. In the recent past, she had drawn the negative into her life.

Darkness was conducive to self-analysis. Maybe the waning moon provided the atmosphere for such reflection. The sliver showed brightly, emerging from the top of a long cloud.

The point of a human life isn't to *never* have a negative thought; *all* emotions should be accepted and appreciated. Passion expands the world, with art, conversation, healthy disagreements and evolution. The idea, Rosemary supposed, was to corral negative thoughts into a virtual recycle bin, to be dumped periodically.

She lowered herself to the top step of the porch and sat on the cement. It was time to dump her virtual recycle bin. She had already recognized her father's human faults, and forgiven and discarded any negative emotions attached to his child-rearing.

She had admitted that it had been her free choice to allow Mark into her life. Though a negative presence, he hadn't been at fault; she could have disallowed his presence. She had to place his memory in the recycle bin, and completely dump that negative space from within her. It was also important that she rid herself of guilt, and discard any residual feelings of that particular life choice.

She swallowed hard. There was still guilt about her pregnancy. She had meant no harm to that soul; she wished only love. It was time to fully forgive herself.

Finally, she felt it necessary to speak out loud one more negative emotion that she needed to discard...

"I forgive you, Lucas." She looked up at the night sky, growing even darker. "I forgive you for taking my father to Hell. It was his choice; you were only his guide. You helped him to heal and now he is free."

It was a comfort to feel the edges of her mouth beginning to turn up, in a small smile.

The darkness of nighttime was beautiful again. She lifted her gaze to the slice of a moon and surrounding stars, inhaling the coolness of a seemingly promise-filled breeze. She closed her eyes and slowly inhaled. Everything would be okay.

The way her foot felt in a properly laced-up, comfortable sneaker

was how her soul now felt inside her body: aligned, secure, relaxed…
and aware.

Fred needed medicine and a bathroom break before bedtime, and
Rosemary stood and stepped down, back to earth. She smiled at the
thought of Fred, Samantha and Rambo greeting her when she opened
the door to her home.

Lucas would *surely* be at the shelter tomorrow morning.

Chapter 19

Rosemary's Miracles

Rosemary had briefly knocked on the door of her neighbor's vacant home, this Monday morning, before heading to work. Lucas hadn't answered. Was he still occupying the house?

He hadn't been at the shelter today, either. It was now eleven a.m.

Sharon said that Lucas hadn't mentioned if he wouldn't be volunteering this Monday.

Couldn't he hear her thoughts, Rosemary wondered? He should know that she was ready to speak to him.

She now stared blankly at the clean floor in front of her, as she sat behind her desk in the lobby, nibbling on the end of a pencil.

"Everything is okay; everything happens as it should," she whispered to herself. A deep breath slowly moved through her nose as she inhaled. She knew her feelings for Lucas were sober and true, but he needed to come to the same conclusion for himself, in his own time.

Sharon walked across the floor, and turned the sign that hung on the glass panel of the front door to *"Open"*.

"Rose…"

Rosemary focused her gaze toward her friend. Sharon nodded toward the glass panel of the door.

"Rose!" Sharon repeated, louder this time.

Rosemary removed the pencil from her mouth. "What?" she called back. She felt her pulse quicken and sat straighter in her chair. She didn't have Sharon's viewpoint, but saw her friend continuing to stare out through the glass.

"Look who's walking this way!" Sharon excitedly said.

Rosemary pushed aside her chair and walked to the lobby floor. She looked out of the window.

Her face seemed to freeze in place, but tears began to warm her cheeks.

It seemed her soul was pulling her toward the front door, but her feet felt as if they were trudging through mud of disbelief.

Lula! Lula May! she mentally screamed.

The woman who had adopted Lula was walking her back into the shelter.

The wetness of Rosemary's tears trailed and caressed her jaw, as though in a joyful embrace. She wiped her face, then continued toward Lula. The woman with Lula opened the front door. Was the woman guiding the dog inside, giving her back to the shelter? Lula May was wagging her fluffy tail as she entered the building.

"I'm sorry," the woman holding Lula's leash said, in a clear voice, "this dog is just too big for our yard. We tried, but we have a small, fenced-in yard, and she always barks at our neighbors and their dogs. She doesn't seem happy. I think she needs more room for her size. I had to bring her back."

A gush of air Rosemary hadn't realized her lungs had been holding exited her mouth, in an audible sigh. She felt her mouth turn upward in an unabashed smile.

She stepped right in front of Lula and took the leash from the woman, desperate to swiftly take ownership. Her mouth opened wide, for the whole world to see her toothy grin, but she tried to pass it off as a kind gesture. Rosemary didn't ask if the family had tried to curb the dog's energy with walks, playtime or obedience training. It was a relief to feel the fur of Lula's big, soft head, as she now held the lead and petted the dog.

"You did the right thing, bringing her back here," Rosemary said. "Thank you."

Sharon smiled as she walked to stand beside Rosemary. "Yes," Sharon agreed. "Thank you, Liz."

"Yes, sorry it didn't work out," Liz said. The woman then turned and left, without patting the dog on its head or giving one last verbal goodbye – due to embarrassment, or lack of connection?

When Liz was inside her car – which Rosemary confirmed by watching through the glass panel – Rosemary dropped the leash and raised her arms in the air.

"Yay!" she cried out loud.

Lula May barked in her deep, husky tone, as she looked up at Rosemary. Her tail wagged forcefully across the tiled floor she sat on.

A new customer had pulled into the parking lot, and was now opening her car door.

"Rose, I'm so happy for you!" Sharon said, hugging her tightly.

The customer opened the front door, and Rosemary greeted her with a full-size smile. "Hello. Welcome to our shelter." She looked down at the large dog. "We are having a good day."

The woman smiled, as Sharon guided her toward the cat cages.

Rosemary stepped behind her desk and pulled a red sheet of paper from the drawer. She then headed to the dog room with Lula. There was one empty pen. Rosemary slipped the *"Adopted"* sheet into the bare binder, then led Lula May inside.

Rosemary lowered to the cement floor. The dog followed suit, right beside her. Rosemary lay down on her back and patted her chest, where Lula rested her heavy head, the dog's loose lips hanging to the sides. The handful of thick, soft fur atop the oversized head felt wonderfully familiar clasped in Rosemary's fingers. She leaned in and kissed the top of the St. Bernard's wide, short nose. She felt pressure behind her eyes, but only a thin droplet of tears slid from the corners.

This was a second chance at love.

Rising to a seated position, Rosemary clapped her hands. "Let's go for a walk, Lula."

The dog's ears twitched as it lifted to a stance. Lula May seemed to dance around the floor as Rosemary continued to clap her hands. She had become accustomed to equating Rosemary's handclaps to treats. Standing, Rosemary reached into her pants pocket and pulled out a piece of beef jerky. She tore off a section.

The beagles in the adjacent pen watched. One sounded a soft, mournful howl.

"Okay." Rosemary tore off two small bites for the beagle girls.

Rosemary got the leash hanging on the peg, near the front table, that she had always considered to be Lula's. Rosemary and Lula May headed outside.

Every time Rosemary's feet touched earth, during their walk, it felt as though another blessing was bestowed on them. Lula May then ran alongside Rosemary.

For each following dog walk of the day, Rosemary found herself smiling, reliving in her mind the astonishment of watching Lula walk back into the shelter.

At 6:30 p.m., Rosemary noticed that her breaths came heavier and faster, as she anticipated bringing Lula home. Rosemary hoped that yet another unfamiliar house would not cause stress for Lula. She would have to slowly introduce the new dog to Fred and Samantha; how would they react? Lula May had never shown aggression toward another animal. Rosemary had even introduced cats to the dog, with no adverse reaction.

"Go home now!" Rosemary heard Sharon shout from the hallway.

Rosemary sat at the front desk, sorting adoption questionnaires from new applicants, according to application date. Lula lay on the floor next to her feet. Sharon walked into the lobby.

"Okay, we'll go," Rosemary told Sharon. She looked down at Lula May. "Ready to meet your brother and sister?"

"I'll lock up," Sharon said.

"Thank you."

Rosemary collected her purse from the closet, then led Lula from the shelter to the truck. The St. Bernard barely fit; her back legs were tucked underneath her rear, and her front legs hung off the seat. She had been given a hefty push to settle her in position.

Taking her place behind the wheel, Rosemary looked over at her passenger's large head, which slightly bobbed from its weight. Soft, white-furred jowls hung with droplets of drool, as the dog returned

Rosemary's glance. Lula's wide tongue licked the front of her own black nose, and she exhaled a heavy breath from it.

On the ride home, Rosemary continued to periodically look at the newest addition to her family. It confirmed her belief in unexpected miracles. If this wonderful thing could happen, then anything was possible. Life would be more appreciated, she supposed, if miracles were *expected*.

Her pulse increased with excitement as she pulled into the driveway. She helped lift the front end of the dog down from the high seat. As Rosemary put the house key in the door, her heart happily sped up. They stepped inside.

Fred's crate was set on the living-room floor, next to the couch, so he would be the first to witness the unfamiliar smell. Samantha must have been asleep on Rosemary's bed.

Rosemary held the leash as she removed her tennis shoes, then walked Lula toward the couch. She sat on the sofa and positioned Lula in a seated position, on the floor to her right. Her legs were between the dogs.

The St. Bernard looked toward the crate, and her fluffy tail swept the rug in two slow wags. The Chihuahua's eyes widened, as Fred watched the large dog sniff the air toward the crate, then shift to a relaxed posture, on her belly. Fred rested his chin on his legs. His head remained still as his eyes followed Lula's movements.

"Good boy, Fred," Rosemary softly said. "This is Lula May, your sister I told you about."

Samantha came into the living room and perched in her usual spot, on top of the couch. Her pupils widened as the newest family member was detected. Though her ears stood erect, Samantha must have felt secure in her aerial position. She did blink when she heard Rosemary's calm voice. Her tail swished abruptly, but slowed with a pet.

"Samantha, Lula is your sister, too," Rosemary said.

The new dog shifted her position, and the cat tensed her shoulders and back, and let out a hiss. Rosemary gently petted Samantha.

"It's okay, 'Mantha," Rosemary cooed.

Samantha blinked and rested, in a leisurely manner. Fred continued to merely follow with his eyes, as Lula May wedged her large rear between Rosemary's legs and the coffee table. She glanced at Fred momentarily, then tilted her chin upward to look at Rosemary. As Lula's large, square muzzle lifted, her soft jowls drooped with drool. Her short, floppy ears framed her deep-set, brown eyes.

Rosemary petted under the dog's chin, lifting the soft jowls.

"I know, Lula. Don't worry; your sister and brother will love you," Rosemary sweetly told her. "It'll just take a little time."

There would be another day or two of this slow introduction. The second step would be the allowance of sniffing one another's rears, with supervision, but no face-to-face contact just yet. The first meeting was positive. Treats were given for praise.

A smile was lifting the sides of Rosemary's mouth. If this reconnection with Lula were possible, if the universe orchestrated this, then anything was possible. Again, the thought seemed to lift any worry from her mind. With practiced positivity, goodness would be inevitable.

*

Lucas had just lit a candle at the dining table. He was then holding Rosemary in his arms.

She felt the warmth of his embrace, and of his breath and lips on her cheek. Lucas was then bent down on one knee, in front of her. "Please be mine for eternity," she heard him ask, presenting a diamond ring, the antique, warm-colored stone centered in an elaborate filigree design. Lucas was then holding Rosemary, as she gazed at the engagement ring circling her finger…

Rosemary woke. Her eyes opened. She was on her side, facing the bedroom door.

She now looked downward and saw Lula May's large body, curled in a relaxed posture, on the rug below the bedframe. Purchasing an extra-large dog bed would be a priority today.

She turned over onto her other side, and stuck her fingertips through the openings of the front of Fred's crate, to pat his bandage-covered legs.

Samantha rested above her, on the pillow. She stretched, and Rosemary could hear the cat's muscles and bones shift.

The darkness of the room suggested that it was too early to rise for work. Looking at the bedside table, the clock proved her assessment: it was 5:46 a.m. The alarm would ring one hour and fourteen minutes later.

Rosemary rested on her back and closed her eyes.

The dream of Lucas was now visualized in her mind.

The dream had been intensely vivid. She had felt his warm breath and lips on her skin. Her soul felt so close to his.

She willed herself back to sleep.

Her new morning routine consisted of feeding four critters.

She felt groggier than at her earlier rise of 5:46 a.m. today, but also joyful.

Rosemary removed her pajama top, and the heat from her body clung to the fabric, as she folded it and placed it on her dresser.

She wished she could share the good news of Lula May's return with Lucas. Where was he? In her heart, Rosemary knew that he'd return into her life.

Walking to the kitchen, she smelled brewed coffee; last night, she had preset the machine. She poured some in a Thermos.

Rosemary inhaled a deep breath, and she tentatively walked to the windowsill. She reached out her hand and picked up Lucas's gold timepiece. She had set it next to the small picture of her with her mother, the evening before *the kiss*. She cupped the round object in her hand, then folded her fingers over it; it was cool to the touch. The vintage watch, a sidewinding piece, had a hairline crack near the center of the glass. Rosemary closed her eyes as she held it. It was an item that meant a lot to Lucas; he loved antiques. It felt as though a piece of his energy resided with her, as she held onto something he had carried with him. She set it back in its place.

She then pulled a protein bar from the cupboard and a water bottle from the fridge.

Rosemary had left Fred's crate, containing a small water bowl, in the bedroom today. He'd need time to grow accustomed to Lula's loud barks, before being left alone in the same room with her. Samantha would stay with Fred. The litter box had been moved into the bedroom, from the cubbyhole in the first-floor bathroom.

Rosemary walked to the front door, and Lula followed her there. Bending over, Rosemary kissed the square muzzle of the dog. Lula May would have free range of the house.

At work, the day seemed to pass quickly.

With no volunteers today, there was no time to socialize. Sharon and Rosemary worked quietly, in sync. Rosemary had told Sharon that Lucas had a work project.

The new beagles had already been adopted into a home with two children. The young dogs would surely be exercised and loved. They would leave for their new home today.

It was always a bittersweet moment when any animal left the shelter. There was hope that the adoption process would go smoothly for the human and the pet. It would be a transition for both.

Rosemary had gone home for a quick, late lunch, needing to let out Fred and Lula for a bathroom break. Sharon was now tending to a customer, as Rosemary walked back inside the lobby. With the lone customer being assisted, Rosemary made her way to the cat area. She entered the stock room and pulled a can of cat food from the shelf.

Slowly, she opened the door to the quarantine room. It was dark and quiet. She had cleaned the room earlier today, but wanted to check on the expectant mom. Brightness filled the area as she turned on the light switch.

"Hi, Mama," Rosemary softly greeted, as she lowered to the tiled floor, in a seated position.

The mama cat lifted her head. She had been napping in her basket, lined with a soft towel. Mama stood and began to walk toward Rosemary; her belly bulged to the sides as she moved. The black cat stopped to stretch her back, then each front leg; Mama then continued her stride toward the awaiting lap.

"I brought the mama-to-be some extra wet food," Rosemary said.

The cat climbed into her lap.

Visually, Rosemary could see bulges in the large belly shifting. She placed her palm on the soft fur and felt movement.

"It's okay, Mama," she whispered. She gently slid her hand along the length of Mama's protruding stomach.

The door to the room opened.

"Rose?" Sharon said.

"Hi, Share. Just checking on Mama."

"Okay. Do you mind if I leave now? I am meeting my mom."

"Of course. Hey, Share…"

"Yeah?"

"Can you please bring me my purse? My book is in it. I think I'll read a little, while I sit here with Mama."

"Of course. Then I'll close up and lock the doors."

Sharon retrieved the purse, then left for home.

Rosemary emptied some wet cat food on a plate, then opened her romance novel. It was a relief to read a lighthearted book. Each page-turn seemed to soothe her mind into deeper relaxation. Mama ate, then went back to Rosemary's lap. Rosemary rested one hand on the cat, while holding the paperback with the other. With one hand, it felt like a trick to be able to fold back the cover, to keep her place.

The cat rose from her lap and walked to the litter box. A soft cry caused Rosemary to lift her eyes from the book.

Mama then returned to her lap and lay flatly across it. She stayed for a moment, then stood again. As she stood, Rosemary noticed droplets of blood on her jeans. Mama walked a couple of steps, then twisted to lick her vulva area.

The strong smell of blood permeated Rosemary's nostrils, as a puddle of dark red suddenly gushed from the cat, onto the tiled floor.

"It's time," Rosemary whispered.

New life was coming. A rush of emotion caused beads of joyful tears to moisten her eyes.

The cat paced from the litter box to Rosemary's lap, several more times. Each time Mama stepped onto Rosemary's lap, she only rested for a few minutes. She now rose and stood just in front of Rosemary.

A clear, jellylike sack began to push through Mama, as her belly bowed to the ground, her back end facing Rosemary. The cat appeared to be only mildly straining to push the object out of her.

Rosemary could now see smashed, black fur, from a tiny head inside the sack. Only the small, rounded head protruded from Mama's body.

With one last push, the gooey sack plopped to the floor, with a little amount of liquid. The glob was dragged around the floor, as Mama turned in a circle. The umbilical cord, still attached inside Mama, pulled the sack along.

Rosemary didn't want to interfere, but her heart began to press harder against her chest.

Mama kept turning, with the baby following behind her, in a circle.

Finally, instincts prevailed, and the black cat now held the small object with her paws and began licking it. Soon, the soft, wet fur of a kitten's head was detectable. As the mama cat was cleaning the rest of the kitten, it began screeching out cries.

The sound was quieted when the newborn found its mother's teats and began nursing.

Rosemary had seen newborn kittens maybe a few hours old, but had never before witnessed the actual birth process. Usually, pregnant cats in the shelter gave birth during the nighttime.

Tiny claws extracted from tiny paws, as the kitten kneaded the soft bulge of the teat. Mama continued to wash the newborn, wetting back fur from the top of the head. She started to nibble inside the miniature ears.

Rosemary inhaled a deep breath, as she felt moisture rebuild in her eyes. It was an honor that the new mother allowed her presence.

Detaching the tiny mouth from her teat, Mama stood, with a concentrated expression. The newborn curled onto its side. Then, Mama's front end directly lowered to the ground as she pushed; her front paws gripped the tile.

Another sack soon emerged. The next kitten's dark head became visible with more pushes. The sack dropped to the ground, attached by the cord.

Mama walked in a circle again, but this time she grabbed hold of the kitten after only one turnaround. The firstborn began crying and wobbling on the tiled floor, and stole Mama's focus for a moment.

After the second kitten was delivered and cleaned, Mama picked it up by the loose skin on the back of the neck; its little limbs hung as she carried it. It was released next to the firstborn.

Mama curled onto her side, next to the kittens, and moved them toward her teats. She continued repositioning her body to line up with the tiny mouths, and she pawed the little heads in the right direction. She licked each baby.

Rosemary witnessed two more births. With each one, Mama seemed to perfect the process, and directly hunched when she felt the urge to push. The circling ended with the second delivery, as she immediately broke the cord with the remaining newborns, after they were pushed outside of her.

For the impending births, Rosemary had placed a medium-sized cardboard box in the room, lined with a thick towel. There was a section cut out of one of the sides, for easy access. Mama now began carrying each newborn into the box. They were all quiet now, as they had just been fed. The cat then lay on her side, as she curled her body around her kittens, and they snuggled up to her belly. Two were black, one was a tabby and one was gray. The gray one kneaded one of Mama's teats as it slept.

Rosemary cleaned the little bit of blood left on the floor, then turned off the overhead light. The nightlight plugged into the bottom of the wall provided sufficient illumination for Rosemary to observe. As she lay on her side, on the hard tile floor, she faced the mama and babies, placing her purse underneath her head for a makeshift pillow. Closing her eyes, she concentrated on the darkness behind her eyelids.

She had just been honored with the privilege of witnessing brand-new life enter the world. Another miracle. She now relished a peaceful nap.

Feeling rested, Rosemary inhaled a deep breath and opened her eyes; she had gotten at least a twenty-minute catnap. She immediately looked toward the box. Mama Cat still lay on her side, with the newborns lined up along her belly. Three of them now nursed.

Mama's yellow eyes turned to Rosemary.

"Hi, Mama," she quietly said. "You did good."

Rosemary's upper left side ached from holding her weight on the tiled floor, and she slowly rose to a seated position. Her left arm was aching, yet felt numb and tingly. She physically moved it to her lap, along with her right hand.

She felt comfortable leaving Mama and the babies now for the night. Everyone looked healthy. The doctor would be called tomorrow morning, to set an appointment for an exam.

When her arm felt normal, Rosemary stood. She took stock of the area. Mama had dry food, fresh water and clean litter. Rosemary added a little more wet food to the empty plate.

Mama sniffed toward the plate on the floor, then directly stood. All the kittens rolled to their backs, but they quickly curled on top of one another and fell asleep.

"Congratulations, Mama," Rosemary whispered. "You did good, Mama."

She petted the cat's back as she ate. Mama purred loudly as she lapped the food. Her back end rose with each pet.

"I will see you first thing in the morning, Mama."

Rosemary gave one last pet, then walked outside the room and shut the door.

The shelter was quiet and dark.

Rosemary and Sharon had learned, from past experience, to keep an extra set of clothes in the storage room. Now dressed in fresh jeans, Rosemary walked quietly to the dog room. She looked at the clock above the table: it was almost 8:30 p.m.

One pup did whine, but Rosemary got outside without waking the whole crew.

Walking to her truck, she heard the slight rumble of thunder. A gust of wind seemed to breathe eerily across her face. She shivered. Her gait increased.

The sky looked almost greenish.

She thumbed through the keys on the orange leather ring, a gift from her mother. She found the vehicle's key and tightly grasped it. As she stuck the key into the door lock and twisted it, her heart fluttered.

Settling behind the wheel and manually locking the doors, she heavily exhaled. What was this ominous feeling?

She was headed to the gas station, just outside of town. Should she continue, or head directly for home? A thunderstorm was usually an occurrence of awe for Rosemary; the greenish sky must have been causing her uneasiness. Rosemary would continue toward town. "Life ain't for sissies," she whispered to herself.

Josephine had preached that a vehicle should always have more than half a tank of gas, for emergencies.

Driving from the parking lot to the dirt road, bright lightning seemed to crack open the darkened sky in punishment, as it zigzagged

425

from above. Thunder sounded, as if growling a threatening warning.

Farther down the road, the wind began to stir up dust from the ditches, while Rosemary's truck traveled the middle of the path.

Suddenly, it felt as though the tires ran over a pothole; Rosemary then felt unevenness underneath the truck. It sounded like the right front tire was flopping heavily against the road.

"Shit!" Her voice filled the cab. "A flat tire? *Now?!*"

Her fingers wrapped tightly around the thin steering wheel, as she hoped to make it into town. There would be streetlights... people.

Lightning lit the sky in a narrow streak, as the tire continued to slowly flop along the desolate path. The sky turned an even stranger light-green color.

"Ha!" she called out. Her great-great-great-grandmother had scared off a pack of wolves, she reminded herself. Surely Rosemary could be brave enough to handle a flat tire in the looming storm. She would choose to be positive, not negative. She would decide to be brave.

Something inside her seemed to rise and shout: "Everything is okay." This dilemma may have happened for a reason, or it may have transpired for no purpose at all. Her reaction would be what determines her future direction.

She had her phone, and her romance book in her purse. The town was now only half a mile away, if she had to walk there.

"Clunk, clunk," she heard, as she rolled down the passenger side window.

Every inch farther she felt a sense of relief, but she knew the wheel would be ruined by continued driving. She drove very slowly, and listened for a worsening of the clunking sound.

Passing the section of seclusion from the shelter to the bordering neighborhood, she smiled. She felt empowered now, as she pulled over to the side of the paved road. Houses lined both sides. The town and cobblestone lane were just ahead. A streetlamp shone security above her head, as she inhaled a deep breath and opened her door.

Walking to the passenger side, she smiled a large grin that felt forced. It began to lightly rain; the wetness felt nice on her skin. The breeze felt cool against her face. A flat tire it was; the flood of light from the tall lamp showed it clearly. She would have to learn how to change one someday; it was a handy thing for a woman to know how to do.

As she began walking back to the driver-side door, a blue pickup truck passed, then stopped just up ahead. The tires slowly backed up, toward her.

The truck stopped.

The door opened. A man stepped out. His head was topped with a ball cap. "Need help?" the man called out to Rosemary, as he walked toward her. The streetlight showed short, blond hair underneath his cap. His skin was fair, like hers.

"I have a flat," she returned.

"I can help with that! Have a spare?" As he neared her, he offered his hand. "Hi, I'm Robert."

Rosemary shook his hand. "Hi, Robert. I'm Rosemary. Thank you for stopping – in the rain, and all."

"Of course. Aw, rain ain't no big deal." Wet drops dripped off the curved visor of his cap.

"I have a spare in the bed," she told him.

427

"Good. I'll get my tools."

The man walked to the back of his truck, and removed a small toolbox from the storage container that lined his vehicle bed. He set it near the front of her vehicle. He then walked to the back of her truck and unlatched the tailgate.

He looked to be her age, or older. His biceps tightened around the hem of his short-sleeve shirt, as he lifted the spare from the bed.

"Looks like the storm's passing," he said.

Rosemary looked up at the sky. The rain had quit. The sky looked dark, but less threatening – not greenish. "Good," she said.

He rolled the spare to the passenger side of the white pickup. Rosemary followed, then stood beside him as he knelt beside the flat. After propping up the front end, he used a shiny, silver tool to undo the bolts that held the flat tire. He removed his hat and set it on his toolbox. His blond hair looked thick and spiky as she looked down at his head, the points gathered in casual disarray.

"I think I ran over a pothole," she said.

"Naw, you got a nail here."

The flat clunked to the ground and he lifted the spare. He began using the shiny, silver tool again; it twisted back and forth. His thighs spread to each side of the tire as he worked. They were clad in faded jeans, worn, with small holes in some spots. His t-shirt was blue.

"All done," he said, facing the truck.

He stood, then bent over to pick up the flat. He walked to the back of the vehicle and set the tire in the bed, with a loud thump. He closed the tailgate and turned to her.

"C.J.'s Diner is right up the road. Will you have a cup of coffee with me?"

"I want to pay you," she said.

"Not necessary. A cup of coffee would be nice, though." His full
lips curved in a small smile. "My hands are a little cold; a cup of coffee
would warm them." He lifted an eyebrow, as if asking his question
again.

"Sure," Rosemary said, "I will get you a cup of coffee. It's the least
I can do."

He started toward his truck, carrying his tool case. "Follow me," he
called back to Rosemary.

"Okay," she called out.

She followed behind his truck, in hers, as she now turned into the
diner parking lot.

It *was* the least she could do for him, Rosemary mused. A fixed tire
definitely warranted a meager cup of coffee.

And he *was* attractive.

She opened her vehicle door and met him at the diner's entrance.
He held open the door for her. He hadn't put his hat back on; his blond
hair looked damp, but still thick and spiky.

The waitress told them to choose a seat, and Rosemary followed
Robert to a small booth near the back window. He smelled of a
pleasant brand of cologne; the scent was more intense indoors. Outside
she had noticed the faint smell, which the breeze had carried to her
nostrils; now she inhaled deeply as they slid into their seats, opposite
one another.

Chapter 20

Lucifer Watches

A smile resonated deep inside Lucifer's soul. He couldn't hear her thoughts, as Rosemary watered her plants in the kitchen, but she hummed. Her spirit was joyful. An antique golden ring circled the fourth finger on her left hand, as she lifted the watering can. She wore a yellow sundress, with little, pink flowers embroidered on it. It swirled around her thighs. A warm patch of sun shone through the window, and rested gently on a section of her hair.

The skin of her neck smelled of vanilla and lemon, as he hugged his chest tightly to her back. His arms snugly wrapped around her, fitting just below her chest. Rosemary's hair moved around her shoulders in soft waves, and revealed patches of the sweet-smelling skin. He tucked his face into her neck and closed his eyes, deeply inhaling through his nostrils. He held her scent there. Parting his lips, he took her smell into his mouth and savored it there. As her scent passed his lips and entered his body, he shivered.

Standing motionless, he allowed every bit of her to linger on his lips, sit in his nostrils and move through his bones. He could taste her, smell her and feel her…

The splendid dream dissipated into blackness…

Lucifer's eyes snapped open. A bedsheet covered his midsection.

His body convulsed, as though an electric shock moved through him. A gray, foggy substance hung like a cloud above him.

430

Lucifer coughed and gasped. His chest ached, as though a thousand pounds lay on it, as he continued to struggle for air. His human body soon became encircled by the haze. He felt immobilized by its thickness. The gray fog was physically suffocating, but also spiritually confining. His soul felt locked inside his human body, unable to rise in the fog.

Uncontrollable gagging was soon followed by absolute paralysis.

He was trapped in the bed, in revulsion; the stench of rotten eggs permeated his nostrils.

His body occasionally shook, but he was still immobile, unable to move a limb.

As if on a wall-sized, 3D movie screen, a pair of red, though human eyes flickered, like an obliterating wildfire. They were an illusion of Ash's.

As Lucifer looked into the pupils, a figure reflected through them. An indistinct figure.

Focusing his stare, he saw Rosemary kneeling beside her truck. The wind was moving through her dampened hair. Blue-white lightning struck against the background of the green sky.

Rosemary!

It felt as though an earthquake broke through Lucifer's chest. His soul was finally free.

The translucent tunnel generated from Lucifer's human chest; his soul left his body and plunged into it.

His orb coiled through the tunnel and exterior colors swirled, as his visualization of Rosemary magnetically pulled him toward her. The vibrations of her voice could be detected, as he got closer.

431

His soul was flushed from the tunnel. He was suspended in mid-air. There she was! Safe.

His nucleus, invisible to the untrained eye, stilled for a moment. He did not reveal his presence.

Lucifer watched.

Rosemary sat inside a booth, at a restaurant. A man sat across from her. She was smiling.

At first, Lucifer assumed the man was Alan, Sharon's friend, but Rosemary called him by a different name. Rosemary's voice wasn't strong to Lucifer just yet; it sounded as though she talked through a fuzzy radio.

Lucifer settled from his disjointed delivery here. His hazy, green aura became adjusted around his soul.

Lucifer watched. He wanted to make sure Rosemary was secure with this stranger.

Was it a date?

"I love all animals," Rosemary said to the stranger across from her. "Do you like animals, Robert?" Her voice was clearer now, and sounded as though she spoke directly to Lucifer, in person.

"I do," the man said.

Lucifer felt his core settle to calmness. Rosemary looked to be at peace.

She smiled. "I co-own an animal shelter near town," she told the man.

"That's wonderful, Rosemary. I've never owned a dog, but would like one someday," Robert said.

"Did you ever own a cat?"

"No, I'm more of a dog person. Plus, I'm allergic to cats. I'd like to have a dog, but one or two would be my limit."

A string of sharp giggles exited Rosemary's nostrils. "It sounds like we're talking about children." She smoothed back the bangs on the top of her head, as she tilted her chin upward. "I'd be open to however many animals God decided to give me." A gush of air came from her nose as she mumbled another giggle.

"Your work sounds very interesting," Robert said.

Rosemary's mouth flattened. "Yes. Always a new animal to meet. A new little soul to care for."

The end would always be right there in the beginning, Lucifer mused. If Rosemary stayed alert to the happenings right in front of her eyes now, she'd know the end result.

This man, Robert, was mannerly. His actions and temperament toward Rosemary were respectable. He spoke affectionately to her. His eyes held sincerity. Lucifer did not sense any malice from this man, Robert. If he treated her honorably now, he would treat her honorably in the future.

"Can I get your phone number, Rosemary?" the man asked. His voice had broken with a grunt. "Maybe take you on a date sometime?"

Rosemary looked into his light-colored eyes and held his gaze.

Her words became muddled again, as the tunnel now extended from Lucifer's core. As he entered the channel, her words fuzzily echoed.

"You are an amazing guy, Robert," she said. "It was so kind-hearted of you to stop and help a stranger."

Lucifer's view of Rosemary was vague, but it looked as though one side of her mouth turned upward. "You are very good-looking, but I do have a boyfriend."

Rosemary appeared to smile awkwardly. She seemed shyly flirtatious as she moved her fingers through her hair. Lucifer appreciated that she was entertaining the thought of dating a nice person.

But Lucifer had to find Ash. Ash had put Rosemary's life at risk, he was sure. The vision had been given to Lucifer for a purpose.

His core felt as though it twisted like a sponge, as Lucifer's energy connected to his brother's.

Lucifer's orb moved through the translucent tunnel, as swiftly as a comet. His green aura extended from behind him, and it followed with gauzy-looking ribbons.

The closer he pulled toward the dark soul of Ash, the uglier the colors of the atmosphere: grays and murky olive greens.

The smell would be repugnant to a human. With no nostrils, the odor wasn't detectable to Lucifer, but instead sent ripples of paralysis through his green aura.

He was now soul to soul with Ash.

His brother's nucleus hung still, with vaporous grays circling it. But now the gray colors had darkened even greater around the aura.

Ash's orb attached to another dimension, which attracted the malevolent. Neither Earth nor Hell offered a magnetic match for the evilness now embedded in his soul. He had intentionally committed a harmful act against a fellow being, with no remorse.

Lucifer's aura turned red. His energy physically rammed Ash's gray-ringed orb and pushed it backward. Gray puffs of cloudlike gases enveloped all sides of both of them.

Lucifer changed his image into that of Lucas.

"It didn't work, Ash!" Lucifer screamed. "You are too weak to harm her! Negative is weak against positive. She didn't even see you! Your thunder and lightning storm were nothing to her. Your evil couldn't touch her! She is good."

Lucifer's aura turned red, all around his image. All his force shoved Ash's orb to Hell. Lucifer focused on the conference room, and delivered them both there.

A long table and chairs extended the length of the middle of the room; they were used when the lineage assumed the human image. Sky showed through ceiling-to-floor window panels.

Gray rings appeared to shatter against the wall, but they re-formed around Ash's orb.

Ash transformed his image into that of the dark-haired young man. But the darkened-gray aura still circled his energy.

"Terrorizing a human, or any soul, is against our laws. You will now be removed from the family, like Nigel! Your malevolent, hateful energy is not a match to the lineage," Lucifer bellowed.

"She was interfering with our family! She had to be dealt with!" Ash returned.

Lucifer's red aura crashed into Ash's gray aura so hard that he tore through it. Again, the gray vapors reconstructed into shape around Ash's image.

Devon appeared, in human likeness: his young, blond image.

"Devon, assemble the lineage! Now! We need an emergency meeting," Lucifer said.

"Yes, cousin," Devon returned.

A family vote would be required for the removal of Ash from the lineage. The unwelcome soul would be abolished from Hell.

There was another place the undesirable, malevolent souls accumulated. It wasn't Hell. It wasn't Heaven. It wasn't Earth. It was in between everything. A place of isolation. A nowhere land. When rejected from every other plane and dimension, not attracted to a place of substance, the undesirables clustered together, as if mold spores.

Seven bright orbs soon gathered in the conference room. Lucifer and Devon each bowed to them.

Ash's image was fixed to a corner of the room. The darkened gray color of his malevolent energy repelled the luminosity of the gathered group. He was no longer magnetically matched to the enlightened ones.

"Grandfather," Lucifer acknowledged, bowing his head to his elder, now beside him.

Grandfather Lucious's nucleus was circled with a purple aura. He directly changed his image into that of an older man, with gray hair.

A fresh, new direction for the betterment of the castle would remain a practice. Though the position as ruler of Hell would periodically change leadership, Grandfather Lucious would always remain the head of the lineage.

Lucifer then bowed his head again, to Grace, as she neared. He felt as close to her now as his original blood mother.

One by one, the incoming, glowing orbs gathered in a circle. Each soul then projected a human image that looked radiantly, ghostly white. A golden cylinder of brightness, from each enlightened soul, formed a peak above each ethereal figure.

Lucifer and Devon joined the group.

Grandfather Lucious and his counterpart, Clara, were there, along with their blood children, Catherine and Grace. Heath, the husband of Grace and blood father of Devon, was there. Daniel and Melanie, blood parents to Heath and Nigel were also in attendance. Nigel was absent, his banishment shameful. Ash was about to become the second member of the bloodline to be banished.

With the nine members of the lineage combined in the circle, the golden cylinders of each soul ignited a ring of fire.

"Thank you for gathering," Lucifer began. His energy spiritually communicated to the group as a whole. There was interaction without words. Each soul was connected by their focus on the intended discussion.

Lucifer bowed to Grandfather. Being the elder, Grandfather would be granted the privilege of beginning the discussion.

"It brings me only sadness, when any soul disconnects from the flow of loving energy," Grandfather began. "There is no joy in witnessing one's disconnect. We can each only pray for realignment." Grandfather then bowed back to Lucifer.

"Ash must be shunned from the lineage," Lucifer said, firmly. "His energy meant harm to a human being."

"Universal law must dictate where Ash's soul dwells," the collective voice of the lineage said. "His soul must be drawn to the darkness, where he must go within."

"Not Earth, nor Hell, nor Heaven will embrace him," Grandfather Lucious said. "Ash's energy must follow the law of the universes. His malevolent energy will only be drawn to the hateful. He will follow his blood father before him."

"All in favor?" Devon addressed the group.

"All agreed," the collective voice of the lineage stated.

Ash's nucleus and the gray aura surrounding it dissipated.

His malevolent energy had been abolished from Hell.

Once the lineage had all agreed, there had been no positivity to allow Ash's energy occupancy in the castle. The troubled soul would spend an eternity in isolation. Maybe other rancid-smelling energies would cluster together with him? Maybe his pungent odor would be intolerable to even the most undesirable soul?

Lucifer, Devon and the counselors spent their subsequent energies rebuilding positive hope for healing in the castle. It had taken a great deal of reassurance to guarantee the residents that the negativity Ash brought inside was now replaced with healthful expectations.

A new curriculum would soon begin, with uplifting subjects such as art, philosophy and science. Group sessions would be offered, to share negative experiences on Earth and also progress in the castle. Role-playing, and acting out past and present incidents, would be added to classes, to help further articulate problems and breakthroughs. Meditation, self-healing and soul travel would be taught to advanced energies.

Having felt his core drained, after the restoration, Lucifer had retreated to the cellar for rest.

The bright-red color of his aura, that had caused the exhaustion, now became absorbed by his usual green. His soul rested, suspended in soothing blackness.

Had it been hours in human time? Days? Or years?

"Lucifer?" a familiar, deep voice sounded inside the cellar, beside Lucifer's orb. "Lucifer, my namesake?"

"Grandfather?" Lucifer telepathically said.

Grandfather Lucious's translucent nucleus, circled by purple, changed to his elder human image. "Yes, it is your grandfather, Lucious."

Lucifer's energy drew from slumber. He then changed his energy into that of his human image.

"Grandfather, what is it? Is everything flowing as it should?" Lucifer asked.

"No, Lucifer, everything is not flowing as it should. You have locked yourself in the cellar. I understand your need for rest, but I also understand your tendency to shelter yourself."

"Grandfather, isn't the castle running smoothly, with our new programs?"

"Lucifer, the new programs are running smoothly. You have been my successor because I trust your compassion and creativity to nurture the castle. Everything is running smoothly under your care."

"You're right, Grandfather: I have selfishly removed myself. I need to resume my duties now."

"You have not sheltered yourself from your duties, Lucifer; you have sheltered yourself from *her*."

"From *her*?"

"You are whole with her. Your core burns a bright gold, just at the thought of her. It's as though the flames of two candles unite and burn

439

as one. Be with her. Love her. Experience everything your human life with her will offer. You will do much greater things with her by your side than you can do alone. Your two energies will spend eternity together now. You have been apart long enough. The first time you saw Margaret, you loved her."

"Her name is Rosemary now, Grandfather."

"Same soul."

"I do not want to ruin the human experience she has planned for her current life. I do not want to be a constant reminder of Hell, a place humans fear. Maybe I should wait…"

"My son, do you not see? You think yourself the most powerful. You are not. You are no more powerful than any other soul in the universes," Grandfather Lucious sternly said.

Lucifer intently listened.

"You do not wish to bring harm to a good soul like Margaret's," Grandfather said, "but, my son, your soul is no more powerful than hers. You are no more powerful than her. You cannot tell her how to direct her own existence. Her spirit is steadfast, like a rooted tree.

"You tell yourself that you are being honorable, by keeping your distance from her, but you are really just hiding," Grandfather continued. "You are acting like a martyr. You tell yourself that you are protecting her, sacrificing your happiness by keeping your distance, but really you are just afraid of living, becoming human and making mistakes, not knowing outcomes, and experiencing every emotion of a human being."

Lucifer's provisional eyes remained steady on Grandfather.

"When you experienced your first human death, as Lucas, and

440

discovered your true identity, you considered yourself unworthy and morally incapable of decency and love," Grandfather continued. "You try to clean your soul by devoting your existence to serving other souls. You have done good works, my son, but maybe you haven't fully understood that your work is partly self-imposed penance.

"My son, you're afraid to live and feel emotions, to not know outcomes and not be in control. But your soul always intuitively knows what it needs. You need to trust – just as you tell the souls here in the castle to. For love, we must take risk. There are never guarantees, only trust. She trusts you, and is willing to take that risk. Do you trust her?"

"I trust her wholeheartedly, Grandfather," Lucifer said. "It's as though our souls were born of the same womb."

Grandfather had always showed his image as the face of Lucas's first blood-grandfather; there was now a teary-eyed, older man projected, looking back at Lucifer through that image.

"Live now! Love now!" Grandfather Lucious implored. "Instead of existing with past memories of your love, make new memories.

"I, myself, loved as a human being, once," Grandfather smiled: "your first blood-grandmother. Our energies still attract. There is no miracle in the universes like love. It heals. You are worthy of love, my son. Just like any other soul, you are worthy. You must go to her now; sometimes, there comes the point when not a second more can be wasted.

"She experienced her intended tribulations independently, to strengthen her will. She is ready for you now. Her aura is much brighter with your presence, as well. You two will brighten the world together.

"You have exceeded your duties here, well beyond my expectations. You have created a loving, healing center. Countless souls have learned and flourished under your care, and gone on. Devon will carry on your work, and he also has good ideas of his own for the castle. You have chosen a capable successor, just as I did."

"Grandfather," Lucifer quietly said, "thank you for helping me see things clearly. I am not more powerful than any soul, especially Rosemary's. I am just a soul, like any other."

"Have a good life, my son," Grandfather tenderly said.

"I will be human, knowing that kindness in Hell exists. Knowing that *you* exist, Grandfather."

"Travel with my love, son. Travel with my love."

A swoosh of bright purple scattered, as Grandfather's presence disappeared.

If he were, at this moment, human, Lucifer knew that he would cry. He would miss Grandfather. Lucifer had no physical eyes to bring about moisture, but he felt a deep ache inside his core.

He then held a picture of Rosemary's face there, in his core, to heal himself. The colors and textures of her beautiful face became clear, as he meditated.

Lucifer focused his energy inward, to transform his image back to an orb. Rosemary's soul felt close to his, as he continued meditating on her energy.

A swirling, translucent tunnel materialized from his concentration, and directed his energy through. The colors and textures of Earth grew vivid, as Lucifer's orb neared the end of the tunnel.

"Stay! Stay! Stay! Stay! Stay, stay, stay!"

Lucifer heard Rosemary's voice, as his core drew to her. The soundwaves were muffled, and seemed to bounce off the walls of the tunnel.

"Stay! Stay! *Stayyyyy!*"

He exited the tunnel, into Earth's atmosphere. Rosemary's cries were loud and clear.

Green was all around her. It looked like a watercolor painting of an emerald forest.

"Stay! Stay!"

There she was. At the park on the bridge. She bellowed, it appeared, to the invisible barrier between planes, beneath the canopy of tall leaves.

"Stay! Stay! Stay! Please, stay."

She was physically unharmed, though her eyes strained to gaze past the sky, toward the tops of the trees, their leaves fluttering green all around her.

He then pictured Lucas's human body. His body.

As if a magnetic pull, his core entered the human body he hovered over. A golden light brightened the chest area, as his soul entered.

He was human. He was Lucas.

Lucas inhaled a long, slow breath. He felt his heart pumping against his chest. A rumbling cough left his lips. Feeling like a rusty engine, he sluggishly began to rouse.

Moisture formed behind his closed eyelids, as his back lay against the mattress and emotions formed. Rosemary. He would be able to touch her. Kiss her.

It was painful to move his heavy arms. He rested a palm atop his chest, to feel his blood pumping fast. His hand rose and fell with labored breaths. His joints made a crunching sound, as he slowly rose to a seated position. Painfully, he stood and dressed. As if shackled, his stiff legs began to shuffle forward.

The more he struggled forward, the more lubricated his bones seemed to become. Blood rushed to his fingertips and toes, nourishing every inch of him.

He made it to his front door and opened it, to view the now-darkened sky. It was early evening.

As he looked down his porch stairs, his grimace seemed to exert a groan, all on its own; it would feel as if descending a mountain. His groin felt a throbbing pull, and his thigh bone resembled a raw slab of meat, but his feet held the weight as he started down. He held the rail tightly.

On a cool, breezy night like this, a long walk into town would be fitting, but not in this stiff body. He drove the convertible to the park.

Standing outside the vehicle, as he shut the door, he could feel her presence nearby.

Only the last tip of the sun's sphere was visible to the west. The trees were enveloped with darkness, and he walked into the deep, dark woods, toward the bridge.

His pace quickened, as he heard Rosemary's voice with his human ears.

The bridge was now in sight.

Though her back was to him, he knew that a face dampened from teary eyes looked into the depth of the darkened trees. Rosemary was on her knees now. Her hands were gripping the posts on either side of her. Rosemary's shoulders and upper back rose as she cried out: "*Stayyyy!* Please, stay!"

"Rose Petal…" he softly uttered.

The beautiful, dampened face turned to him.

Rosemary's lips parted; her pupils dilated. She stood, as more tears watered her eyes.

Tears filled Lucas's eyes, too, as he stepped onto the bridge. His gaze stayed steady on Rosemary, as he walked toward her.

Rosemary's eyes wouldn't stray from Lucas's as he watched her. Her spirit was steadfast, like a rooted tree.

"I'm here, if you'll have me," he said.

"You'll stay? Forever?" she asked, her voice hopeful. Her lips were still slightly parted, and a small intake of air caused an inward gasp.

"Yes, Rose Petal."

His heavy legs walked over to her, and he pressed her to his chest, tightly. His fingertips pressed against her warm skin, as he held the side of her face against his.

Rosemary folded her arms around his back.

"Your soul resembles a dove's feather," she whispered: "luminous, healing, encompassing brightness and love."

She had whispered the most beautiful words that had ever graced his ears.

He moved his mouth to hers. His lips felt the softness of hers as he pressed onto them. Inhaling deeply, he took her essence inside of him.

When the long kiss ended, she looked up at him, while he held her.

"You told me in a poem to follow my inner light," she whispered in the darkness.

"Yes."

"My inner light guided me here. My inner light guided me to you. To *your* light."

"Rose Petal, from the moment I first looked into your eyes, hundreds of years ago, I fell in love with you," he said, looking down at her. "I am Lucas now."

"Will you miss the castle?" she asked.

"I will miss Grandfather. I will miss the castle. But... life should be exhilarating. I need to have *you* in my life, to live an existence of exhilaration. You are blue waves crashing on the shore. You breathe fresh, clean light inside of me. I've always needed you. Even when not in your presence, you've always been the one who brightens the light inside of me."

"Life will be us sharing sacred moments, every day," she breathed.

"Yes," he smiled, as he looked down at her. "You know, Rose Petal, Chuck will fit nicely into our little family."

She smiled up at him. It felt as though the golden flames of two candles united energies, and burned as one.

Made in the USA
Columbia, SC
05 August 2024

39482836R00271